THE
MOON
POOL

SOPHIE LITTLEFIELD's novels have
won Anthony and RT Book Awards
and have been shortlisted for Edgar,
Barry, Crimespree, Macavity, and
Goodreads Choice Awards. Sophie
lives in Northern California. This is
her UK debut. Visit her website at
www.sophielittlefield.com

Also by Sophie Littlefield

House of Glass

Garden of Stones

The Moon Pool

THE MOON POOL

SOPHIE LITTLEFIELD

HEAD
ZEUS

First published in 2014 by Gallery Books, a division of Simon & Schuster, Inc.

First published in the UK in 2014 by Head of Zeus Ltd.

9 7 5 3 1 2 4 6 8

A catalogue record for this book is available from the British Library.

ISBN (HB) 9781781856840
ISBN (XTPB) 9781781856857
ISBN (E) 9781781856833

Printed and bound in Germany by
GGP Media GmbH, Pössneck

Head of Zeus Ltd
Clerkenwell House
45-47 Clerkenwell Green
London EC1R 0HT
WWW.HEADOFZEUS.COM

For T-wa and Little C:
scrappers, both

acknowledgments

THIS BOOK ASKED more of me and took me further than any before. I am forever grateful to Barbara Poelle and Abby Zidle, my agent and editor, who encouraged me mightily before leaving me to my task—and then, when I brought back a first draft, stayed the course until it became *The Moon Pool*.

A special thank you to Heather Baror-Shapiro and Danny Baror for never giving up on me, through all these years. I'm honored to have a place in your suitcase full of stories.

Many other people helped me create this book. My thanks to Rachael Herron for helping me get the dispatch details right, and David Kozicki for law-enforcement guidance. To Susan Baker for medical information. To the real Scott Cohen, Vicki Wilson, and my pal Shay, for use of your names. To Kurt Billick for his insights into the oil industry. To the men and women working in Williston who were kind enough to share their experiences with me, including Shane Sparks, Terry Kellum Jr., Joe Mondali, and Jason Gartman.

one

COLLEEN MITCHELL'S WORLD had been reduced to the two folded sheets of paper she clutched tightly in her left hand. She'd been holding them since leaving Sudbury at four thirty that morning, even when she went through security at Logan, even during the layover in Minneapolis, where she paced numbly up and down the terminal. The paper was slightly damp now and softened from too much handling.

Nobody wrote real letters anymore. Especially not kids. All through middle school, Colleen had forced Paul to write thank-you notes by hand every birthday and Christmas; the monogrammed stationery was still around somewhere, up in the dusty shelves of his closet. Once high school started, they had bigger battles to fight, and she gave up on the notes.

When was the last time she'd even seen her son's blocky, leaning handwriting? There must be papers—class notes, tests—in the boxes he'd brought back from Syracuse, but Colleen hadn't had the heart to open any of them, and they too were stacked in the closet. Nowadays Paul texted, that was all, and in Colleen's hand was a printout of all the texts from him. God bless Vicki—she'd figured out how to print them in neat columns so they fit on two double-sided pages and had emailed Colleen the file too, "just in case."

Colleen had read them a hundred times. They went back four months, to last September. All the communications from her son since he left—and they fit on two pages. One more indictment of her parenting, of what she'd done wrong or too much or not enough.

SEPTEMBER 27, 2010, 2:05 PM

Got it thx

That was the oldest one. Colleen couldn't remember what Paul had been thanking her for. Probably one of her care packages—she sent them all throughout last autumn, boxes packed with homemade brownies and Sky Bars and paperback books she knew he'd never read. But when Paul came home for Thanksgiving (well, the week after Thanksgiving, but she and Andy and Andy's brother Rob and Rob's girlfriend had delayed the whole turkey-and-pie production until Paul could be there; Andy had even taped the games and waited to watch them with him), he made it clear that the packages embarrassed him.

Next was a series of texts from her:

OCTOBER 28, 2010, 9:16 AM

Hi sweetie dad has enough frequent flyer miles for u to come home when you're off

OCTOBER 29, 2010, 7:44 AM

When are you off again?

OCTOBER 30, 2010, 11:50 PM

Wish u were here for hween the flannigans have the pumpkin lights in the trees

Like he was *eleven*, for God's sake, and off at sleepaway camp, instead of twenty, a man.

A small sob escaped Colleen's throat, an expulsion of the panic that she'd mostly got under control. She covered the sound with a cough. In her carry-on was half a bottle of Paxil, which Dr. Garrity had given her over a year ago before they settled on a regimen of red clover extract and the occasional Ambien to treat what was, he assured her, a perfectly normal transition into menopause. She hadn't liked the Paxil; it made her feel dizzy and sometimes sweaty, but she'd packed the bottle yesterday along with her own sleeping pills and Andy's too. She hadn't told him, and she felt a little guilty about that, but he'd be able to get a refill tomorrow. She'd leave a message with the doctor's answering service when they landed, and then all he'd have to do was pick it up.

Colleen refolded the papers and rested her forehead against the airplane window, looking out into the night. The plane had begun its descent. The flight attendant had made her announcement—they'd be on the ground a few minutes before ten, the temperature was one degree, winds at something. One degree was *cold*. But Boston got cold too, and it didn't bother Colleen the way it did some people.

Far below, rural North Dakota was lit up by the moon, a vast rolling plain of silvery snow interrupted here and there by rocky swaths where the land rose up in ridges. Colleen tried to remember if she'd ever been to either Dakota. She couldn't even remember the names of the capitals—Pierre? Was that one of them?

A flare of orange caught her eye, a rippling brightness surrounded by a yawning black hole in the snow. And there. And there! Half a dozen of them dotting the bleak landscape, blazes so bright they looked unnatural, the Day-Glo of a traffic cone. Colleen's first thought was forest fire, but there were no trees, and then she thought of the burning piles of trash she saw sometimes in Mattapan or Dorchester. But people didn't burn trash at night, and besides, there were no houses, no town, just—

And then she saw it, the tall burred spire like an old-time radio tower, and she knew, even as they flew past, that she had seen her first rig. The plane was still too far up for her to make out any details except that it looked so small, so flimsy, almost like a child's toy—a Playmobil oil rig play set with little plastic roughnecks.

The plane tipped down, the engine shifted, and so did the men, the tired-looking, ill-shaven lot of them who'd boarded with her in Minneapolis. They turned off their iPads and crumpled their paper coffee cups and cleared the sleep from their throats.

Colleen closed her eyes, the image of the rig imprinted in her mind, and as they approached Lawton, she thought, *Give him back, you have to give him back to me.*

two

LAWTON'S AIRPORT SEEMED to be composed of several trailers welded together and sided in cheap plywood, plunked down in a large, frozen parking lot. Colleen filed past the flight attendant, wondering if she imagined the look of pity in the woman's eyes, and down the metal stairs. The cold hit her hard, nostrils and lungs and ears instantly brittle with the ache of it, and she shoved up the hood of her down coat. Once she reached the ground, the men shuffled away from her so she was at the front of the group waiting for baggage. They stood there quietly, patiently, their bare hands hanging at their sides; none of them wore gloves. She'd noticed their hands in the airport: weathered and raw and red. Maybe they no longer felt the cold.

There it was, her roll-aboard with the hot pink luggage tag she bought for their anniversary trip to Italy last year. Colleen lifted it from the cart and headed toward the building. Sharp crystals of icy snow stung her face, a drift from the roof or perhaps blown up from the ground by the wind. Her boots echoed on the ramp, and then she was inside, surrounded by warmth and a vaguely chemical smell.

The ticket counter—only one—was shuttered and dark. Same with the rental car counter. The entire operation was smaller than her family room. A man in a reflective vest was doing something at the front doors, kneeling near the bottom hinges. Outside, she could see the parking lot, half the vehicles heaped with snow. Beyond were the lights of town; a tall truck-stop sign down the road advertised showers along with the price of gas.

"Excuse me," Colleen said to the kneeling man. He stood with some difficulty, as though his knees bothered him, wiping his hand on his pants.

"Ma'am." There was a faint tinge of the South in his voice, which caught her off guard even though it was one of the first things Paul had told them about the place: everyone was from places like Arkansas, Mississippi, Georgia.

"I need to call a cab. Can you recommend one? A company?"

"A cab?"

He looked puzzled. In his hand was the sort of knife Paul had carried ever since he started Boy Scouts: not so much a pocketknife as a collection of little tools on a central axis. "Well, now, where are you headed?"

Colleen shrugged, impatient. "A hotel. I need to go to a hotel."

"Which one?"

"I—I'm not sure." She had been planning to save this discussion for the cabbie, but this man—who seemed kind enough—would do. "I don't have a room. I know they're booked up, but I was just hoping that—I have a lot of hotel points. A lot. And money isn't a concern."

"Hotels be full up, ma'am. All of 'em."

"Well, I know that. I did call, but my thinking was that there might be a cancellation, at the last minute, someone who didn't show up, I thought they might release the room now that it's . . . now that it's getting late." There was *always* a room to be had somewhere, she didn't add; the expensive rooms—the suites—often went begging, and she was willing to pay.

But as the man continued to regard her with polite consterna-tion, Colleen had to admit what she'd been putting off thinking about: maybe there really *were* no rooms to be had. That was the issue with the private detective she'd tried to hire—he'd searched for a hotel room and said the only one he could find was more than two hours outside Lawton. He had managed to book a room for a week from now, and Colleen told him to go ahead and keep the reservation and if—God, she could barely stand to think it—if Paul hadn't been found by then, the detective would have a room waiting for him when he came out to North Dakota.

Andy thought they should give it a few more days. He'd actually used the term "vision quest" at one point and reminded Colleen that he'd gone off on his own the summer after his freshman year and not bothered to tell anyone where he was going. Andy had spent the better part of a month in Yellowstone with his guitar and a single change of clothes, come back with a beard and a case of crabs, and—the way he told the story, anyway—his parents had barely registered his absence.

But that was different. It was before cell phones, and Andy had been the artistic type, at least to hear him tell it, and Paul definitely was not. And Andy had something to get away *from*—his parents were in the middle of a messy divorce and his mom had developed a pill habit—while Paul insisted he loved working on the rigs, so why would he cut and run? It didn't add up, and every day that they delayed, they risked his trail growing colder.

Once Colleen made up her mind, she moved fast. She'd spent most of yesterday getting the flights lined up and finding someone to cover for her at the school. When Andy got home from work he'd watched her finish the laundry and pack, drinking a beer out of the bottle and saying little. He didn't try to talk her out of going, but he didn't volunteer to take her to the airport, either. When the car service came for her early this morning, he was still asleep.

"There hasn't been a room around here in months. Every one of them full up, some with whole families."

Colleen blinked and took a deep breath. Andy had asked her the same thing—what would she do if she couldn't find a room?—and she'd told him not to be ridiculous, worst case she'd sleep in the airport and find a room first thing in the morning, never believing for a second she'd actually have to do it. But it was obvious she wouldn't be sleeping here: even if the tiny airport wasn't about to close, there were only a few seats, and nowhere to stretch out. The other passengers had exited the building while she stood there talking, clomping out into the cold in their heavy boots. In the parking lot, trucks were coming to life, their headlights illuminating the mounded dirty snow and exhaust clouding from their tailpipes as their owners chipped ice from the windows.

"Still, I can try." She forced a smile. "I'll have the cab driver take me around, and if there really isn't anything, I'll have him take me to an all-night restaurant."

"Well . . ." The man tugged at his collar, clearly wanting to say more. "Call Silver Cab, then, I'll wait until he comes. Shouldn't take him too long. It's just seven-oh-one-five-S-I-L-V-E-R. But you best tell him . . . you know."

Impatience flashed through Colleen. "Why? The longer he has to drive me around, the more I'll end up paying."

"It's just, the Buttercup, that's the only restaurant that stays open all night besides the truck stops, they won't let nobody stay in a booth all night no more. Not since folks started trying to sleep in them. They cracked down."

"Well, I—" Colleen wanted to protest that she wouldn't be like them, those other people, trying to sponge off the restaurant. She was only even considering it out of desperation. She'd leave a very large tip, payment for the time she spent there, the pot of coffee, the restroom, all of it. "I won't sleep, then."

She tapped the number into the phone and waited, forcing a smile, staring at the man's shirt. The vest gapped open, and Colleen saw that above the pocket was stitched the name Dave.

The phone rang and rang. After six or seven rings, Colleen gave up and lifted her gaze to Dave's face. His expression had gone from concerned to something more like dread. She supposed he thought he was going to get stuck with her.

"Didn't answer, huh?" Dave didn't wait for her to respond. "They get busy. Him and the other outfit, Five Star. Doing runs from the bars, see. They'll be pretty busy from now until after closing time. Which is one a.m.," he added.

"I understand, but—" The feeling of panic that had been simmering inside Colleen threatened to burst into full bloom. "I wonder. Is there any way—I mean I would pay you, of course, and I'll wait for you to finish here, but could you just give me a lift to that restaurant? The one you were telling me was open all night? I'll wait there until the cabs are available."

The building was eerily quiet save for the buzz of some fluorescent fixture. A moment passed, Colleen's fingers tight around the handle of her suitcase.

"I'll be glad to take you," Dave finally said, sounding anything but, "but do you mind me asking what you're doing here? In Lawton?"

Colleen had prepared an answer to that question, but she'd hoped she wouldn't need it until later, after she'd settled in. In the morning, when she came back to rent a car, they would ask her where she was taking it. She had planned to say she was visiting relatives, but now it seemed painfully clear that she could never have relatives in a place like this. Who would live in a place where the nearest civilization was two hours away, where there were only two flights in and out per day?

"I came . . ." she said, and tried to come up with another story. If she invented relatives, she had a feeling Dave would insist on driving her to their house. If she made up a job, a company whose business brought her here, he would want to know why they hadn't booked her a room—and besides, what could she possibly say she did? She knew nothing about the oil industry, only what Paul had told her, and that had been precious little.

Dave waited, and the fluorescent light buzzed, and the smell of exhaust reached her. All of it harsh, all of it wrong.

"I came to find my son," she blurted. A huge sob bubbled up from inside her, taking her breath and leaving her gasping, and her eyes filled with tears.

"Hey," Dave said, alarmed. "Hey. Here." He plucked a box of tissues from the rental car counter and offered it to her. "Did your son come up here to find work?"

Colleen nodded, pulling tissues from the box and dabbing at her eyes, but she couldn't seem to stop crying. "Back in September. He got a job right away, with Hunter-Cole Energy. He stays at the Black Creek Lodge. He was just home over Christmas. And then he came back here and we didn't hear from him and that's not like him . . . last week my husband called the company and they said he hadn't come to work. No one let us know. I'm sure he would have listed us, an emergency contact at the very least, but they didn't call or anything. They didn't tell anyone. If Andy hadn't called them . . . And he hadn't been in his room at the camp, either, Andy talked to someone at the lodge, they gave away his room. Paul wouldn't do that. He wouldn't just . . . quit and not tell anyone. They said, the police said they can't do anything about it. So I'm here. I've come to find him."

A change had come over the man's face. He already knew the story, Colleen could tell; recognition mixed with concern in his eyes. Well, so at least people up here were talking about it. The cops had made it sound like boys went missing all the time, but that wasn't true, and this man Dave knew it.

She put her hand on his arm, feeling the warmth of his skin under the rough cotton of his shirt. "Do you know something? Have you heard something?"

"I heard . . . I mean, I don't know if it's the same one, if it's your son, but they say two boys went missing from the Black Creek camp a couple weeks ago. Hunter-Cole Energy boys—one was still a worm. Went by Whale and, uh, can't remember the other boy's name."

"Paul. My son is Paul." She didn't know about any other boy. The police, the men from Hunter-Cole Energy—she'd kept calling until they transferred her all the way to the company's headquarters in Texas—had never mentioned that. She didn't know what he meant by *worm* and *whale*, and what did it mean that there were *two* of them—that had to be worse, didn't it?

"All I know is the handles they used up here. I'm sorry, I shouldn't even, I don't know if it's the same ones."

"When did these ones go missing?"

The man squinted, as though the question caused him pain. "Let's see, I heard it Thursday last. They were moving a rig out Highway Nine east of town, the boys didn't show. I got a friend on Highway Patrol, is how I know."

"It's him, then! He went missing the same day, that's the first day he didn't come back to his room."

"Well, listen. There's someone you maybe ought to see."

"You know something? Anything. Anything at all, please tell me."

The man took a deep breath and let it out, shrugging off his vest. He folded the vest in half and began to roll it up, not meeting her eyes. "I don't know a damn thing. Wish I did. But *she* might, and I'll take you to her right now."

"Who?"

"The other mom."

three

DAVE CALLED HIS wife to tell her he'd be late. As he drove, he told Colleen he had moved to Lawton from southern Missouri during the last boom, in the late 1970s. He met a local girl, married her, and stayed. The airport job was a good one, and he didn't miss the work on the rigs, or the prospect of losing his job when the boom started to fade.

The snow was coming down more heavily now, dusting Dave's windshield between each swipe of the wipers. His truck smelled pleasantly of oil and tobacco. It seemed like the only traffic on the road was trucks—pickups like Dave's, bigger than those Colleen saw around Boston, many of them jacked up on larger-than-life wheels, but mostly long-bedded vehicles both empty and loaded with equipment. Traffic moved slowly, giving Colleen a chance to watch the town go by outside her window.

Lawton seemed to be one long stretch of four-lane highway, lined with gas stations and restaurants and lumberyards and storage facilities. A huge Walmart looked like it was open for business despite the hour and the weather. They passed two motels, both with brightly lit NO VACANCY signs and parking lots full of pickups.

Dave hadn't actually met the woman he was taking Colleen to see. He only knew where to find her because his wife's sister worked at the same clinic as the woman who'd rented the other mother her motor home.

"But how can she be staying in a motor home in this weather?"

"Generator." He didn't seem inclined to say anything more on the subject.

Dave pulled onto a street lined with shabby ranch houses at the edge of town; the cars and trucks in the driveways looked old and battered. He drove slowly, reading addresses on mailboxes. Televisions flickered in windows.

"This'll be it," he said at the end of the block, pulling in front of a small house with white siding. Parked at the side of the house was the motor home, several feet of snow piled on its roof.

Colleen felt her stomach twist. "Would you—I mean, you've done so much for me already, and I insist on paying you, of course . . ." She dug in her purse for her wallet. "But could I ask you to come with me? To make sure she's here?"

"Put your money away," Dave said roughly. "Of course I'll go with you. Let me come around, it's a big step down."

Colleen's stomach growled as she waited, and she realized she hadn't eaten anything since a protein bar in the Minneapolis airport, many hours earlier. Dave offered his hand and she took it, letting him help her out of the cab.

He got her suitcase from the back and waited for her to walk ahead of him. Colleen's boots made neat prints in the snow that had fallen since the drive was last plowed. She tugged her scarf tighter around her neck so that only the center of her face was exposed to the bitter chill. Once she got close, she could hear voices from inside the motor home. She took a breath and knocked on the door.

It opened almost instantly. Standing inside was a small woman in a navy blue sweatshirt several sizes too big for her, printed with a tornado and the words FAIRHAVEN CYCLONES FOOTBALL. Bleached, kinked hair was loosely piled on top of her head; much of it had come loose and cascaded around her shoulders. She had startling blue eyes ringed with thick black eyeliner. Colleen got a whiff of the air inside—pot and pizza. The television was on; that's where the voices were coming from.

"Brenda called over," the woman said. "You must be Whale's mom."

THE WOMAN ACROSS the tiny table looked as though a tap with Shay's little pink craft hammer would shatter her into a thousand pieces. Which you might expect, except Colleen Mitchell looked like she'd been this way forever, long before the boys went missing. You didn't get lines as deep as the ones between her eyebrows and around her mouth in a single week.

"You're lucky you found someone to drive you," Shay said. "We're supposed to get six more inches by morning."

"Lucky," Colleen echoed, like the word was in a foreign language.

Dave took off as fast as he could without being rude. Shay knew how *that* went too. Most people didn't like to be around bad luck; it was as though misfortune was contagious. But the men here in Lawton had surprisingly old-fashioned manners. In the three days since she arrived, strangers had opened doors for her, let her cut in line at the coffee shop, and even offered to carry her groceries to her car.

"I know what you need," she told Colleen.

"Oh, I—I couldn't," Colleen said quickly, eyeing the bottle on the table. Shay had been drinking weak Jack and Cokes, smoking and thinking, before Brenda called, and she hadn't put the bottle away because there wasn't anywhere to put it.

"Oh, no, I didn't mean that, though a drink might not hurt. You need something to eat. I'll make you something."

"No, thank you so much, but I'm not hungry."

"Yes, you are," Shay said patiently, the way she'd talk to Leila. "Come on. You been on a plane since, what, this morning? Probably didn't have any lunch?"

"I had something," Colleen said miserably. Her eyelids were crepey, makeup collected in the creases. Her lips were pale and flaking. She gave off a faint smell of fabric softener and sweat. And she looked like she was about to cry.

"Well, now you're going to have something else. What time is it in Boston, anyway? An hour ahead, right? That's almost one in the morning."

Shay kept up a steady stream of conversation while she got the bread out of the little fridge, the ham, cheese, mustard, and put a sandwich together. Colleen answered a word or two at a time, her voice dull. Both plates were dirty, so Shay served the sandwich on a folded paper towel. She poured a glass of milk and set that down on the table too.

"Eat."

Colleen picked up the sandwich and took a bite, chewing with her eyes glazed. Shay doubted she tasted a thing. The woman still hadn't taken off her coat and scarf, though the RV was so cold that Shay didn't blame her; she herself wore long underwear and a sweater under Taylor's old sweatshirt. And that was *with* the generator blasting almost constantly. Brenda had come over after work to complain for the second time that Shay was running it too high. But since weather.com said it would get down to minus three degrees overnight, she'd decided to just turn it back up and let the bitch complain.

Shay gave the glass of milk a gentle push, and Colleen picked it up and drank. Like some kind of robot, like worry had taken away her will. That wasn't good. It was way too early for that, and Shay—veteran of crises since before she could walk, though nothing like this—should know.

"Okay," she said, keeping it friendly but firm. "So let's figure this out."

Colleen set down the sandwich. A crumb clung to her bottom lip. "I didn't even know there was another boy until tonight. That seems . . . I'm sorry. I'm sorry about your son and the way I came barging in here."

Shay shrugged. "The company doesn't want you to know. Why would they? All it can mean is more trouble for them."

Colleen's frown deepened, emphasizing the groove in her forehead. "I don't understand."

"The company? Hunter-Cole Energy? Look, think about it. How many accidents have you heard about up here in the last couple years? Workplace accidents, where they lost workers?"

"Accidents?"

"Come on, you use Google, right? I have an alert set up on Hunter-Cole." Shay waited for Colleen to process what she was saying, because people like her never expected women like Shay to be able to do anything with a computer. Which admittedly had been true until a couple of years ago, when she started selling her boxes on Etsy, so there was that. "Any time a guy gets hurt on the job, they have this whole team that tries to bury the news, but it still leaks out if you know where to look. It's hidden, but it's there."

"You mean like the man who had the seizure?"

"Well, sure. That. But everyone knows about that one." In August, a fifty-two-year-old grandfather had a seizure, his first, and fell from the platform. He died in the helicopter en route to Minot. It might have escaped national attention—Shay would bet the lawyers were working their asses off doing damage control—but *People* magazine ended up doing an article. The man's daughters were pretty, his grandchild adorable—shit like that sold. "But there's been others. More than you'll ever know about if you don't keep your eyes open."

Colleen's chin trembled. "And you think our boys . . ."

"Whoa, whoa, whoa, I didn't say that." Too late, Shay saw the panic in Colleen's eyes and realized her mistake. "No, come on, honey, you are *not* going to go there. I don't for a minute believe our boys were hurt on the rigs. I mean, there's protocols they have to follow, they have to call the next of kin—"

She seized Colleen's hand and felt the tremor pass through her wrist. Her fingers were waxy and cold, her polished nails sharp against Shay's skin. *Next of kin,* she shouldn't have said that.

"If our boys had been hurt at work, they'd be busy trying to buy us off. There'd be a pack of lawyers sitting here, and instead all you got is me. It wasn't an accident. That's not what this is."

Shay felt Colleen relax fractionally. Her shoulders slumped and she stared at the sandwich.

"That's right, eat," Shay said softly. She waited until Colleen took another bite before continuing. "So, think like the company would. The boys go missing. It could be a hundred things. Guys don't last out here, the work's not what they think it'll be, they don't like the cold, they miss their girlfriends back home. Whatever. Say twenty percent of them quit the first week, right? And that's a conservative guess."

A little color had come back to Colleen's face. "I didn't know," she said quietly. "I don't know anything. Paul didn't—doesn't—tell us. And I didn't know where to look, who to ask. We don't have anyone else, any friends, any of his friends . . . we're the only ones, with a son who came out here to work."

"Damn, not me," Shay said, with feeling. "I know half a dozen families with sons up here."

For a while there, it was all the kids could talk about—the rig or the service, the only solid opportunities for boys who graduated from Fairhaven with bad grades and a blemish or two on their records. Fairhaven—a stupid name for a central valley town whose population was half illegal immigrants and the other half competing with them for shit wages. It wasn't any kind of haven and it sure as hell wasn't fair, but that's what they had. Taylor and another boy, Brad Isley, had gone the weekend after graduation; by the end of summer, three more boys had followed them. Two were already back—homesick, overwhelmed, just plain broken by the hard work. "Anyway, the company doesn't care, it's just a hole to fill. They need another worm, so they hire and move on—"

"*Worm*," Colleen said, interrupting. "I've heard that twice today. What does it even mean?"

"You don't know what that means?" Thinking, *What kind of boy doesn't share that, the first thing they learn on the job?* "It's what they call the new guys. First couple months on the rig, they do all the work no one else wants to do, they're worms. Later they become hands, like the rest of the guys. Roughnecks, roustabouts. You know."

"Oh."

"Anyway, the companies up here are hiring as fast as they can. A lot of times they don't even process the applications until the boys are already on the job, just get them to sign all the releases and send them on to HR. And you know HR is in some office building in another state, and meanwhile up here where the work is getting done it's all about getting the boys in a hard hat and on the floor. So a couple of them go missing, they don't care, they don't have *time* to care, all they're worried about is they don't want any more bad press. So they hand it off to the suits, and they do *their* thing and keep it out of the news."

Colleen looked like she was trying to decide whether to confide something. "They called us," she said after a moment. "Hunter-Cole did. They called Andy at work."

"Andy—that's your husband?"

"Yes. He's a partner at his firm, his name's on it, so I guess he was easy to find . . . anyway, the Hunter-Cole management tracked him down. They offered their support, said they would help in any way they could."

Shay snorted. "Yeah. I bet."

Colleen nodded wearily. "They didn't have any specific suggestions. So then when we decided to hire our own detective—"

"You hired a detective? To look for your son?"

"Well, yes." Colleen evaded Shay's gaze; she looked embarrassed. "Someone to supplement the efforts of law enforcement up here."

"Law enforcement up here couldn't find their ass in a can. Sorry," Shay added, regretting the way it had sounded. She was bringing her own issues into this, something she'd promised herself not to do.

"I just thought that someone who was dedicated to the task, who wasn't juggling a lot of other cases . . . anyway, I had Andy call the guy at Hunter-Cole back. Just to tell him, you know, that Steve Gillette, that's the detective, would be giving him a call? And suddenly the Hunter-Cole guy got really evasive. Started backpedaling . . ."

"They're trained to do that," Shay said. "Like they learn it in law school or something."

"So *I* called." Colleen straightened in her chair. "I called the Hunter-Cole offices myself. I repeated the same thing Andy said, that Steve Gillette would want access to whatever they could show him—time cards, employment records, like that. And the whole narrative changed. They were polite, but it was like a wall went up. They didn't so much answer my questions as promise to look into them. Get back to me later. That sort of thing."

The anger in her voice—that was good; that's what she would need. "That's why you're here, right?" Shay asked. "They told you no once too often?"

Colleen looked directly into Shay's eyes for the first time since she knocked on the door of the motor home. "Yes. Yes. Andy wanted me to wait. He said . . . he said we should give Paul a few more days, it was probably all a misunderstanding."

"Fuck that," Shay said before she could stop herself. "You're the *mom*. You know when something's wrong."

"Yes. That's what I tried to tell him." Colleen nodded. A moment passed, and then she rested her hand on the bottle and turned it so she could read the label. "I don't believe I've ever had Jack Daniel's."

"You want me to pour you one?"

"Maybe. Yes. Do."

LONG AFTER COLLEEN'S breathing had gone deep and even on the opposite side of the motor home, on the bed Shay had made by flipping the dining table and chairs, she lay awake, thinking. Part of the problem was that she was cold—she'd given Colleen most of the blankets, saying she'd be fine in her layers and second pair of socks, which wasn't quite enough to keep the chill off—and part of it was Taylor.

During the last conversation they'd had, Taylor had talked about a girl. Charity, Chastity, some old-fashioned name like that—Shay wished she could remember. But it probably wouldn't help; there was always a girl. Taylor never stayed focused on them for very long; they came and went, affably and without drama, a series of pretty, smiling, exuberant girls who held no grudges and remembered him with affection. "Say hi to Taylor," they all said when Shay ran into them at the grocery or the bank, and she promised to do so, though she could never keep them all straight.

Her tall, broad, handsome son, cocaptain of the Fairhaven football team, had never lacked for female company. So when Shay listened to him talking about his latest, driving to work with the phone tucked between her ear and shoulder and an eye out for cops because she damn sure couldn't afford another ticket, she hadn't been paying attention. Nowhere near enough attention, considering it was the last conversation she'd had with him before he disappeared.

She remembered that Taylor had talked about this girl's skin. Well, sure, didn't every twenty-year-old girl have beautiful skin? Shay certainly had—people used to stop her all the time to ask her if she modeled. There was a time when Shay had taken comments like that for granted. And maybe this girl did too, this girl who was among the last to see him.

As for the rest of his life, Taylor reported that it was all fine, nothing new, the job was a job, the guys were great. Taylor was never one to complain; the thing he said most often was "you do what you gotta do." Which was amazing because his father used to say the very same thing, may he rest in peace. Maybe it was in the blood, though Shay liked to think she'd had a hand in turning out a boy who wasn't afraid of hard work. Lord knew she'd done her share.

Deep in the night was the only time Shay couldn't keep the fears away. She listened to Colleen breathe; she heard a dog bark somewhere. The generator cycled on and off; the heater blasted hot, dry air. She'd be glad to get out of this tin can, but she had no idea where to go next, a fact she hadn't yet shared with Colleen.

The other mother. She'd known there was one—assumed, anyway—and it was even on the list Shay was keeping, written on the outside of a manila file folder. "Other parents"—it was right below "Call Lawrence." Lawrence was Brittany's husband's uncle, a lawyer. Shay had met him at a wedding. Maybe he could help somehow.

But Shay hadn't gotten that far on the list yet. By the second day Taylor didn't call her, she knew something was wrong. By the third day, she was frantic. She quit her job on the eighth day, after the guy at Hunter-Cole stopped taking her calls and the police sergeant who'd been assigned her case told her tersely that he'd let her know the minute they had anything and to stop calling. And on the morning of the ninth day, before the sun rose in California, she was on the road, drinking truck-stop coffee and listening to preachers on the radio.

Twenty-two hours in the car, with just a few hours' sleep in her backseat at rest stops—a trip like that wasn't for the weak. Shay had a hundred and thirty-five dollars in her purse and her last paycheck ought to hit her account tomorrow. It wasn't much, but she'd been down that far plenty of times before and frankly it didn't scare her much.

What scared her was the fact that North Dakota seemed to have swallowed up her baby—whom she'd raised tough like her, tough enough to play the last quarter against Noble Hills with a torn oblique—and left no trace behind.

But fuck North Dakota. Fuck the cops and fuck the oil company and fuck everyone and everything that stood between her and what she needed. Shay would not stop until she found her son—or died trying.

four

T.L. WAITED FOR the sound of Myron's key in the front door. It didn't come until twenty minutes after midnight, and T.L. did the math quickly in his head. Ten minutes to close the store, ten to get to Griffon's, ten to get home—so his uncle would have been at the bar only forty-five minutes.

When had it all turned upside down like this, with Myron going out late and T.L. waiting up like a nervous housewife? Of course T.L. knew exactly when. On the day that changed everything. Only it wasn't that simple, was it? Because if he'd never met her . . . if the Wolves varsity baseball team hadn't made the finals in the NDHSA West tournament . . . if she hadn't shaken her blue-and-silver pom-poms in the frosty spring air as he came up to bat for what would turn out to be the game-winning triple.

If he hadn't got that hit—surely then. T.L. knew what he could do and what he couldn't. The triple was a fluke. He could draw an eastern cottontail so realistic it looked like it might leap off the page; he could unload and stack three dozen eight-pound baler bags of ice into the freezer in ten minutes; he could rattle off the name of every elder who'd served on the tribal business council since 1997, the year his mother died and Myron took him in. But what he could not do, on an ordinary day, was capture the attention of a blond-haired, blue-eyed pom-pom girl from Lawton High and so impress her that she got her friends to give him her phone number. The triple had

made the difference: there were several hundred people in the Lawton High stadium, more than had turned out for any other game of
the season, stamping their feet in the stands and shouting. Nearly
forty of those people packed the visitors' area, Myron and his buddies
and a few of the guys' moms, and they all started chanting "T.L."
Then someone on the other side picked it up, and his name echoed
back and forth across the field, and everything in the world had
seemed possible, including a girl like Elizabeth walking across the
parking lot toward him after the game.

Right there. That would have been the moment to freeze in
time.

T.L. leaned up on his elbows. The curtains didn't close all the
way, and light from the parking lot leaked through, casting a narrow
stripe of yellow across his bed. That stripe had been there for thirteen of his nineteen years. He had once driven his Matchbox cars
along it, long after Myron told him to go to sleep.

He heard Myron's keys landing in the dish on the hall table, his
boots heavy on the linoleum, a glass of water being poured at the
sink, seconds later the empty glass being set down on the counter.
The walls in the house were thin, the doors hollow. Myron had
bought the place for nothing, after the first boom was only a memory,
when he got back from serving in the Gulf: a shitty house set back on
a badly poured parking lot with a two-pump service station and convenience store fronting the highway. Myron struggled for years, but
now it was boom times again and the location, right past the turn-in
for the reservation, was genius: shift workers passing by four times a
day, on the way to the rigs, on the way back to town. They might not
always gas up, but they stopped for cigarettes, tall boys and jerky and
sleeves of cashews, cupcakes and skin magazines and Red Bulls.

Myron's boots, on the way to his room. Steady. Slow. Worn-down . . . T.L. could hear it in the tread. Pausing outside T.L.'s door, only for a moment.

Forty-five minutes at Griffon's, for Myron that was one beer. He might not even have finished it. T.L. lay back down and closed his eyes. He'd sleep now. This new vigilance, as unfamiliar as a Sunday suit, wasn't costing him any rest that he'd be getting anyway, not with the shadows and specters and fears that jammed his mind. Myron had come home drunk only a handful of times, and he was a calm drunk, usually getting a ride home. Besides, if his uncle decided to start leaving his money on the bar, what could T.L. have done about it?

He had no idea, but he still had to be vigilant. *Someone* had to stay on guard. To keep hidden things hidden and danger at bay. T.L. was a man now, and he meant to do a man's job.

five

COLLEEN WOKE TO the remains of some fitful dream splintering and vanishing, leaving behind only a scattered sense of dread. Next came the terrible realization that Paul was missing, the running calculus of his absence ticking up automatically to nine days, and she felt the loss of him like a gaping hole inside her.

Only after the waking and remembering did her other senses kick in. Everything was wrong and unfamiliar. The surface she was lying on was cold and hard. The air she breathed held an unpleasant mélange of her own odor and faint notes of spoiled milk and industrial cleaner. And there was a rumbling that she not only heard but also felt, a mechanical, knocking-engine sound.

Generator. Colleen remembered. She opened her eyes and recognized the inside of the motor home faintly lit with gloomy dawn. There, maybe eight feet away, was Shay, huddled into a lump under a pile of clothes and a single blanket. Guiltily, Colleen realized she had the lion's share of the blankets, a fact she hadn't registered last night, when the whiskey had gone down all too easily, followed by a fluster of preparations in which she hadn't exactly participated. She hadn't been drunk. But she hadn't been sober, either. Nothing but the protein bar and the half sandwich, the milk Shay insisted that she drink, and the whiskey. Then peeing and brushing her teeth in that tiny closet of a bathroom. In fact the last lucid thought Colleen remembered having was to wonder where the water went when she flushed, while she rinsed the toothpaste down the sink.

No, wait. A hand-lettered sign taped to the mirror—Sharpie on a lined index card—read USE AS LEAST WATER AS POSSIBLY PLEASE, and Colleen's *last* lucid thought was the one she always had when confronted with grammar mistakes on public display, which was to wish she had the ability to fix them without anyone ever knowing. A Johnny Appleseed for the postliterate generation, she would sow grammar skills everywhere she went.

Colleen sat up slowly, trying to make no noise. If there was light in the sky, it had to be nearly eight o'clock, didn't it? Which was what—nine her time?

What time had they gone to bed last night, anyway? It had been after eleven on Dave's dashboard clock when she climbed in the truck, she remembered that. She and Shay had stayed up talking for maybe an hour. Colleen couldn't believe she had slept seven hours straight, something she hadn't come close to managing the last few nights. Was she simply exhausted? Or could it be a sense of relief at having someone to share her burden with? Immediately Colleen felt guilty. It was only because another boy was missing—and another mother frantic—that she wasn't alone.

And then she felt even more guilty because she wasn't alone, at least not as alone as Shay. She had Andy. Who she had forgotten to call last night. He would already have been up for nearly two hours this morning. She eased her legs over the side of the bed—not a bed, but the motor home's tiny table, which Shay had somehow flipped over to create a sort of cot—and immediately felt the cold air slide into her sleeves and under the legs of her pants. The floor was freezing, even through her socks. Wedged in the narrow space between table and kitchenette was her suitcase. She remembered pawing through the contents last night to find her toiletry case; when she'd returned from the bathroom the table/bed was made, the lights were turned off save a dim overhead night-light, and Shay was sitting cross-legged on top of the tiny bed, as though the two of them were at sleepaway camp. Colleen had considered digging through her clothes for her nightgown, but that would mean changing in front of Shay, and she was too tired to contend with her own modesty, her embarrassment at her pouchy abdomen and jiggling upper arms and thighs.

She'd left the suitcase open and crawled gratefully under the covers, mumbling a good night. She must have gone to sleep immediately, because she remembered nothing after that.

Now she considered Shay's sleeping form while she slipped her boots on, pulling up the zippers slowly so as to make no noise. She wondered if Shay had looked through her suitcase or her purse. Had it been her, she wouldn't have attempted the suitcase, mostly because it would be hard not to muss the contents yet leave no evidence that she'd been snooping. But she might have looked in the purse to see if there were any obvious clues. Shameful, but true.

Shay's purse, if she had one, was nowhere to be seen. Besides the bottle of whiskey, the cigarettes, and the small CorningWare ramekin she was using as an ashtray, there was a mound of folded clothing, a laptop plugged into the only outlet in sight, two Mountain Dew cans, and a stack of magazines.

Colleen tiptoed to the narrow counter and dug her phone from her purse. There were three calls from Andy, but just one voice mail. Colleen hesitated for only a moment before taking her coat from the foot of the bed and slipping it on, winding her scarf around her neck.

Despite her caution, the door squeaked and rattled. Colleen didn't look at Shay; if she'd woken the woman, she hoped she'd have the courtesy to feign sleep until Colleen got outside. Just these few moments of privacy, just long enough to talk to Andy.

As she eased the door open, she spotted something she'd missed the night before: tucked into the window, curling from the moisture condensing on the glass, was a photograph of a young man. Colleen's breath caught in her throat: Shay's son, Taylor, was beautiful, broad-shouldered and strong-jawed, with the same startling blue eyes as his mother. His dark blond hair was so thick it refused to stay flat. He had a tan and a smattering of freckles across his nose, which, combined with the dimple at one corner of his confident grin, gave him an air of wholesome mischief. He was the sort of boy you wanted to believe in, the boy who was a shoo-in for class president and dated the prettiest girls.

As Colleen slipped out the door, pulling it gently shut behind her, her heart withered as it had a thousand times before. *You're every bit as good as him*, she whispered to the wind, to her lost boy, and deep in her weary heart she waged her forever battle to believe it hard enough to make it true.

THE COLD WIND hit her like a sheet of metal, slamming into her lungs, crackling her nostrils, and assaulting her bare hands. Despite Shay's prediction, only another inch or two of snow had fallen since her arrival; she could still make out her footsteps and Dave's larger ones. Light peeped between blinds in the house's front windows. A gust lifted snow from the ground and swirled it around her face, stinging her cheeks, and Colleen hurried around the corner of the trailer, out of the wind. From this vantage point, she faced the side of the house as she made her call.

"Col, what happened?" Andy said before the phone finished the first ring. "I called you half a dozen times."

"Yes, sorry, I'm fine," Colleen said, thinking, *Three, it was only three.* "I didn't—it got so late and . . ."

"Where are you? Did you find a room?"

"Well, not exactly. I mean, yes, I had a place to sleep last night." It occurred to Colleen that Andy didn't know about the other boy, the other mother.

"You didn't call, and I got up this morning and there wasn't a message. I was about to call the airline."

"Oh, Andy." Something crumpled inside Colleen, and she felt like she might cry. But her first day in North Dakota had barely begun, and she couldn't afford tears. So she rubbed her eyes and focused on the cold leaching through her boots and freezing her ears and nose. "There's another boy. They went missing together. He's also twenty, and his name is Taylor, and he and Paul worked on the same rig and they both stayed at Black Creek Lodge." She told him the rest: arriving to find the airport closing for the night, Dave taking pity on her, driving her to the trailer. Shay sharing her blankets and food.

She left out the whiskey, the photograph of Taylor wedged in the window.

"But Hunter-Cole never mentioned the other boy," Andy said, skipping right over Colleen's ordeal, her introduction to Shay in the middle of the night. "Surely they must have been aware there were two of them."

"I *know*, Andy, there's something wrong here. Shay says that the oil companies routinely cover up workplace injuries. When we talked to the corporate office, they were giving us the runaround."

"Wait, hang on. Is Shay an attorney or something? Does she have a connection in the industry?"

"No, she's a . . ." Colleen thought, trying to remember if Shay had said what she did. *I told my boss something came up and hit the road*, she'd said, and Colleen—dazed and exhausted—hadn't bothered to ask her what job she'd left. "She did some research online."

"Well, I spent quite a bit of time online myself the other night."

Colleen hadn't stopped to wonder how Shay had been able to find things out that Andy hadn't. Her fingers flew so fast over her laptop keyboard; she seemed to type as fast as she thought. She was full of contradictions, something Colleen didn't have the energy to explain to Andy.

She looked down the street. Wisps of smoke wafted from chimneys; lights shone weakly from kitchen windows. Gusting drifts provided a snow globe whimsy at odds with the dispirited houses and shabby cars, the leafless black trees.

"I don't know where Shay got her information," she said, too tired to make the effort to protect his feelings. "But she said she'd read about all these accidents and workplace injuries. Things that weren't reported. Or weren't compensated, anyway."

"All right," Andy said, and in his tone Colleen detected the skepticism that had been present from the moment she first suggested coming out here. "Tell you what. Are you writing all of this down? If you email it to me, I'll keep it organized for Steve. He's supposed to call me today, he was going to make some calls to towns within a hundred-mile radius just double-checking on the hotel situation. Not that there are many to call—there's only a dozen towns in the whole state with more than a few thousand people."

The door of the house opened, and a figure stepped out, pulling a knit cap down over his ears. *Her* ears, Colleen corrected herself, as the flat-faced woman strode toward her more quickly than Colleen would have thought possible in unlaced Bean boots and a flapping parka. Her face was set in a determined scowl. In her bare hand was a wooden spoon.

"Listen, I need to go," Colleen said. "I'll call you later today."

She hung up and slipped her freezing hand into her pocket as the woman came to an indignant halt a few feet away, huffing white breath. She had a smear of something at one corner of her mouth, and graying blond hair pulled back in a plastic clip. She was around sixty and badly in need of a good moisturizer.

"Who the hell are you?"

"I'm Colleen Mitchell. I'm the—the other mom." She extended her hand, but the woman made no move to shake it. "I'm sorry I arrived too late to introduce myself last night."

"Jesus. I looked out and saw you out here, you could be anybody." She looked only slightly mollified.

"I thought— Shay said you'd called over . . . Brenda, right?"

"Yeah, I called to say you were in *town*, after Lee called me. I didn't tell her you could *stay.*"

Colleen struggled to keep up, blushing. Lee: Dave's wife's sister, if she was remembering right. "There're no rooms. I tried, I was going to stay in a hotel room and I . . . I am very sorry to inconvenience you."

Her voice sounded hollow even to herself, because really, how much inconvenience could she possibly be?

"Look. I'm real sorry for your loss, but—"

"My *loss*?" The word felt like a slap, and Colleen staggered back as she echoed it. "My son is *missing*, he's not—he's not—"

Brenda waved her hand. "Right, sorry. I meant I'm sorry for what you're going through, but it's a code issue. Having two people in there? With the generator and the tanks running like that?"

"I hardly imagine it's legal to have even one person living in your driveway, but I notice you took Shay's money," Colleen snapped, too stunned by Brenda's remark to censor the haughtiness that was her first defense when she felt attacked. "So perhaps *codes* aren't the issue."

Brenda crossed her arms over her chest, her scowl deepening. There was something stuck to the spoon, maybe oatmeal. "Look, you want to talk issues, let's talk about her smoking in there when I clearly told her not to, let's talk about the *cigarette butts* I found out here yesterday, let's talk about her running her computer and her hair dryer and I don't know what in there."

"Look, I'm sorry. I'll talk to her. If my presence is an issue, I'll be glad to add a per diem."

"A per what?"

"An increase in the rate you are charging her. To make up for the added use of your resources."

"Well, all right, then, because tanks are going to have to be taken care of twice as fast, plus there's all that gas. And look, I could've called the cops on you. Almost did, look out my kitchen window and seen a stranger standing in my yard."

Colleen bit back a retort and forced a tight smile on her face. "I'm so glad you didn't. I just had to call my husband, and I didn't want to disturb Shay."

"That woman's still *asleep?*"

"Is it any of your business?"

They both turned to look at Shay, who'd come out into the yard with a plaid blanket draped around her shoulders, her cigarettes and lighter in her hands. Her hair was a wild halo around her face. Smudged makeup ringed her eyes. "I'm not paying you rent to keep track of when I sleep, Brenda."

"I didn't tell you she could stay," the woman huffed. "And I told you no smoking, it's a fire hazard."

Shay walked to the alley that ran behind the house and calmly lit up. "Don't worry, I won't smoke on your property. 'Sides, the stove doesn't even work in this shitty tin can."

"You don't like it, good luck finding something else."

The argument had an air of lifelong hostility, as though Shay and Brenda were sisters, not strangers. "We're grateful to be staying here," Colleen said quickly. "If you'll just let me know about the per diem . . ."

"And make sure you don't run that generator all around the clock," Brenda added, turning her back on Shay. "You don't have to have it on all the time. You're just wasting gas and it won't make it a speck warmer in there."

"All right," Colleen said. "Thanks so much." She waited until Brenda went back inside to go stand with Shay in the alley.

"Fuckin' cold out here," Shay said. "Look, I wish I could offer you some coffee, but the stove—"

"Doesn't work," Colleen finished her sentence with a game smile. "Um, I know it's gauche to ask, but just how much are you paying her to stay here?"

"Well, I gave her two hundred on Tuesday and I told her I'd give her another couple hundred tomorrow. That's three hundred for the week plus a deposit on next week so she doesn't rent it out to someone else."

"Three *hundred* a week?" Colleen was stunned.

"Yeah. Now you see why I hate that bitch? Here's the thing that makes it worse—it never even occurred to her to rent it out until I got here. Then the minute she sees she can make some cash on it, she jacks up the price."

"How did you even find her?"

"So this is the best part. When I was on the road I started calling up here. Taylor had told me about the housing shortage, but I went ahead and tried the motels anyway."

"I did too," Colleen admitted.

"Yeah. Fat lot of good that did. Then I called city hall. Took me three tries to even get anyone to answer over there, and then they tell me I'm crazy to try. Suggested I try Minot. That's a good hour and a half from here, but by the time I hit Montana I was desperate enough I tried them too. Figured worst case I'd drive over during the day, drive back to sleep."

"Let me guess—nothing there, either?"

"Nope. Only when I got hold of the chamber of commerce there, they told me that they got whole families sleeping in the basement of a church, and that gave me an idea. I pulled over the next place that had Wi-Fi and I started calling churches in Lawton. I got this one lady who sounded nice. Like she gave a shit, you know? And then I told her about Taylor, and . . ."

Her voice trailed off and she stared out past Colleen's shoulder. The day was slowly brightening, and a few rays of sunlight glinted off the windows on the opposite side of the street. "Well. It's hard, talking about him, you know? Yeah, you know. Anyway, this lady at the church is the mother-in-law of this girl Brenda works with, and she knew about the motor home because I guess Brenda's ex-husband used to hunt with her boyfriend. So she knew it had a generator and all, and she called Brenda up for me. 'Course I doubt she has any idea what Brenda's charging me."

"Look, I'll be glad to pay it," Colleen said briskly. "I mean, you did all the legwork, and you let me stay." A thought occurred to her, and she flushed. "I'm sorry, that—I mean, is it all right if I stay? I'm absolutely happy on the, um, table and I'll buy more blankets today, and I can—"

"Shut up," Shay said. "Of course you can stay. What else are you going to do? Besides, we need to work together now. It doesn't make any sense for us to duplicate our efforts, you know? With two of us, it'll be harder for people to close doors in our faces."

Colleen thought about her vague plan from yesterday, to rent a car, set up a headquarters for her search in her motel room. It all seemed ludicrously naïve now. "Do you already have next steps in mind?"

"I figure best thing is for us to get a shower and something to eat and go over what we both know. Maybe we'll come up with something that way. Then we can head over to the lodge. There's a guy there that might talk to us today—I got shut down when I tried yesterday. I figure someone over there has to know something. The Hunter-Cole crew, someone on the staff, something. And also they have Taylor's things; they were hunting them down for me. I bet they have Paul's too."

Colleen flinched at the thought of collecting her son's belongings. Wouldn't that be tantamount to admitting he wouldn't be coming back for them? She could sense the despair slithering into the cracks in her composure. But that couldn't happen. She couldn't fall apart; she'd been in Lawton less than twelve hours.

"A shower sounds good," she said briskly. "Will Brenda let us come into the house to use hers?"

Shay laughed. She had an unexpectedly lush laugh, at odds with her voice, which was cigarette-rough and almost coarse. "She didn't offer. But I've got something better. You're in for an education."

six

SHAY CARRIED HER toiletries and a change of clothes in a pillow-case. Colleen used the laundry bag that matched her luggage. Shay gave her a washcloth she'd bought at Walmart, a thin orange one that she said was buy one, get one free.

"Now that's luck," Shay said, and Colleen couldn't tell if she was kidding.

Shay's car turned out to be the old white Explorer parked across the street. As she worked on the windshield using an ice scraper with the price sticker still attached, Colleen noted a mismatched side panel and several dents that had been patched and primed but not painted.

She watched for a couple of minutes before she couldn't stand it anymore. "Will you let me do that?"

Shay handed her the scraper, eyebrows raised. Colleen, wishing she'd brought thicker gloves than her thin leather driving ones, scored a crosshatch of scratches in the ice with the point of the scraper, then chipped away the segmented areas with brief, hard jabs of the blade. A fine dusting of ice blew in her face as the ice came off in chunks, her body warming to the task.

"Damn," Shay said admiringly.

"I didn't get to park my car in a garage until I was thirty," Colleen said, feeling awkwardly proud. "I've been scraping windshields since I was a kid. My dad used to give me a quarter to do his before work."

"Where did you grow up?"

"Maine. Little inland town called Limerock. My dad worked for the railroad."

Inside the car, they put their hands in the blast of the heating vents, waiting for the wipers to sweep away the last of the snow. Colleen tried not to look like she was checking out the interior. The leather seats were worn and split, the seams popped and the foam visible underneath. A feather-and-bead ornament swayed gently from the rearview mirror. In the console were a handful of coins, a half-empty pack of gum, and a cheap lighter. The cup holder bore a dried coffee ring.

But other than the ring, the car was surprisingly tidy. Colleen had anticipated crumpled fast-food bags, a smell of stale coffee and unwashed flesh, dirt in all the crevices. Instead, it was every bit as clean as her Lexus back home.

Shay eased the Explorer into drive and did a tight three-point turn, heading back into town.

"Jesus, how can you stand to drive in this stuff? I'm a nervous wreck," she said, turning onto Fourth Avenue, Lawton's four-lane main street. Behind them, a truck bore down at what seemed an unsafe speed, tapping the horn as he passed.

"You get used to it, I guess," Colleen said, watching the scenery go by. The town looked cleaner in the light of day, dusted with fresh snow, but also less appealing. The busy traffic didn't make up for the fact that the buildings they passed were run-down, low-slung brick and cinder-block shops appointed with modest signage and fronted with slushy parking lots. A huge billboard over a church parking lot advertised a cigarette shop. A school bus passed in the other direction, its wipers resolutely pushing off the swirling snow that had started up again.

Shay pulled into a massive gas station with two sets of bays, one for trucks and one for cars. Pickups mostly kept to the car side, but a jacked-up model with enormous tires idled next to the pumps on the truck side. A sign large enough to be seen from the other end of town said STAR SUPER PLAZA FUEL—SHOWERS—DINER—HOT COFFEE—24 HOURS. The word CLEAN flashed in neon underneath.

Shay found a space up next to the restaurant and cut the engine.

"Here?" Colleen asked.

"Yeah, what did you expect?"

"I don't know." Actually she'd thought Shay might have found a health club, perhaps even a nice one. "Women can go in there? I mean—are there separate facilities for men and women?"

"Nope, it's just one big showerhead that sprays in every direction. You have to be aggressive, find yourself an opening and squeeze on in." When Colleen was too horrified to respond, Shay flashed her a tight grin before opening her car door. "Come on, of course they have separate. You get your own private bathroom. Free shampoo and conditioner too, but I like to bring my own. And definitely you're going to need some shower shoes, because I don't trust them to disinfect enough after some of these guys, no matter how clean it looks in here."

In the convenience store, amid aisles of snack foods and coolers full of soft drinks, Colleen found rubber flip-flops and a package of hair elastics, and joined Shay in line.

"Don't buy those, I've got plenty," Shay said, eyeing the elastics.

"Oh. Well. I kind of need one now, to put my hair up."

"You're not going to wash it?"

"Um . . . maybe not." Colleen washed her hair only every few days; it was part of a regimen recommended by her colorist to preserve her color, rinsing only with cool water and using sulfate-free products.

"Well, here, then, you can have mine." Shay twisted her own po-nytail out of its band and handed it over. A few long curly strands were knotted to it.

"Thank you," Colleen said, looping it over a finger, trying not to show her distaste.

"It's probably going to be half an hour before our names come up. We might as well get some coffee."

"You mean for the shower?"

"Yeah, lot of these guys are living in their cars. They come in here to clean up after work."

"*After* work?"

"Yeah, night shift gets off at seven. So they get back to town and come here for a shower and a meal, then go crash."

"But they can't sleep in their cars—not in weather like this!"

Shay laughed. "I'm not saying I'd want to do it," she said, as they neared the head of the line. "But I would have if I had to, if Brenda hadn't come through. I talked to this one guy, he wasn't hardly older than Taylor. He's been in his car all week, got a job his first day up here but there was a delay on his room in the camp. Says he turns the car on three times a night and runs the heater to warm up and goes back to sleep. 'Course if it was me, I'd be having to pee every time I woke up. I'd probably pee in a Big Gulp cup rather than open the car door and let all that cold air in. Yeah, two showers," she added, to the harried-looking clerk.

"I'll get those," Colleen said primly, laying the flip-flops on the counter along with her credit card.

"You don't have to," Shay said, a slight edge to her voice. "I have money."

"Oh, I didn't—I mean, I'm happy to," Colleen stuttered, as the clerk waited. She gave the credit card a little push, willing the clerk to pick it up. After a painful moment, she did. "We can settle up later," Colleen said quietly.

Shay muttered something unintelligible, turning away. Colleen signed the slip quickly and followed her to the restaurant, where a waitress thrust laminated menus at them.

"Anywhere you can find, dolls," she said as she moved down the counter, refilling coffee cups. "I'll send Petey out to bus soon's I get a minute."

Every table in the place was occupied, but two men were in the process of leaving. Colleen inhaled deeply: coffee, bacon, a not-unpleasant note of burned potatoes. And aftershave—a masculine smell she associated with her father. Paul took after Andy, the pair of them insisting she buy only unscented soap and deodorant and shaving cream, and the shock of the forgotten scent kept her rooted to the spot for a moment, her father's memory startlingly present.

Martin Hockemeyer would have been at home here, a thought that made Colleen wistful. She had never been particularly close to her father, and he had died when Paul was in grade school after their visits had diminished to once-yearly trips to Florida. Even in old age, Martin had been a man's man, puttering around their trailer park wearing a tool belt and fixing things for the widows while her mother gardened in her sunhat, beaming with thin and flinty pride.

"Move," Shay said, digging into the small of Colleen's back with a knuckle. "Else we'll lose that table."

But the waiting customers stepped respectfully aside. "Ma'am," one said as they passed, touching his cap in such a perfect imitation of Martin that Colleen briefly wondered if she'd conjured him from her imagination.

The men who were leaving wore bulky earth-colored coats over jeans and enormous boots. One of them pulled on the kind of hat that some of the kids used to wear at Paul's high school, what Colleen thought of as a Berenstain Bear hat, corduroy with a plush lining and ear flaps. At home they were a style statement, if a clumsy one. Here, she suspected they were strictly utilitarian.

"We left a mess for you girls," the man in the hat said in a rueful drawl. He pulled a wad of napkins from the dispenser and wiped at the toast crumbs and syrup smears on the table.

"Don't worry about it," Shay said, tossing her hair over her shoulders before plopping down in the chair and unzipping her coat. Colleen had noticed that Shay became unconsciously flirtatious around men, her voice throatier and a sashay in her walk. "Drive safe."

Colleen slipped off her own coat and draped it over her chair. She hung her purse over the coat and, after a brief hesitation, set her laundry bag on the floor, since there was nowhere else to put it. She avoided looking at the plates stacked at the edge of the table; a brief glance at the bright yellow smear of yolk, the rinds of a pancake stack, had made her faintly nauseous.

A busboy came by with a tub and cleared everything away in a clanking flurry, followed by a sweet-faced waitress with a red ponytail and at least half a dozen earrings in each ear. She wiped the table with a rag that smelled of bleach and Windex, lifting the salt and pepper shakers to clean underneath. She pocketed the tips—one of the men had left a ten, the other a fan of ones—and dug her pad from her pocket.

"What are you having?"

"We just got on the shower list," Shay said. "Think we have time to eat before we come up?"

The waitress looked over at the kitchen and squinted at the row of orders clipped to the warming lights. "Yeah, should be fine. They got it under control back there."

"Okay. I'll have a western omelet, biscuit, potatoes fried well. Can you do that?"

"Sure thing. You, hon?" She looked at Colleen expectantly.

"Um—toast?"

"White, wheat, rye?"

"Wheat, please."

"Give her a couple of scrambled eggs too," Shay said. "You sure you don't want a biscuit? No? And potatoes, cook them like mine. You got any decent melon today?"

"Sure, got the honeydew."

"We'll have some of that too."

The waitress left with their order. Shay dug in her purse—really, it was more like a tote bag, a large rectangular brown canvas affair with an appliqué of pink birds—and took out a plain gray notebook. More digging produced a cheap mechanical pencil. Shay opened the notebook to a clean page and pressed it flat on the table.

A different waitress came by and turned their cups right side up, pouring steaming black coffee without asking. "I'll get your creamer in a second, or you can just fetch it," she said, already moving on to another table.

Shay got up and grabbed a little metal jug of cream off the counter. Colleen saw how men watched her move, their eyes both hungry and glazed. Shay was wearing the same jeans she'd had on yesterday, dark denim with a loop of sparkling topstitching on each back pocket, curving over her narrow rear. Colleen felt even more self-conscious, dressed in her wool pants and silk and mohair sweater. She took a sip of the coffee, hot enough to scald. She blew on the cup and took another, longer sip. It tasted so good she thought she might cry.

"Just black?" Shay asked, pouring a long stream of cream into her coffee until it was pale as caramel. "Okay, let's talk about money. I don't mind keeping track. We can split it all down the middle, the shared stuff. You got the showers, they're twelve dollars—I know, they jack you—and I can get breakfast, but I got to be honest, I'm getting to the bottom of my cash so if you could chip in for your half of the trailer that would be . . . let's see, it was Tuesday to Tuesday, you got here . . ."

Colleen watched uncomfortably as Shay wrote a neat column of numbers, her pencil flying over the numerals. "Four days out of seven, at three hundred, that's eighty-five dollars and change if we split it. I don't mind covering the deposit."

"Shay . . ." Colleen said. "I don't—this is—let me just get it all. I brought a lot of cash."

Shay was already shaking her head before Colleen finished speaking. When she frowned, the brackets around her mouth and the fine lines along her top lip made her look older. "Let's just keep it square, okay?"

"I just want to find my son. Our sons. I don't—"

Shay slammed her hand down flat on the table, making the coffee cups jump. Some spilled over the edge of Colleen's, sloshing onto the table.

"Don't you think that's what I want?" Shay demanded. Her eyes shone with tears, but she brushed them angrily away with the cuff of her sweater. "Don't you think that's what I'm thinking every second of the day? There's so much of him in my head, I just have to—I have to—"

She looked down at her numbers, carefully closed the loop of an 8, drew two lines below the total. "I have to keep my brain moving. Okay? If I don't—oh, God, I don't know. I just do things, keep busy.

That way everything, Taylor and all those little moments when I'm so terrified I want to scream, they just kind of stay aboveground a little. I do this"—she tapped the paper with the point of her pencil—"and it helps for a minute. So humor me here. Let me do my math."

She picked up her own mug with two hands and drank deeply, the heat of the coffee evidently not bothering her.

"I understand," Colleen said, though she didn't, not really. But if the numbers on the pad helped Shay, she wasn't about to argue.

The first waitress was back with their food. "Careful, it's hot," she said. "Ketchup? Hot sauce?"

"Hot sauce for sure. You got any strawberry jam?" Shay asked. "Col, you want anything?"

Colleen shook her head. No one but Andy had called her Col since college, but she found that she didn't mind.

"Eat," Shay said, salting her potatoes. Colleen's stomach rumbled. Hunger felt like a betrayal. She picked up her fork and poked at her scrambled eggs, pushing a thin string of egg white out of view under the toast. She took an experimental bite of potato. It was good, salty and hot and crispy, the sort of thing Colleen never ordered. Breakfast, when she had anything at all, was usually a protein bar or oatmeal, but she preferred to wait as long as she could before eating. She had lost thirty pounds on Weight Watchers three—or was it four?—years ago, but all but five were back, and she had been vaguely planning to try again to lose it this spring.

She took another bite.

"You wanted to go to the police station this morning, right?" Shay asked. "They open at nine. We can go straight from here."

"I just thought an in-person visit might, uh, underscore . . ."

"Yes. Definitely. We want to be a burr on their ass. Then I want to go back to Black Creek. When I was there the other day I couldn't get anywhere with the desk girls. Dumb as stumps. The manager's supposed to be there today, and we can get the boys' things. You got your ID, right?"

"Shower for Capp . . . Capp . . ." a female voice came on the intercom.

"Capparelli," Shay said. "It's not that hard! Listen, you go ahead and take the first shower if you want. Finish eating, though, let them wait a few minutes, they won't give it away."

Colleen crammed down the eggs and a single triangle of toast. She took her things and headed back to the counter, where the clerk pointed down the hall. "Number four."

Inside was much better than she had expected. It was like a hotel bathroom, except that every surface but the ceiling was tiled. On the floor, one corner dampened and stuck to the tile, was a rectangle of paper labeled BATH MAT in blue lettering. A blue plastic trash can with a fresh liner was the only other industrial touch. A long counter held a folded towel with a paper-wrapped bar of soap on top.

Colleen took a deep breath and looked at herself in the mirror. The past few days had taken a toll on her. The bulb in the motor home bathroom had been blessedly dim, so she'd been able to pretend the dark circles and sunken flesh were the result of bad lighting. Here, under the bright fluorescents, every wrinkle and pore was on display. The whites of her eyes were bloodshot, the lids puffy, the lines at the corners like her mother's before she died. Her skin looked like it had been carved from wax, yellowish and sagging. Her lips had no color, disappearing into her face like an old woman's.

Was this what grief looked like? Colleen reached out and touched her image with her fingers, leaving a smudge. She took the washcloth Shay had given her and wiped the glass. She was a wiper of smudges. A cleaner of countertops. A vacuumer of crumbs. Only . . . it was Paul's fingerprints, his jam smears, the remains of his pizza crusts to which she had devoted herself for so long. Since the day he left for Syracuse a year and a half ago, his absence had withered her, scouring out what was left inside and draining any traces of youth that remained on the outside. She'd been fifty when he graduated from high school, Zumba-fit and pampered, the envy of her friends, the recipient—still!—of the occasional drunken pass at neighborhood dinner parties. Now she was . . . this.

And if he was really gone? Forever? What then?

Colleen gasped, doubling over, elbows on the cold countertop, unable to breathe. She closed her eyes and murmured *no, no, no*. Because she didn't mean gone. She meant dead.

Dead.

She hadn't allowed herself to think the shape of the word until now. It had hovered, slinking around the edge of her consciousness, ever since the missed Sunday call. A mere shadowy wraith first, as the hours and days passed, it had become more insistent, waiting for her to slip, to forget for one second, to fall into incautious sleep. But she'd been so careful. So careful! Under her clothes her thighs and inner arms were bruised from where she pinched herself. Because that's what she did. Every time that cursed thought threatened—*dead*—she punished herself until the pain forced it to recede.

But here, in the mirror, was evidence that she hadn't escaped the fear at all: the proof was in her face's wornness, its ugliness. Colleen pushed herself up from the counter and tore at her clothes. One of her blouse's buttons popped off in her clumsy fingers. She yanked her panties off along with her pants. She unsnapped her bra and ripped it off her arms and threw it; it landed behind the toilet. Her socks ended up nearby. There. *There!* Naked and pale and useless, the mother of no one, nothing. It was hard enough to fight the terror without the noise, that terrible racket echoing around the small room, and Colleen covered her ears to drown it out and it was only when someone started pounding on the door that she realized that the sounds were coming from *her*. She tried to stop, the wailing turning to gulping breaths, and someone—a man—was saying in a muffled voice, *Ma'am, ma'am. Are you all right, ma'am?*

And then there was Shay's voice, firm and hard. "Colleen. Open the door. Let me in *now*." Colleen stared at the doorknob for only a few seconds before picking up the towel and holding it in front of herself and opening the door a fraction of an inch.

Shay's blue eye, the smell of coffee, the din behind her. "Colleen," Shay repeated calmly. "Let me in now. Okay? Open the door. I'm coming in."

And then she did just that, pushing the door open wide enough to squeeze through before Colleen had made up her mind. Once inside, Shay closed the door nearly all the way and put her face to the opening and said, "We're fine in here, don't worry." Then she closed and locked the door.

Colleen folded her arms over her breasts. The towel was ridiculous, it hung in front of her, concealing part of her stomach and thighs but leaving her hips exposed, the sagging dollops of flesh at her sides.

Shay didn't blink. She didn't reach for Colleen, either, which was good because Colleen wouldn't have forgiven that, even if she'd been dressed.

"So this is where you thought you'd fall apart?" Shay demanded, in that same steely voice. "With an audience? Honey, they're not going to forget that. You just got yourself talked about for the rest of the week."

"I don't *care*," Colleen said. Because she didn't. And wasn't that odd? Not to care what all those strangers thought? But she had finally admitted to herself that she was only a husk, a shell, a used-up woman, and maybe there was some freedom in that.

"You let yourself think worst-case," Shay continued. "That was your mistake. Want to know where I fell apart? Because I did the exact same thing as you're doing now. Well, I kept my clothes on. It was somewhere in Nevada and it was about three in the morning. I'd stopped because the highway sign said there was an Arby's, twenty-four hours, and I hadn't eaten all day. Only it was shut down, the Arby's. Sign busted and everything. There wasn't *shit* at that exit and the next one was forty miles. There was some kind of mom-and-pop diner and a gas station with some old toothless perv staring out the window. And I parked and got out of the car and I picked up a rock from the flowerbed and I was going to throw it through the window, I *swear* I was, was going to wipe the sneer off his face. And then I just let that rock drop down on the ground, and I started screaming. Worse than you, actually. I screamed and cried until there was snot all over my face and my voice was just about gone. I thought about Taylor and the last time I talked to him, and I went down on my knees and when I couldn't cry anymore I lay down. *Facedown*, right on the asphalt, and I took my nails and dragged them over the road. Here. *Here*, look at this." She put her hand up in Colleen's face, and the nails were broken off and the nail beds red and scabbed. How had Colleen not noticed?

"I got sand and shit up under my nails and I didn't care. There was sleet or rain or something coming down and I just lay there, all cried out, and then I started to worry that the guy had called the cops, which, come on, wouldn't you? I know I would. I got up and got back in the car and got on the highway and drove that forty miles, and there was a Shell there with a bathroom and I cleaned myself up. I got a coffee, and when the guy asked me how I was doing, I said fine. I said I was *fine*, Colleen."

After a minute Colleen nodded, because it seemed as though Shay was waiting for a response. She adjusted the towel.

"So that's once for each of us. But that's *it*. That's all you get. You are not going to fall apart on me again. Because I'll cut you loose, Colleen. I swear I will."

Colleen nodded again, because it suddenly made sense. Grief was an indulgence. A weakness. She'd been careless and she'd let it come too close.

It helped, knowing Shay had done it too. Even if she was lying. Even if she'd made it up for her.

"I'm fine now."

"Yes. You are." Shay narrowed her eyes and considered her. "You got any makeup with you?"

"No, I—I left it back at the trailer. I didn't think—"

"Okay. You shower and get dressed. You only get twenty minutes and if you go over, you have to pay for another full twenty, so be fast. I'll wait. It's getting late enough in the day there's a couple of showers free, so whenever you get out, I'll go in."

Shay looked around the bathroom. She bent down and picked up all of Colleen's clothes and laid them out on the counter, turning the socks right side out and retrieving the bra without comment. Then she let herself out the door, squeezing it shut so no one could see past her into the bathroom. And Colleen was alone again.

She ran the shower hot and didn't bother to get her shower gel out of the toiletry bag. She unwrapped the soap and tied up her hair in the elastic Shay had given her, and stepped into the shower enclosure. The water sluicing over her felt shockingly good, and she let her breath out in a long sigh, closing her eyes and letting it cascade over her breasts and shoulders and neck. She made an effort to punish herself for taking pleasure from the heat and the spray against her skin, but she was too weak to resist.

seven

SHAY KEPT AN eye on Colleen as they drove the mile to the police station, gauging her reaction. Colleen watched the old downtown go by, her lips pressed together and her hands clutching the strap of her purse. Shay wondered what the streets of her town looked like—probably a far cry from both the ice-crusted, dreary streets of Williston and the dusty brown hills around Fairhaven. This trip was the farthest east Shay had ever been, and she had a made-for-TV notion of New England—horse-drawn wagons, crusty Maine fishermen, maple syrup, charming cobblestone streets lined with expensive little shops. In a way, Williston was just Fairhaven with snow and natural resources; for Colleen, it must be as foreign as another planet.

At least she had come out of the shower with her shit together. She kept her chin high and didn't acknowledge the curious and pitying glances from the other customers. Shay wondered if Colleen realized that the moment they walked into the place, everyone knew who they were. It was the third morning in a row Shay had eaten breakfast there, and twenty minutes into her first visit, she had made sure everyone in the miserable little place knew exactly who she was and what she was looking for. She'd held on to a faint hope that someone would be able to help that first day, that one of the customers or waitresses had been keeping a secret or a confidence. That when she laid Taylor's picture flat on the counter next to the cash register, and they saw his big blue eyes and megawatt smile, they'd realize how badly she needed to find him, and they'd step up and say . . .

It's a hell of a thing. Can't believe it got this out of hand. Can see how you must have been worried sick. Boys will be boys . . .

Some caper, a case of bad judgment, a terrible misunderstanding. *Something.* Shay hadn't told Colleen the whole story, how after the Arby's parking lot episode, for the next forty miles she'd bargained hard with God while her fingers bled, letting Him know that whatever Taylor had done, she would forgive, if only he was alive and safe somewhere. A night in jail, she could accept that. A knocked-up girlfriend. A lost weekend in the Indian casino. A barroom brawl, a case of the clap, a fight that ended with the other guy in the hospital—she'd forgive all of those. By the time she crossed the North Dakota line the next day, she'd upped the ante. Would she forgive Taylor for being involved with a hit-and-run? Drugs? A shootout? Yes, yes, and yes, and there she was to prove it, laying his picture down, ready for the truth.

Only she'd been met with one blank stare after another.

The police station was blocky and modern, maybe fifteen years old, more glass than brick. It looked out of place on the corner where it hunkered, across from a shuttered movie theater and a Meineke muffler shop. Shay found a parking spot out front and dug quarters from her console. Fifty cents an hour; she doubted they'd need even the first quarter, but she put three in the meter just in case.

At the door, Colleen hesitated. "You've been here already, right?"

"Yes."

"And they stonewalled you."

"Yes."

"All right." Colleen nodded to herself and squared her shoulders, tipped her chin up, and went in. Shay followed her to the receptionist's desk, but Colleen ignored her. She pulled off her gloves and laid them down on the counter before saying, "My name is Colleen Mitchell. I'd like a word with the chief of police, please."

The receptionist, a young dark-haired woman with thick-fringed eyelashes behind plastic-framed glasses, gawped at her. "He's pretty busy. He mostly only sees people with appointments."

"I understand," Colleen said calmly. "Please let him know that I have come all the way from Boston to talk to him. About a private and sensitive matter," she added, speaking over the young woman's protest. "I'll wait right here."

"You can sit over there in those chairs—"

"I prefer to stand."

As the receptionist disappeared down a hall, other people in the warren of desks behind the reception area glanced up curiously. Shay, who hadn't been permitted to talk to anyone but the on-duty sergeant when she visited two days ago, considered Colleen. She was nice-looking in profile, with her expensively styled hair and good skin. She had probably been gorgeous twenty years ago, and now she was the kind of woman Shay made fun of. The kind of woman who could afford to buy anything but settled for shapeless, boring old-lady clothes. Whose makeup case held three shades of concealer and no eye shadow.

But she had something. An . . . elegance, Shay supposed, or else just a knack for giving off a rich vibe without trying. Here she was without any makeup on, her boots rimed with salt and her clothes wrinkled from the suitcase, and she could still probably walk down Fifth Avenue and have people waiting on her hand and foot.

The receptionist returned. "Chief Weyant says he can give you a few minutes before his next appointment. Just wait over there."

"As I said, I'll stand. Thank you."

Shay took a chair, picked up a brochure from a stack on the table. "Towed, Stored, and Abandoned Vehicles." She scanned it without reading the text, put it back. Colleen stood motionless, gazing at the wall above the desks, appearing not to notice everyone staring at her. When the chief came down the hall, she gathered up her gloves and purse and extended her hand.

"Mrs. Mitchell?"

Shay's first impression of Chief Weyant was that he had the right look for a difficult job, projecting unflappable calm while his department tried to keep a lid on behind-the-scenes turmoil brought by the boom. Fortyish and fit, Weyant had the ramrod-straight posture and bland good looks to carry off the polyester uniform shirt without giving up an ounce of authority. He was probably six one, six two, and his dark, thick hair was just a shade longer than a military-style brush cut, a bit of silver showing at the temples.

Colleen flashed him a smile so brief it might have been imagined, and shook his hand. "Thank you for agreeing to talk to me and Ms. Capparelli."

The chief glanced over at Shay and acknowledged her with a nod. If he knew about her prior visit, he didn't let on. "Sure thing. Come on back. Get you ladies some coffee? Water?"

Colleen declined, murmuring her thanks, and they followed him to a large office at the corner of the building. The windows looked out over the street where they'd parked, and then past the downtown to the old houses and barns and vacant lots at the edge of town, beyond which the white-and-tan landscape stretched to the horizon under an oppressive gray sky. The snow had stopped, only to seem to be gathering for a greater onslaught later.

The women took the chairs facing the chief's desk. Weyant rested his hands on the laminate desktop and regarded them gravely.

"Let me start by telling you the same thing Sergeant Sanders told Mrs. Capparelli. We are concerned that your sons have been out of communication, and we are devoting as many resources as we can to locating them. But we can't rule out the possibility that there's an explanation other than them getting into some kind of trouble. We've seen too many of these boys light out of here without giving notice, just to show up a few weeks or months later in another state entirely. You know how it is when you're that age."

"Not really, no," Colleen said coldly. She sat very erect in her chair. "Please share a little more about your line of thinking."

"Oh. Well—all I meant was, you got a twenty-year-old, especially a boy, a male, there's going to be a lot more hormones and such than common sense at work. If I had a nickel for every fight we had to break up in the bars—and this is *after* these boys come off a twelve-hour shift that would knock me out, I'm not afraid to say it—well, I'd be a rich man. Then we got the casinos barely an hour away, or—and this happens more often than we like to admit—they just get tired of the guy-to-girl ratio around here, they take the money they've made and go looking somewhere else. Find a girl and an easier job and don't get around to writing home for a while."

His speech concluded with a shrug, the chief looked relieved, even a little pleased with himself. It was a better, smoother version of the speech that Sanders had given Shay two days earlier. Clearly, Weyant had put a little thought into it, adding the bit about the boys coming off long shifts, for instance—that was a nice touch. Maybe he saw the writing on the wall, figured he'd be using the speech on a regular basis. Heck, maybe it really was true, and he already had.

Colleen didn't say a word. She watched him expectantly, barely blinking, her face giving nothing away. The chief put a finger under his collar, loosening it, and cleared his throat, waiting for one of them to say something. But Shay decided to take a page out of Colleen's book and stayed silent.

"So," Weyant finally said.

"My son has not left town for a *girl* or a *casino*," Colleen said, her voice tight. "He and his friend Taylor are missing. Instead of focusing on the unimaginative list of possible scenarios you've come up with, I am wondering why you and your men aren't doing any actual police work in an effort to find them." She held up a hand to stop Weyant's protests. "I understand that your resources are finite. I can only guess at the demands on your staff. I'm not a police officer. But I damn well expect my son—*our* sons—to get at least as much attention as a liquor store holdup or highway accident or domestic dispute. And you haven't told me one concrete thing you've done to find out where they are."

"As I told Mrs. Capparelli—"

"And that's another thing." Fury had gradually shaded Colleen's face a deep red. Shay marveled at the change in her. Somehow she'd pulled her shit together, turning from the blubbering mess in the truck stop to a fearsome bitch. "It's *Ms.* Capparelli. Not Mrs."

Weyant looked from Colleen to Shay and back again. "Look here," he started.

"I am interested in everything you have to say," Colleen went on, opening her purse and searching through the contents. "In fact, I want to make sure I get it all down."

"I'll take notes," Shay said, grabbing her notebook out of her own handbag. Later there would be time to resent Weyant for being intimidated by Colleen after dismissing her. For now, they needed to benefit from the momentum. "You talk."

"Thank you." Colleen returned her purse to the floor. "Let's start with which officers are involved with the case, or assigned to it, or whatever the proper term is."

"I don't have to . . ." Weyant wiped his forehead, shaking his head, before starting over. "I wouldn't want to say without checking the duty roster. But you can consider me your liaison. I don't want you contacting my officers, disrupting their work. You need something, you come to me."

Colleen raised an eyebrow. "Noted."

"That's not what Sanders told me before," Shay muttered.

"It's all right, Shay," Colleen said, giving her a bland smile. "We can revisit that later if we need to. Now, what steps have your officers taken? Who have they interviewed; what leads have they tracked down?"

"When *Ms.* Capparelli notified us of her concern, officers were sent out to the Black Creek Lodge—"

"Not the *first* time I called," Shay interrupted, as she wrote. "Took you all three days."

"They interviewed staff there and confirmed the boys hadn't been around for a few days," Weyant continued, testily. "They talked to their employers. Believe they went out in the field. They'll have the names of the supervisors they talked to. But the upshot is, no one on the rig knew anything. The boys simply didn't show up for work."

"The officers spoke to the men who worked closely with Taylor and Paul? Their coworkers?"

"I'm sure they did," Weyant said, looking not very sure at all.

"What about other men who were staying at the lodge? Restaurants or other places they were known to go?"

"Well, now you're getting into a gray, that is to say, an area where we don't devote more resources until there's a reason. Something to suggest a direction to go."

"You mean, like them still not turning up?" Shay snapped.

Weyant turned on her, his irritation obvious. "Like an indication that harm has actually been done to them. Your son's vehicle hasn't been seen at the lodge since the day you reported him missing, which to me says there's a good chance he drove out of here on his own steam."

"*Truck.* Not vehicle. My son drives a white Chevy Silverado. And what about the fact he left his things in his room?"

Weyant shrugged. "A few changes of clothes and some deodorant? There wasn't anything valuable. He could easily have replaced it all. Or maybe he took what he cared about with him. I don't see that meaning a whole lot one way or another."

"What about the boys' phone records?" Colleen said. "Have you looked into who they spoke to? Whether there have been calls since they disappeared?"

"Let me guess," Weyant said wearily. "You like watching cop shows. No, look, don't get all in a twist. It's just, to put it mildly, they can give you an unrealistic idea of how that sort of thing proceeds. Even if we had the boys' phone numbers—"

"Gosh, too bad they wouldn't have been all over the lodge's records," Shay interrupted. "Or their employment applications, for that matter. Or in Sergeant Sanders's notes, since I told him."

"Even if we had the numbers," Weyant continued, ignoring her, "they're likely to be with out-of-state carriers, and we can't just fax them a picture of our badges. It's a little more complicated than that."

"Well, I'll tell you what," Colleen said, reaching across the desk to a little bronzed stand holding the chief's business cards. She handed one to Shay and jotted a phone number on the back of another, along with the word *Sprint.* Then she added her own name and phone number. "We'll give you their phone numbers right now. Carriers, too. There, we just saved you two steps. I put my phone number on there too, so you can reach me whenever you have something to report. Feel free to share it with your officers. Now, what happens next?"

Weyant blinked, looking both angry and a little overwhelmed. "What happens next is I thank you for your input, and I go back to doing my job, which is to put my limited resources and budget to work the best way I can see. Yes, I will follow up with these numbers and I will review the case with my staff. But you want to be the one to explain to all these people"—he smacked his hand down on a stack of folders stuffed with paperwork—"why you're more important than they are? You want to know what else I'm dealing with? How about a woman whose boyfriend hit her so hard her teeth went through her lip? Or this one, we got a six-year-old who disappeared Tuesday, and his father's missing too, and he's got a known meth problem and a gun."

He was breathing hard, leaning over his desk, looking like he wanted to sweep the folders to the floor. It was time to go. They'd pushed as hard as they were going to get away with—for now.

"You'll follow up and let us know," Colleen said, standing with dignity. "We appreciate that. But let me add one thing. I can mobilize the press in my own hometown easily. Maybe you don't care much what they're saying about Lawton and its police department in the greater Boston area. But my husband is a respected attorney with contacts all over the country, and he won't hesitate to involve the media if we feel that the police are not giving our son's disappearance sufficient attention."

She turned and headed for the door. Shay stood too, as did Weyant. "As for me, I may be nobody," Shay said, "and I don't have money and I don't know anyone important. But I won't go down quiet. This is my *son* who's missing. I'm his *mom*, and I don't have anything to lose."

She closed the door behind her, harder than she intended, the sound getting the attention of everyone in adjoining offices. Shay could feel her face burning as she strode after Colleen, refusing to meet the eyes of the people they passed.

They didn't speak as they exited the building or on the way to the car. Shay slid into the driver's seat and put the key in the ignition, but she didn't turn it. Colleen put her seat belt on and sat with her arms folded, staring straight ahead.

Then she started to shake. Shay watched Colleen's careful composure disintegrate, torn between sympathy and the knowledge that it was going to get a lot harder before it got any easier.

"You did good," she said quietly, as silent tears streamed down Colleen's face.

Colleen nodded, not bothering to wipe the tears away. "He was just so . . . I don't know. Smug? Supercilious?"

"I don't have any idea what that second one means, but I don't like that fucker. Only it doesn't matter how we feel about him. We need to *use* him, Col, you hear? Him and everyone else who can help us. Nothing else matters. Now, we going to the lodge? You ready for that?"

"Yes," Colleen whispered fiercely, digging for a tissue. "Yes, I am."

eight

SHAY WAS A good driver, Colleen had to give her that. She'd adapted to the road conditions and didn't make any of the beginner mistakes that caused so much trouble back east. She hovered under the speed limit, left ample room for the cars in front of her, and dropped back whenever the ubiquitous long-bed trucks passed them.

They drove back through town, block after block of strip malls and lumberyards and churches now familiar. A few more times back and forth and she'd have the whole town memorized. What was it Paul had said, during his first trip home? That it was easy to feel like you fit in. Something like that. He'd been irritated when Andy called Lawton a one-horse town. Andy hadn't meant anything by the description, but something had already changed between them: it was as though for the first time in his life Paul had found something that was his alone, and he guarded it jealously.

By then they'd accepted that nothing they did or said was going to change Paul's mind. Any hopes that the first few weeks of hard work would convince Paul of the absurdity of his choice were dashed when he returned home even more enthusiastic than before he'd left. He paced the house restlessly during that first visit, and if he didn't complain out loud that he couldn't wait for his days off to be over, it was only because they'd all retreated into a state of forced politeness, the aftermath of the violent arguments before he left.

How Colleen had longed to touch her son during that visit. To put her arms around him, to inhale his scent, to reassure herself that he was still hers. But something was broken in their relationship. Oh, for heaven's sake, she knew exactly what was broken, because she'd been the careless one who broke it. She was the one who delivered ultimatums and demands, years and years of them, thinking she was building him into something stronger and better, believing that someday—eventually—he'd come around.

If she had other sons, she would know what to do next time. Colleen understood now that a boy of eighteen or nineteen might not be a man in every way, but he wasn't going to let anyone tell him what to do. Her belief in her own authority struck her as ridiculous and even pitiable now, proof of a careless ignorance, which felt, in the worst moments, like the sin that had driven him away.

She'd been the one to find his note that morning, the morning Andy was supposed to drive him back to Syracuse to start his sophomore year, which was actually his second attempt at his freshman year, though they didn't discuss that. It should have been Andy who found the note, because he was always up first. He made the coffee and got the paper while she was in the shower, then came up and took his turn in the shower while she dried her hair and dressed. But Colleen hadn't slept well that night. She woke at three o'clock and tried to get back to sleep until five, turning one way and another trying to get comfortable, alternately too hot and, after she cast off the covers, too cold. Andy slept through it all, as she replayed the week's arguments in her head, Paul's anger and their objections and pleading, the plans she thought they'd all agreed to at the therapist's office, his grudging agreement to stay on the Concerta and Pristiq.

At five, she gave up. She padded down the hall in her bare feet and briefly considered looking in on Paul, one last chance to watch her son sleep before he left, abandoning the idea mostly because she didn't think she could open the door without waking him. She went downstairs and got the coffee out of the freezer and a filter from the cabinet and had been about to fill the pot with water when she saw the piece of paper centered next to a bowl of apples on the island. Paul's handwriting, blocky and childish and slanted down the page. She hadn't even begun to read when she knew he was gone. Her fault, her fault, all her fault.

The road out of town seemed carved by a router that dug wide ditches on either side, for reasons Colleen couldn't fathom. One wrong turn and any of these trucks could catch a wheel and tumble in, like soldiers into a moat. The land was not as flat as it looked from the air; a long, gradual ascent led them past empty fields, stalks of some dead crop poking through snow, and warehouse-size buildings that seemed cobbled together from sheets of metal. Once they crested the top of the hill, more of the same was laid out in front of them as far as she could see: squared-off fields, graveled drives that led to roundabouts before heading back to the road, small squat clusters of industrial vehicles.

Shay signaled and eased over to the shoulder, taking a slow right turn. There was a bridge, pavement edged with rocky earth, over the ditch or culvert or whatever it was.

"This is it?" Colleen asked as they pulled even with a guard shack. Downhill from the shack, on the other side of a parking lot the size of the one in front of Walmart, was a grid of long, low buildings that reminded Colleen of the chicken farm in Vermont she had visited once as a child, the stench of the cramped open-air buildings worse than anything she had ever smelled.

When Shay rolled down her window, the only scent on the air was of the cold. A man bundled head to toe came out of the shack with a clipboard in his hand. He was wearing cloth gloves with the fingertips cut off, clutching a pen.

"Me again," Shay said. "Shay Capparelli. I'm here to see Martin."

"He know you're coming?" The man spoke from underneath a fleece hood with a mask covering the lower half of his face. The shack must have no insulation at all.

"Yup." The two stared at each other for a moment, the wind blowing snow up from the ground and into his eyes, then the man waved them on and retreated into the shack.

"I said I'd be back," Shay said defensively. "So yeah, he *ought* to know."

The parking lot was only about a third full, but many of the spaces had recently been occupied, judging from the snow pattern. Shay parked next to one of the few scraggly trees in the lot, the Explorer dwarfed by the massive pickup trucks on either side. Colleen followed Shay to a cedar-sided lodge at the intersection of the long, plain buildings. The doors and railing were festooned with dry brown pine garland, and a wooden deck and steps out front had been shoveled and salted.

"They put some money into the main building," Shay said grudgingly. "It's pretty nice. You know what the dorms are made of, though? Shipping containers. Just like they send over from China. They freight them in, weld them together and cut holes for windows, and put up the lodge practically overnight. Martin, he's the manager we're going to see, he says when they dismantle this place you won't be able to tell it was ever here."

"Paul told us this boom will last for twenty years. At least. That seems like a long time for a temporary structure."

"Yeah, Taylor said some people are saying that. But the boom in the seventies? That ended pretty much overnight, left a lot of people out of work," Shay said in disgust. "I had an uncle, down near Galveston, showed up one day and the company was gone. Not just the rig, not just the portable office, the *whole company.* He was out a month's pay, didn't find work for the rest of the year. That's why these camps are all temporary now, nobody wants to get stuck with a building down the road."

Their boots clanged against the metal tread embedded in the steps. They entered a tiled vestibule with another set of doors leading inside, a sort of air lock that kept the wintry air from blowing into the building. In a box on the floor were dozens of pale blue fabric booties and a hand-lettered sign reading WATCH YOUR FEET! WEAR BOOTIES PLEASE! THIS IS YOUR HOME—ACT LIKE IT!

"Wow," Colleen said, reaching in the box. "Just like at an open house."

"That doesn't mean you," Shay scoffed. "That's for when the guys come in with mud all over their boots. Believe me, you don't qualify."

Colleen tried to ignore a flash of irritation as she stomped off as much caked snow as she could. She was growing tired of Shay pointing out the chasm between them every chance she got. Inside, two girls who couldn't have been more than twenty-five sat on high stools behind a rustic wooden counter. They had been laughing together, but they went silent when they saw Shay. The one whose plastic name tag read BRIT got off her stool and busied herself with something under the counter. The other one blushed and looked at her nails. She was wearing a lot of eye makeup, dramatic wings of silver shading to black, and had tried to cover up the ravages of acne with heavy foundation that didn't quite match her skin. Her name tag read JENNIE.

"Martin said to tell you he's sorry but he can't talk to you anymore," Jennie said without preamble.

"That right?" Shay said, slamming her purse down on the counter.

"He said. Um. I'm just telling you what he told me to tell you. He said he'd call the cops if he had to this time."

"Well, you can tell him to—"

Colleen grabbed Shay's arm. Shay twisted away from her and shot Colleen a look full of raw fury and aggression, but Colleen held on. Shay blinked a few times, breathing noisily through her nostrils, and then the intensity was gone. Colleen was learning the rhythm of Shay's temper, and now she tugged her away from the counter, grabbing Shay's purse and slinging it over her arm.

"They can't tell me I can't—" Shay muttered.

"Stop it," Colleen hissed. "Now come on."

She pulled Shay back to the vestibule, waiting until the first set of doors closed behind her before speaking. The air felt barely above freezing after the warmth of the lodge.

"What happened when you came here before?"

"The manager—Martin—I don't know. I mean, I maybe pushed him kind of hard, I mean, just *talking*, but nothing to make him react like that. I swear."

"It's just, I don't think he would have threatened to bring the police into it unless something *happened*. Would he? I'm not judging," Colleen lied—in truth she wished she could slap some tape over Shay's mouth. "I'm just trying to understand what the situation is."

"Yeah?" Shay's eyes blazed, but in seconds she dropped the stormy glare. "Okay, look. I got kind of mad when they wouldn't let me see Taylor's room. They said they'd already rented it out."

"They probably had. With the occupancy rates what they are . . ."

"All I wanted was a *look*. I wasn't going to touch anything. I told him he could come with me and watch to make sure I didn't disturb anything, but he kept talking about liability. Like whoever had the room would even notice. And if he did, he wouldn't care. I mean, these guys are working twelve-hour days and coming back to a shared shower and cable TV. Quality of life isn't like their main concern, you know?"

Colleen bit her lip, trying to figure out how to handle this. She'd known Shay less than twenty-four hours and she already could trace the arc of her volatility. And it was easy to imagine that in whatever low-paying job Shay worked, conflicts were probably settled with direct confrontation.

But throwing a temper tantrum would quickly burn through strangers' sympathy. Since arriving, Colleen had learned nothing that could lead her to Paul, and due to Shay's behavior this could end up being another dead end. And she didn't have a whole lot of other ideas. They had to make this work.

"Let me try. I'll talk to the girls. And fast, before they decide to go tell their manager we're here."

"Trust me, they aren't going to listen to you. You don't have any idea how places like this run. They got the girls out here for one reason and it ain't what's between their ears. It keeps the men settled down."

Colleen tightened her mouth. "All right. Duly noted. Now will you just let me try?"

Shay rolled her eyes and then gave a small, tight nod. "Fine. Knock yourself out. I'm going to smoke outside."

She held out her hand for her purse, which Colleen had forgotten she was holding. Shay stomped outside onto the deck without another word. Colleen took a moment to breathe deeply and figure out what she wanted to say. Then she faked a pleasant smile and went back inside.

"I'm sorry about that," she said before the girls could speak. They gaped at her with more curiosity than suspicion. "You have to understand, we're mothers, we get emotional."

Her face felt brittle. She wasn't sure how much longer she could keep it up. But she'd learned the technique—smile before speaking, even when disagreeing—at a conflict-resolution workshop she'd taken back when she was on the PTA regional board, and it really did help. Something about tricking the brain, redirecting one's impulses. "Did either of you know my son Paul? Paul Mitchell?"

The girls glanced at each other. Brit wouldn't meet Colleen's eyes. But Jennie twisted her long blond ponytail and nodded. "I knew him a little. Just to say hi. He was nice."

Colleen's heart skipped—she hadn't been expecting that. "You knew him from working here? Or socially?" she asked, knowing it was the wrong question, asked out of her hunger for Paul to be well liked, to have made friends. But it was as irresistible now as it was when she volunteered in the third-grade classroom and watched her boy shyly approach the table where his boisterous classmates sat, her heart full of longing on his behalf.

"Just from here. He was quiet, you know? But real sweet. Sweeter than most."

"We really *are* sorry they're missing," Brit said. "Only Mrs. Capparelli, she like threatened Martin or something, and now we aren't supposed to talk to her."

"He called Alaska," Jennie said. "That's our main office? I heard him on the phone with them. They don't want the publicity."

Colleen nodded, aware that it was only a matter of time before Martin or someone else saw her and Shay on site and then this narrow window would be closed.

"Listen," she said, "is there somewhere we can go to talk in private? Please? I don't want you to get into any trouble. I promise I would never tell anyone you talked to me. I swear it. But I haven't talked to my son in over two weeks—" Her voice wobbled, and she paused, steadying herself. "And I'm just so worried about him."

"Jennie," Brit said reprovingly. "We can't."

A look passed between them. "I didn't take my break yet," Jennie finally said. "Come *on*, Brit. It's his *mom*."

It was that last plea that seemed to make the difference. Brit huffed a breath and turned away, typing furiously on the keyboard.

"Listen, around the corner is the rec room and past that's a little meeting room they use for Bible study. Go in there and wait, okay? I'll come in a few minutes. Martin comes out to the coffee machine all the time, you don't want him to see you. And make sure *she* doesn't come back in." She pointed at the front entrance.

"Got it. Thank you." A couple of men had come in, stomping snow off their feet and putting on the required booties, joking loudly. The girls ignored Colleen to focus on the men, and Colleen walked briskly around the corner with her head down, hoping not to attract attention. The halls were quiet. It was already after one p.m.; the men who'd gotten off work at seven, and would return to the rigs this evening, were surely asleep now.

The rec room was spacious, a row of windows looking out to the parking lot on one side. A giant timber-manteled fireplace burned gas logs in front of an arrangement of sofas and chairs and coffee tables. On the other side of the room were pool and foosball tables, poker tables, and bookcases full of board games and paperbacks.

Colleen found the small meeting room, its door standing ajar. It held the same sort of furniture, tweedy sofas and a couple of La-Z-Boys and oak tables. On a side table were a Bible on a stand, a vase full of silk flowers—tulips and daffodils, which seemed especially out of place in the wintry setting—and a stack of flyers reading "JESUS in the Camps" and, in smaller letters, "He wants to hear from YOU!"

Colleen chose a chair in the corner that couldn't be seen from the rec room. She dialed Shay.

"Hello?"

"Shay. One of the girls is going to come talk to me. You can't come back in here, okay? You have to wait out there, if they see you I don't think this is going to work."

"Do you have any idea how cold it is out here?"

"Well, sit in the car and run the heater if you have to."

"That'll burn so much gas, my car doesn't—"

"Forget about the gas, I'll pay for it. Come on, this is important."

"You think I don't fucking *know* this is important?"

"I didn't—"

"Just don't talk to me like I'm a child, okay?"

Colleen took a breath, let it out slowly. "I'm sorry."

"And I can pay for my own gas."

"I'm *really* sorry." Although she wasn't—she was angry and frightened and resentful and probably a lot of other emotions she wasn't even aware of.

After a pause, Shay said, "Okay, look. Remember, they have the boys' things. That fuckwad Martin let it slip when I talked to him. See if you can get them back."

"How am I going to do that?"

"I don't know, Col—maybe you could *buy* them?"

She hung up and Colleen was left staring at the phone. But there wasn't time to worry about feelings. Besides, the money thing was ridiculous. If throwing money around helped find their sons, Colleen would do it and not apologize.

And maybe she *could* buy a little help. When Jennie arrived a moment later, Colleen was still working out how to frame the offer.

"I got the keys to a room that was vacated today," Jennie said. "Maid service hasn't been through and they're on their lunch, so we have a little time, is that okay with you?"

"Yes. Perfect."

"Look . . . I don't think anyone's going to try to talk to you, but best if you didn't let on who you are. I guess headquarters got on Martin pretty hard. They don't want it getting on the news that the boys were here if . . . if it turns out it's something bad. Sorry."

Colleen knew what she meant by "something bad." The fear fluttered and tugged around her as she followed Jennie down a hall that intersected an even longer one, branching out in corridors of rooms on both sides. There were no windows, only the soft glow of muted fixtures every few yards. Colleen tried to get oriented, to figure out where they were in the warren of rooms.

"How many rooms are there?"

"Four hundred, most of them singles. We have a few doubles, but the guests don't like them. Guys prefer to have a space of their own while they're here, especially since they have to share the bathroom."

"Paul said he liked his room. He said it was really nice."

"Oh, yes, ma'am, we have the nicest ones of any of the camps," Jennie said sincerely. "Everybody wants to stay here, but we're booked out. Companies buy up whole blocks. Okay, turn here."

Under Colleen's feet, the carpeted floor felt hollow, and she wondered how much insulation had been laid between the floorboards and the bottom of the unit. Between steel and earth, the winds would rush and the snow would blow all winter long, but it was almost too warm inside.

On either side of the hall, metal numbers marked plain gray doors. Men's and women's restrooms bore signs reading QUIET, PLEASE! FOLKS SLEEPING!! On a few of the doors, cartoons and photographs had been taped up. One had a pair of tiny stuffed toy reindeer arranged in a pornographic pose, held in place by duct tape. About a third of the doorknobs held PRIVACY PLEASE tags, and Colleen imagined the men inside, blinds drawn, sleeping through the daylight hours.

"Here we are," Jennie said, unlocking a door. She stood aside for Colleen to enter first.

Inside the room was the faint but unmistakable funk of male sweat. The bedding was strewn haphazardly, pillows and blankets on the floor. Besides these two details, Colleen's first impression was that it resembled a hospital room more than a hotel. The space was small, a double bed with no headboard wedged in one corner and a small laminate desk and chair in another. In the remaining two corners were narrow metal lockers, just big enough to house a few changes of clothing and stow a duffel bag. Hooks on either side of the door served for towels and coats. A single window faced across a fifteen-foot expanse of unmarred snow at the neighboring wing. The only decoration in the room was a TV suspended from the ceiling; its position suggested the best viewing would be from the bed, not the desk chair, which struck Colleen as sad.

The departing guest had left clues to how he'd spent his leisure time. A half-empty bag of Doritos shared space on the desk with a beef jerky wrapper and several empty Styrofoam cups. On the floor were copies of *Road & Track* and *Penthouse.*

"Sorry about the mess," Jennie apologized. She grabbed a corner of the sheets and yanked the remainder of the bedding off the bed before sitting down. "You go ahead and take the chair."

"This room . . ." Colleen placed her hand on the laminate desktop. It was warm from the heat blasting from a fixture in the ceiling. "It's not what I pictured."

"But you should see some of the other places," Jennie said defensively. "Everything here was new when they set up. I mean, we have maid service twice a week and they can have new towels anytime they want. And people are good about keeping it quiet. We're real strict about that. We got cameras on the halls, nobody ever tries to break the rules here."

"What are the rules?" All Paul had said, last Thanksgiving, was that nobody partied at the camp. The more Andy ribbed him about it, the more he clammed up, refusing to talk about what he did with his free time.

"No alcohol or drugs, no women in the rooms except the staff, no gambling, and keep it quiet. I mean, right there, that keeps the partying out. And the guys know if they break the rules and get barred, they aren't going to have anywhere to stay."

"What do they do when they're not working?"

"Depends how far they're going to the job site. The rigs can be an hour or more away, especially in bad weather. So mostly it's just the younger guys on in-close jobs who go out. If it's a big game on or something, they'll get together and watch it in the rec room. The kitchen does something nice on special occasions and holidays. Like for Super Bowl? They're going to fly in king crab."

"But the younger ones," Colleen pressed. "Like Paul. They go to bars?"

"Well, the guys work twelve-hour shifts, so a lot of 'em, the ones with families? They just want to get through their hitch and go home. The younger, single guys, yeah. There're a few places in town. *I* don't go," she added. "I'm engaged."

"Could you give me a list of places they go? Did you ever happen to hear Paul or Taylor saying where they were going?"

"No, ma'am, I'm sorry, I never did talk to them like that. But yeah, I'll write down a few for you. I wish there was something more I could do."

"Jennie, listen. Is there anything you could think of, any guess of what might have happened to them?"

The girl's expression turned not so much wary as sad. She twisted a button on her sweater and seemed to be trying to decide how to phrase what she wanted to say. "We talk about it," she finally said. "Me and the girls. This one girl, Megan, thinks one of them got hurt, and maybe the other one was going to report it. If he was the only one who saw, and the supervisors thought they could keep it quiet . . ."

"Hurt how?" Colleen demanded. "What kind of injury?"

"Well, they were with Hunter-Cole, right? And Hunter-Cole works their crews real hard, and they got a reputation for safety problems. They lost three men last year, it was in the papers. Had the inspections and all; OSHA was out here making a fuss, they put a ton of money into fighting it. I mean, I don't know all the details, but supposedly they have guys in Washington trying to get the rulings reversed and it ain't anywhere near over."

"Three men *died*? How?" Colleen's mouth tasted bitter—just saying the word took effort.

"Well, one fell. He didn't have his harness on, that was straight regulation failure and they took a hit for that. I don't even know how much the fines ended up being. The other two, though, the families signed an agreement they can't talk about it, so I don't really know. I mean, there's rumors and all, but people talk all kinds of crazy."

"They signed an *agreement*?" Thinking, *Who would do that, who would get in bed with the devil that killed their loved ones?*

"You got to understand, Mrs. Mitchell, they autopsy the bodies, and if there's any drugs in their system then they don't have to pay out. It's in the contract they all sign. And it can even be something like Ritalin, some of them take it just for the energy to get through their shift. Anything at all."

"But that would never hold up! No jury would let a corporation off the hook." Not if the victim was attractive, anyway. Flash a picture of a young man in the prime of his life—her mind went to the picture of Paul on her refrigerator at home, her favorite, in which he was holding up a plastic fish in a souvenir shop in Cozumel, pretending he'd caught it.

She forced the image out of her mind.

"Ma'am," Jennie said quietly. "What you got to understand is some of the families don't have the money for the hospital bills. And the burial. If the company ain't going to cover it, it's a powerful reason for them to make a deal. I'm not saying they're happy about it. I got this friend from school, her boyfriend got his hand crushed last year, he can't work now. She told him to sue, but the company lawyers sat him down and laid out how if he took them to court they were going to get this whole team from Minneapolis to fight it, and even if he eventually won they'd make sure it took years. And they got a baby coming. So he took the settlement. And it was a lot of money, almost two hundred thousand dollars. They're building a house south of town."

"But—" Colleen did the calculation—a few hundred thousand dollars was no compensation for the years ahead that the boy wouldn't be able to earn. She didn't know what to say. She settled for, "I'm very sorry for your friend's boyfriend." It hardly seemed adequate.

"Mrs. Mitchell, can I ask you something?"

"Yes, of course."

Jennie took a breath and looked down. "Did your son have some sort of like . . . problems?"

Colleen froze. The habit of years, the defensiveness, surged up instantly. *He's just an active boy, just like all the other boys*—the old chant, the one she recited in her mind like a mantra since pre-school, echoed in her brain. This was it, the thing they spent all the money on, making sure he could pass for *just like everyone else.* Money and a raft of tutors and coaches were what allowed him to get into the college prep track and then—miracle of miracles—Syracuse. His success was proof it had worked. No teacher had sent home notes with the names of specialists in the last few years; Paul hadn't returned home despondent over teasing since before puberty. But paradoxically, the more successful the ruse became, the more insistent the voice: *Please just make him like all the other kids, don't let them notice.*

"Can you be more specific?" she asked faintly, stalling for time, trying to figure out where the greater betrayal lay—telling his secrets or letting even the tiniest sliver of a clue slip through her fingers.

"I'm sorry, I don't mean anything by it, but did he like to gamble? Like did he have a gambling *problem*?"

"What? Oh, Lord, no," Colleen said, her relief so great she lost her composure. "I mean, he's never gambled, that I know of. Maybe a few slots in the Las Vegas airport."

"Oh. Because why I ask is, there's been a few guys that get hooked on the casino up on the reservation. It sounds crazy, but they'll go up there and run through their whole check and keep going. I just thought, I don't know. If he'd got in trouble that way. Him or Fly."

"Fly?"

"I mean Taylor. Sorry. It's these nicknames they give each other."
She smiled sheepishly and shrugged.

"Jennie, why did they call my son Whale?"

"Well, because of those shirts," Jennie said with what seemed like
fondness. "With the little whale on them? Nobody had ever seen those
before. Especially that one he had? It was yellow and blue, I think."

Colleen got it. The shirts she bought at the preppy little shop
downtown, the one that the local kids were so crazy about. They
were way too expensive, seventy-five dollars for a polo shirt, but Colleen had always felt it was well worth it to buy the trappings that
would help Paul fit in. The yellow and blue—well, yes, she could see
why that one wouldn't play well here, color-blocked and turned-up-
collared and looking like a parody of a Ralph Lauren ad. But Paul
had never cared about his clothes—he wore what Colleen bought
him and, that night when he'd lit out for North Dakota the first time,
he would have simply taken the bags he'd already packed for Syracuse, the suitcase full of preppy clothes.

"Does he still wear those?" she asked softly.

"Oh, no, ma'am, not after the first couple of weeks."

Oh, Paul. Colleen felt regret for her error, longing to go back and
do it right. If only she'd known that she couldn't keep him from Lawton, she would have found out what they wore up here and made
sure that her boy had it, that he had everything he would need to get
by. Suddenly she understood why Paul had refused Andy's offer, over
the holidays, to take the Cayenne since Andy was getting a new car.
Paul was bound and determined to buy a truck when he got back to
Lawton. A truck! It had struck her as so outlandish, when they were
offering him a vehicle that could handle the weather, and all he had
to do was drive it out there.

But now she got it. Everyone else had trucks. So Paul would have wanted a truck.

Jennie dug her phone out of her pocket and checked the time. "I'm sorry, I just have to make sure I'm back in time so they don't wonder where I got to. But we have a few more minutes."

"Jennie, listen. Ms. Capparelli says that the boys' things might have been saved. Their belongings, from the rooms."

"Well, what I heard, the police are supposed to pick up F— Taylor's stuff, only they haven't come by yet. And ma'am, there wasn't anything in your son's room."

She looked away when she said it, embarrassed or reluctant to add to Colleen's pain.

"What do you mean, there wasn't anything?"

"Like he packed up before he left? I didn't see it but I talked to Marie, she's the one who cleaned the rooms on their wing that Friday, the day after they went missing. They clean on Tuesdays and Fridays. And she said Paul's room was done up neat, he made his bed and left the towels hung up off the floor and there wasn't anything else in the room, not even in the trash."

"Oh," Colleen said. The news felt significant, but what did it mean? In a way, it was hopeful: her son had deliberately packed his things and taken them away. He'd *planned* to leave, in the middle of a hitch. But why? And why were Taylor's things undisturbed?

A sharp twist in her stomach signaled a very specific terror, and she pushed back against it. No. No, she was *not* going to allow her mind to leap to fantastical conclusions, scenarios she had no business entertaining, given how little information she had.

She had to focus on what she *could* do, now. One step at a time. The past was done, and the future, if she could influence it at all, was going to require all her attention.

"Listen," she said. "I don't know how to say this to you, Jennie, and I know we just met and you have no reason to trust me. But I am going to ask a favor of you, and I just have to hope that you'll understand I am asking you as a *mother.* You're—you're someone's daughter, and I hope your mother loves you and would do anything to keep you safe. So. I know this is breaking rules, a lot of rules, and exposing you to risk—but could you give me Taylor's things?"

Jennie's lips parted in protest.

"Wait, wait, don't say no yet. Hear me out. We've just been to see the police. Chief Weyant, he practically came out and told me they don't have the resources to work on this case. You know they aren't going to be happy to investigate what you just told me, the possibility that someone at Hunter-Cole is covering up safety issues. I mean, that doesn't even sound like a police thing, that's got to be federal or OSHA—or, I don't know, but if the boys got tangled up in something like that, the Lawton police aren't going to be any help at all. But Shay—she *knows* her son. Knows him the way only a mother can."

She paused, trying to gauge the effect her words were having, desperately hoping Jennie's mother wasn't one of those women who turned their nearly grown children out into the world with indifference, who'd parented her with resentment or worse. "If there's anything, any clue, to be found in his things, it's Ms. Capparelli who will be able to figure it out, don't you see? If there's something out of the ordinary, something that showed he strayed from his habits or got into something new—if there's names on his phone that she doesn't recognize—things like that."

"But . . ." Jennie wouldn't look at her. "There could be DNA . . . all kinds of evidence. I don't think you're even supposed to touch stuff without gloves and, I don't know. It's supposed to be *processed.*"

Colleen nodded, wincing because the girl had a point. Maybe

she was making a mistake here, risking destroying clues that could lead to the truth.

But Weyant had been very clear: no one was lighting a fire to process the things Taylor had left behind. Even if they had the lab, the equipment, they weren't making an effort to examine a bunch of dirty laundry for clues. And they wouldn't, unless the unthinkable happened . . . and then, what would it matter?

And the other, the terrible little voice inside her nagged. The other reason. The one she would *not* give credence to, that she would not entertain for one second, because it meant a breach of faith in her son so wide and deep that she wasn't sure she could ever come back from it.

"Sweetheart, I think that's mostly on TV," Colleen said shakily. And then she told a lie which, since it was a point of some honor with her to be as truthful as she could, always—a core family value, so to speak—surprised her with the ease with which it tripped off her lips. "I saw a documentary where they were saying that eighty percent of what we see on those shows is either impossible or police departments aren't equipped to handle it. In most cases evidence ends up in lockers and is never even looked at unless a case goes to court, and even then it gets lost or damaged way more often than you'd think. And I just can't—Taylor's mom and I can't take the risk of that happening. You understand . . . don't you?"

Jennie bit her lip, but she didn't look away.

"There's one more thing," Colleen said, reaching for her purse. "Now I know you'll try to say no, because I can tell you were raised the way I raised my own son. You want to help just out of decency, but I also know you're a young woman starting out, and it's so hard these days, isn't it? I am going to give this to you whether you decide to help me get Taylor's things or not. It, well, it means something to me, more than you can imagine, that you remember Paul and that you—"

Her voice broke, and suddenly the line between lie and truth blurred, and she was speaking more deeply from her heart than she'd intended. "That you said he was a nice boy," she finished in her broken voice. She took Jennie's hand and pressed the folded bills into her palm, closing her fingers over the money and squeezing. It was three hundred dollars, everything she'd withdrawn from the ATM.

"Oh, ma'am . . . I couldn't," Jennie said.

"Yes. Yes, you can, sweetheart. Let me do this. Let me do a nice thing for you, it will help *me*, don't you see? I need—I need to do something nice for someone today. To make a difference, even a little. If you like, you can use it to buy a nice gift for your friend's baby," she added with a smile.

For a moment their hands stayed clasped, and Colleen thought, *This—this is enough*, this knowing that she could be what a child needed.

But the young woman who tucked the bills into her jeans without looking to see how much, who stood up resolutely while digging the keys from her pocket, who paused with her hand on the door and turned to nod briefly at Colleen, was not a child at all.

"Stay here," she said. "I'm going to get what you need."

nine

SHAY HAD MANAGED not to smoke a second cigarette. Well, third, counting the one first thing in the morning. Just two, and it was almost noon. Half a day. Two in half a day, four in a whole day; if she could manage that, it was all right. Not perfect, not by a long shot, but under control.

She jumped when Colleen rapped on the passenger window. She turned the ignition on and leaned across to unlock the door, the automatic control having quit on her last year.

Colleen slid into the seat. In her hand was a large plastic Walmart bag.

"Is that the boys' things?"

"Yes," Colleen said tensely. "But can we go? I don't want to look at them here."

Shay headed up the road out of the camp and back through town. She focused on staying under the speed limit. Halfway back, Colleen spoke again. "It's only Taylor's. Paul's was—there wasn't anything in his room."

"He took it all with him? Or someone cleaned it out?"

"Well, it wasn't there, that's all we know. Whether he took it or . . . or something else."

There was something in her voice, some sharp splinter of fear, and Shay didn't push. Instead, she thought about what it might mean. The boys disappeared the same day, as far as anyone knew . . .

but the maid didn't come until Friday. Could Paul have stayed back, for some reason? Or—it seemed impossible—could it be unrelated, some fantastic coincidence, the boys deciding separately—for their own different reasons—to leave? Maybe not even aware that the other—

But that was insane, wasn't it? What was it Sherlock Holmes was supposed to have said—something about eliminating the impossible and whatever was left had to be the truth. Two boys, good friends, independently deciding to leave without a word, on the very same day—that was so unlikely as to be impossible.

But still. Events were splitting off into two directions. Differences were appearing. The two boys were *not* the same. Maybe they had made different choices. And even though Shay was no closer to knowing what had happened, she had to tread very carefully, never forgetting that the obvious could be a trick.

"I DON'T TRUST that bitch," Shay said, lowering the dented mini-blinds over the motor home's long side window. Brenda's car was in the driveway. She'd worked the three-to-eleven every day this week, and apparently she had the same shift again today. Unless it was her day off, in which case they'd have to deal with her staring out the window at them all night.

Colleen set the Walmart bag on the table. Shay slid into the seat across from her and reached for the bag. "Okay," she said, dumping out its contents. Clothes—wadded and faintly smelling of body odor and Axe—tumbled out. A paperback copy of *Game of Thrones* that looked like it hadn't been read. A baggie with two compact nuggets of weed, and a little glass pipe. Shay recognized that pipe—she'd threatened to throw it out over Christmas when she found it, to which Taylor had said, "Really, Mom?" with that amused lazy smile of his, the one that said she was taking herself too seriously. Besides, it was only a couple of years since Taylor had found *her* little stash one day when he was looking for Advil and they'd had the talk about being grown up and respecting each other's choices and besides it was only very occasional and blah blah blah.

Shay glanced at Colleen, gauging her reaction. "Is that—" Colleen asked, then blushed. "I mean, I don't mean to judge. I don't—I know that—"

"Yes, it's what you think. It's marijuana. I knew he had it." She set it aside, picking up a smaller Walmart bag, the top twisted and knotted, its contents clanking. Tearing the bag open, she felt a tendril of dread, but inside were only the things she would have expected—a toothbrush, toothpaste, dandruff shampoo, body wash, deodorant, condoms, ChapStick. She laid these things out in a row and the two women examined them together.

"Paul used that same body wash," Colleen said. "That Axe brand. I always thought it smelled so nice. I was surprised, you know? That a . . . well, a drugstore brand could smell that good."

"Seriously?" Shay poked her fingers into the corners of the plastic bag, turning it inside out. Nothing, not even leaked soap. "You don't buy your husband's soap at the drugstore?"

"I mean—yes, sure, it's just Kiehl's makes this really nice one—"

"What's missing?" Shay interrupted, a little more sharply than necessary. "His wallet. His keys. Sunglasses, except I think he always kept those in his truck. What else? What else do boys carry around with them?"

They were both silent for a moment. "Paul has a bottle-opener key chain," Colleen said. "He got it when he was a freshman. But it would be with his keys."

"Taylor has these flip-flops with the bottle opener built into the sole. But they're back home. He left all his summer stuff there. I kept his room just the way he left it. I mean, he's pretty neat, he wouldn't want me moving things around anyway."

"Wow, not Paul. He's so careless with things. I wish— I should have made him do more. But we always had the cleaning ladies, and I never minded doing laundry. I kind of liked it, actually." She looked so forlorn that Shay forgave her the cleaning lady comment. "Maybe that's from just having the one. Every stage, every birthday, you're always thinking how he's that much closer to leaving."

Shay barked a laugh. "Hell, not me. I made Brittany learn to do her own laundry when she was eight. Taylor would have been four, and he used to help her. I had two jobs back then, and Frank, that was Taylor's father, he wasn't around much."

"See," Colleen said. "That was so good. They learned because they *had* to learn. With Paul, I never had the opportunity to teach him that kind of self-reliance. Everything was always done for him; he never really learned to look out for himself."

"It wasn't that hard," Shay said. "If they wanted to eat, they had to figure out how to make the macaroni and cheese. Don't you think I would have rather been home doing it all for them?" She shook her head at the memory. "I was supposed to take six weeks after Taylor was born, but my boss called me after three and paid me time and a half to come back early. We couldn't say no to that, not back then." She dug back into the pile of Taylor's things. "Oh, this was his favorite shirt," she exclaimed, holding it up. It was soft from being washed over and over again, a faded green cotton T-shirt he got from working at the Y sports camp. On the back was his name, Capparelli, spelled out in block letters.

She kept going through the clothes. There was the belt Brittany gave him for Christmas. A pair of shorts. Socks paired and rolled, which made her smile—at home he just dumped them into his drawer, but here, so far from home, he'd adopted her habits.

She came across a shirt she didn't recognize, a silky collared shirt with a stripe of pale green against a navy background. She held it up to her face, but it smelled only of detergent. Had he bought it for going out? To show off for a girl? She closed her eyes and touched the soft fabric to her cheek, trying to conjure an image of the girl who'd caught his eye, who was special enough to warrant this kind of purchase.

She put it back on top of the other things, then put them all carefully back into the Walmart bag. "Nothing," she said. "Nothing out of the ordinary, anyway. I guess that was a bust."

"I don't know." Colleen folded her hands and rested her chin on them. "For now, maybe. But let's put it all aside and maybe later it will mean something. Let it—you know, let it simmer in your mind, in your subconscious, and maybe something will come to you."

"So. You now know everything I do," Shay said. "You've seen the cops and the man camp. I was going to try to go out to the rig where the boys were supposed to be working, but Hunter-Cole won't tell me where it is. I looked on the Department of Mineral Resources website, and Hunter-Cole has got nine of the twenty-seven active rigs in Ramsey County. I mean, I guess we could start driving around to all of them, but it would take a while."

"We'd have to find the crew right away if we want to talk to them," Colleen said. "From what Paul told us when he left, they were supposed to work every day through the twenty-sixth. I put it in my calendar. Today's the twenty-second. That only gives us four days and then all the workers will scatter for the next couple of weeks."

"Well, so we have to figure out how to find these guys. I think going to the supervisors was the wrong angle. One-on-one, most of these guys are okay. We just have to get them on their own to talk to them."

"Did Taylor tell you any of his friends' names? Other workers who might have known him well?"

"Yeah, but the problem is that they all go by nicknames like Dukey and Tailbone, and I never asked him for last names. I mean, why would I?"

"Shay, listen." Colleen picked up one of Taylor's T-shirts that had fallen to the floor and started to fold it, her movements smooth and efficient. "I've been thinking. You found this place, right? Even though they said there wasn't anything out here."

"Well, yeah, but only because it had never occurred to that dim-wit Brenda to rent it out. Not to mention there's no way it's up to code and it's a piece of shit. You can bet she'll have a sign out there the minute we're gone, asking twice as much."

"Well, what I'm saying is, if there was one . . . opportunity like this, there's bound to be others. Right?"

"What are you getting at, Col?"

"Look. I want to bring our detective out here. The man my husband and I hired? I can have him on the next plane as long as I can promise him a place to stay. And he'd be looking for *both* our boys, Shay, not just Paul."

Suspicion coiled in Shay. "Wait a minute. Are you about to ask me to hand over this trailer to him? Because I am not—"

"No, no, that's not what I'm saying. Just—it's what, four o'clock, and if I start calling now—I'll try all the motels again first but I thought, while I was doing that, you're better at—well, I mean, you found this place. Maybe you could try to see if there's something else. Talk to the guys at the truck stop, you'll do better with them than me. If we can find a room, we could get Steve here in twenty-four hours."

"What do you mean, I'll *do better* with them?" Shay snapped. "You mean because I'm trailer trash? Want me to flash some tit or something?"

Colleen looked shocked. "That is not what I meant—"

"Sorry," Shay muttered, wondering what was wrong with her, overreacting to everything Colleen said.

"I only meant because you're pretty and outgoing."

"Sure," Shay said, waving the comment away. "But if we get him here tomorrow, then what? What exactly do you picture this guy—what's his name again?"

"Steve. Steve Gillette."

"Okay, *Steve*. So you get him here and he does what? Goes to see the cops, goes to see the camp—which I might point out you already stole evidence from—then he's sitting on his ass just like you and me, trying to figure out his next step, only a couple days have gone by, and how is that better?"

"He's a professional." Colleen's tone had turned pleading, but the look in her eyes was even worse. Panic. Fear. Two emotions that could easily erode any momentum that they'd managed to build.

"I'm *not* stepping aside," Shay said. "I am not about to sit on my ass while some mall cop whacks off on our dime."

Colleen winced, and Shay regretted her choice of words. It was one of her anger responses, one that she wasn't particularly proud of, but it had always worked for her and Taylor, who knew how to handle her. That easy grin . . . that "Really, Mom?" He knew her bark was a hundred times worse than her bite. If only he was here . . .

"He's ex-police," Colleen said quietly. "Eleven years on the force in Boston."

"I don't care if he's an ex-fucking-Navy-SEAL. It's not *his* kid who's missing, and there's no way he can care enough."

"Shay, please." Colleen looked like she was about to cry, and Shay pressed her lips together and let her speak. "I'm not saying he would replace what we're doing or that we would step back at all. He would just supplement what we're doing, and maybe he could provide structure . . . you know, share his insights and experience, outline a game plan. That we would have final approval of, of course. And I'll pay for the whole thing. Don't be mad," she added hastily. "I am not trying to throw my money around. It's just, it's a tool, it's something we can use. Just *let* me. All right? It's something I can do, so please, let me."

Shay managed to bite back her retort. Colleen had finished folding the first shirt and tugged several more from the bag and was folding them into perfect rectangles unlike anything Shay had ever produced in decades of doing laundry for the many people who'd come in and out of her life.

"Okay, look," she said. "Here's a compromise. You make your calls. Call every damn hotel in the county if you want. I'm going to lie down. When you're done, we'll go into town, get some dinner, talk to people. I have an idea where to go. If—*if*—we get what we need, which is to find out where the boys' crew is, then we can use the rest of the night to ask around for somewhere to stay for your cop."

"He's not my cop," Colleen said, and then, "but thank you. I have all the phone numbers printed out, it won't take me all that long."

"Here." Shay dug her iPad out of her bag. She tapped out a quick search and spun it around on the table. "Just in case you missed any."

She gathered up the folded clothes and put them back in the bag, all but one, the green one with Taylor's name on it, hiding it with her body. She lay down on the cot with her phone, slipping in her earbuds and launching into her "last ditch" playlist, the one she saved for the worst days. Lucinda Williams came on, singing "Those Three Days," and Shay turned the sound up loud enough to drown out Colleen's voice, loud enough to crowd out her own thoughts, and rolled over on the bed and pressed her face into the pillow, shutting out the light.

She pressed the T-shirt to her face and inhaled through the worn cotton, wishing for some trace of him, some faint remnant that would take her back. But Taylor had done his laundry with some detergent Shay didn't use, and though she wished with all her might, the shirt smelled like some other mother's son.

ten

THE WALLEYE WERE heavy on the line, melting crusts of ice cling-ing to their scales. T.L. had gutted them on the frozen lake next to the hole he'd cut with Myron's hand auger, leaving their entrails glisten-ing in the blood seeping into the ice. They shone like treasure, scales and blood reflecting the sun among the ropes of guts. Next time he went back, in a week, the guts would have been eaten by scavengers and the bloodstain would be skimmed over in frost and ice.

T.L. slapped the fish down on the steel counter. Four fat ones, all the Swann's chef wanted, enough for the special. That left a cou-ple for T.L. to take home, one for tonight and one to freeze. The manager, a thin, blinking man in his fifties named Cory, handed over three crisp twenties from the drawer. "Appreciate it," he said. "Might take an extra next week, we see how this sells." T.L. nodded, all the time looking through the kitchen to the window where the girls picked up the plates. Looking for Kristine.

Finally, after he listened to Cory complain about a dishwasher who hadn't been on time all week, and washed his hands in the prep sink, he gave up. "Kristine around?" he asked as casually as he could manage.

"Sure. We're not busy yet, go out on the floor and say hi, if you want," Cory said, already heading back to his office. The cook whose name T.L. could never remember, the one who had a tattoo on his throat like an extra set of teeth, had already slid the fish down the counter and opened one up with a meaty, scarred hand, flipping up the rib cut and planning where to section it into servings. They slapped on a Parmesan-garlic crust, charged thirty dollars for it. T.L. didn't mind. For him, it meant sixty bucks for an afternoon on the ice, a Saturday afternoon he didn't have anything else to do with, anyway.

T.L. took a breath and dried his hands on his jeans. They were soiled where he'd knelt to gut the fish. He was wearing his old jacket, which was warmer than the North Face parka Myron had given him for Christmas; his wrists jutted two inches past the cuffs, and the lining was ripped, but the matted-down chamois lining kept him warmer than the new one. T.L. looked like he'd been doing exactly what he'd been doing, and this was the one place in town where even an oilman wore his good clothes. Not that many came: it was mostly the suits here, the men who flew in from corporate offices in Texas and California.

He couldn't do much about the way he looked. He pushed through the swinging doors and saw her with a dark-haired girl over by the coffee station. Kristine was kneeling, pulling filters from a box on a shelf below. The other girl was separating and stacking them, counting out loud.

"Kristine." T.L. stood back outside the waitress station, hands jammed in his pockets. The dark-haired girl glanced at him and smiled, pushing her hair back behind her ear. Kristine took her time peeling off a clump of the filters before she stood up.

She was ready for him. The look she gave him wasn't a smile, but it wasn't a frown either, it was just a bland expression that tele-graphed *Don't bother*. T.L. figured she got plenty of mileage out of that look working here, especially after she'd served a guy his second or third drink.

"Thought we could find a time," he said wearily, as though he'd asked her a thousand times already. In truth it had been only once before. "When I could come over."

"Dinner rush is starting," she said, even though there were only three occupied tables. In another hour the place would be packed and it would stay that way until closing.

"I could call you."

"Sure," she said, but they both knew the lie was only for the benefit of the other girl. If he called, Kristine wouldn't pick up. It wouldn't matter how many times he tried.

"Okay, then," T.L. said, turning to go.

"I'm so jealous," the dark-haired girl said, and they both turned to look at her. She was the kind of pretty that had another ten years to go before her hair lost its sheen and she started thickening through the neck, the arms, the waist. She spoke in a careful, awkward way that was meant to cover her teeth, which were not straight.

"Because of L.A.!" she clarified, blushing. "I've never been farther than Colorado."

"Oh," T.L. said. This. He thought everyone knew. He stared at the coffeepot that had been set on the burner with its handle out; if someone bumped it at the wrong angle, there would be hot coffee everywhere. "I'm not going. I decided . . . not to."

"You're kidding!" The girl gaped. "But I thought it was like a full scholarship to the art department? Like for minorities? I've seen your stuff, when they had that show at the library. You're really good."

"Yeah . . ." Another uncomfortable shrug, T.L. backing toward the swinging doors. "Maybe next year. I'm going to take a few classes at Minot this fall. I need to stay and help my uncle out."

He pushed open the doors with his hip, meeting Kristine's eyes before he turned away. They were cold and hard. But none of it had been his fault. How could she not see that?

eleven

SHAY NAPPED THROUGH most of Colleen's ever-more-frustrating calls, her small body still and peaceful-looking on the bed, curled up and facing the wall. One of the motels Colleen called didn't answer at all. Another had a message saying "We are currently at full occupancy and do not anticipate any rooms being available for the week of January seventeenth." When Colleen spoke to actual humans, the message was always the same: nothing, as far as the calendar stretched; everything had already been booked by companies and individuals.

She was still going down the list—Shay had searched motels in a fifty-mile radius—when Shay got up and changed clothes. Or rather, changed her shirt from the soft jersey cowl-neck she'd worn earlier in the day to a gold-flecked, cut-out-shoulder top. Shay took her cosmetic bag into the bathroom and stayed there long enough for Colleen to call Andy, tell him about their day, and learn that he had nothing to report. When Shay came out, she trailed a cloud of perfume and was wearing a lot of eye makeup and sticky-looking dark pink lip gloss, and her hair cascaded around her shoulders in a nest of curls.

Colleen didn't dare ask why she'd gotten dressed up. Dressed, not to put too fine a point on it, like a tramp, but maybe that was just a California thing. She felt like everything she said had the potential to set Shay off, even those things that seemed neutral. She understood that she had come barging into Shay's life, into her hell-bent search for Taylor. It was very generous of Shay to allow her to stay with her. And it was awkward to try to repay the kindness with the only currency Colleen had, which was her money. Still, she was determined to keep trying. They needed each other.

So instead of mentioning the makeup, the evening top, Colleen got her own cosmetic bag and added some lipstick, some eyeliner, a swipe of mascara. Not satisfied with the result, she got out her concealer and did her best to camouflage the circles under her eyes.

They were pulling away from the house, Shay flipping off their unseen landlady, when she finally admitted they were headed for Walmart.

"I was afraid you'd refuse to come along," she said, and Colleen couldn't tell if she was making fun of her.

"I've shopped at Walmart tons of times," she protested. "There's one in Salem. We always go on the way to the beach."

"Yeah, well, this Walmart's a little different. Supposedly it's the busiest one in the whole country. Everyone, I mean *everyone* in this damn town seems to go there. The guys getting off at seven all stop by on their way back to wherever they're staying."

"But how are we going to talk to them?"

"Look, Hunter-Cole is one of the biggest employers in town right now. How hard is it going to be to find someone who works for them?"

"That doesn't answer the question of how we'll *talk* to them, though."

Shay glanced over at Colleen, bemused. "You never started a conversation in the garden department? I met a guy that way, we dated for six months. I asked him for help picking a garden hose."

"You didn't."

"Hell yeah, I did. Didn't need the help, but he came through with the hose, if you see what I'm saying."

Colleen felt herself blushing, her skin warming.

"Sorry," Shay said after a moment. "I didn't mean to embarrass you. Do you mind me asking, how long have you been married?"

"Twenty-two years. Our anniversary was last October."

"Damn. That's an accomplishment."

"And . . . were you married for a long time?"

"No, we only made it a few years. We were awfully young . . . and, well, I was looking for a baby daddy."

"Oh—you were pregnant?"

"No, I mean for my first. My daughter, Brittany. I had her when I was seventeen. She's twenty-three now. Her dad was never really in the picture. I lived with my mom when she was a baby, but by the time she was two I was ready to get my GED and get a real job, and I didn't want to live with my mom for the rest of my life, so when Frank proposed I kind of figured all the pieces were falling into place. God bless him." She said the last bit with a fond smile.

"You and he stayed close, then?"

"Yeah, until he died. Taylor was only two at the time, and I was twenty-three. We'd already gotten divorced. And it was a hell of a thing because I would have qualified for his service benefits, but the dumbass was stupid enough to die on leave, driving his motorcycle while drunk, instead of over in Iraq. Woulda, shoulda, story of my life back then. But yeah, I always did love him, and we were kind of talking about getting back together."

"Oh, my God, I'm sorry," Colleen said, thinking, *Two kids by two men, all by the time she was twenty-one years old, practically still a child herself.* She and Andy hadn't had Paul until she was thirty-three, and then only after two rounds of IVF. "Do you . . . is there . . . I mean, it's none of my business."

"Am I seeing someone? Not really. Which I guess means only

when I've had too much to drink." Shay laughed, but Colleen thought she detected a note of sadness. "I mean, don't get me wrong, I don't take people home from bars or anything. Just, if I get lonely, I know who to call. Old friends, you know? But mostly, I'm on my own, and I have been for almost all of Taylor's life. I mean, I had guys I saw for a while here and there, but nothing ever got serious, especially because I never wanted to introduce the kids to a guy unless it was the real thing. I used to tell myself that when Taylor got out on his own, I'd look . . . you know, for real. Maybe try the online thing, seems like everyone's doing that. I have girlfriends who found guys, got married, even." She was silent for a moment, and Colleen searched for something to say, but before she could think of anything, Shay added, "Maybe I've just been independent for so long, it's too late for me to live with anyone again. Too used to having my own space and making all my own decisions. Hell, I don't know."

"I met Andy in college," Colleen said impulsively. "I was twenty-one. He was my first real boyfriend. I mean, I dated a few other guys. But still."

"Do you love him?"

It wasn't the audaciousness of the question that caused Colleen to freeze up—it was something else, a tiny hesitation before she said, "Of course." During that split second, she realized that she had no idea if she still loved Andy or not. She said "I love you" every day—had made a point of it since early in their marriage—but the words felt like nothing, a casual gesture like wringing the dishrag out before hanging it, or the way Andy always rubbed his shoes twice on the coir mat at the front door. Habit. Ritual. Both important to humans, maybe especially important to Colleen, who was dependent on the repetitive nature of the rhythms of her life for serenity—but was it love? Especially in the last year or so, when the distance between them seemed to be widening into a chasm, something Colleen had blamed on the tension with Paul—had they moved so far apart they couldn't find their way back?

"I *do* love him," she repeated. "He's a great husband. And father. He's . . . good with Paul."

"Paul's lucky, then. Okay, here we are."

They had arrived at the Walmart, Colleen too wrapped up in the conversation to notice. The snow was coming down again, big fluffy flakes clinging to the windshield between swipes of the wipers. Underneath the new snow the lot was slick with ice; Colleen saw a man slip and almost fall as he walked toward the store.

"We can't risk you getting hurt. We need to get you some new boots."

Colleen laughed, then realized Shay was serious. "These will be okay. They're really comfortable."

"The salt'll ruin the leather. Besides, it doesn't matter how comfortable they are if you don't have any traction. Look, we can't afford for you to break a leg."

"How do you know so much about snow, anyway?"

"Fairhaven is only an hour and a half from Tahoe. I used to take the kids up there in the winter."

"Skiing?"

"No, too expensive. But there's a stretch along the highway where people park, and there's a slope they turn into a sledding hill. We'd take lunch and they'd sled all day, and warm up in the car when they got cold. I brought extra mittens and stuff for when they got wet. But eventually they'd get soaked through their snow pants and we'd have to call it a day. Then they'd sleep all the way home . . . I loved driving home with them asleep in the backseat." She smiled at the memory. "Okay, so, boots. And I bet you didn't bring thick socks, right? And then we need more food if we ever plan to eat in the RV. And maybe some beer. What else?"

"I don't—I don't think I need anything."

"If we head out to the rigs, you're going to need better gloves and a hat."

"My coat has a hood," Colleen said, lifting it to show her.

"That thing? Come on, it doesn't look like it would even stay up."

"But we're not going to be outside, are we?"

"The rigs aren't exactly luxurious. The guys working outside are exposed to the elements. Taylor told me stories of guys freezing to death when they went out to the shed and couldn't find their way back to the rig. And inside they run some sort of heater, but he said it was freezing in there. Besides . . . I'm not counting on a big welcome, are you? So we need to be ready to stand outside if we have to."

"Okay." Colleen nodded. She could do this. It was just a pair of boots.

They moved slowly through the parking lot, keeping their heads down against the wind and stinging snow. Twice Colleen slipped and narrowly avoided falling, and she took to bracing herself against the vehicles they passed, hanging on to the beds of pickups, the big steel bumpers.

"Why would anyone park back there?" she asked, pointing at the far end of the parking lot, where a dozen vehicles were lined up.

"Those are the ones who are sleeping in their cabs. The ones who don't have anywhere to stay. The lady at the church told me that in the fall there were so many, Walmart had to kick most of them out so the customers could find parking."

"I can't believe that's even legal."

"Oh, no, Walmart allows that all over the country. Me and Frank, we borrowed a camper for our honeymoon, pulled it behind his Jeep down to Mexico. We stayed in Walmarts on the way. Once you get there, you can stay right on the beach . . . it's beautiful. Here, let's grab that cart."

She took a cart from a man who was finishing unloading his purchases. When they got to the doors, Colleen saw why: there were no carts left in the corral. There was a line of people waiting to get through the door. Nearly all of them were men, just like everywhere else they'd been.

Inside, a blast of warm air hit Colleen in the face. This Walmart was much bigger than the one in Salem; the entire right side of the store was a giant grocery. In front were bins full of merchandise: T-shirts with the logo of the Minot Muskies hockey team, carelessly mounded with no regard to sizing. A special on Blazin' Jalapeño Doritos.

"Keep moving," Shay said, grabbing her arm and propelling her toward the produce aisle, but not before a man stepped in their path and said, "Evening, ladies." Shay steered around him, ignoring him. Colleen raced to keep up.

They made it as far as the dairy aisle before another man—a fortyish, thickset redhead with a couple days' growth of beard and a bad case of hat hair—put his hand on their cart to stop it and stepped in front. "God, you have beautiful eyes," he said to neither of them in particular.

"Yeah? Fuck off." Shay drew the cart back and then rammed it against his shins, causing him to curse and jump back. Even then he called after them, "Feisty, huh? Come party with me and my friend!"

"The checker warned me about this when I was here the other day," Shay said, grabbing a carton of milk. "She says most women won't even come at night. There's been rapes in the parking lot. So they say, anyway. Man rape too."

"*What?*" Colleen was aghast.

"Man on man. Because they're desperate, you know? But I think that's just urban myth."

"No, I mean . . ." Colleen felt dizzy. "Why does she even work here? The checker?"

"Well, for one thing, she's about seventy and has a face like leather, so maybe they leave her alone. And for another, they pay double here what they pay at any other Walmart in the country, plus a signing bonus if you stay a full three months."

Colleen shook her head, trying to wrap her mind around it all. Up ahead she noticed a stocky man pushing his cart into the office supplies aisle, reaching for a box of envelopes. It was his cap that caught her attention—or rather, the logo stitched on the front: a stylized palm tree above a swirled flourish.

Hunter-Cole Energy's logo.

She raced after him before she could change her mind, leaving Shay with their cart. He had moved on, down the aisle and around the corner, before Colleen caught up with him. She found him pondering a wall of snack foods, dozens of brands, hundreds of bags of chips and pretzels.

"Excuse me."

The man looked around in surprise. He was fit looking, in his late thirties, Colleen estimated. He'd taken off his bulky coat and gloves and tossed them in his cart. Resting on top of the coat were the envelopes, a package of cheap pens, a six-pack of Gatorade, a box of Slim Jims—and a mop-top doll with floppy fabric sneakers.

"Me?" he asked, looking around. The aisle was empty other than the two of them. "Help you with something?"

"You work for Hunter-Cole, right?" Colleen pointed to his hat, and the man's hand went to it self-consciously.

"Yes, I do . . ."

"Did you know the boys who went missing? Paul Mitchell and Taylor Capparelli? Fly and Whale?"

The man's expression went wary, and he began backing away. "You from the news?"

"What? No. I'm his mom. Paul's mom."

The man stopped edging away, and his expression morphed into pity. "Oh. Well, I'm real sorry about all that."

Shay came around the corner, pushing the cart ahead of her. The man glanced at her. "Is she—"

"Taylor's mom. Listen, can we talk to you?"

"What about? I didn't actually work with them. I was on a different rig. Worked with Taylor once last fall, but I got rotated out when my dad died. When I got back they put me on another crew."

"But you've been with Hunter-Cole this whole time, right? Please, could we talk to you? Ask you a few questions?"

"I don't know what I'd be able to tell you. I haven't seen him since then."

"Just general questions. I understand you didn't know them well, but we just need a place to start."

"Look, ma'am. We all sign nondisclosures, you know? I could lose my job if I talk to you."

"But we won't tell anyone we talked to you, I promise." Colleen felt tears of frustration building. "Every day—every *minute* that passes, the trail's getting colder, do you understand that? Please. You have children, Mr. . . ."

"Oh, Jesus, it's Roland, okay? Just Roland. Yes, okay, I got a daughter, she's four. She's back in Ohio with my ex-wife and I go my whole hitch without seeing her, but they depend on my paycheck. I feel for you, I really do. But the last guy who talked to the media about safety problems on the rig got fired and their legal team came down and threatened to sue him. They didn't let up until he was finished here, couldn't get a job anywhere after that. I can't afford that, okay?"

"Then let's go somewhere." Shay pushed forward, abandoning their cart. "Look, we'll meet you anywhere. Just tell us where."

"I don't even have much to say . . . it's not like I know anything about your sons. I mean, if that's the impression you have, you're going to be disappointed. None of us know anything. And everyone's been talking about it. So if there were rumors I think I would have heard them. All I could do is tell you what happened . . . what they *say* happened . . . to other people."

"That's all we're asking," Colleen said, resisting the urge to touch his arm, to somehow cement the tenuous connection. "That's plenty. It's a start."

"Give me an hour. I don't want to go anywhere public. I got to clear this with a friend of mine; if she says it's okay, we can go over to her place. She won't say anything. Look, I'll text you the address, okay?" Already he was backing away from them, scanning the aisle behind him, where a couple of men were putting bags of chips in their carts. One of them looked curiously in the women's direction, and Roland looked like he was going to bolt. Shay pulled a pen from her purse and grabbed a price tag from the shelf, yanking it out of its plastic holder and scribbling her phone number on the back. She handed it to Roland and he jammed it in his pocket as he hurried down the aisle.

SHAY GRABBED THEIR cart and headed in the other direction. "So, let's find your boots," she said loudly.

"He was so skittish," Colleen said as soon as they were out of earshot of the other customers. "I can't believe it's really that risky. I mean, just to *talk* to us?"

"Hunter-Cole isn't fucking around. Think of how they've been treating us, right? You said the minute you explained what you wanted, they shut you down."

"They talked to Andy . . ." Colleen said uncertainly. "I should get the name of the guy. He told Andy that he should call with any questions, that he would serve as a liaison to the company's own investigation."

"Right." Shay's tone was grim. "The investigation they only said they were starting *after* you talked to them, right? And your husband told them he's an attorney?"

"Well, yes, but he does intellectual property law, which isn't . . . but how would they even know?"

Shay rolled her eyes. "What you got to realize is, this isn't a company run by a bunch of redneck wildcatters. Sure, the guys on the ground drive trucks and chew tobacco, but you got to believe there's a bunch of guys in suits running the numbers and doing damage control. You know what I found out about Hunter-Cole?"

"No . . ."

"They've had twenty-seven OSHA citations in the last two years, and six fatalities in the last fourteen months. It's all in the public record, but how much of that got in the news? Hardly *any* of it, all because they spend a fortune on legal fees and buying off the victims' families. They're serious about this shit. Okay? And don't think they haven't looked us both up. At this point, if they consider you a threat, you can bet they know everything about you, from your bra size to what brand of toaster waffles you buy. And since they know I'm here, they've got all my dirty laundry too. Now, there's nothing we can do about that."

"There's nothing interesting to know about me," Colleen said. She wasn't good with computers, didn't really know what was possible to discover online. "Nothing anyone would care about."

"Yeah, well, that's our culture now, so you better be sure. I mean, look what kind of shit we know about celebrities' private lives. So it's no wonder this guy Roland is scared. But we just have to hope he calls. Okay. Look at that, just what we need. Temperature-rated to minus forty for twenty-seven bucks, I'd say that'll work. Size?"

Shay had led her to the racks of shoes at the back of the store. On the end of the row was a display of women's rubber-soled snow boots, their black nylon uppers topped by a cuff of fake fur.

Until today, Colleen wouldn't have been caught dead in them. "Eight and a half," she said.

"Nope. Whole sizes only. So you're a nine." Shay dug through the stack of boxes, many of them open and torn, until she found the pair she was looking for. "What kind of socks do you have on?"

Colleen unzipped her right boot and slipped it off. "Um, just these wool-blend ones . . ."

"Hang on. I'll be right back."

Colleen stood, holding on to the cart for balance while she stood on one foot. The floor looked clean, and after a moment she put her shoeless foot on the floor. The smell of synthetic leather was strong.

Nearby, a woman with a little boy was forcing his foot into a boot decorated with some sort of cartoon warrior. The boy was beginning to cry, protesting as his mother tried to wriggle the boot onto his foot. The problem seemed to be that the Velcro straps were stiff and unyielding and didn't leave enough room for his foot to slip into the boot; the harder the mother tried, the more the little boy protested.

Abruptly the woman yanked the boot off and threw it at the shelf, where it knocked a box onto the floor. "All right, all right, all *right!*"

she burst out, shocking her son into silence. A second later, as he began to wail in earnest, she pulled him into her arms and said, "I'm sorry. Goddamn it. I'm sorry." She stood up with her son in her arms and hurried away, leaving the boots and boxes in disarray on the floor.

Colleen's heart went out to the woman. How well she knew that moment. She had never yelled in public, had never thrown anything. But there had been so many times, when Paul was little, that she yelled at him in private, at home. When she dug her fingers into his arm so hard that her nails left little crescent moon marks. When she wished for a fraction of a second that she'd never had him at all, then suffered for the rest of the day with the guilt.

Long before Paul was ever diagnosed with ADHD and—for want of anything that precisely fit the diagnostic criteria and, she suspected, because she and Andy had spent a hell of a lot of money on a battery of tests and weren't about to walk out the door without a diagnosis— with oppositional defiant disorder. Long before she had accepted that it wasn't just a rough-and-tumble preadolescence that Paul would out- grow, she had privately admitted to herself that she wasn't the mother she'd anticipated being and her son wasn't the child she'd expected. When a couple of years of trying went by without another pregnancy, she and Andy decided—in a brief conversation where she suspected neither admitted the real reasons—that they would be content with just one child. If Andy had suspected what she was really thinking, that she couldn't handle another one like Paul, years of sleepless nights and screaming tantrums that nothing would quiet, he never condemned her for it. Quite possibly he felt the same.

But now. Oh, now. To go back to when he was the age of that lit- tle boy—three, maybe four—knowing what she knew now. She'd do everything differently. Because what she had done hadn't worked, had it?—even though she'd tried everything, paid every specialist, consulted every physician, tried every medication, every special camp, every education expert—had practically bought Paul's way into Syracuse with that shockingly expensive "admissions consultant" who essentially wrote his essay for him.

If she were given the opportunity to start over, Colleen would give away all her breakable things—her crystal and china and art and good furniture and every single knickknack in the house—and pad the walls and put an extra lock on the door, for safety, and then she'd let him run as wild as he needed to and never complain. She'd sit down and learn to play that zombie video game with him, she'd let him play lacrosse despite the potential for injury, she'd throw rocks into the duck pond with him all day long and ignore the posted rules. She'd move to some other community—somewhere like where Shay came from, maybe—where no one expected kids to sit still and take conversational Mandarin and join the debate team and score in the top percentile on standardized tests. She would have let Paul break a few bones and wreck a car and get into fights when he was in elementary school, before years of chafing at the restraints imposed by his overprotective parents made him do something so much worse.

"You okay?" Shay was standing in front of her, waving a hand in front of her eyes. "You zone out or something?"

"Sorry." Colleen forced a smile and turned her mind away, something she had taught herself to do when the churning of her thoughts proved too much to bear.

Shay held up a pair of socks, thick gray with a stripe of pink. "Here. Try these."

"You mean, open them right now? Before we pay for them?"

"Yeah, who's going to care?" Shay yanked off the cardboard band, tossing it into the cart.

Colleen put on the socks and boots. They were stiff, a little low on the instep, but otherwise fine. Already she could feel her feet warming up.

"Might as well put the other one on and wear them out of the store," Shay said. "Parking lot's only going to have got worse."

Colleen hesitated only for a moment. She rolled her old socks and tucked them in her leather boots and put them in the box. Her pants broke awkwardly over the top of the new boots, so she tucked the cuffs into them. She was certain she looked absurd.

With Shay's help she picked a pair of heavily padded nylon gloves in a shade of deep pink, and a matching synthetic scarf and knit hat that were surprisingly soft. In the checkout line, Shay tossed in a couple of tabloid magazines, gum, and mints. Colleen maneuvered herself in front of the cart and, handing over her credit card, pushed away Shay's fistful of bills. "It's all my stuff," she protested.

"Not the magazines and the—" Her phone went off and Shay pulled it out of her pocket, stepping out of the line. "Hello? Yes. Thanks so much for . . . okay . . . no, but I can remember . . . yeah, that's fine. And thanks, really."

"Ma'am?" The checker was trying to get Colleen's attention. The belt was rolling, the customer in front of her pushing his cart toward the exit, and Colleen had failed to notice.

"I'm sorry." She piled her purchases on the belt, explaining about the boots and socks; the checker accepted the box and wrapper without comment.

"Roland gave me an address," Shay said. "Here, I'm texting you so I don't forget. He said he'd be there at nine. So that gives us almost an hour. Let's head next door."

"Next door where?" Colleen said, signing the credit card slip.

"You didn't see when we came in? Liquor department has a separate entrance."

Colleen hadn't noticed, and she didn't really want to brave another gauntlet of lonely, horny men with their appraising eyes. But maybe it wouldn't be as bad in the liquor section: perhaps the men would feel chastened by the nature of their purchases, like kids caught reading comic books in Sunday school, and they'd keep their comments and gazes to themselves.

The Walmart liquor department was easily as large as the Tip-Top Liquor store back home in Sudbury, but in place of the wood-crate and plastic grapevine décor at the Tip-Top, the hand-lettered "staff picks" cards with the *Wine Spectator* ratings, there were shelves stacked with enormous bottles of spirits and cases of beer. More beer in the refrigerators lining the wall; the wine was limited to a paltry selection of cheap California labels.

Shay picked up a twelve-pack of Coors Light. "What about you?" she asked. "You want anything?"

Colleen debated for a moment. "I'll get a bottle of wine."

She made her way over to the refrigerator and scanned the bottles. The only labels she recognized were the cheap table wines, the Glen Ellen chardonnay and Beringer chenin blanc.

"What a nice change of pace," a man next to her said. "A woman with a little class. Don't see enough of that around here."

Colleen was about to turn her back and leave without picking a bottle when she noticed that the man was nothing like the others she'd seen in the store: for one thing, he was freshly shaved, with a conservative haircut. For another, he was wearing a suit and a cashmere overcoat, the effect only mildly spoiled by lug-soled boots.

"Sorry," the man immediately amended. "Forgive me. You spend a few days here and you completely lose track of your manners. Jesus. I feel like a jerk. You just don't look like . . . well, like Lawton material."

"It's no problem," Colleen murmured, and stepped politely aside to give him access to the case. She was about to head back to the front of the store when a thought occurred to her.

The suit. Clearly not from here. Who wore suits in Lawton? Executives, that's who. Oil company executives. And safety compliance inspectors. And lawyers.

A riffle of revulsion mixed with fury kept her rooted to the spot. And then . . . an idea so bold and so unlike her that she threw herself into it before she could hesitate.

She curved her lips into a smile and turned back toward the man. "Allen . . . right?"

Confusion passed over his face. "No, I'm Scott. Scott Cohen, White Norris?"

"Oh, I'm so sorry!" Colleen laughed as though embarrassed. "I thought—but no. I see it now. Not much resemblance at all. It's been a long day. I'm Vicki. Vicki Wilson, Slocum Systems."

Immediately she regretted using her best friend's name; she felt like she was dragging Vicki into something sordid. But it was the only thing that came to mind. Colleen really had worked for Slocum Systems once, during a college internship. She offered her hand; Scott had a nice handshake, firm but not crushing.

"Nice to meet you. Even under questionable circumstances." He smiled, circling a finger in the air to take in the Muzak, the heat blasting from ceiling vents, the depressing lighting and industrial shelving.

"Oh, I know. I wouldn't dream of coming here, but the hotel where I'm staying doesn't carry anything decent."

Scott laughed. "What a coincidence. I'm at the Hyatt—best hotel in town, and the nicest thing on the shelves in their bar is a bottle of Cutty Sark. Stuck here another few days. And there's only so much bad pinot a man can stand—you know?"

Colleen smiled, reaching past him into the case and picking up the most expensive bottle she saw. Her mind raced, trying to think how to extend the conversation without seeming too obvious.

"So, what brings you to Lawton?" Scott asked. Colleen glanced at his left hand—yes, wedding ring.

"Oh, Black Creek Lodge is one of our accounts. Slocum's in food services."

"We have some of our boys over there, I think. A couple of drilling crews. I'm from the head office, so I'm not real familiar with operations on the ground."

"Oh, then you heard about the boys who went missing." Scott's expression went instantly wary, and for a moment Colleen thought she'd pushed too far. "I have a son that age, is why it's on my mind," she added hastily. "He's away at Cornell."

"Terrible thing, really." Scott seemed to relax. "Boys that age, no sense at all, probably halfway to Vegas. So, Vicki . . . any chance I can talk you into sharing this nice bottle of"—he reached for the same shelf that Colleen got her own bottle from—"Navarro pinot grigio with me? The Hyatt's got a nice lounge. Nicer than any of the other hotels around here, anyway."

Colleen felt her smile tighten on her face. No one had tried to pick her up, explicitly or otherwise, in over a decade. Maybe closer to two. But there was something about the vibe in this town, a desperation and carelessness fueled by the terrible weather. Scott didn't even look abashed.

But Colleen felt her heart constrict. What was she doing? What was happening to her? She hadn't spoken to her husband for more than a few tense moments in days; her son had been missing for over a week. And not to put too fine a point on it, but she hadn't had sex in nearly a month, and the time before that had been only because she'd had too much to drink at a holiday party. Not that she had any interest in an affair or even flirting with a stranger. Although that was what was called for, wasn't it? She'd come this far, and she'd promised herself she would do anything for Paul; wasn't this just the next step? Drink with this stranger, keep her ruse going, tease out whatever details she could—and end the evening early. It wasn't a crime. He couldn't accuse her of being a tease; even a mild flirtation had to beat another night of pay-per-view and room service.

"I'm so sorry; I've been up since four a.m. East Coast time," she found herself saying. "And I've got early meetings tomorrow."

"On a *Sunday*?"

Shit. *Shit.* Colleen had completely lost track of what day of the week it was. She tried to smile. "With my team. Some of them came in from the West Coast, and we've only got tomorrow before we go see a new account."

"Yeah? Which one is that?"

"It's—well . . . I'm afraid I can't say. It's all very preliminary right now."

"I'm sorry, I shouldn't have asked," Scott said. "We're under pretty tight confidentiality restrictions ourselves. But hey, there's lots of development going on; I'm sure it's boom times for your business. So tell me, how long are you here for?"

"The rest of the week. We've got . . . a couple of pitches."

"Well, listen, then." Scott tucked the bottle under his arm and reached inside his coat, taking out a leather card case. He extracted a card and held it out to her. "My info's on there. Email, and that number'll forward to my cell. Why don't you give me a call if you get an evening free? No sense both of us dying of boredom up here, is there?"

His smile was just crooked and self-conscious enough to lend him a sort of charm, and Colleen slipped the card into her purse and thanked him. "I'll do my best. I have to see how the presentation goes."

"Tell you what—for now, let me buy you a drink anyway." He took the bottle from Colleen's hands and walked to the register. The cashier looked at them with faint interest while she rang him up.

"Two bags," he said, and she put the bottles into separate brown bags, twisting the paper over the tops, and then slipped them into the ubiquitous plastic Walmart bags.

"Here you go, then," Scott said, holding the bag out as though it was a box of long-stemmed roses. "Can I walk you to your car?"

Colleen searched for Shay, but she had disappeared. The only people on either side of the glass doors were men dressed in work clothes.

"Oh, thanks but I . . . have to pick up a couple things in the other side," Colleen said.

"All right, then. Uh, I'll be looking forward to hearing from you. Have a good presentation."

"Thanks for the wine." Colleen headed out into the cold and walked toward the other set of doors without looking back. Inside, she ducked to the right, to the darkened Subway counter, where she was hidden from view. She waited, her heartbeat slowly settling down.

Her phone rang. Shay.

"Hello?"

"What are you up to, girl?"

"I'll explain. Uh . . . can you pick me up by the main entrance?"

"Yeah, I just watched you walk back in there. After I watched you with that guy long enough to figure out you didn't need me horning in. Give me two minutes."

twelve

"WHITE NORRIS," SHAY said thoughtfully. "How many rigs do they run in Ramsey County?"

"I didn't ask," Colleen said, sounding exasperated. "Maybe you could've gotten him to just turn over his industry secrets on the spot, but I'm not used to talking to strange men in liquor stores."

Shay resisted rolling her eyes, and after a moment Colleen apologized. "I'm sorry. I'm just a little tense, and . . . well, thanks for coming to pick me up."

"It's no problem."

Shay concentrated on her driving. It had started snowing hard while they were in the Walmart; now the flakes made a blur in the taillights of the truck in front of her.

The directions Roland texted her led to a duplex on a street not much different from Brenda's, visibly run-down even under the cover of snow. There were already three vehicles in the driveway, so they parked on the street. As they stepped into a plowed pile of snow on the sidewalk, Shay guessed Colleen was glad to be wearing her new boots.

They trudged up the steps. The door on the right side of the duplex opened before they had a chance to knock. Roland was waiting, dressed in a Steelers jersey and a pair of sweats.

"Come on in, don't let the cold in," he said, ushering the women inside, where they stamped snow onto the towel-covered mat in front of the door. They added their boots to a pile that filled a huge Rubbermaid tote next to the doormat. The house smelled of microwave popcorn. As they were shucking off their coats, a woman with oversize glasses and a ponytail sprouting from the top of her head came into the room with a tray of mugs.

"Hi," she said. "I'm Nora. My daughter's asleep in the back of the house, so I hope you don't mind talking in the front room. I made y'all some coffee."

"Thank you," Shay said.

"I'm really sorry to show up like this," Colleen said. "You and Roland—we appreciate it so much."

"No, listen. If something happened to my daughter . . . I don't know what I'd do. Okay. Y'all need anything, just holler. I'm going to go work on papers in the den." Roland took the tray from her, and she put her hand on his shoulder and squeezed. A look passed between them.

"She teaches at the high school," Roland said gruffly. "She's got to grade papers. Here, go ahead and sit."

He set the tray on a worn oak coffee table, and the women sat down on the couch. He pulled an armchair closer to the table.

"You know anything about the Fort Mercer reservation?" he asked without preamble.

"You mean the Indian reservation?" Shay asked.

"Yeah. Upward of five hundred thousand acres an hour east of here, mostly Oyate. Got a casino, a couple of one-stop-sign towns, and a lot of unhappy folks living in trailers. Oh, and a fair amount of oil just sitting there under their alfalfa fields and grazing land."

"Why aren't they selling it?"

"Well, that's the big question, right? Turns out that through a series of incredible screwups, some of them their own fault, they've managed to sell the rights at a fraction of what they're worth. Like in some cases, less than one-one-hundredth of their value when you figure in the bonus and royalties."

"How does that even happen?" Shay asked.

"Well, the tribal council is supposed to negotiate on behalf of its members and distribute the profits from the tribal leases. But that ain't been happening, and things are getting out of control."

"I'm sorry, I don't understand," Colleen said. "What are the tribal leases? And bonuses and royalties?"

"The mineral rights? You know how that works, right?"

"No, I . . ." Colleen reddened.

Shay tried to curb her impatience. After all, most of what she knew about this stuff came from Taylor; it didn't sound like Paul had told his parents the first thing about the job. Still, she was surprised Colleen hadn't been curious enough to learn on her own. North Dakota oil was showing up in the national news more and more often, and a single Google search brought up thousands of results.

But maybe Colleen had tried to ignore it, hoping that would make it all go away. Maybe she figured that if she refused to acknowledge the oil boom that had lured Paul far from home, from the tidy little life she and her husband had planned for him, he'd eventually give up and come home.

But it hadn't exactly worked out that way, had it?

"Okay, well, just because you own surface rights to a piece of land, you don't necessarily own the mineral rights," Roland explained. "Like if you own your house, right, you're in charge of your yard and the water and electric lines that come into it and all. But you don't necessarily own what's beneath it, including the oil. People who own land out here, they lease out the mineral rights so companies can come in and drill, and they can make a lot of money that way. The big companies almost never own the land, just the rights, and then they pay royalties back to whoever holds the lease and a bonus when the well goes into production. A well might have an active life of twenty, twenty-five years, so it adds up. And since most people don't have the ten million dollars it takes to drill their own well, they have to go that route and let the companies do it.

"But what happened on the reservation got all fucked-up— excuse me. The tribe still holds the rights on a lot of the land out there, and they've got a tribal council that's supposed to negotiate for the best interests of all the members, and then the profits go back to the people. But so far no one's seen a dime. The council leased the land a few years back to a number of individual speculators at incredibly unfavorable terms, and then it turned out they were all acting on behalf of Hunter-Cole, which turned around and bought the leases from them, and now Hunter-Cole holds the leases for like a quarter of the drillable land up there. There's a guy on the council who made a shitload of money on the deal, and if you ask me, that's the real crime in all this, since he was the one that green-lighted the deals in the first place. Hunter-Cole bought and paid for him. But tribal lands are still held in trust by the US government, so the thinking goes that the government should have stepped in to stop this all from going down. Save them from themselves, so to speak. And now they've got three or four lawsuits challenging the leases."

"But I still don't understand how this could affect our boys. Or anyone working on Hunter-Cole rigs. I mean, none of them had anything to do with these deals."

"Yeah, but get this . . . these leases? They were nearly all for three years, which is the standard term. And they're going to start expiring soon. The way it works is that as soon as a well starts producing, the company has the right to work it as long as they're still bringing oil up and paying the royalties. But if Hunter-Cole hasn't put wells into production, the tribe has the right to let the lease expire and resell it."

"Shit," Shay said, as it all suddenly came together. "And let me guess what could get in the way of Hunter-Cole drilling."

"Safety violations?" Colleen guessed, her face going pale.

"OSHA investigations?" Shay said. "Rig fires in the news, footage of bad accidents?"

"OSHA . . . hah," Roland said bitterly. "Most people don't know this, but OSHA can only level fines. They can't actually shut down a rig. Hell, there was a Nabors rig out here, they had three guys die over eleven months, and the thing's *still* running."

"So it has to be . . . individual lawsuits?" Shay guessed.

"Yeah. And so far they've controlled things pretty well, but all it's gonna take is one guy—or his family—willing to tell Hunter-Cole's lawyers to jam their tiny settlements up their ass and go public. I doubt they could shut down existing operations, but you get a big enough lawsuit, with enough exposure—throw in allegations of a cover-up—it could halt new drilling. So, the Indians' wet dream is someone gets hurt and has the balls to raise a stink."

"My husband is a lawyer," Colleen said. "What if he threatened to start looking into the violations unless they cooperate with us to find the boys?"

"I don't know," Roland said doubtfully. "As long as your sons are missing, there's no threat to them. It has to be someone who can actually prove they've been hurt."

"And who doesn't need the money for hospital bills," Colleen said, her voice barely a whisper.

"Look, this is all speculation," Roland said. "I have no way to back any of it up."

"What's your angle, anyway?" Shay asked him. "How do you know so much?"

"Know what I used to do, back in Ohio?"

"No," Shay said. She had a feeling that the answer wasn't going to be a pretty one.

"I taught high school civics. When my daughter was born, she had a rare skeletal condition that's going to require a dozen surgeries as she grows up. We thought, at least we've got great health insurance. And then the school district started cutting costs and my wife and daughter didn't qualify for their insurance anymore. We were on the hook for almost fifty thousand dollars in bills by her first birthday." He scowled. "We were divorced by her second birthday. By the time she turned three, I was up here trying to make a dent in what I owe. I come home covered with drilling mud, but somewhere under there I guess I'm still kind of a news junkie."

Roland took a sip of his coffee. Colleen gripped her mug tightly but didn't drink. Shay thought through everything he'd said.

"Back at Walmart, you didn't want to talk about any of this."

"Well, think about it. I got debt back home, and my girlfriend moved here to teach. What happens if I lose my job? I'm fucked. And if anything happens to me, everyone I care about is fucked too."

"What do you mean? What would happen to you?"

"I knew this guy, derrick hand on my first job. Friend of his died when the hand brake on a geronimo failed. So he started making a fuss about the routine safety checks not being performed. A few weeks later, he died in a snowmobile accident on the reservation."

"Are you saying . . . was there something suspicious about his death?"

"I can only tell you what I heard, because they kept the whole thing hushed. But supposedly he was found at the bottom of a hill with the snowmobile turned over a few feet away. But what killed him was getting hit on the *back* of the head. They say his brains were leaking out of it. And you don't get hit like that running into a tree. Also, what was he doing on the reservation? It's not like people go up there recreationally. Unless they were trying to send a message . . ."

"Didn't the police investigate?"

"The *Lawton* police?" Roland snorted. "Gimme a break. They blame everything on budget and staffing issues, but whenever anything happens on the worksite, they're nowhere to be found."

"But what about their own police? Don't they have their own law enforcement?"

"Oh, now that's a whole other can of worms. Reservation law enforcement's a joke. They can't do much more than hand-slap their own. And if any outsiders are involved? It's out of their jurisdiction and you have to get the staties or the Feds in. So what happens is they hardly ever prosecute anything. I'm no fan of the tribe, but what you hear about them raping women up there, taking guys out of their cars and beating the shit out of them—it's mostly the opposite that's true, because if a white guy commits the offense, then the tribal officer's hands are tied."

"So you're telling me no one's even looking into this whole angle?" Shay demanded.

"What if we contacted other agencies ourselves?" Colleen said, mostly to Shay. "Cut out the Lawton cops and see if we can find someone else to pick up the case, since it potentially involves the Indians. I mean, maybe we could even get FBI, right?"

"Shit, I don't know," Shay said. "That's a stretch, isn't it? No matter what our boys were up to, why would they have any connection to the reservation?"

"I don't know. But maybe someone up there could tell us more about who's making trouble for guys who are too vocal about safety issues."

"Just be careful," Roland said. "You don't want Hunter-Cole thinking you're up to anything at all, because they're willing to throw money and manpower at every little problem that comes along. There's a rumor they're setting up a satellite office here in town so their guys don't have to keep flying in from their headquarters in Houston."

"Earlier, you said the boys' crew was still working in the same place. Can you tell us how to get there?"

"Yeah, I can give you the coordinates. I'll text them to you. But they're not going to let you on site. And if they get wind you're even close, you'll just draw their attention and make them hypervigilant."

Shay looked at Colleen. "Maybe we save that for now."

"No—we can't hold anything back. It's been *nearly two weeks*."

"All I mean is, we've got a couple more things to look into now, thanks to Roland. We have the reservation angle. And maybe we come at it from the side too—from your friend."

"You got a friend in management?" Roland said, startled.

"No, no, she's exaggerating. I met a guy in the Walmart. Legal counsel at White Norris. I lied and said I was in town for business."

"We're getting very good at lying," Shay muttered.

Roland nodded. "Wait long enough, you'll meet everyone in the Walmart. The devil himself walked through those doors, wouldn't surprise me."

Colleen and Shay thanked Roland, promising to keep everything he'd told them to themselves. Colleen wrote her own phone number down, as well as Brenda's address, and told him to contact her or Shay at any time.

"If you need to get in touch, go ahead and text me. But if I run into you somewhere, I'm going to pretend I don't know you, got it?"

Roland's girlfriend made another brief appearance as they were putting on their coats. "Roland able to help you out at all?" she asked sleepily, pushing her glasses up on her forehead and rubbing her eyes. "We'll both be praying for you."

"Something I got to ask," Shay said, pausing at the door. "You're a teacher, right? I'm guessing they didn't double teacher wages just because every fast-food joint in town's paying fifteen bucks an hour, right?"

Nora laughed drily. "Hell no. They've proposed raising our salaries, but that kind of change moves especially slow these days, now they can't figure out what to do with the budget surplus."

"So why are you still doing it? When you could be making so much more money doing just about anything else?"

Nora glanced over her shoulder, down the hall. "Reason's sleeping in that back room. I stay with the school system, I'll be able to pick her up after preschool, get my summers off. I want to be there for her."

Shay understood. Back in the day, she'd passed up more than one promotion—once when she was working as a bank teller and once at a gym—because the hours would have kept her away from the kids too much. Which was why her career path was more of a career checkerboard. And why she was down to a few hundred dollars in her checking account and a roll of the dice for a retirement plan.

Roland went to stand next to Nora, his arm around her. "You two drive safe and take care," he said. "Let me know if you need anything."

thirteen

WHEN THEY GOT back to the motor home, Colleen checked her phone. "Andy called," she said, surprised. "It's after midnight there. I wonder—"

Paul. Someone had found something out. Or Paul had called him. "Oh, God," she whispered, dialing. When Andy picked up, she didn't wait for him to say hello.

"Andy! Tell me—"

"Nothing happened," he said quickly. "And I don't have anything new to report."

Relief and dread tangled inside her. There wasn't bad news, and for that she was grateful. But what would she have done for good news? What would she have traded?

Had she dared to hope, for a moment, to pretend that Andy would say, *Guess who just showed up on our doorstep, in need of a shave?* That it was all a terrible misunderstanding, that Paul and Taylor had decided to go skiing or camping or, who knew, visiting someone he met last year in Syracuse, and was now back, sheepish and cranky and ready to get his life back on track.

"What," she said hoarsely, the voice of a ghost, a used-up thing.

"I called in some favors today." Andy was businesslike. "Two things. I've got a hotel booked for Wednesday on. It's yours as long as we want it. You can move into it, and if I come out I can join you, or you and Shay, now that I think of it, or we can give it to Steve, if you feel you want him there."

"Yes. Steve."

She could sense, rather than hear, his frustration over the phone, in the lengthy pause that followed, in the careful way he spoke again. "I understand why you feel that way, you want as many resources devoted to the search as possible. But I still wonder if this is the right move. Having Steve there, the cops are going to see it as a challenge to their investigation."

"There *is* no investigation. Don't you get it? They aren't doing anything."

"Look, Col." Andy sighed, and Colleen recognized the faint note of condescension that set her teeth on edge. "You have to have a little faith in these guys. Whatever abbreviated account the chief gave you was probably in the interest of saving time and, frankly, not causing a couple of hysterical moms any more worry than necessary. He wasn't—"

"Were you *there*?" Colleen demanded, clutching the phone tight in her anger.

"No, but I talked to him myself. Just about an hour ago."

"*What?*"

"Don't get all worked up, Col, I just felt I should weigh in too, to, you know, bolster our side of things. And he reassured me—"

"I can't talk to you about this right now," Colleen said, feeling like her breath had been forced from her lungs. Fury ignited a sharp pain behind her eyes, and she squeezed her free hand into a fist. "You have no right to—to—"

But what had he done, exactly? Another voice to nag the police, more weight behind their demands that attention be given to the case. Andy was an attorney; he was male; he was powerful. Those were things that could be used, especially with someone like Chief Weyant. So why did it infuriate her so much?

"I have *every* right," Andy snapped. "Don't you *dare* shut me out of this. Paul is my son too. I've been busting my ass here, me and Vicki. She's been down here practically since you left, setting up the Facebook page, helping me make calls. It was her idea I call Klipsinger in the first place—and he just got back in touch. You want to tell your best friend she doesn't have any right, either?"

Colleen's anger quickly turned to remorse. John Klipsinger was Vicki's ex-husband's law school roommate—and now a Massachusetts congressman.

"Vicki talked to Klipsinger?"

"To someone on his staff, anyway, and he's going to talk to someone in the North Dakota attorney general's office." Andy sounded chastened too. It had to be the pressure, the incredible stress making them turn on each other when they needed more than ever to be united. "I mean, it's a favor, for sure, and without any serious threat behind it, any cooperation they give you is just a courtesy. But it's a start. Klipsinger's guy says this should at least get us more manpower on the investigation, and some coverage for you and Shay if you feel threatened. So you're not going around leaving yourself open to who knows what. And if we need to escalate, we can do that too."

"Tell . . ." Colleen licked her parched lips. "Tell Vicki thank you."

"You might want to tell her yourself," Andy said shortly. "She's barely gone home to shower. She's really knocked herself out."

"I will." A faint alarm was ringing in Colleen's head, but now wasn't the time or place to pay attention. "I'll call her, as soon as things settle down for a minute. Right now I have to get some sleep. I'm exhausted."

"All right." There was an awkward pause. "Oh, I almost forgot. Vicki's putting together a flyer. Can you get a picture of Taylor? She says she can have it done overnight, and she found a place in Lawton that'll batch-print them priority. You can pick them up by ten."

"Shay," Colleen said. She looked up from her iPad. "Can you email Andy a picture of Taylor? My friend Vicki is putting together a flyer."

"What's his email address?"

Her fingers flew while Colleen recited it. "Two minutes," she said.

"Vicki even thinks she found someone to put them up around town, someone the shop owner referred her to," Andy said. "She went ahead and ordered a thousand. I know that's probably too many, but better too many than too few. And tonight she's going to post it online—she found all these sites, I guess. Blogs and Facebook pages, sites the camps maintain. And listen, Col, WHDH is sending over a reporter tomorrow. I said I'd talk to him. I mean, anything to drum up attention, right?"

"I guess," she said. "It just seems like there's hardly anything that anyone can do from there, really. All our leads—I don't know what else to call them—the reservation, the safety issues, that's all here in Lawton."

"All right, I'll let you get back to it," Andy said, sounding exhausted. "Let's check in tomorrow."

They said terse love-yous and good-byes. As Colleen hung up, she tried not to think about Vicki stopping by with the printout of Paul's texts, dressed in those shimmering yoga pants, the tight jacket, her makeup perfect even though she said she was going to the gym. Of how often over the past few months she seemed to time her visits for when Andy was home, coming by on the weekends with an extra jar of jam she picked up at the farmers' market, or asking to borrow the short stepladder to change the light in her foyer. "A divorcée's problem," she'd laughed ruefully.

Andy had laughed along.

"I sent him three," Shay said without looking up, dragging Colleen back to the present. "A head shot and two others. Now, for tomorrow, how does this sound? Let's drive out to the rig first thing. Roland sent me the coordinates, and all I had to do was put it in the map and it gave me driving directions. I don't care what he says, I want to see that rig. And it's on the way to the reservation, kind of. Shouldn't add more than a half hour to the trip, anyway."

"Yes. Good."

"You look like you're about to fall over. You can't do anything more right now. Get some sleep, Colleen."

"What about you?"

"In a minute. I just need to check a few things. I've been reading all these blogs and I got on Facebook and found six people who either work for Hunter-Cole now or have in the past. I mean, some of them are private so I can't learn much until they friend me back, but it's a start. I'm looking at the reservation site now."

"My best friend back home is doing that too. Andy said she's been trying to get the word out."

"What's her name? I'll friend her and see if we can join efforts."

"Vicki—Victoria, actually. Victoria Wilson."

"Victoria Wilson, Sudbury, Mass? Oh, here we go . . . good, got it."

Colleen set her phone alarm for six, knowing she'd be up even earlier. She was suddenly unable to keep her eyes open as she slid down under the blankets.

VICTORIA WILSON WAS about what Shay expected—a slightly flashier version of Colleen, same smooth haircut, same understated earrings, trendy eyeglasses.

She was also a night owl, at least this week. She accepted Shay's friendship request within moments. Shay was about to message her, explain who she was, but then for some reason she hesitated. Instead, she scrolled down through several pages of updates and other people's wall posts. It looked like Vicki had cranked up the effort as soon as Colleen had left Boston. Vicki had posted on websites and blogs for every school Paul had ever attended, from the looks of it. Community bulletin boards. Neighbors, friends, old teachers—all of them were adding their best wishes and prayers on Vicki's wall.

A woman named Laura Schmidt-with-a-D had set up a Caring-Bridge page, which, from the looks of it, was designed to feed Andy. Already three weeks' worth of "healthy meals and snacks" had been signed up for, his preferences—did Laura already know them, or had Colleen's friends conferred, putting together the information from years of acquaintance with the Mitchells?—listed for all to see. "No lamb or shellfish please. Low-fat where possible. CHOCOLATE always welcome! Please no white flour."

Vicki was no slouch. From the looks of it, she'd managed to find most of the same resources that Shay had, and several she hadn't. Of course, she had an advantage—she was doing this around the clock, probably from some *Better Homes and Gardens* kitchen while the nanny took care of her kids.

"Stop it," Shay whispered to herself. God, she could be such a bitch. She was lucky to have Vicki on her side, even if only by proxy. She read through enough of the comments to see that Vicki mentioned Taylor in nearly every comment and post in which she mentioned Paul. Already, pictures of the boys were popping up, along with dozens of prayers and "thinking of you" comments by strangers.

Shay blinked and took a sip of her beer. She really ought to get some sleep. She clicked over to her Etsy account; there'd been half a dozen new orders in the last couple of days. She'd set up an auto-responder before she left California, explaining to would-be customers of CaliGirl Designs that due to personal issues, her orders were backlogged. Which was going to be hell on her business. But fuck it. Until she got Taylor back, all of that had to wait, even if it meant she had to start over from zero.

"Love the Medium Box with Curved Drawers," a woman named MitzyD wrote. "I was wondering can you make me one custom for my daughter. She is graduating from 8th grade. Can you put an S in the middle of the design and some of the ruby crystals because ruby is her birthstone. Also she loves horses flute and dance."

Shay stared at the note for a long time, trying to imagine the little girl. The custom work wasn't cheap; the Swarovski crystals cost a bundle even through the wholesaler, and Shay had increased her prices as her customer base grew. For one of the medium jewelry boxes, with either images that the customer sent or that Shay selected, she charged two hundred dollars. It took a while, because every step of the paint and découpage process had to dry for the right amount of time, and Shay didn't take any shortcuts—didn't skimp on the sanding, made sure the fittings were secure, added her own custom paint work.

Still, she cleared about a hundred seventy in profit, money that she could really use, even if Colleen did keep picking up the tab for everything. But it wasn't just the money that kept Shay's attention fixed on the note. MitzyD's tiny little square profile picture didn't reveal much—a cartoonish pose with outsize glasses and a pink wig. A cool mom, then—a fun-loving mom who celebrated her kid's milestones and made her feel special. Shay approved.

She dug in her purse for her cigarettes and put one in her mouth. Not to smoke, not to light up. Maybe if Colleen wasn't here . . . But Brenda was being such a bitch; Shay was pretty sure she was over there in the house thinking about what she could charge the next person to rent the motor home. Too bad she didn't realize Colleen would pay her whatever she wanted. Well, Shay wasn't going to be the one to tell her.

She rolled the cigarette back and forth in her lips, inhaling the smell of the tobacco. They ought to make a perfume out of that. Tobacco and whiskey and maybe some vanilla or something to bind it all together. No—throw in some Polo Explorer. The thought of Mack's aftershave traveled through her tired body, making her miss him so powerfully it was like the memory of him was more real than this moment, this trailer, this image on the screen in front of her. Mack wore aftershave only on days when he had to put on a tie and go up to the office in Sacramento, but those were good days because he could usually see her on the way back; Caroline never expected him home for dinner on those days. Sometimes, he got away on weekends, and then he came to her smelling of woodsmoke and grass clippings and sweat, and Shay loved that even more, drinking him in, inhaling him, trying to make him last.

He'd email her again tomorrow. He emailed every day. But she wouldn't be weak, she wouldn't go looking for comfort rereading his note, not when she had this job to do. They were grown-ups. God, how many times had they reminded each other of that? They weren't teenagers. Hell, he was going to be fifty in the spring; Caroline was talking about throwing him a huge party when the kids came home from college for the summer. It was good. It was fine. Mack was a piece of her life that Shay goddamn well deserved, that she refused to feel guilty about, but she wasn't about to go making him into something he wasn't. And he wasn't the man who held her when she couldn't go on—because Shay never, ever let herself get to that place.

"Fuck," she whispered. Quickly she typed a note back to MitzyD, saying that she was sorry she couldn't commit to a custom piece at the moment but that she'd be in touch as soon as she was able, and would throw in a 20 percent discount for her patience if she was still interested.

"Congratulations to your daughter," she added, and when her throat went a little thick and her eyes watered, she hit Send more savagely than necessary and took a fake drag on her unlit cigarette.

The Facebook window was still open. There had been three more comments since she last looked. Two more God-be-with-you wishes.

And one in all caps that read, "HOW DOES IT FEEL NOW, COL-LEEN?"

fourteen

SHAY LOOKED OVER at Colleen, who slept with her hand on the pillow next to her cheek, prettily, like somebody posing for a mattress ad.

Her heart was pounding as she clicked over to Nan Terry's profile. It wasn't private; Shay was able to view her photos (twenty-two photos in two albums, profile pictures and everything else lumped together) and her posts (infrequent; she played Bubble Safari and Candy Crush and was fond of reposting inspirational pictures) and her friends (124 of them). She was married to Gerald Terry, whose profile was even more sparse. She was mother of Caryssa Terry, age seventeen and a junior at Sudbury High, and Darren Terry, age twenty, attending Massasoit Community College.

Shay enlarged Darren's profile picture as much as she could. He was a nice-looking kid with a shock of reddish hair that would mellow to auburn as he aged, a smattering of freckles, and a wide, confident grin.

And a scar that traced from one temple down past his cheek, ending an inch short of his jaw. It was faint, almost invisible, but as Shay clicked through his pictures it was more apparent in some of them, when his profile was turned toward the camera.

Shay looked at the time: almost two a.m. She started searching in earnest.

The motor home was completely silent other than Colleen's occasional sighs and the wind against the windows. It had stopped snowing, and outside she could catch a glimpse of stars. The cold crept up through the floor, through Shay's feet, and now and then she tugged the blankets tighter around herself.

It took nearly half an hour, and dozens of blind alleys and dead ends, before she found it, and it wasn't in any news item or community posting, but rather in a Facebook post from a kid who'd gone to a high school that apparently had a rivalry with Sudbury High, where both Paul Mitchell and Darren Terry had played football their freshman year. Darren had been moved up to varsity halfway through the season, and Paul, who never made it past the freshman team, wasn't tagged in any of the same pictures as Darren and wasn't his friend on Facebook, but apparently they had once known each other.

In what would have been their junior year, a kid from Medfield wrote a long post that was commented on by dozens of kids from both high schools, in which he talked about an upcoming game between the Sudbury Panthers and the Medfield Warriors.

> There wide receiver can't block worth shit. Remember when he was a freshman that retard nearly killed him he couldn't even take him in a fair fight. Paul Mitchell your my hero bro even if you are messed up. Go tell your boyz watch out because the WARRIORS are coming to fuck them up. Oh but dont hit TERRY again I want to take him down myself.

Adrenaline surged in Shay's veins. She narrowed her search to the months the boys would have played football their freshman year, tried a variety of search terms. Nothing. Then she turned her attention to the online white pages.

It was nearly three when she put her coat on and went outside. First she smoked the cigarette, its filter damp and limp from being chewed on. She tossed the butt on the ground and toed snow over it. A truck drove by, trundling slowly, loaded with steel pipe. Shay barely registered the cold against her face.

She dialed.

"Hello?"

"Mrs. Terry?"

"Who is this? It's barely four o'clock in the morning."

"I'm really, really sorry to call you like this. I don't want to intrude on your privacy. But it's kind of important. Please don't hang up."

There was a silence. Shay imagined the woman in her fancy New England home, clutching her nightgown around her, heart pounding from the middle-of-the-night ringing of the phone. She took a breath. She was about to lie, to betray. But it was the morning of the thirteenth day since her boy went missing, so Shay made herself not care. It wasn't the hardest thing she'd done by a long shot.

"My name is Anne Hutchins. I'm calling because my son Ben works with Paul Mitchell in Lawton, North Dakota." Betting that Nan Terry wouldn't know a California area code when she saw one. Betting that she'd be unable to hang up when she heard what Shay said next. When her voice broke, she wasn't entirely faking. "Ben's in the hospital. He's beat up bad, Mrs. Terry. My husband and I . . . we just want to know what happened."

"Oh, my God. He's done it *again*. Oh, God, I knew this would happen."

"Done what?"

"I . . . can't talk about it. Look. That boy is dangerous, that's all I'll say. I'm legally obligated not to talk about it."

Icy dread took hold of Shay. "Please. I won't repeat what you tell me to anyone, I swear it. I'm just trying to understand what happened. I won't mention your name, I won't—"

"If I talk to you, it's completely off the record, do you understand? If anyone contacts me, if you get a lawyer, I'm going to deny I ever talked to you—"

The woman's anguish was clear even two thousand miles away. "I understand. Please, just tell me what you can."

"When my son was a freshman in high school, he said something to Paul Mitchell in the locker room after football practice one night. There were three of them getting dressed, and the other boy started it. He was making fun of Paul because of his dyslexia, calling him a retard, but it was only when Darren joined in that Paul snapped. What Darren said, it was a stupid thing to say, but you know how boys are at that age. I mean, God, they were all of fifteen. Darren's not a mean kid, and the other kid started it, but Paul came at him with both fists and kept pounding Darren even after he was down, and then he switched to kicking him. With his *cleats*. There was blood *everywhere*, I saw the pictures. By the time the other guy pulled Paul off of him, Darren was already unconscious. He lost three teeth, his jaw was broken, his eye socket was fractured, his face—oh, God, if it had gone to trial and they'd let the jury see those photos, they would have sent Paul away. If he'd been eighteen . . ."

Shay couldn't speak. Paul Mitchell, who her son had befriended, who he had called his *best* friend, was more than just the sweet-faced, shy boy in the picture his mother carried. He was capable of violence, and he'd lost control before.

"The lawyers laid it out for us. With Paul being a minor, we didn't have a chance, especially because the school had just started this huge antibullying campaign and there were a number of kids and teachers willing to testify that Darren and the other kid, who was way worse, had a clear and demonstrable habit of taunting Paul. And the Mitchells had their lawyers, I swear to you, before you could blink. They threw money at this like . . . and the other boy's father was out of work and they didn't have money for a defense, and Darren ended up needing some therapy that our insurance company wouldn't cover. My husband . . . the Mitchells' lawyer was offering to pay for everything, all his therapy, they promised to make Paul go to anger management and quit the football team, and the school worked it out so the boys would never even have class in the same wing."

"Sweet holy Mary," Shay said weakly. "Did he ever do it again? To anyone else?"

"Not that I know of, but who can say? His mom watched him like a hawk after that. Look. I'm not saying, you know . . . I mean, it's her son, what's she going to do? But she never contacted us, never an apology. My husband says we have to let it go, because of all the legal stuff, but I've seen her at Safeway, she turns her cart around and walks away, she won't even look at me. First her son almost kills Darren and then it's *my* fault?"

"I . . . appreciate you telling me this. I won't mention your name."

"Thank you. Can I ask, what set him off this time?"

Shay thought fast. She couldn't afford to raise any more suspicions. "My son was friends with a boy named Taylor. They were popular on the rig, kind of the ringleaders. I guess they pulled some sort of harmless prank on Paul, and he reacted badly."

"Yeah, that sounds about right," Nan said bitterly. "Look, I'm as sorry as the next person for the kids who don't fit in. But it doesn't make it the fault of the ones who do, does it?"

fifteen

AT SEVEN THIRTY, Colleen was wondering if it was too early to wake Shay. She'd already made up the bed and packed her bag for the showers and tried to read the book she'd brought, but she'd been up for an hour and a half and hadn't been able to get through more than a few paragraphs.

Someone tapped softly at the door. Colleen jumped off the vinyl bench, her heart pounding. She opened the door and found Roland's girlfriend standing outside, her breath making clouds in the sunless morning air.

"Nora, right?" she said. "For heaven's sake, come in, it's freezing out there."

"I'm so sorry to just show up like this. Oh—I didn't realize—"

Colleen followed her gaze. Shay was propping herself on her elbow, rubbing sleep from her eyes.

"No, please, it's okay. Shay, Nora's here. Roland's girlfriend."

"Uh-huh." Shay's voice was throaty from sleep.

Colleen shut the door behind Nora and they sat at the dinette table. Colleen was glad she'd tidied up, but the close quarters smelled of sleep and morning breath, and Shay's clothes lay on the floor where she'd shucked them off.

"I'll only stay a minute. It's just that there's something I think you should know. I didn't hardly sleep last night, trying to figure out if I should tell you."

"If you can help us, I don't care if you move in." Shay pulled the covers up over her shoulders, her hair clinging to them, charged with static electricity.

"Look, Roland doesn't know I'm here." She took a deep breath and let it out slowly. "Actually . . . there are a few things Roland doesn't know."

"What do you mean?"

"Okay, look. Before I explain, because you're going to think I'm a horrible person, there's a few things I have to tell you. My ex is out of work, and Roland sends just about every penny home to *his* ex after he pays his bills. You know I don't make much money teaching. And I can't switch jobs, not if I want to be there for Ellie. So a while back, when my rent went up almost double what it was, one of the other teachers, someone I've got close to, told me about a way to make some money."

She dropped her gaze to her lap, her hands twisted together tightly. "Her husband works on the rigs too. What happened was, he got pulled into this mess where a guy was threatening to sue the company for an injury he said was caused by failure to install the right equipment. My friend's husband went on record saying that wasn't the case. He was just telling the truth. But then . . . well, a guy came out to their house and handed him an envelope. Said the company really valued his integrity and wanted to thank him, and to let them know if there were any other . . . areas of dissatisfaction where the company could do a better job of meeting its workers' needs. Right? Like, using really vague language. And in that envelope, there was five thousand dollars in *cash*. Well, he wasn't stupid. He knew exactly what they were looking for. He gave over a couple of names, a few details."

"You're saying that he turned in his coworkers who were . . . what, threatening to sue?"

"Not even that, necessarily, just the ones who were potential problems, either because they complained a lot at work, or talked about filing complaints or contacting lawyers or the news. Anything, really. They wanted to know who the 'troublemakers' were"—she made air quotes—"and then they handled it. My friend said the guys her husband turned in ended up being let go before too long. They just got jobs on other companies' rigs, but management didn't care because they weren't *their* problem anymore."

"So you're saying that Roland—"

"Not Roland," Nora said fiercely. "*Me.* I made the call. I met the guy in a Starbucks over in Minot and all I had to do was pass along a few names that Roland mentioned to me. He promised that nothing would go on their permanent record, that there were a dozen different ways they could be let go and they'd be working again in a week, somewhere else. I made seven thousand dollars in one afternoon. That's how I paid for Christmas and caught up on my rent. I even flew my mom up here."

Her voice had taken on a defiant edge. Colleen waited for Shay to blast her for what she'd done, but Shay merely watched her, twisting her hair around her finger.

"Look, I'd never have done it if I thought anyone would get *hurt*. And honestly, I don't think the company's doing anything, you know, real bad. I *don't* believe they would ever hurt any of their employees, for what it's worth. But I thought you should know, okay?"

She was already standing up, tugging her purse strap over her shoulder.

"I . . . thank you for coming to us," Colleen said.

"You're not going to say anything to Roland, are you?"

"No, of course not."

"Good. Thank you. And I . . . I'll be praying for you."

As the door closed, Shay lay back down and pulled the covers up over her head, her voice muffled as she said, "Amazing how easy it is to buy people these days."

SHAY SAID LITTLE during their drive to the truck stop, breakfast, the wait for the showers. Colleen figured they both were entitled to silence when talking didn't suit them, but when they finally were on the road again, headed for the rig, she couldn't stand it anymore.

"Is there anything I can do? Do you want to talk about it?"

Shay said nothing, staring straight ahead at the road. The sky was a vivid, clear blue and the sun blazed down on the wintry landscape, softening the top layer of snow despite the temperature hovering around ten degrees. Her mouth seemed tight, her profile especially tense. Colleen was about to ask a second time when Shay let the car drift over on the shoulder, braking slowly until they came to a stop. The landscape was eerily uniform on all sides: endless rolling fields of white, weed stubble poking through here and there, snow crusted with grit piled at the edge of the row.

Colleen was digging in her purse for tissues, getting ready to offer comfort, when Shay said coldly, "I know about Darren Terry."

Darren Terry. The name was daggers, ice picks, chain saws. Colleen had worked so hard to bury the memory that its invocation was like a rock shattering glass, leaving shards everywhere. Neither she nor Andy had spoken that name aloud since they met in their attorney's office to countersign the settlement four years ago.

They had talked about moving away from Sudbury, and sometimes, when Colleen glimpsed Nan Terry driving around town in her little BMW or running along the Blue Hills trail, she still wondered if it would have been better if they had. But that would have meant forcing Paul to start over at another school for his sophomore year and finding all new therapists and a new psychiatrist, just as he'd finally gotten comfortable with the current ones. And besides, no one knew, besides the Mitchells and the Terrys and the lawyers and the school administration, which was the whole point.

No one knew. But Shay, who had known her less than forty-eight hours, was staring at her with revulsion and fear, just like Nan Terry had looked at her at the Safeway last fall the one time Colleen broke her own rule and didn't make the trip over to the Norfolk grocery, just in case.

"How—"

"*Fuck* how," Shay snapped, cutting her off. "Tell me *exactly* what Paul did and why."

"He . . ." Colleen's mouth moved, but nothing came out. How many times had she had this conversation with herself? How many times had she told herself this story in an attempt to find some new angle, some softening, some abatement—to soothe herself?

"Paul is severely dyslexic, and he has ADHD. And he also used to suffer from oppositional defiant disorder."

"Oppositional *what?*"

In that word was reflected all the skepticism Colleen herself had ever felt, every bit of Andy's resistance, every conversation with Paul's teachers through the years when she pleaded for a little extra understanding, a second chance, a do-over.

"I know it sounds . . . made up, but it's a real diagnosis. It's often linked with dyslexia and attention deficit. For kids like Paul, ordinary schoolwork can be incredibly frustrating. Especially in adolescence. Everyday things we take for granted are really difficult for—"

"Lots of kids are frustrated," Shay said, her voice thin steel. "Lots of kids suck at school. And they don't have half of what you were able to give your kid, and they still don't go around beating the shit out of other kids."

"You don't understand," Colleen said, feeling the remainder of her composure crumpling. She was having trouble breathing, her gut tightening. "They teased him. Every day of his life since kindergarten, someone was always picking on him. Ever since they started learning to write and Paul began to understand that he was different. All through school, and we come from an incredibly competitive district, the kids are attuned to the expectations—"

"*My* kid got teased. *Every* kid gets teased. All through fourth grade Taylor got called Shrek because he was tall and his ears stuck out. But you just tell them to *deal* with it."

"It's . . . it's something you're born with," Colleen continued doggedly. "He was . . . he didn't hurt Taylor. That's what you're thinking, isn't it? That he hurt him?"

Tears flooded her eyes, making her vision blurry. Her hand found the tissues in her purse, and she pulled out a clump and pressed them against her face.

"How can you say? After he nearly killed that boy? Over a little teasing?"

Colleen twisted in her seat so she could look directly at Shay. "It wasn't just a *little* teasing! It was every day at football, every single day. Calling him a retard. A *monkey.* Darren and the other kid, Tanner, he was even worse. It wasn't even about the dyslexia, anyway, it was over a girl Tanner had been interested in, this girl Paul took to the homecoming dance, and he'd known Paul since back in grade school when Paul used to have a specialist shadow him in second grade. I mean, it had been almost a *decade,* but when Tanner got upset about this girl, he just brought it up again like it was yesterday, and Paul reacted."

She knew that Shay must have heard the evasion, the desperate denial in her voice. "And Paul and Taylor were *friends*. You said it. You said Taylor told you about Paul. That they were—that they were close."

"But Paul never told you about Taylor. Right?"

Colleen's mouth hung open as she tried to think of what to say. Had he? Had she somehow missed it, maybe he hadn't used Taylor's name, maybe some mention or allusion that she had missed or glossed over? Maybe he'd talked to Andy and not her, one of the times the two of them went out to get firewood or pick up wings or Chinese, hadn't there been a few times they'd been out much longer, Colleen saying nothing because she guessed Andy had taken him to the Hub for a beer and hadn't told her because he wasn't legal yet?

"Maybe Taylor *thought* they were friends," Shay said, "and all along Paul's thinking something else. It's festering, it's growing . . ."

"Stop," Colleen begged. "Please. Look. We were on our way to the rig, right? We'll find people who knew them. We'll ask. Just, please, reserve judgment."

"Your *detective*. Does he know? Did you tell him?"

"Steve?" Colleen said, stalling, but of course she couldn't get out of it, she had to tell. Shay with her Googling, her finding of facts, ferreter-out of secrets; somehow, she couldn't keep anything concealed from Shay for long. "It hasn't come up yet, but if it does, if there is any reason to mention—"

"There's a *very fucking good* reason, as far as I'm concerned. My *son*. Who trusted your son, befriended him, without knowing anything about his past, about what he'd done. No, don't talk." She held up a hand to stop Colleen from speaking. "Here's how this is going to work. If we haven't found them, haven't figured all of this out by tomorrow afternoon, either you tell the police or I will. And you're going to tell Steve before you ever fly him out here. Else we part ways, we both go on our own. But that'll put you out here with no car and nowhere to stay."

Colleen nodded dumbly. How had this even happened, how had it gone so wrong? The car continued to idle, the rumble of the engine occasionally interrupted by a tick or a pop.

She couldn't do this without Shay. She wouldn't be able to venture out here, on these nameless back roads, searching for oil rigs, wouldn't know where to start on the reservation, who to talk to, where to go. With Shay, things just seemed more . . . possible. She was fearless in ways that Colleen could only imagine.

"It's got to be something with Hunter-Cole," she mumbled. "The safety violations. Or it could have been something we haven't even thought of yet."

"Are you seriously going to try to tell me those are better options? Is that what you're praying for when you close your eyes at night?" Shay eased back onto the road. "Our boys are still missing. All I care about is finding them. Far as I'm concerned, what Paul is is one more possible explanation. For both their sakes I hope he didn't do something. But I just don't got enough give-a-damn to worry about your feelings, so don't ask me to."

Colleen nodded again. So they had a new understanding. And she had something terrifying to worry about.

Because the only thing worse than her son and Taylor going missing was the possibility that it was Paul's fault. That despite the years of therapy and medication and mindfulness training, despite all the progress he'd made, he had gone into a rage so powerful that— like what happened once before—he wouldn't even remember how he ended up with blood on his hands.

THEY PULLED OVER where the new road had been cut from the earth and churned with snow and mud. Dead stalks poked out from the tread marks made by dozens of trucks, evidence that not long ago, this land was undisturbed.

A few hundred feet away, the rig rose high into the air, painted the primary colors of a child's toy: the tower was white lattice with a bright yellow core; equipment clustered around the base was yellow and red. It cast a shadow that seemed to go on forever. Four cobalt blue holding tanks were lined up like beads on a necklace. A perimeter road had been carved out; inside it the earth was raw and criss-crossed with tire tracks. Half a dozen trucks were parked haphazardly. A few men moved between the vehicles and machinery; no one seemed to be looking toward the road.

In the passenger seat, Colleen stared, glassy-eyed and so miserable she was practically vibrating with pain. But Shay couldn't let herself care. She imagined the separation between them made of something solid—Lucite, or very thick glass, a boundary neither of them could breach. Colleen was not the enemy—but she might be something even more dangerous. Because if Shay allowed herself to feel pity or even compassion, it might cloud her thinking.

So, back to the rig. A few of the men were walking toward the road. Or was that her imagination? Were they trying to see through the windshield, taking down her license plate? Had the supervisors been warned to be on the lookout for her and Colleen, ever since they began searching for their boys?

Shay felt conflicting impulses. If they did nothing, they would learn nothing, except for the fact that the rigs were bigger up close than she'd ever imagined. If they got out of the car, they risked getting in trouble for trespassing, and alienating management further, making them even less likely to lend assistance. On the other hand, hadn't they already announced their intentions by making the calls to Hunter-Cole in the first place?

While she was mulling over her options, a black pickup truck made a lazy, wide turn on the cleared land and started driving slowly toward them down the access road. The women waited without speaking. When the truck stopped a dozen yards away, Shay squinted at the driver, but other than wraparound sunglasses and a baseball cap, it was hard to see much through the windows. After a few minutes the truck pulled even so that his driver's-side door was only a few feet from hers and he rolled down the window, motioning her to do the same.

The blast of cold air was instant and bracing. Now she could see his whole face: unfamiliar, lined and sun-weathered, colorless lips, and a sandy brown growth of beard.

"You ladies lost?"

"No. I know exactly where I am. I'm staring at a rig where a bunch of men who worked with my son are making piles of money for Hunter-Cole." Despite her bravado, Shay felt her heart pounding under her shirt.

The man took his time removing his sunglasses. His eyes narrowed against the sun, revealing a nest of wrinkles at the corners. This man was no stranger to the outdoors, and judging from the wear on his suede coat, he actually worked for a living. "Who are you?"

"I think you know who I am. Either that or you're dumb as a stump. Who are *you*?"

Now the man smiled, a tight and mean-spirited smile. "You're starting to hurt my feelings," he said softly. "I'm the safety compliance officer. One of the *good* guys."

"Show us your ID," Colleen said from the other seat. Shay gave her a quick glance, surprised she'd come back to life.

The man chuckled. "This ain't *Law and Order*. We don't have badges. But I can tell you, you're starting to get on the nerves of my bosses. And while that may not flutter your wings, I'll tell you something else that you ought to care about. You are barking up the wrong tree. Nothing happened to your boys on the job. I give you my personal guarantee."

"Really? Are you on every job site every minute of every day?" Shay demanded. "Were you there last fall when the wireline went through one of your employees' guts? Or when two guys fell off the same platform in one month because Hunter-Cole didn't put up the regulation guardrail? Were you there when your lawyers bought off their families?"

There was the slightest flicker in the man's expression, a tic at his eyelid, which quickly disappeared. "Give the little lady a medal," he drawled. "She knows how to use Google. Only you got a ways to go, because if you'd read everything on the subject you'd know that we settled. Not because we were guilty. But to make it go away."

He waved his hand, as if shooing away an annoying fly. "That's what Hunter-Cole does, you know. When whiners start making a lot of noise like whiners do, and it becomes a threat to productivity, they settle. Except you two, you don't really pose much of a threat at all, do you? Two ladies in a girlie little SUV—unless you get out of this car and take your tops off, you're not even providing much entertainment."

Shay was trying to work up a comeback when Colleen unsnapped her seat belt and opened the car door. She was out of the car in seconds and plodding unsteadily through the shin-high snow, around the car to the road. When she reached the flattened snow, she made better progress, striding toward the rig.

The man cursed and backed up, spinning snow under his tires.

He executed a sloppy three-point turn and began following Colleen, his front bumper inches from her backside. She paid him no attention.

"He's going to run her down," Shay said out loud, and then she was out of the car too, running to catch up. Or rather, slogging through the snow as fast as she could. She came abreast of the truck and slammed her fist into the side, instantly regretting it as pain traveled through her wrist and arm.

"Take a video if he runs me over," Colleen yelled. "Post it online."

It was a good idea. But Shay used her energy to catch up instead. They arrived at the periphery of the cleared area, and a handful of men gathered at the base of the rig, watching them.

A bearded man in an orange vest over a brown coverall came unhurriedly down the stairs. He waited, with his arms folded, as they walked the rest of the way, the truck close behind them. When Shay and Colleen were a few yards from the small crowd of workers, the driver parked and jumped out of the truck. He was out of breath when he jogged around to join them.

"This is how you contain them, Pardee?" the bearded man at the front of the group asked. To Shay and Colleen he said, "I need to ask you to leave. This is a hazardous environment and you're not dressed or trained for it."

"We'll take that risk," Colleen said. "Some of you worked with our sons. Did any of you know Paul and Taylor?"

There was murmuring among the crowd of men; the man in the vest turned around and glared at them. "Back to work," he said. "This ain't no tea party."

"Hey!" Shay yelled, as they began to disburse. "I'm Taylor Capparelli's mom. *Fly's* mom. This is Colleen and her son is Paul Mitchell, or you might know him as Whale. If you know anything about where they are or what happened to them, you need to tell us. Please, do the right thing and tell us!"

"That's enough now, ma'am, you're making a fool of yourself," the man in the vest said, taking her arm. Emboldened, the man who'd driven the black truck came around and grabbed hold of Colleen. "We're going to escort you back to your car so you don't hurt yourselves. Now don't fight me, or someone's liable to get hurt."

"You all have mothers!" Colleen called, struggling to get out of his grip. "Wives and daughters and sons. People who love you. If you were missing, they would want to know what happened to you!"

An idea occurred to Shay. "369-648-2278! Call me, please! Anytime. If you know something, call!"

"471-216-9669!" Colleen yelled, and then they took turns repeating their phone numbers while the men dragged them back to the Explorer. Shay let her body go limp. Though she weighed only a hundred twenty pounds, the coat and boots must have made her hard to handle because the man dragging her cursed harder and sweat formed on his brow despite the cold. When Colleen caught on, she did the same thing, all the while screaming their phone numbers even as the group of men dispersed and disappeared into the rig.

At the car, Shay shook off the man's arm and opened the driver's-side door and pretended to get in. At the last minute she twisted and slammed the door hard against the man. The edge cracked against his elbow.

"Fuck! Are you insane?" He jumped around for a minute, massaging the elbow, and then he grabbed her arm and pulled her from the car, pinning her against the door. Shay knew what was coming; they were hidden from view of the rig. She worked up a gob of spit and let it fly a split second before he hit her, and as her head slammed into the window she had the satisfaction of seeing her saliva land on his cheek.

She tasted blood when she fell to the ground, but she laughed anyway, getting up on her hands and knees. She felt around her mouth with her tongue: didn't feel like any of her teeth had been knocked out or broken. Probably just cut on the inside. Colleen was screaming something and running around the truck to help her, but Shay pushed her away.

"Bet you've got my number memorized now," she yelled, getting to her feet and dusting herself off as the man walked disgustedly back toward the rig. "Don't be a stranger!"

sixteen

"AT LEAST LET'S see if there's a clinic," Colleen fretted as they drove toward the edge of the reservation. "There's got to be one somewhere here."

"Don't need it," Shay said for the second time. "It's just a little cut. He didn't hit me that hard—probably because if he broke my nose or blackened my eye I'd have proof he assaulted me."

"You *do* have proof! I saw the whole thing!"

Shay laughed. "They're gonna be real attentive at the police station when you demand justice for me, right? After they told us to mind our own business? You can bet that Hunter-Cole has someone on the payroll over there, anyway. In fact, I wouldn't be surprised if the next person to get in our face is a cop."

The scattered buildings—prefab housing, mostly, with a few battered-looking shacks and cinder-block buildings here and there—gave way to a tiny business district, the main road bisected by two other streets and a single stop sign. A general store had several neon beverage signs in the window. There was a feed and hardware store and a secondhand shop. A gray-sided building with a green roof was the nicest-looking structure, the sign lettered onto the side reading INDIAN AFFAIRS.

"Nobody around," Shay observed, taking her time deciding where to park. She drove to the end of the two-block cluster of buildings and made a wide U-turn before coming back and parking in front of the Indian Affairs building. "Of course, the fact it's ten degrees out might have something to do with that."

"Who do you want to talk to?"

"I thought maybe I'd take a break from talking." She touched her mouth gingerly; the flesh above her lip was swollen and puffy. With her tongue, she could feel the ragged place where her teeth had cut her cheek. "I haven't been all that effective so far, have I?"

"Well, but what are we trying to accomplish here? How can we get anyone to talk to us if there's as much hostility up here as Roland said?"

Shay didn't answer. The headache that had arrived on the heels of being hit wasn't the worst she'd ever had, but combined with a lack of sleep and the anxiety from what she'd discovered online, it was all she could do to keep from biting off something sarcastic. Besides, why did she have to have all the ideas?

Colleen seemed to have arrived at the same conclusion because she started tramping over the snow to the entrance. A bell affixed to the inside handle chimed when they opened the door.

A woman sat at a desk with a sheaf of papers in one hand and a mug in the other. Talking to her with one hip resting on the edge of her desk was a man dressed for the outdoors, his unzipped parka being the only concession he'd made to indoor heat. Both stopped talking as the women entered.

"Hello," Colleen said loudly. "My name is Colleen Mitchell and my son is missing. He worked on a Hunter-Cole rig until two weeks ago, and no one has seen him or heard from him since. His friend is also missing. This is his mom, Shay. Our sons are twenty years old. We heard a rumor that there's a lot of bad feelings about Hunter-Cole up here, and I don't have time to apologize to you for everything that is wrong in your world, so can you please tell me how to figure out if anyone around here knows anything about our kids?"

Shay was surprised and impressed, even if Colleen went a little wobbly there at the end. The man edged his ass off the edge of the desk and stared at them, saying nothing. The woman cleared her throat and moved her mouse an inch.

"I just got hit in the face by some Hunter-Cole asshole," Shay said. "If you got some issue with them, you won't get any disagreement from me."

"I don't got issues with them specifically," the woman said grimly. She looked about fifty, with a no-nonsense haircut that made her look older. A silky floral top over a turtleneck concealed her extra pounds. "But I don't know anything about your sons."

"Can you help us find out who to talk to?"

"How about fuck-off-dot-com?" the man said. His face had darkened with anger. His graying hair was cut short, making him look ex-military. "You figure your boys got into trouble, they had to have had help? You don't think they could have gone off the rails themselves, so you come up here to point the finger?"

"I'm doing no such thing," Colleen said. "I'm trying to explore every avenue. Look, I'm from Boston. In the past seventy-two hours I've taken a shower in a truck stop, slept in a motor home, and eaten more fried food than I've had this whole year. Now I'm on an Indian reservation. I haven't done any of those things before and frankly if my son hadn't disappeared I doubt I ever would have. But I'm running out of ideas and it's been thirteen days, and I don't know who to talk to. One of the men from the rig said there were rumors that workers who get hurt are being bought off and the ones who complain are getting into trouble, all because Hunter-Cole is trying to hold on to leases on your land. And he says there's a lot of bad feelings about outsiders making money off what's rightfully yours. Maybe my son got in a spot, made someone mad. I doubt he meant to, if that was the case."

The pair exchanged a glance. "City council convenes once a week. It's open to the public. You want to know more about all of this, you could show up."

"When's that?"

"Friday mornings at ten. They're usually there until lunch."

"It's *Sunday*," Shay said. "You honestly want us to come back in *five days*?"

"Look, I don't know what else to tell you. I guess you can go around knocking on doors if you want. You're going to hear the same thing, though."

"Can you at least tell us who around here's the type to make trouble?" Colleen said. "People who can't seem to stay out of it . . ."

"Yeah," the man said. "*Me*. I did, anyway. I'm forty-eight years old, and twenty-five, thirty years ago I used to knock heads the last time people tried to get their hands on this land. 'Course, last time they didn't sell our rights out from under us."

"What are you talking about?"

"A hundred and fifty years ago we had twelve million acres up here. Thirty years later the government had taken all but a million, and it didn't take long for white farmers to steal half of that while the government sat on its ass. In the 1950s they took a third of what was left to build the dam."

"That's all too bad," Shay said. "But I don't see what it has to do with oil."

The man regarded her evenly. "When the first oil boom came around in the seventies, speculators started trying to pick up mineral rights cheap, and a lot of families around here didn't know what they had and practically gave them away. I guess you could say it was their fault for being a bunch of dumbass prairie niggers, but the way some people up here look at it, you take it up the—"

"Hey," the woman at the desk said. "Enough."

"Sorry." The man blew out a frustrated breath. "There's only so many times you can lose everything, is all I'm saying. People are angry, but we got traitors on the inside trying to sell us out, we got plenty of other problems to deal with. Your boys come over here to raise hell at the casino, yeah, there's going to be trouble. But if they stayed on their own patch, any trouble they got into, nobody around here knows anything about it."

Colleen reached into her purse and took out her fussy floral notebook and carefully tore out a piece of paper. "I'm going to write down our information," she said. "I would consider it a great favor if you would keep us in mind if you think of anything—anything at all—that might help us. If you could spread the word that we are try- ing to find out what happened, and we're no friends of Hunter-Cole. That's all we're asking."

"All right," the woman said tiredly, rubbing the pouchy skin under her eyes. "I can't promise you anything. But we can do that."

The room was dense with grim pessimism while Colleen wrote.

THEY WERE ALMOST all the way back to Lawton when Shay's phone rang. She picked it up and squinted at the screen. "Don't know who it is and no idea what that area code is. Answer it, okay? I don't want to end up in a snowbank."

Colleen took the phone. "Hello?"

"This one of the ladies from the rig today?" A male voice, thick with a Southern accent, polite.

Colleen's fingers tightened on the phone. "This is Colleen Mitchell. Paul's mom. Whale's mom."

"Oh, sorry." He sounded disappointed. "I wanted to talk to the other one. Fly's mom."

"Don't hang up. Please. She's driving, the weather's bad and we can't pull over. We're in this together." Colleen blinked; it was the first time she'd said it out loud, the first time she'd claimed it. "Maybe you can talk to me? What's your name?"

"No, ma'am, no names," he said quickly. "I got enough trouble as it is. I'm on probation right now, I could lose my job 'cause I reported a violation last month. I'm calling you from the crapper so I got to make this quick."

Colleen blushed. "I—I appreciate your candor. You knew Taylor?"

"Yeah, me and him worked together last summer and then we got put on opposite shifts. I only met Whale the one time. He seemed real nice, Mrs. Mitchell. What I want you to know, the day them two went missing, me and Fly was supposed to go fishing. But he canceled on me because he said something came up. I thought it was because he knew what I wanted to talk to him about. I was trying to get him to go to the authorities with me. See, there was this accident the month before when the rig crowned out. One of our guys got hit with a thirty-pound piece of drill pipe and ended up in the hospital with permanent brain damage. Taylor actually saw it all. He told me how it happened, but he didn't want to say anything because they had this meeting where the bosses said they were taking care of Morty, he's down in Alabama where he's from, they set up a whole fund for his medical and his kids. That's what they said, anyway. In the meeting they said what happened was a driller lost his concentration and hit the top of the rig with the blocks. But Taylor, he said there was a problem with the crown saver that had been reported but they hadn't done anything about it, they didn't even check it at the start of the tour. So what I said to Taylor, this shit's gonna keep happening as long as management gets to write the reports any way they want. Safety compliance crew hasn't been out since November, it's a joke."

"So you were going to go to the authorities, and you wanted Taylor to go with you?"

"Yeah, I told him we couldn't trust Hunter-Cole management. So my idea was, we'd go straight to the state Justice Department. I even called in advance, didn't identify myself, asked if we could set it up so we could conference-call and our identity would be protected. Taylor was real insistent that unless we got some sort of guarantee we couldn't do it, because they already shit-canned a few guys for complaining. I mean, that's why I got written up."

"They can do that? They can discipline you just for reporting a violation?"

"Well, they don't call it that, Mrs. Mitchell," the young man said. "The way they did me, it was for coming in late. Reason being there was a couple times I forgot to punch my clock. I was there on time, my shift supervisor knew it, everybody knew it. But I get another one, I can be fired. They want to go after someone, you can bet they'll find a way."

"And Taylor . . ."

"He's got a mouth on him sometimes, I guess you know that. He got written up for real, way back last fall, time he got into it with this assho—excuse me, ma'am, this fellow we worked with. So he had that on his record and he was real worried about losing the job. I just thought if we went fishing, had some time to sort it out, I could talk him into it."

Shay was motioning to Colleen to hold the phone closer so she could hear. "Listen, I got to go," the young man said. "There's some-body waiting to get in here, and they're standing outside in the cold and I already been in here a long while and everybody's all tense around here since you came by."

"Can we call you? If we need to?" Colleen said in a rush.

"I really would rather you didn't. I'm sorry." And then the phone went dead.

"What the hell?" Shay demanded.

Colleen did her best to fill her in on the conversation.

"And he never said who he was?"

"No, but I have the number on my phone now. If we need it, we could call back. It shouldn't be too hard to find out who got hurt, if we go back and look."

"Taylor told me about that one," Shay said. "I knew he was downplaying it because I'd worry. I looked it up, though. Crowning out is bad, but it happens all the time because you got all that heavy machinery in motion combined with all that well pressure. Taylor acted like it was the guy's own fault, but the floor just isn't that big, there's no way you could get out of the way if you're in the wrong place at the wrong time."

They rode in silence for a while, each lost in her own thoughts.

"What we have is a lot of hearsay about the safety problems," Colleen finally said. "But if we could get a look at the leases, that would be something concrete. If we could see exactly what Hunter-Cole is up against."

"Well, that shouldn't be too hard. They're public record."

"They are?" Colleen wanted to ask how Shay knew. In a way, she was afraid it would be one more detail Taylor had shared with her, that Paul had never told his own parents. Another bit of proof of the distance between them.

"Yeah. Maybe we can get someone at the library to help us."

"You think they're open? Back home, our library closes at four o'clock half the time due to budget cuts."

"In a state with three percent unemployment? Hell, yes, they ought to be open—state assembly probably can't spend their money fast enough."

seventeen

THE LIBRARY, A pleasant 1970s facility that seemed to be half children's area, was indeed open until seven. Colleen stayed outside to make a call while Shay went inside.

It was a call she had been dreading—not because she didn't want to talk to Andy, but because she was afraid of what he might say. But she couldn't look at Shay anymore without remembering her expression when she confronted her about Darren Terry.

Colleen found an alcove on the side of the building where the winds didn't reach. The ground was tramped down and littered with cigarette butts; this was clearly the smokers' retreat. She hoped none would come while she was on the phone. It was almost six thirty in Sudbury; Andy would be home, putting dinner together from whatever he found in the fridge. Or maybe the dinner brigade that Laura had set up had dropped something off. Helen with her famous lasagna, maybe; or if it was Vicki—

She's been down here practically since you left. Wasn't that what Andy had said? Working on the Internet and creating the flyer and making calls. Keeping Andy company, offering solace, reassurance . . .

"Colleen." Andy sounded out of breath. "I'm glad I heard the phone. I'm out here shoveling the drive. We're getting another three inches tonight. How are you doing?"

Terrible, she wanted to say. She pushed thoughts of Vicki from her mind, but it was impossible to pretend that she wasn't failing here. She hadn't succeeded in getting any closer to finding Paul, other than opening up possibilities that might make things even worse.

She was going to have to tell him about Shay finding out about Darren. Besides, she needed someone now. Andy was Paul's *father*. They ought to be drawing on each other's strength, comforting and supporting each other, talking and listening. Even if things had been less than perfect between them, Andy would be better than what she had now: a virtual stranger, who was hostile and suspicious, sharing a freezing-cold motor home with no shower.

"There's something I have to ask you," she said. Better to get straight to it, or she might lose her nerve.

"Sure, anything."

"That Wednesday last August, before Paul left . . ."

"Oh." It came out as a groan, and Colleen knew it pained Andy as much as it did her to remember.

The three of them had argued over breakfast, the same tired fight they'd been having ever since Paul came home from Syracuse in the spring, having gotten two Ds the first semester of his freshman year and withdrawn from the second semester when it became clear he was going to fail several classes. Andy's last words to Paul that morning had been along the lines of, "Considering I just sent Syracuse a twelve-fucking-thousand-dollar deposit, you're damn well going back."

Paul had stood up from the breakfast table, and for one terrible moment Colleen had thought he was going to hit Andy. He was that close, that angry, his hands clenched into fists. But instead he had said, his voice strained, "Why do you even want me to go back if I let you down so bad last year?"

And Colleen had started to protest, to remind him that he'd been able to withdraw from the worst classes, so he still had the 2.6, he didn't have a failing grade on his transcript, and if he retook algebra and met with the tutor like they'd asked him to . . .

But neither Andy nor Paul paid her any attention. Andy got out of his chair and faced Paul down, and Colleen realized that Paul had passed Andy sometime that spring, he was now slightly taller. And muscular from the garden center job he'd taken, it seemed to Colleen, to spite them. If it *did* come to blows, Andy didn't stand a chance—then she felt terribly guilty for even thinking it. Disloyal to both of them.

"Please," she begged, but they didn't listen.

"You didn't let *me* down," Andy said, in that irritatingly condescending voice of his. "You let *yourself* down. You let yourself down every time you don't study, every time you give up because it's too hard, every time you don't go to office hours or call the tutor. Those are *choices*, Paul, and if there's one thing I wish you'd get through your thick head it's that you get where you end up because of the choices you make along the way."

"I'm not *you*, Dad," Paul retorted. "I can't do those things. I can't be who you want me to be."

"Fine," Andy said in disgust. "You know what, I can't stand to have this conversation one more time. So you win. You're right. Effort wouldn't make a goddamn bit of difference. You're doomed to fail. None of our suggestions are worth shit." He slammed his coffee cup down on the table, spilling over the edge. "I'm late. Somebody's got to earn a paycheck to pay for you to go up there and sleep through your classes."

Seconds after Andy stomped out the door, Colleen raced after him, but he'd already pulled out of the drive. She didn't want to be alone with Paul, with their argument, and instead she went straight to the school, where she spent the next six hours in the literacy office, preparing for the returning student evaluations.

When she got home, she entered the house with a sense of dread, ready to take up the terrible talk again, to try to intervene on behalf of Andy, to apologize to her son for his father. But Paul was on his knees on the kitchen floor. He had a bucket of soapy water and a rag and he was washing the floor under the cabinet. When he looked up, his eyes were puffy from crying.

He admitted that after Colleen and Andy left, he'd broken every dish on the breakfast table, hurling them all to the floor, the juice and milk upturned, the syrup pitcher smashed. When there was nothing left to break, he sank to the floor and sat there long enough, Colleen gathered, to remember how much he loathed himself. He stripped, leaving his clothes in the kitchen, showered, and changed. Then he went to Target and replaced everything he'd broken, using the money he'd earned at his job, and came back and started cleaning.

She'd cried and hugged him and told him she loved him and promised that they would all try harder, and silently thanked God that he'd at least finally gotten it all out of his system.

But she'd been wrong.

"Did you see it coming?" she asked Andy now. "Because I didn't. I though it would be all right."

Andy was silent for a moment. "You *have* to believe that," he said, bitterly. "You're his mother. You have to always believe in him. You're the self-appointed keeper of hope."

Colleen cried silently, not wanting Andy to know. "But you knew. You knew he wasn't done, you knew the other shoe was going to drop."

He didn't deny it.

"So what I have to know—please, Andy, tell me the truth, because I can't trust my own feelings. Do you, in your heart of hearts, think it could have happened again? That he could have had one of his—his rage episodes? Maybe hurt someone . . . maybe hurt Taylor?"

This time the pause was even longer. When Andy spoke again it was barely more than a whisper.

"I don't know. God help me, I just don't know."

COLLEEN STAYED OUTSIDE as long as she could stand it. She didn't want Shay to see her eyes red from crying. She also didn't look forward to the prospect of waiting around, unable to help, while Shay displayed more of the hardscrabble competence that made Colleen wonder if she'd wasted the twenty years since she herself had held a full-time job. In the volunteer position at the school, she wrote the newsletter, but someone else formatted it to go online. She submitted her receipts and budget, but someone else keyed them into the spreadsheet. Her skills were pretty much limited to email and reading the news. And shopping . . . she did a lot of online shopping.

Finally, she went inside the library. And of course she found Shay sitting at one of the tables with a stack of books and her laptop, typing madly.

"They have a printer," Shay said, barely looking up. "A nickel a page. I've found this database that a Bismarck newspaper put online. It's not complete or anything, but so far I found a couple leases that seem to be on reservation land. It's printing now."

"Oh," Colleen said. She felt oddly formal, standing and looking over Shay's shoulder, holding her purse across her chest. "Thank you for doing that."

"There's something else. I found this blog where they report on workplace accidents. I can't tell who's behind it, and a lot of it seems like it could be made up. Here, want to see? Only, some of it's pretty bad."

Her fingers stilled over the keyboard and she finally looked directly at Colleen. Her eyes were full of doubt. Colleen understood—Shay didn't think she could handle it.

She didn't like the tilt in their relationship. And it wasn't just that Shay suspected Paul. It was an imbalance in competence. Shay did everything. She found their lodging, she knew about the showers. She came up with the plans for where to go and who to talk to. And she had the skills to investigate.

So far all that Colleen had added was smoothing over the communication with the girl at the lodge after Shay insulted her, and getting Chief Weyant to meet with them. So score one for Colleen's impeccable tact. That was what she had to show for the last twenty years—no, make that four decades, ever since her own mother, bitter with disappointment from her rash decision to marry down, started steering Colleen toward Junior League and Bryn Mawr, reminding her that it was all well and good to have a career, but she needed to prepare for the life she would create for her family. And that had been Colleen—*she* had wanted the family, she had been so happy to sink into its comforts, its luxurious bosom, once their bout with infertility had finally been over.

She'd done damn well in her role too, even with Paul's challenges, even with the effort it had taken to smooth his way, to create a place for him in the community and, later, at Syracuse. It had been exhausting much of the time, but she'd done admirably. Her friends called her a rock, said they didn't know how she did it. She'd even allowed herself to believe it—some days, like when she watched her

son cross the stage on graduation day, with the 3.4 GPA that they'd
all slaved over.

And what did that meager skill set do for her now? How was it
helping her find her boy? Absolutely nothing, that was what. A way
with words, an expensive wardrobe, the ability to talk to people in
positions of authority, a faultless sense of social commerce—none of
that was worth a thing.

And here, in a public library in the middle of nowhere, wearing a
coat lined with pink acrylic fake fur, typing with fingers bearing
chipped crescents of glitter nail polish, Shay had come up with hard
evidence in half an hour.

"Let me see," Colleen said between clenched teeth. She yanked
off her coat more roughly than necessary and flung it over the table,
then pulled out a chair and sat down.

"You're sure. I mean . . ."

"I'm *sure*."

Shay tried to shield the screen with her body while she typed.
"Let me just find one . . ."

But Colleen had seen it, a glimpse of it, anyway, a man's arm,
blood running down and dripping from the fingers. "No. Go back to
that one. The one you were looking at. I can handle it. I have to see it."

Shay was still for a moment and then reluctantly moved her
mouse to the Back button and clicked.

It was an arm . . . but it wasn't connected to a body. It had been
severed at the middle of the forearm, and some remnant of the skin
that peeled away from the innards of the arm had caught in the machinery from which it hung. The long sheets of metal were connected to pulleys of some sort, the machinery taller than a man,
bigger than the photograph. Blood pooled on the floor. In the background, incongruously, was a man turned away from the camera,

wearing a nice plaid shirt, a shirt like Andy wore to the office on casual Fridays.

Colleen thought she might be sick. She pressed her hand over
her mouth, but she didn't look away. *Here.* Here was what was real.
She had boldly, stupidly come to this place on the strength of a
promise to her son, a promise she'd never voiced out loud, a promise
to find him. She was *not* going to fail him now, the first time she was
forced to look at something she didn't want to see.

She swallowed the bile, the contents of her stomach. She swallowed again, forcing down her shame and her fear. Her mouth tasted
terrible. She'd clenched her fist so hard she'd hurt the flesh of her
palm. "All right," she said in a voice that would fool no one, a parody
of calm. "And that is, the nature of that—accident—"

"Caught in the gears," Shay said. She sounded wobbly herself, so
there was that.

"Mmm-hmm. And the next one?"

Shay clicked the arrow. This one was of a windowless room full
of incomprehensible machines, pipes and ladders and other parts littering the floor. It was all covered with a brownish slime. Only after
staring at it for a few moments did Colleen realize that some of the
debris on the floor were the bodies of two men, faint patches of yellow showing through the dirt-covered hard hats.

Mud bucket explosion, the caption read. *Drilling mud caught fire.*
"Click on that link. Please."

The link took them to a glossary page. Colleen read: *Drilling
mud—heavy drilling fluid that lubricates drill bit, keeps pressure on
reservoir to prevent oil/gas escape.*

Shay clicked back to the image and they stared at it together.

"That's the inside of the rig, isn't it?" Colleen said. "I mean, that's
where our boys worked, right?"

"Yes."

They cycled through the images. There were grainy videos among the photographs, heart-stopping clips of explosions, snapping chains, falling equipment. Men jumping from burning derricks, men falling from platforms. Some of the accidents had taken place on offshore rigs, the drilling mud and broken equipment littering the "moon pool" – the opening in the bottom of the hull that allowed access to the ocean below – rather than a rig floor.

"There's no proof these are all Hunter-Cole," Shay finally said. "I don't think they are. The blogger's anonymous. Says he worked for Hunter-Cole, but there's no way to know. Listen. I can't look at this anymore."

"We've seen enough," Colleen said. "I mean, we've seen enough to know that there were a lot of accidents. Probably still are. We just don't know how much is due to negligence."

"It wouldn't even have to be, right?" Shay said, closing the browser window. "It could be just that the company wants to keep these images from ending up in the news. Even if they're not liable, right?" She rubbed her temples. "God, I need a drink. Come on. Let's go get something to eat."

"Listen," Colleen said slowly. "What if I call Scott? The man I met last night. I could tell him we're having dinner, see if he'd come meet us. I could . . . I could try to find out more about how the companies are dealing with safety problems."

Shay was already standing and putting on her coat. "What did you tell him you did?"

"I said I was with a food service company. Back before Paul was born, I worked for Slocum Systems for a while. It was just what came to mind."

"Not sure how you can tie that into asking him about safety."

"I'll think of something," Colleen snapped, irked that Shay doubted her ingenuity. "Let me text him now."

She sat down at the computer again and brought up Yelp. She searched on Lawton bars and taverns that served food, picked the one with the highest rating. Put the address in her phone. Shay had gone to go pick up the pages she'd printed. While she was waiting in line to pay, Colleen composed a text: Scott—Long day in the salt mines! Are u up for a drink? Headed to the Oak Door Tavern with work people now. Maybe dinner later?

She read it twice before finally hitting Send. Immediately she felt a dizzying sense of remorse. No, *fear.* What she felt was fear, and she had sworn off fear, at least while she was on this mission.

Shay was at the front of the line. Colleen reached for her purse, to get money to pay for the pages. Then she slowly put her wallet back.

Colleen could pay for thousands of copies and never even notice the effect on her bank account. Shay was struggling.

But Shay had doubted Paul. She had made it clear that they were no longer necessarily aligned.

And that made her, if not an adversary, not an ally, either.

She could pay for her own damn copies.

eighteen

T.L. WAS HALFWAY to the door when he stopped and looked again: Myron's truck in the drive, even though it was Sunday. The *third* Sunday.

The third Sunday of the month meant football if there was a game on that anyone cared about, and poker the rest of the time, over at Wally Stommar's place. Myron had taken part for the last six years, ever since he decided T.L. was old enough to mind himself at home. Myron and Wally and the other guys had known one another since they were all kids on the reservation. It was a hard thing to imagine, these full-bellied, gray-whiskered men ever having been boys, but Myron came back from these evenings in a good mood.

It had to be something big to keep him home from poker. T.L. set his keys in the brass dish with extra care, making no sound. If he was quiet enough, he might gain a minute to think, a minute to consider all the things that might have happened, all the ways things could go sideways, and how Myron might have found out. This was why he'd been trying to talk to Kristine. To make sure that things that were buried stayed buried.

"T.L.?"

"Yeah, I'm back."

T.L. followed his uncle's voice to the living room. The room was a rectangle, the furniture old and boxy and arranged in a square. Plaid sofa perpendicular to the recliner, anchored by the oak coffee table. Bookshelf with the TV on it, a big, heavy son of a bitch—Myron had been talking about replacing it with one he could hang on the wall, he was just waiting for the prices to come down. That was a matter of unshakable faith with Myron—he believed if you just waited long enough, everything electronic got better and cheaper.

Myron was sitting in the middle of the sofa in his khaki pants and button-down shirt and a V-neck sweater T.L. had given him on Father's Day a few years back—his special occasion clothes. For once, the TV was off. There was a magazine open on the couch next to him—looked like *Autoweek* from where T.L. was standing. A mug of tea was going cold, sitting on a cork coaster.

"You didn't go to Wally's." T.L. felt guilty, like he'd flunked a test and tried to hide it from his uncle. But all he'd ever tried to do was the right thing. He'd tried to take responsibility, to be a man, and it wasn't his fault that she'd lied to him. Nothing that had happened was his fault, and he'd been the one to suffer, and now he resented the guilty feeling even as it was replaced by dread.

"Listen," Myron said. "Darrel called me, from over at the council office. He just wanted to talk about the merchants' association meeting, but while we were on the phone he told me they had some visitors over there today. Those two women, the mothers of those boys who went missing."

T.L. kept his expression carefully neutral, not meeting Myron's gaze. He reached for the closest object at hand, an empty glass sitting on top of the old television. A faint film of juice stuck to the bottom. It would have been T.L. who left it there; Myron would never leave a dirty dish out. He never nagged or complained, either, just cleaned up T.L.'s messes and carried his belongings to his room—the backpack he was always leaving on the kitchen table, the shoes he took off and left in the living room.

Myron had given his life away so many times already, becoming quieter and steadier with each passing year. T.L. always suspected he'd suffered more in the Gulf than he ever let on, only to come home and have to clean up the messes his sister left behind when she died, T.L. being the biggest one of all. Myron never voiced a single regret, but if things had been different, there could have been a woman for him, a family. A different job in a different place, maybe. Instead, he had T.L. and the store, the Sunday poker and the overnight visits to Minot every couple of months, where T.L. was pretty sure he went to see a hooker.

All of that. All of that was why T.L. had lied. It wasn't to protect himself, because T.L. didn't care what happened to him. He could go to court, go to jail, and it wouldn't be so different from the life he'd been leading already, waiting for the truth to come out—that was a prison too. He hadn't painted in months, not since Elizabeth broke up with him. He didn't care what food tasted like or what the snow looked like on his windshield or what anyone said at school.

He cared about the truth, but T.L. was a realist. He doubted he could convince anyone of his version of what happened. He had thought he understood people, but it turned out he didn't—he thought Elizabeth was his, but he hadn't known her at all—but one thing he still believed was that there was an order to the world that you couldn't fight. That there were rules about how things ended up being presented in the news and online and in the conversations people had while waiting in line to buy a cup of coffee. Rules about who could be believed and who was guilty before they even opened their mouths.

In the credibility department, pretty white girls were fairly high up. Chief of police—well, that was hard to beat. As for someone like him, maybe he could walk around L.A. or New York and blend in, but up here people took one look at him and figured they knew something about who he was and they would never let him forget it. They wouldn't trust a thing he said or did.

But Myron would believe him. T.L. had a choice to make, because whatever he said now Myron would accept it. That was how it had always been.

"You had dirt on your pants that day," Myron said. His voice was heavy and dull, without accusation, without any emotion at all. "Your boots were soaked through. Your jacket—there was blood on it."

"You saw it." T.L. felt cold. He'd left the clothes on the floor of his closet, meaning to wash them himself, but Myron had gotten to them first. Later, T.L. had seen the jacket hanging from the pole in the laundry room, dripping into the tub. He'd convinced himself the stains hadn't been noticeable on the dark fabric.

"Wasn't much. Almost missed it. I didn't think anything of it at first. I thought you must have got that jacket dirty cleaning fish. I was starting the wash when I remembered you didn't bring any home. And you didn't say you'd been by Swann's. I thought—I don't know what I thought. I mean, I thought about that girl." *That girl*—he hadn't said her name since T.L. told him, his voice cracking, that it was over, last fall.

"You thought I *hurt* her?"

"Of course not." Myron waved his hand impatiently. "Not for a second. But I was your age once. I got into scrapes. I busted up my knuckles on another guy's face. I figured you needed to work something out, you took care of things. I figured if it was bad enough, you needed . . ."

He closed his right hand into a fist, brought it down heavy on his left. His meaning was clear. Myron trusted that if T.L. had fought someone, he'd had a good reason.

T.L. set the juice glass down carefully on top of the television and watched his hand tremble. "Myron." His mouth tasted like chalk. He stumbled two steps and sank to his knees in front of the coffee table. He put his hands on the scarred oak and stared at a ceramic dish he had made in second grade, which had been on the table ever since. On the bottom, he had scratched Myron's name in the wet clay before it was fired.

"It's worse than you think," he whispered. Then he forced himself to look at his uncle's face and told the rest.

Myron rested his hands on the couch cushions while he listened, his face tight and grim. When the story was over, T.L. waited—for condemnation, for commiseration, to finally have someone tell him what they were going to do next. When T.L. had arrived at the front door of this house at the age of six, with his clothes stuffed into a dirty red suitcase that had been his mother's, he had not expected to be soothed. Living with his mother had taught him not to hope for much.

"Oh, son," Myron finally said, his voice heavy with sadness. "Come sit with me."

T.L. went, and Myron opened his arms and made a place for him. T.L. pressed his face against the acrylic sweater, trying to hide his tears, and Myron held him tight and murmured and rocked him, like a baby, as he had never been held before. Somehow the warmth reached the place inside T.L. where he stored all the losses and the pain, and they came out like a beating of wings and filled his chest and pressed against his lungs, making it hard to breathe. He pushed his knuckles to his eyes and tried to stop crying, but Myron held on, and finally T.L. gave up trying to keep any of it in. He sobbed and soiled his uncle's shirt with his tears and snot, holding on for dear life.

"It's over now," Myron said softly, after a long time. But still he didn't let go.

nineteen

COLLEEN DIRECTED SHAY to the bar. They were inching through what passed for rush hour, the shift-change traffic of men heading out to start their workday as darkness enveloped the town. They were almost to the address when she glanced at a light pole and saw Paul grinning back at her.

"Oh, my God," she said, and Shay braked, hard. The car behind them laid on the horn.

"*What?*"

But by then Colleen realized what she'd seen: the flyer Vicki had made, the one she'd ordered a thousand of and had posted all around town.

"Pull over," Colleen said, her hand already on the door handle.

"I can't just—there's nowhere to park!"

Colleen opened the door and got out, slamming it fast. She sprinted the half dozen steps to the pole and tore down the sign. Both boys were pictured, Taylor's smiling team photo from football on the bottom, his shoulders broad and his smile confident, his jersey a brilliant green. By contrast Paul seemed to be asking the camera permission in his photo, looking a little to the side, his expression somewhere between defiance and dismay. Even his shirt, a slubbed cotton in what Colleen had thought was a beautiful shade of slate blue when she bought it, looked washed out next to Taylor.

HAVE YOU SEEN US? the sign read, in large, stark lettering. Below,

Andy's phone number was prominently displayed, along with the number for the Lawton Police Department. *Missing since January 15*, it read in italics at the bottom.

Shay had managed to pull into a handicapped spot at the end of the block. Colleen didn't hurry on her way back to the car. She wasn't in a rush to share the poster, but when she got in the Explorer, Shay leaned across and took it from her hands. She stared at it, frowning, for a long time.

Then she set it gently on the dash. Neither woman said anything. Around them, a few pedestrians shuffled, heads down against the wind and drifting snow, taking care not to fall. Lawton didn't have the sort of downtown that invited casual shopping and dining, unlike, say, the affluent enclaves of Waban or Newton, in which Sur La Tables and Anthropologies rubbed elbows with yarn stores and artisanal cheese shops, and the movie theaters had been restored to show art films. In Lawton, there were two blocks—plus a few side-street enterprises clinging to the center commerce like barnacles on a sinking ship—of no-nonsense restaurants and clothing stores, dotted with shuttered and empty businesses.

"Your husband did a good job," Shay finally said. She cleared her throat. "Paul is a nice-looking kid."

"Vicki made it. All Andy did was—" *Pay for it*, she was going to say, but of course that wasn't true. Andy did what he knew how to do, marshaling all the resources in his reach, dispatching and delegating for the greatest possible efficiency. Because that's all it was with Vicki, wasn't it? An efficient use of resources.

Her phone buzzed with a text. Drink sounds great, will try to get away ASAP. Stuck in meeting! Yrs, Scott

"I guess that's our cue," Colleen said shakily, but Shay was already pulling away from the curb.

They saw half a dozen more of the posters on the way to the restaurant. Most unsettling, there were six of them framing the double wood doors of the place, affixed with what looked like packing tape. Someone had made little yellow bows out of cheap ribbon and taped them on each of the posters.

"Look at that," Shay said. She reached for the poster, touching her son's image gently with her fingertips before going inside. It reminded Colleen of her mother dipping her fingers into holy water, all the Sunday mornings of her childhood, until the church renovated and removed the old marble fonts.

She waited until Shay went inside, holding back until the door had almost shut behind her. Then she traced a cross on Paul's forehead with her thumb and made a quick, covert sign of the cross on her own forehead, chest, and shoulders, something she had sworn she would never do again after declaring herself agnostic at the age of nineteen. "God," she whispered. Behind her there was a conversation going on in the parking lot, two men trying to settle some sort of bet. The snow landed on her bare neck, since she hadn't bothered to pull her hood up. Inside was her next best hope, and it didn't seem like much at all. "God," she whispered again. "I need you. For real this time."

Then she went inside.

Shay was hanging her coat on a long row of hooks along the entry wall. Colleen did the same, and then they approached the hostess.

"Good evening," the girl said. She had the look that Colleen was beginning to identify with Lawton girls: young and far more fresh-scrubbed than their East Coast counterparts, favoring pastels and a lot of hair spray. "Will you be dining with us tonight?"

"No, we're just going to the bar," Shay said.

"I thought you said you were hungry—"

"Bar's fine, come on, Colleen." She grabbed Colleen's arm and pulled her toward the bar area, which looked to Colleen like a TGI Fridays with a slightly different theme—hard hats and old, rusted pieces of metal equipment shared wall space with antlers and ball caps and license plates. Every seat at the bar was taken, and as more men arrived, the bar tables were beginning to fill up too. Shay grabbed one of the last tables and sat down, and picked up the table tent advertising a variety of fried appetizers and cocktails.

"Listen, Shay. If Scott comes, I was thinking . . . I told him I was with work people."

"Uh-huh. Oh." Shay glanced at Colleen and then away, her jaw set. The waiter picked that moment to come over, and she muttered without looking at him, "Bourbon and soda, lots of ice."

Colleen ordered a glass of wine and waited until he left.

"Are you hungry?" she asked. "You said you were, earlier . . . do you want to order something? Maybe calamari?"

"Let me just make sure I understand," Shay said tersely. "To be sure. You're worried I don't look like we could work together. In, in a job where you . . . fly places."

"It's just, you know." Colleen didn't know what to say. She rested her hand near her neckline. She was wearing a ribbon-trimmed crew sweater over a white pinpoint cotton shirt. Not business wear, by any stretch, but certainly more formal than anything anyone else was wearing in the bar.

Shay, on the other hand, was wearing a V-neck cotton top with a woven-lace inset. Colleen could see her bra through the lace. Her earrings dangled amethyst drops almost to her shoulders, and her wild pale hair was escaping its clip, which was the only way Colleen had seen it so far, which made her wonder if the effect was deliberate. Shay's eyeliner was smudged, and had been since she got slugged at the rig. Remarkably, she'd escaped a shiner or any evidence that she'd been hit. She looked amazing for a fortyish woman, it was true, but also like she worked behind a bar herself.

"Look. You can say I'm your secretary. Or assistant, or whatever you want to call it. And when he comes, I'll make my excuses and go. I'll say you gave me a ton of work to finish by tomorrow."

"I really feel uncomfortable—"

"What, lying?" Shay's eyes flashed angrily. "Why, because you're *really* a corporate executive? Come on, none of that matters anyway. We're doing this for the *boys*."

The waiter returned with their drinks. Colleen felt her face burning with embarrassment. "We'll take the calamari," she said. "And bruschetta and . . . and I guess that's it for now."

"Yes, ma'am. The boys over there picked up your drinks."

Startled, Colleen looked where he was pointing; at the end of the bar, a pair of middle-aged men in work clothes raised their beers in a toast. Shay gave them a little wave. She probably had drinks sent to her all the time, Colleen thought, staring into her glass.

"It's okay, you can drink it," Shay said after the waiter walked away and she had taken a sip of her own drink. "You don't owe them anything."

"I know that." Colleen picked up her glass and sipped. The wine, in theory a chardonnay, tasted thin and moldy. "I *know* that," she repeated, setting it down.

"I'm just saying, you need to loosen up if you're going to be convincing."

Neither of them said anything. Someone turned the lights down a few notches and turned up the music. At least with the pounding bass, it felt less awkward not to talk; conversation would have been difficult.

More men had poured into the bar, and now there wasn't an empty seat in the place. So Shay really wouldn't have any option besides leaving. Of course, then Colleen would have to find her own ride home. Or call Shay to come pick her up.

Or accept a ride from Scott.

She was getting ahead of herself. The prospect of speaking to him made her nervous, and when a second round of drinks came— unordered, and this time when the bartender pointed to their benefactors, Colleen didn't even bother to look—she drank quickly.

"I have to make some notes," she announced abruptly. But when she looked up, Shay wasn't there. Maybe she'd gone to the ladies' room.

Colleen dug in her purse for her little notebook. The folded sheet of Paul's texts fell out and she felt unmoored, discovered. She pressed it fleetingly to her cheek, thinking, *I love you, baby, I'm doing this for you*, and then slipped the pages into one of the zippered compartments inside her purse.

Then she wrote, pausing after each line to think.

Leases—Indian, which companies?
Legislation/lawsuits? Pending? Dropped?
Bribery?
Police involvement, FBI?
Injuries, which company worst record
Fatalities, same

Colleen looked down at what she'd written. "*Oh,*" she breathed, the word staring back at her. *Fatality.* Death. An accident, a moment of inattention, a small neglect that snowballed into a major error—

and some boy or man didn't go back to his family. His wife. His kids. His *mother*. She groped at the table for her glass, unable to tear her eyes away from the words she had written. To her surprise the glass was full again. She must have been so intent on her list that the waiter didn't even bother to announce himself this time. A fresh bourbon and soda sat across the table, but Shay hadn't returned.

"Excuse me," a man's voice said. Colleen steeled herself for Scott, pasting a fake smile on her face, before she turned. But it wasn't Scott. It was a man with a beard, a biker beard, his ponytail silver and a wide web of wrinkles around his eyes.

"I'm meeting someone," she said quickly, letting the smile drop.

"Well, ain't that a shame, but it's no surprise, a beautiful lady like you," he said, bowing before he turned and walked away.

When he was gone, Colleen checked her phone: nine fourteen. No text. She'd been stood up. She slid her stool back from the table. Apparently, all their drinks had been bought for them, but just in case, she peeled off a couple of twenties and left them in the middle of the table.

The bar crowd now spilled over into the restaurant. The music had switched to country, and a drunk-looking couple shuffled in a circle in the corner. There were three bartenders working behind the bar now, and they were having a hard time keeping up, judging from the way they rushed back and forth between the bottles and taps and the customers. The air smelled of smoke, even though Colleen didn't see anyone smoking. She was suddenly desperate to get outside, to get away from here.

But she didn't see Shay anywhere. The few women present— half a dozen, maybe ten—were all younger, girls with their hair in po- nytails, at least half of them wearing the same sort of work clothes as the men. Colleen decided to check the bathroom, but as she passed the couple dancing in the corner, the woman moved under one of the light fixtures and Colleen saw the bright, pale hair.

It was Shay. She'd taken off her top and now she wore only a camisole. She had her arms draped over the shoulders of a man a good ten years younger than she was. He was trying to tell her something, it looked like he was yelling right into her ear, but she moved lazily with her eyes closed and a half smile on her face.

Colleen shoved her way through the crowd, not caring who she ran into. She grabbed Shay's arm and pulled her away from the man.

"Hey!" he said, looking more startled than angry.

"Oh, hi," Shay said, her smile crumpling. "Scott ever show? Is he here now?"

"*No*, he never came." Colleen realized she had yelled it. Too late, it occurred to her that she didn't know why she was angry, exactly. "I want to go."

Shay raised her eyebrows and put a hand on her friend's shoulder. "This is McCall. That's his first name. That's kind of cool, isn't it? What did you say your last name is?"

"Whittaker." He was looking at Colleen like a boy who's dropped his ice cream cone down the storm drain. He and Shay both had that look, in fact, of having something taken away from them.

"Yeah, that's right. McCall Whittaker. He's from South Bend, Indiana."

"I don't— I don't *care* where he's from." The wine had rushed to Colleen's head all of a sudden, and she felt overheated and dizzy. "I'm sorry. I didn't mean it like that. But Shay . . . we have that, ah, meeting tomorrow, that I asked you to prepare for . . ."

"She's my boss," Shay said. "She's right. I have a shit ton to do before tomorrow. But it was nice to meet you."

Colleen turned and started wading back toward the entrance,

which was all the way at the other end. There were no men in suits here. She wondered if Scott had ever intended to meet her at all, if he was just toying with her. If, somehow, he had divined her true purpose, read the madness on her face that was the sole domain of the desperate mother.

She kept going until she was standing outside. Her breath made clouds in the air. The parking lot was nearly full. What day of the week was it? Colleen had to think for a moment before determining it was still Sunday. But it almost didn't matter. These men, here on twenty-day hitches, she bet they lost track of the days too, since they had no days off, no weekends. Instead of counting Monday through Thursday, they probably had a week that began day one and ended when they got on the plane. A twenty-day week, so that maybe day seventeen was like Thursday night, when freedom is so close you can almost taste it.

Shay was taking her time. Colleen stamped her feet on the ground and waited, trying to control her impatience. She was doing everything she could think of, and it wasn't enough.

twenty

COLLEEN DIDN'T STOP to think about about how much Shay had had to drink until she destroyed Brenda's front yard.

When they got back to the motor home, there was a new padlock on the door, and half a dozen white plastic garbage bags were stacked on top of their suitcases in a pile on the driveway. Snow had drifted onto the bags, giving them an eerie, sculptural effect. A piece of paper had been taped to the door above the padlock. The lettering had run a little. It read FOUND YOUR POT I WILL NOT HAVE DRUG-GIES IN MY HOME YOU ARE EVICTED.

They'd both gotten out of the car, and when they were done reading the note, neither of them said anything for a moment.

"That *cunt!*" Shay said, and kicked the door, making a small dent in the metal. She turned to Colleen. "She can't go through our stuff! I can't believe she went in there. She had to have been waiting, watching through her little windows, spying on us to see when we left. Goddamn it. She can't kick us out like this."

Colleen remembered the smell from the first night, the faint skunky odor. She bit down her impatience; it wouldn't help anyone. "Let me talk to her."

"And say what? She doesn't want us here. It's clear. She knows she can get more money is the only reason she's doing this."

"And I can *pay* her more! Come on, Shay, *think* for a minute. We lose this place, we have nothing." Colleen took a deep breath. Now she had to tell her about the room Andy had found, and it felt like she was giving up the only card she held. Because she couldn't let Andy come now, not if it meant Shay would be without a place to live. "Look, I should have told you earlier. Andy found us a room starting Wednesday. That means we just have to make this work for three more days and we can move into a hotel."

Shay stared at her. "You weren't going to *tell* me that? What were you planning to do, just move out? Were you even going to leave a note?"

"Shay, listen, I hadn't decided what to do. Andy said he might want to come, I told him I might still want to room with you, if—if we were getting somewhere with the search—"

If we were still speaking to each other, she didn't say. If she learned to live with the faint accusation in Shay's eyes every time she looked at her. If she could convince Shay—because that's what she had hoped to do, though the understanding didn't come to her until just that moment—that her son was *good,* that he was worthy of Taylor's friendship, of membership in this club that he had chosen for himself, defying her and Andy. That his bid for a life of his own hadn't been a failure.

She'd needed time to make Shay see that. But how? What difference would a few more days make?

"I don't need you," Shay muttered, backing away. She stalked to the front door of the house, cutting across the frozen lawn. She didn't bother with the bell, just started pounding with her fist.

"She's not home!" Colleen ran to catch up. "There're no lights on and her car is gone. Shay, she's at work."

"Then I'm going there."

"Shay, stop! We can't make trouble with her. We can't get the cops involved in this or they'll be even less likely to help us. If you don't want me to try to talk to her, we need to put our energy into finding somewhere else to stay."

Shay didn't respond. She walked over to the Explorer, opened the tailgate, and started tossing the garbage bags in, not bothering to brush off the snow first. Colleen helped; she could hear things rattling in the bags. The suitcases were empty; Shay threw them in last. Then she slammed the hatch and went around to the driver's side. "You coming?"

Colleen had barely gotten in the car when Shay revved the engine twice and drove onto the lawn. While Colleen scrambled to get the door shut and her seat belt on, Shay drove to the other side of the lawn and then backed up. The tires spun on the icy grass and the engine whined. Lights went on over the neighbor's porch, but no one came outside.

"Shay, stop it! Come on, you're just making it worse!"

"How could it be worse?" Shay drove over the garden bed, the car lurching as it went over the little decorative fence. She plowed through the bushes, backed up and drove over them again. The branches brushed and scratched against the side of the Explorer, but she kept going until she'd managed to flatten them all.

Colleen said nothing, sitting rigid, braced with her hands on the dashboard. Finally Shay finished with the lawn. Deep gouges had kicked up frozen clumps of grass and dirt. She turned the wheel and Colleen saw it coming, closed her eyes before Shay drove into the mailbox. When she backed up, the thing was leaning nearly to the ground, the pole bent and the concrete pad clinging to the base.

Shay drove around it and out into the street. She stayed to the speed limit as they headed for town.

"I can't believe you did that."

"I can't believe you wanted to just pay her off! Is that how you solve every problem in your life? Never mind. I guess I already know the answer to that."

Colleen waited just a beat and then she couldn't help herself. "What the hell is that supposed to mean?"

"That means that instead of being a *mom* to your son, you were so worried about what people would think that you bought his way into everything so you wouldn't have to deal with it! Even in Fairhaven we got a few mothers like you. The other kids don't like their kids, they go out and buy Happy Meals for the whole class. Have parties at the jumping gym and spend more on the goodie bags than I ever spent on Taylor's whole birthday! How much did you have to pay to get him into college? Huh? How much to keep the admissions people from knowing he nearly killed another kid?"

"*Stop it!*" Colleen screamed. "Stop it, oh, God, let me out! Let me out!" She reached for the door, unsnapping her seat belt. She saw the asphalt moving underneath the car as Shay slammed on the brakes, and when her feet hit the ground, the momentum made her stumble. She tottered and fell, the shock of the impact shooting pain through her hip. Her purse had fallen upside down and emptied itself on the street.

"Are you fucking *crazy*?" Shay yelled. "Do you have a death wish?"

"Leave me alone!" Colleen pawed at her wallet, makeup case, keys, stuffing everything back into her purse. "You don't know anything about my relationship with my son!"

"I know that my son told me he was hanging out with Paul as a favor because no one else wanted to!"

"That's a *lie!*" Colleen was on her knees, trying to grab a lipstick that had rolled a few feet away. She tried to stand, slipped and fell again, this time on her knee. The pain was breathtaking. "Paul had a ton of friends!"

"Maybe back east. You probably bought those too. That's not how it works here. I mean, look *around* you, Colleen. You think anyone's paying these guys to just show up? Everything here you have to earn. Maybe if you'd left him alone, Paul would have finally figured out how to be a man. Maybe that's why he disappeared, he couldn't get away from you even up here!"

Colleen abandoned the lipstick. She finally got to her feet and stumbled toward the sidewalk. They were in front of a storage facility, its parking lot surrounded by tall fencing. She grabbed at the chain link for balance as she tried to get away.

"Are you out of your mind? Get back in the car!" Shay shouted.

Colleen kept walking, tears streaming down her face. She was sobbing, unable to catch her breath. After she'd gone another twenty feet she heard the screech of tires and Shay peeled off down the street.

She thought Shay would turn around, make a U-turn and come back to harangue her some more. To rip at the open wound. Thinking of what she'd said about Paul . . . Colleen couldn't stand it. She covered her ears with her gloved hands and made sounds to cover up her thoughts, horrible wailing sounds of pain, but she couldn't obliterate them.

Ahead, in the next block, was the truck stop where they showered and had breakfast. The sign still blinked SUPER STAR PLAZA FUEL—SHOWERS—DINER—HOT COFFEE—24 HOURS. Half a dozen trucks and a few cars were parked on the side; all but one of the pumps were occupied. Even the car wash was going, steam rising into the night as the hot water blasted away the snow and grime and salt.

Colleen shied away from the light. She followed the edge of the parking lot, along the fencing. The snow covered shapes of dead plants. In the summer, they probably grew geraniums here. Marigolds, begonias. Hardy plants you could buy cheap at the hardware store.

There was a bench, awkwardly placed by a planter that contained nothing but cigarette butts, some of them recent. Colleen brushed the snow off the bench and sat down, hoping no one would glance her way.

After a while, the sobbing slowed. The tissues had fallen out of her purse along with the lipstick, so Colleen had been forced to wipe her nose on her sleeve and the back of her glove. Her hair was matted to her cheeks. She was terribly cold, but she welcomed it, wished for the pain that was setting into her fingertips and toes to spread. She wanted to feel the pain everywhere. Maybe she would freeze to death here. They would find her body frozen to the bench. With her long coat and her hood pulled up, she would look like the Virgin Mary in prayer. And this would be her pietà, her final sign of devotion to Paul. Because in the end, she defended him alone, no matter how much Andy loved him, no matter how he wrestled with his own demons. A boy grows into a man and leaves his father, to return as an equal. But a mother is always his mother.

She remembered holding Paul in her arms when he was a baby, cradling him with that head full of downy dark hair nestled in her elbow, marveling at the beauty of him, the perfection of him. Even as an infant he'd been angry and restless; even then, if Colleen was truly honest with herself, she knew there was something different about him. But look at him! God, he was so beautiful.

Yes. Dying here, now, with this image in her mind, this would not be so bad. God would forgive her this. She had done her best; He would judge her kindly. Andy would move on, eventually. Everyone would forgive him. They always forgive the men. He would find another woman, who would adore him, who would remind him that it was never his fault, none of it was ever his fault. She might spare Colleen some compassion; she might allow Colleen's photo to stay on the mantel. But deep down she would know what everyone knew: somehow, it was always the mother's fault.

Because what Shay had said before she drove away was true. She *had* tried to buy Paul's way in the world. All the tutors, the personal coaches, the Ivy League summer programs, the therapist and psychiatrists and private school counselors—with what she had paid them, they could have bought a summer home on the Cape. If there were a lever you could pull to flush another child's future away so Paul could have succeeded, she would have been first in line.

And then, at the end, she'd had to face her failure. The expression on Paul's face that morning, as he scrubbed the floor, trying to erase the stain of his own rage—guilt and shame and fear and despair.

Colleen was guilty of so many things. She couldn't stand herself. No matter how much Shay loathed her, Colleen loathed herself more. And somehow, despite all her failings, she'd taught her son one solid lesson: how to loathe himself as well.

Take me, Colleen whispered, hoping the wind would carry her plea to God's ears.

twenty-one

SEX WASN'T THE best form of self-obliteration, but it would do. Especially when the buzz Shay had worked up earlier in the evening had faded, leaving behind its chalky, dulling aftereffects. Shay knew from her hard-drinking days that it was possible to light a second wave and get hammered all over again, even after neglecting the buzz for several hours, but it took work and generally you wanted to stay in one place after, and she wasn't up for either of those things.

When she got back to the Oak Door Tavern, it was eleven thirty and the crowd was holding strong. She found a parking place wedged between two giant pickup trucks and went inside, stepping around a rowdy group of revelers clogging the doorway. She headed for the ladies' room; she'd had to go ever since they were at the trailer.

Thinking about the trailer made her furious all over again. She'd known so many sanctimonious women like Brenda. Go to church on Sunday and judge everyone all week long. Shay'd been used to people judging her since she was just a toddler, when her hippie mother let her hair grow down past her butt and dressed her in Indian-cotton dresses she tie-dyed herself. These days she figured she was a hell of a lot better adjusted than most of the women she knew. She bought a little weed now and then from a boy who'd once mowed her lawn; she had Mack when she wanted a warm body in her bed. She had a beautiful grandbaby, and her daughter and son-in-law came over every weekend because they *wanted* to, not because they needed a handout or felt obligated.

And she got along great with Taylor, which was more than a lot of those uptight women could say about their relationships with their own kids. Which made her think of Colleen.

The things she'd said. Christ, the things she'd said to Colleen.

After she dried her hands, she reached into the pocket of her jeans and pulled out the poster. Paul was a nice-looking boy. You could tell he was shy from the way he looked at the camera, or rather didn't look at it.

Taylor had taken Paul under his wing the way he always did. He was such a mother hen, always scouting the outskirts of any party for the wallflowers, the tender ones, and folding them into his sparkling orbit. What he had actually said about Paul was that he seemed to be having trouble making friends, but it was because he was *bewildered*. Not disliked, as she'd implied to Colleen. "It's like he's never seen anything like us before, Mom." Taylor had laughed after telling her about a prank in which Taylor had convinced Paul to drive their shift supervisor's truck up onto a flatbed. Shay hadn't completely understood the story, but she did understand what Taylor was doing, even if *he* didn't—teaching Paul the way things worked, giving him the ticket to belong. Just like when he'd patiently taught Javed Suleman the rules of American football in the backyard before tryouts back in sixth grade. Or Paul's nickname, Whale. Taylor had been the one who gave it to him, and it was his gentle way of showing Paul how to fit in, how his fancy, expensive East Coast clothes weren't doing him any favors in the camp.

What Shay hadn't said to Colleen was that after that, it was always "Paul and I" and "Paul was telling me . . ." and never again was there talk of him not fitting in.

A girl came into the bathroom, talking on her cell phone, and Shay hastily shoved the paper into her pocket and headed back out into the crowd. She didn't see McCall Whittaker from South Bend, despite taking her time circling the bar. Well, it probably hadn't been her best idea ever anyway, even if it might have bought her a place to spend the night in addition to a few hours of release. Tomorrow was still going to be tomorrow, and Taylor was still going to be missing, and she needed to have a clear head to figure out what to do about all that, and Colleen too.

Actually, what she really ought to do was go back and find Colleen and make sure she was okay. Shay sighed deeply, wondering when she was ever going to learn to think first and speak later. Even though it was looking like she and Colleen weren't going to be able to work together, Shay couldn't just leave her out there, where, it occurred to her, she was as vulnerable as her own son had been when he showed up, a fish out of water.

She was heading for the door when she saw a familiar face. It took a second to click: the man from Walmart, the one Colleen had been hoping to meet up with here earlier. He looked uncomfortable, standing at the end of the bar, staring at his phone. He was the only man in the bar wearing a suit jacket, though his tie had been loosened, and he was also the only man in the bar with a wineglass in front of him.

Shay hesitated, not knowing what to do. They couldn't afford to miss this opportunity. She got out her phone and dialed Colleen, but there was no answer—and she wouldn't have been able to hear her in the din of the bar anyway.

She slipped the phone back in her pocket, thought for one more minute, then headed outside. In the back of the Explorer, she dug through the bags and found what she needed. She didn't even bother returning to the ladies' room to change, just threw her coat into the back and shrugged Colleen's cashmere sweater over her own clothes, pulling it down over her hips. She twisted her hair into a chignon with an elastic from her purse and wiped most of her makeup off with a tissue—and then, on second thought, reapplied her lipstick.

Then she headed back to the bar. She was ready as she'd ever be.

COLLEEN NEVER GOT to the part she'd read about in the Jack London story, the part where you just want to go to sleep, when all the pain leaves you and you gently drift. On the contrary, it just got colder and her shivering more violent, until the numbness in her fingers and toes was too painful to ignore.

But that wasn't the reason that Colleen finally got up off the bench, her coat pulling away with a tearing sound since it had frozen to the metal.

She got up because she had no proof that Paul was dead. And as long as he wasn't dead, she was on duty. It didn't matter what he'd done. It didn't matter what bad decisions he'd made. There wasn't anyone else, and so she got up.

Her face stung, and she was sure she looked frightening. She pulled the hood tighter. She'd go freshen up, and then she'd get a cup of coffee and figure out what to do next.

Two more posters were taped to the glass doors. Colleen stared at the photo for a moment. Was this how it would be, now? Every door she went through, was she going to have to confront this image of Paul, which had been ruined for her now from what Shay said? Why had Andy used this photo, why couldn't he have used the one from the Cape two years ago, when Paul was laughing and tan and holding up a crab by its pincer?

Because no one else needed to see evidence that he had once been happy, Colleen answered her own question. Only *she* needed that.

She opened the door and stepped onto the mat. The smell of coffee and bacon drifted to her nose. The music was quiet, some country song she vaguely recognized.

Other than the waitress, it was all men. They were sitting by themselves, at the counter, at tables. The digital sign showed that only two showers were in use. No waiting. The only sound besides the music was the clack of a spatula on the grill and the quiet thud of a coffee cup being set down.

Everyone was staring at her. Colleen's hand went to her face— she must look worse than she thought. But to get to the ladies' room, she would have to walk past every customer in the place. She looked down at her pants—they were crusted with dirt from when she fell and there was a tear over the knee, rimmed with dried blood. She hadn't even noticed she was bleeding.

"Ma'am, are you all right?"

It was the waitress, a girl scarcely older than Paul. She was standing behind a row of ketchup bottles. Some had other ketchup bottles balanced precariously on top, the last of the spent bottles draining into the new ones.

"I'm . . ."

She couldn't seem to get the words out. *I'll be fine. I just need a moment in the ladies' room. Oh, and could I have a cup of coffee, please? Just black is fine. You're a lifesaver. I'll be right out.*

"I just . . . I need . . ."

She looked from face to face; older men, mostly, their faces creased with worry lines, their bodies thick with years of hard labor. Maybe this was the only place to come if you didn't want the noise, the partying, the strangers jostling you. Maybe this was where you looked for peace.

"I'm Colleen Mitchell." She wasn't sure why she said it. Her voice sounded broken. Her fingers and toes, as they warmed up, ached intensely. "My boy is one of the missing ones. Paul Mitchell. We put up those posters . . . well, my husband had those posters put up—I don't know what else to do. I don't know where else to look. I don't know where to go."

No one moved. The men's expressions didn't change. They had seen things before. Things had happened to them. They weren't young; they were cautious. That was all right. She didn't want their pity or even their compassion.

"Mrs. Mitchell, I knew your son," the waitress said quietly. "I think you better sit down."

THE WAITRESS'S NAME was Emily. She told Colleen that when she got back from the bathroom, there would be a cup of coffee and a turkey club waiting for her.

Colleen had been here only fifteen hours earlier for a shower and breakfast. The first time she'd looked in the truck stop's mirror, she'd been shocked by what she saw, by how much she had aged since this whole ordeal began. Tonight, she was not shocked at all. She understood the bargain she'd made: herself for Paul. And if the devil or whoever had been sent to collect had left behind the lines around her mouth, the purple hollows under her eyes, the sagging lifeless skin, she knew it was all part of the trade.

But that didn't mean she couldn't fight back. She splashed water on her face and dug into her makeup kit. Repaired what she could and combed her hair. Dampened a handful of paper towels and wiped the mud off her clothes. Pulling up her pant leg, she inspected the bruise and torn skin. She dabbed at it with soapy hot water, and welcomed the sting.

Back at the counter, the sandwich was indeed waiting, cut into four perfect triangles, with a tiny sprig of parsley and a lemon slice on the side. The men had resumed what they were doing—reading the paper, watching a game playing silently on the TV hung from the ceiling—and didn't even glance her way. Emily watched as Colleen forced herself to take a bite and wash it down with water.

"I am so sorry for what you're going through," Emily said.

"You knew him?" Colleen felt a little better. She had been hungrier than she realized. "You knew Paul?"

"Only a little. My friend's roommate was his girlfriend. I met him at a party once."

"Paul had a girlfriend?"

Emily's expression softened. "You didn't know?"

"He . . . he never said."

"Okay then, well, what I have to tell you is going to be kind of a shock, I guess. I wouldn't say anything, I mean, I feel like it's not my place or whatever, but you have a right to know, especially since, well, because of whatever happened." She took a deep breath and said, "He and Kristine started dating last fall, and, well, she's pregnant."

"*What?*"

Pregnant. The word tumbled in Colleen's mind, spinning and bouncing against all the impossibilities. Paul had never had a girlfriend, not for more than a few weeks at a time; he never had any trouble getting girls to go to dances with him, and Colleen had always felt that they might have been interested in more, but for some reason Paul had never let things go further. While he was at Syracuse, she'd had the impression that there were a couple of girls he dated, but he never talked about it at home.

And since he came to Lawton, it hadn't occurred to Colleen even to wonder. The ratio of men to women up here . . . *that* she was aware of, it was mentioned in every news article about the place. She'd assumed that all the girls would pair up with the more outgoing boys, the ones who knew their way around a place like this, who were more confident and charismatic.

But Paul had found someone. Even as Colleen tried to wrap her mind around the situation, there was a tiny flame of pleasure inside her, a relief that he'd had this happiness.

They'd made a *baby*. Even now, with Paul missing, his trail going colder, the piece of him that he'd left behind here in Lawton was growing. His child.

"How far along?" she asked faintly.

"I don't know, Mrs. Mitchell. I'm not supposed to know. They aren't telling anyone. Way I heard was, I guess Paul was drinking with some friends and he kind of hinted around that he got her pregnant, and one of the guys told Chastity. When she asked Kristine about it, she got all upset and asked her not to say anything. And she'd only told me, and I don't think she's told nobody else and neither have I. I don't like to spread rumors. But I thought you should know."

"I can't . . . I just can't even believe it." Colleen stared at the food on her plate. The idea of eating was impossible now. "Could you put me in touch with her?"

"I don't have her phone number, but I can tell you where to find her. She works at Swann's, her and Chastity both. Chastity got her the job."

"What's Swann's?"

"It's a restaurant, the only really nice restaurant around here.

Steak and seafood and stuff like that. They make good money over there; they get all the corporate types."

"How late are they open, do you know?"

Colleen saw the look that passed over Emily's expression before she answered, knew what she was thinking. In her state, she was hardly at her best, especially to meet the girl who was carrying her grandchild.

"I think they're usually open until eleven," she said. "Do you want me to try to call over there for you?"

Colleen considered: how would this girl, this girlfriend, feel about meeting her? If she loved Paul—and God, Colleen discovered that she wanted this girl to love Paul—she must be frantic with worry. But she hadn't tried to contact her or Andy, and presumably Paul had told her where he was from. Although Mitchell was a common name . . . But she couldn't afford to scare her off. "No, I think it would be better if I didn't, if she didn't, um . . ."

"I know this has to be a shock," Emily said. "But if it helps, Kristine seems really nice. I don't know her all that well, but she's always been real polite to me."

"Thank you," Colleen said faintly. She noticed that Emily didn't try to talk her out of showing up unannounced. What girl would want that, to meet her boyfriend's mother in these circumstances, the future grandmother of her child . . . if she was even keeping the child? Oh, God, she hadn't thought of that. Especially now, with Paul missing, maybe she would get rid of it. Maybe she already *had*. Colleen was astonished to experience a jolt of loss at the thought—that a baby she didn't even know had existed until moments ago had instantly come to mean something to her, a connection to Paul, a child of her child.

"Do you want me to tell you how to get there?" Emily asked.

"I can find it," she said. "It's just that . . . I don't have a car."

"Did someone drop you off here?"

"I . . ." How to explain? That forty-eight hours after meeting Shay, joining up with her to find their boys, she had managed to destroy that relationship and lose their place to stay and all of her possessions?

"Someone did, but it's not someone I can ask for a ride."

"Well, where are you staying?"

"I'm . . . I don't currently have a room." She realized that Emily probably thought she was deranged, given the way she looked when she came in, the fact that she had no bags with her. "There was a miscommunication about where I was supposed to stay," she tried, figuring that a lie was easier than the truth. "And my luggage has been lost. I need to figure out my next steps, but I don't want to wait to talk to this girl. Every day that passes . . ."

Her voice broke, and Emily surprised her by reaching across the counter and taking her hand. "I'm so sorry, Mrs. Mitchell. We've all been praying for the boys and the families, down at my church. I just feel in my heart that you're going to find them."

"Thank you," Colleen whispered.

"Tell you what . . . let me call Kristine myself. I'll text Chastity for her number." She got her phone from her pocket and her thumbs flew over the screen. "Look, I'd invite you to stay with me, but I'm with my folks and my mom's sick. She doesn't sleep good at night and—"

"I wouldn't dream of imposing," Colleen said. "Please, I have several options, I just need to sort them out."

Emily apologized again and excused herself to go take care of her customers, and Colleen forced herself to eat the sandwich and drink the water and coffee. The food felt like lead going down, but she hadn't been eating much and she couldn't afford to collapse from hunger.

Emily returned, coffeepot in hand. "Chastity texted back. I didn't tell her why I needed Kristine's number, but she didn't ask, so that should be all right."

Colleen entered the number into her phone. Emily moved down the counter, checking the ticket on an order she'd taken. Colleen knew she was giving her privacy, but years of nagging Paul not to talk on the phone in public places made her get up and go stand in the lobby by the restrooms and the vending machines.

She hit Send before she could think about it too much. Even so, she was shaking when the girl picked up.

"Hello?"

"Is this Kristine?"

"Yes . . ."

"Kristine, I'm so sorry to be calling late at night. This is Colleen Mitchell, Paul's mother."

There was the sound of an intake of breath, not quite a gasp. "Mrs. Mitchell . . ." she said faintly. "I get off in a few minutes. I'm just doing receipts now. Would you like to meet?"

"Yes, very much. I'm . . . I'm at the truck stop down by the storage place. I hope it's all right that Emily gave me your number."

"That's fine. I'll get there as soon as I can. Just give me a half hour."

twenty-two

SCOTT PEELED THE foil expertly from the bottle before opening it. The cork made a satisfying pop. The sweat patches visible through his starched cotton shirt had almost dried, now that they were back at the hotel, away from the noise and din of the overheated club.

His suite was nice; the hotel couldn't have been more than a year old, the newest one built to accommodate the boom. It had a minifridge that he'd used to chill the wine. The wine he'd intended for Colleen, Shay reminded herself, keeping the playful smile fixed on her face. It hadn't been too difficult to get him to forget all about being stood up, especially not after she'd told him how tired she was of the unwashed and ungroomed men in Lawton, considering that she worked as a physical therapist and took her work seriously. Shay didn't know a lot about physical therapy, but she did know how much men liked to talk about themselves, so it didn't much matter. In the bar, he'd been happy to talk her ear off about his job and his golf game and the trip he was planning to take down to the Keys with some guys he knew.

She pretended to listen, laughing at the right times, occasionally touching his hand. She tried to mimic Colleen's ramrod-straight posture: maybe guys like this liked the chase, preferred the ice-princess type. When he finally got around to asking her about herself, she implied that she was getting over a breakup, while accidentally brushing against him, easy enough to do given the press of the crowd at the tavern.

It was entirely too easy, especially considering the fact that she was wearing Colleen's shapeless sweater and mimicking her frosty demeanor. Either the guy was truly desperate or he really did go in for the frigid housewife look. Different strokes for different folks. Maybe, Shay thought, she should have a little compassion: it couldn't be much fun to be stuck up here, away from family and friends, week after week. It was probably lonely and definitely boring. But then there was that ring on his finger, the phone calls he kept ignoring, checking his phone and then putting it away, until finally, when they got back to the room, he silenced it and tossed it onto the desk facedown.

Just like Mack, a voice inside scolded. But no. This was nothing like Mack, who came to her when Caroline turned away from him, who tore himself up with guilt and longing whenever they lay twined together after. Who'd been in love with her for years, longer than a lot of marriages lasted. At least, that was the story Shay clung to hard, and she wasn't going to give it up now, not because of one expense account douche bag who'd probably already forgotten her fake name.

"Look, I hope this doesn't seem out of line, me inviting you up here," Scott said, handing her a glass of wine. She was sitting in the club chair in the suite's living room, leaving him the sofa. He sat down close enough that their knees touched. "I just was having trouble hearing you in the club, and that shit they serve there could wear a hole in your gut. This is a pretty nice pinot, by the way. New Zealand, 2008."

Shay made an appreciative sound as she sipped.

"So," Scott said, setting his glass down and inching slightly closer. Now their knees were pressed together, and it would be awkward for her to move them. "You said you wanted to ask me about something in the bar. I got to say, the lawyer business can't be half as fascinating as what you see every day, working in a rehab clinic."

"Well, I'm sure that's not true. You've seen one torn Achilles, you've seen them all."

Scott laughed as though she'd said something hilarious. By Shay's estimate, he'd had at least three glasses of wine so far—the one he'd been finishing when she spotted him and the two since then. Depending when he'd arrived at the bar, possibly more. She'd had a weak gin and tonic, most of which she'd left at the bar.

"It's just that when you said you were a lawyer for White Norris, well, I thought I could ask you, since it doesn't involve your company. And my friend Rose is having the hardest time getting answers."

"She got a legal problem?"

"Not her, but her son. He's twenty. Last December, he got in an accident out on one of Hunter-Cole Energy's rigs. What happened was, some drive chain broke and snapped back, and Ricky lost a couple of fingers." Shay was quoting from the anonymous blog, as well as she could remember. The image accompanying the post, taken at the hospital—the man's hand bloody, the stumps ragged—was impossible to forget.

"One of the Hunter-Cole guys came to see him in the hospital and told him Hunter-Cole was picking up the bills and throwing in ten thousand dollars for his future medical bills, on top of what he'd get from disability."

Scott nodded. "Sounds about right. They generally have some discretionary funds to help out with cases like this, try to make things right when a guy's going to be out of work for a while."

"Well, that's just it. Ricky can't go back to being a derrick hand, and he can't earn anywhere near that kind of money doing anything else. I know from my job that he's got a lot of occupational therapy ahead of him. And he's got a couple of friends willing to testify that there was all these safety violations. I guess the cable hadn't been oiled and it was all clogged with dirt, and that was what caused it to snap."

Already Scott was shaking his head, frowning. Shay knew she probably wasn't getting the details right but she was counting on him chalking it up to her ignorance. She rushed ahead before he could interrupt her. "One of his friends took pictures on his phone of the logbook where they were supposed to initial that it was getting oiled, and there were all these gaps, whole weeks with no entries. And this thing was dated with the supervisor's signature. So Ricky's mom, my friend, she's wondering if she's got a case? If she hires a lawyer?"

"Look," Scott said. "I shouldn't even be talking to you about this. You got to understand, I don't just answer to my own boss, I've signed so many confidentiality agreements you could paper this room with them. I'll guarantee you right now there's not an attorney in this state who would give your friend the time of day."

She was losing him, she saw; his expression had turned wary and his posture had gone rigid. Suspicion clouded his expression and he looked at his watch.

"I know that," she said hastily. "I know it's an uphill battle, my friend is just so worried. Ricky and his wife bought a house, they just moved in before the accident, and their second baby is on the way. They're desperate." She made her voice soft and tremulous, brushing away an imaginary tear.

"Aw, now, hey," Scott said. "Look. What you got to understand, rig work's dangerous, it's just the nature of the job. Then you got

OSHA coming around changing the game every few months, half the time we can't comply simply because we haven't got the latest updates to the standards and procedures. I know everyone's ready to point the finger at the big bad corporation, but the truth is, and you can ask any hand worth his salt, that ninety percent of accidents on the rig are just plain human error. Inattention, shortcuts, whatever you want to call it, it's when the guys themselves don't follow company procedure. Case in point, your friend's son. And I'm not even saying that the state of the draw works is what caused it, because it's frankly impossible to know, but even if it was due to maintenance gaps, whose fault is that? I mean, was it the company president's job to get out there and oil the damn thing?"

"Well, I guess that—"

"No way, it's not. That's a case, and again I don't mean to generalize, but a lot of your younger hands, they're finding what you might call *chemical* ways to tolerate the twelve-hour shifts where your more experienced guys know how to pace themselves, you see what I'm saying? I'm not trying to tell you that your friend's boy was using uppers, but you wouldn't believe how many of them do, and *that's* where you get your procedure failures. Skipping steps like that."

He shrugged, as though that closed the case for him.

"I don't think Ricky was the type to do drugs," Shay said doubtfully. "I mean, I'm really grateful you're talking to me about this, telling me what her chances are. It beats paying some guy three hundred bucks an hour to hear the same thing."

"Yeah, which is exactly what would happen, if she could even find someone to be honest with her. Trouble with a lot of these personal injury outfits, they're not going to shoot straight. Hell, they might manage to get a couple thousand more out of Hunter-Cole, especially if they're willing to sign a covenant not to sue, but where do you suppose that's going to end up? Lining the lawyer's pockets. Seri-ously, if I was you, I'd tell your friend to save her money."

Shay took a sip of her wine, waiting until Scott did the same. She had to push him just a little bit further, and she wasn't sure he'd follow. While she was hesitating, he put his hand on her knee; his fingers made slow circles around her kneecap.

She figured she had nothing to lose. "I know this is going to sound crazy," she said. "But Rose says a guy came to see her and told her to drop it. She says he threatened her. That if Ricky's friends didn't back off about the maintenance logs, they'd regret it. She asked if they were going to get fired just for making a report, and she says he said something like, not just their jobs. Like their *safety.*"

Scott's fingers stilled on her knee. "Rose has always been kind of dramatic," Shay said, pretending she hadn't noticed. "So I don't even know what to believe. I mean, it sounds kind of crazy, right?"

"I got to say, I've just about had enough work talk for today," Scott said stiffly. "I mean, you're asking things way out of my exper-tise. And frankly it sounds a little suspicious."

"No, you're right," Shay said. "God, I'm sorry. I feel like an idiot. I mean, I don't think Rose is trying to take advantage or anything, but yeah, she's kind of hysterical about this whole thing." She gave him an apologetic smile and placed her hand on top of the one resting on her knee. "Don't mind me."

"Yeah, sounds like you're better off staying out of this one," Scott said. His fingers traveled an inch up her leg, kneading the flesh through her jeans. "I mean, they don't call this the Wild West for nothing. Hunter-Cole has a reputation for playing hardball. You don't see the same culture at White Norris. But that still doesn't mean anything, and believe me, these things change slowly, if they change at all. There's not a man on either side of the desk who's a fan of

OSHA. So. Now, can we put this behind us and try to enjoy what's left of the evening?"

"Mmm," Shay said, giving him her most winning smile. He leaned forward and put his hands around her waist and pulled her onto his lap. She could feel his erection through his pants. His face was at the level of her breasts, and he bent forward and nuzzled at her cleavage.

"Will you excuse me," Shay said, extricating herself gently, caressing his face with her hand as she stepped over his legs. "If I don't visit the little girls' room now, I'm afraid I'll get too . . . distracted."

Scott leaned back against the couch, a dazed grin on his face.

"Maybe we can check out the bedroom when I'm done," Shay said, backing toward the bathroom, unbuttoning her blouse as she went, giving him a good look at her bra and the white skin of her stomach. She grabbed her purse off the coffee table and took it with her.

In the bathroom, she closed the door and looked around quickly. She'd lucked out: a monogrammed kit sat on the counter. She dug her phone out of her purse. There were two missed calls and a text from Colleen: Please call me. I need your help. Please.

Shay was flooded with worry and remorse, but Colleen would have to wait. She picked up the kit and snapped a picture of herself holding it in the mirror, letting her hair obscure her face but making sure her unbuttoned blouse showed, as well as the monogram *STC*.

When she came out of the bathroom, Scott had moved to the bedroom. He was sitting on top of the bed, as naked as the day he was born, with one hand behind his head and the other at his crotch. Shay made sure she got close enough for some fine detail before she took the second picture.

Then she put her phone in the purse and started buttoning her blouse.

"What the *hell*?" Scott said, grabbing the sheet and pulling it up over his pale, flabby gut.

"Settle down," Shay said calmly. "We just need to have a conversation. I'm not here to make trouble for you. I don't want anything from you other than your room."

"My . . . *what*?"

"This room. I need it. I need you to call down to the desk and prepay it through the end of the week and let them know that your employee will be staying here. And don't say they won't let you, because I've done it before."

She hadn't, actually, but Mack had done it once when she went up to Sacramento to see him while he was at a conference. He'd had to leave early when his daughter fell off her bike and broke her leg, but he made sure she was set up for the rest of the week in case he could come back.

"Where the fuck am *I* supposed to stay?"

Shay shrugged. "Not really my problem, is it? You told me you had a whole team here, you made sure I knew that all those guys reported to you. So send one of them home and take his room. Look, it's already almost one. You can probably crash in the lobby until morning. Or call one of your guys and bunk with him, whatever, I don't really give a shit."

"You're out of your mind. Who the hell *are* you, anyway?"

"Start getting dressed and I'll tell you. Oh, and don't forget your things from the bathroom. I got a picture of myself and your little bag in there. You know, the one with your initials on it. Gift from your wife?"

All the color had drained from Scott's face. He got out of the bed, dragging the sheet with him. As he struggled to get his underwear on without letting the sheet drop, Shay edged toward the door.

Scott, with his soft hands and embossed business cards, hardly looked like the violent type, but safe was way better than sorry.

"I'm going to give you the benefit of the doubt and tell you the truth now. Maybe it will make you less upset with me. I'm the mom of one of the missing boys."

Scott had been tugging his pants on. At her words, he stopped, and stood up slowly to stare at her. "The Hunter-Cole boys?"

"Yes. I'm trying to find my son. I found out there's been some safety issues that a few of the boys wanted to report. One of my son's friends said he'd been threatened. I want to find out if my boy got into trouble with Hunter-Cole."

Scott swallowed, then resumed dressing. He didn't say anything until he'd got his shirt on and was fastening his belt.

"If your son is half as crazy as you, if he was making trouble around the rig . . . Look, there's no way I believe they'd hurt anyone, even over at Hunter-Cole. But a payoff? Money to get them to leave town, lie low until they can cover their tracks? Maybe. I'm not saying it happened, or that I've ever seen anything like it happen, but it wouldn't surprise me."

He went into the bathroom, emerging a moment later with his toiletries, which he flung into his suitcase. He pulled his shirts and suit coat from the closet and threw them in, not bothering to fold anything. He picked up his phone and stuffed it in his pocket, and got his coat from where he'd thrown it.

"Look," he said, as Shay backed away from him, giving him access to the door. "Christ. Why didn't you just ask me about this? Why all the . . ." He gestured at the wine, the half-empty glasses, the sofa cushion that had fallen to the floor.

"Right. Like you would have told me?" Shay shook her head. "This is my *son* who's missing. He's been gone thirteen days. His odds are shit. Don't you think I know that? I'm balls to the wall here. And if I hurt your feelings, well, I guess I'd be sorry if I had the time. But I don't. So why don't you run along now? I'm going to call down in fifteen minutes for room service, so I'll know if you took care of things like a good boy. If you did, you won't hear from me again. If you didn't, well, let's just say I'm good with a computer and I'll be able to get these pictures to your home address by tomorrow after-noon.

"The name to put the room under is Capparelli," she added. Then she spelled it for him, twice, slowly. "And, just in case you're wondering, my son's name is Taylor. Now if you don't mind, I think I'd like to be alone."

twenty-three

KRISTINE ARRIVED IN fifteen minutes. She was unwinding the scarf from her neck and unzipping her coat when she came into the restaurant. Her gaze found Colleen immediately.

Colleen jumped up from her stool. "I'm Colleen Mitchell." She put out her hands, and when the girl hesitantly gave her one of her own, she squeezed her cold fingers. "Please, come sit down."

Emily came over to the booth, bringing two cups of coffee without being asked. "Hey, Kristine," she said.

"Emily, thanks."

"I don't even know where to start," Colleen said when Emily walked away. "I mean, I guess, maybe . . . I'm not really myself right now." She touched her face self-consciously. "I've been sleeping in a motor home, though it's been hard to sleep, and I've been worried sick and—oh, God, let me just get right to it, you were with Paul?"

"Yes," the girl said carefully. She seemed frightened. "He and I . . . since last Halloween."

Colleen wanted to touch her, just to feel her skin, the hands that had once touched her son. "I'm—his dad and I—well, I can't even begin to tell you. We just . . . anything you can tell me. Anything."

"It's just that I didn't see him that day. Honestly, Mrs. Mitchell, I wish I could tell you something about where he went. I'd give anything . . ." The look of anguish on her face.

Colleen couldn't help the feeling of disappointment that settled into her. God, she was just so tired. Her hopes had been raised and the exhaustion felt bone-deep as they receded. What had she expected—that the girl would be able to explain it all away? Lead her directly to Paul?

"Kristine . . ." she said carefully. The last thing she could afford to do was to scare the girl off. "I'd love to know a little more about you. Are you from here?"

"Yes, ma'am, my family lived here while I was growing up, then they moved away when I was a senior in high school, but I wanted to finish with my class, so I stayed with relatives. I went to Mayville State for a year, but it, you know, it wasn't for me. So I came back here last year, been working. The money's good. I might go back to school, I'm not sure."

Go back to college . . . while carrying her grandchild? Colleen felt a flush of anxiety. But the girl probably had no idea that Colleen knew about the baby. "Can you tell me how you and Paul met? If you don't mind?"

Kristine flashed a brief, tense smile. "Well, there was a party last Halloween. I went with Chastity, my roommate. She dated Taylor for a while, you know, the other one . . ." She didn't finish her sentence. Colleen knew she probably didn't want to say *missing*. "Anyway, Paul was there. He was more . . . polite than the rest of them. You know? I mean they're all good guys, don't get me wrong, but Paul was kind of shy and, like, he went and got chairs for all us girls, and he went to get the drinks. He—" She shook her head, her voice going thick. "I'm sorry. I'm so sorry."

"No, really, please." Colleen reached automatically for her tissues, then remembered that she had lost them when they fell out of her purse. "If you knew how much crying I've done in the last week . . ."

Kristine grabbed a few napkins from the dispenser on the table and dabbed at her eyes. "I was just going to say, I don't know if this will even make any sense. But we have this one friend? A girl from where I work? And she's kind of, she's not the best socially. I think she has some kind of Asperger's or something? And sometimes people don't understand and they . . . I don't know. Also she's, like, big? But when people started dancing, Paul asked her first. You should have seen her. She was so happy."

A memory of cotillion flashed through Colleen's mind. Paul had hated it; they'd had a huge fight over it. Andy wanted to let him quit, but Colleen was desperate for him to learn the social skills he'd need in college. Now she saw how ridiculous that was . . . she'd had some crazy idea that Paul would get into one of the Ivies, that he'd meet girls from old families and get invited to the sort of places . . . God, she was disgusted with herself, especially because she and Andy weren't those people, they never had been. It was just some leftover fantasy from her own youth, from her mother. Because he'd looked so nice in his navy jacket, tailored for his fast-growing frame the summer of eighth grade . . .

. . . and Andy had taken him aside before the first dance and taught him to tie his tie, and then told him that he'd better never find out that his son refused a girl's request to dance. And then he went one step further and told him that the mark of a gentleman is making sure that every girl gets to dance. Colleen, listening from the kitchen, had pressed the dish towel to her cheek and felt something for her husband that she hadn't felt in a long time.

Tears coursed down her face now. "Thank you," she whispered.

"Oh, Mrs. Mitchell, I just feel so bad about all of this." The girl looked genuinely distressed.

"Kristine, I hate to ask this now, when we've just met, and it's a terrible violation of your privacy and, and I just hope you'll forgive me because of what . . . has happened. But . . ." She drew a breath, not knowing how to ask, her heart thudding unevenly. "It's just that I understand that you and Paul might be expecting a baby."

Kristine froze. Her eyes went wide with surprise. She slowly lowered her hand to the table. Then she picked up her purse and pressed it to her chest. "I'm so sorry," she said, her voice barely more than a whisper as she slid out of the booth. "I'm so sorry, but I have to go."

"No, please," Colleen said, wanting to chase after her. "Please don't go, I shouldn't have brought it up, I—"

"I'm sorry," Kristine said again, and then she was sprinting for the door. Emily called after her, but she didn't turn around.

Colleen got out of the booth, staring after her, unable to breathe.

"Mrs. Mitchell, are you okay?" Emily was ringing up a customer at the register, but she left off in the middle of the transaction and came around the counter. "Can I help?"

"No . . . no, I'm fine." Colleen stood up straighter and reached for her purse. "You've been so very kind, and I know you have your hands full." She avoided Emily's gaze, digging in her purse for her phone.

Reluctantly, Emily went back to the register. Colleen checked her messages. A text from Shay: Call me ASAP

Before Colleen dialed, she sent a text to Kristine, taking care with the wording, trying to strike a tone that wouldn't put her off. Please forgive me for bringing up a subject you may not wish to discuss. Could we please talk again?

Then she called Shay.

Once again, Shay was all Colleen had.

SHAY GOT TO the truck stop in less than ten minutes. She drove up on the sidewalk in front, leaned across, and opened the door. "Look," she said before Colleen could say anything, "it's too late and I'm too tired to get into it again right now. So just get in and let's both keep our mouths shut until after we get some sleep."

"Did Brenda change her mind?" Colleen slid gratefully into the seat. Suddenly she felt like she was about to pass out from exhaustion. The clock on Shay's dashboard read two forty-two.

"Not exactly. Look, I'll tell you the whole story in the morning. I got us a hotel room. We have it through Thursday."

"You . . . how did you do that?"

"Aren't you *listening*? Shit, I'm sorry. Look, it's kind of a long story."

They rode the rest of the way in silence. Shay's irritability weighed on Colleen, but it was tempered by the secret she was holding. She would have to tell Shay in the morning, but for now it was hers alone, a precious bit of hope in the desperate landscape of her mind.

Colleen had seen the Hyatt from the plane when they landed, the biggest and newest hotel in the area. It was brightly lit, the parking lot full. Shay drove right up to the circular drive, where a sleepy-looking bellman hurried to open her door.

She handed him the keys. "Hey, Col, do you have a few bucks for a tip?"

twenty-four

COLLEEN WOKE AT nine thirty to the vibration of her phone alarm, which she'd set last night and left on the nightstand. Sun streamed through the hotel room's windows. They'd been too tired to close the drapes last night, too tired to pull out the sleeper sofa, too tired to do anything but fall asleep in their clothes.

Across the expanse of the king-size bed, Shay slept in the same compact, motionless little ball in which she'd slept at the motor home. She snored faintly on the exhale, but Colleen envied her peaceful sleep. She'd woken a couple of times from nightmares that immediately vanished, leaving only unease and dread in their wake.

Colleen closed her eyes and said the prayer she said every morning now: *Please, God. Please.* She knew there should be more, faulted herself for being unable to come up with the words, but it was the best she could do. This time, though, after focusing on Paul's face, she allowed herself to think—very briefly—of the girl, of the baby she carried.

The word slipped into her mind, past the hasty, inadequate defenses she'd built. *Grandmother.* She was a grandmother, at least in this moment. And from there it was an irresistible leap to the baby itself, probably no larger than a pea, a bean so far. Kristine had the fair complexion that was heartbreakingly lovely on young girls but didn't age well: her straw-yellow hair was thin, her milky skin already creased at the eyes. But she had dimples when she smiled, and a sweet Cupid's-bow mouth: an old-fashioned, innocent kind of pretty.

Combined with Paul's olive skin and his good proportions, the baby couldn't help but be beautiful, could he? Or she? Paul's hair had come in curly; Colleen couldn't bear to cut it until his first birthday. How many thousands of times had she twisted the curl at the nape of his neck around her finger, just for the joy of watching it spring free? To do so again—a girl, perhaps it would be a girl, with her mother's blue eyes?

"Stop it, stop it," Colleen whispered to herself. Imagining had left her breathless: it was a dangerous exercise, the return from even a fleeting fantasy far too painful. If Kristine wasn't going to keep the baby, Colleen needed to know now, so she could take the temptation out of the equation as she searched for Paul.

She checked her phone. Nothing. Before she could think better of it, she messaged Kristine again: PLEASE. I only want to help.

KRISTINE FINALLY TEXTED back when they were having breakfast in the Hyatt's dining room. Colleen had showered and dressed before waking Shay, and it was nearly ten thirty now.

Can you come to my apartment at 12:20? It has to be right at 12:20, sorry. Will explain.

"Anything important?" Shay asked.

"I . . . I'm not sure." She wasn't ready to tell her about the baby yet. Maybe Kristine wanted to tell her she had decided not to keep it. Colleen didn't think she could bear the pain of having to talk about another loss; she wouldn't tell Shay unless it turned out that Kristine was planning to keep the baby. Maybe Kristine had class in the morning and only a brief break before her shift; that would explain the timing.

As Colleen texted back, asking for the address and promising to do her best to get there, a young man in a wool overcoat dragged a roll-aboard to the hostess stand. "Could I get a cup of coffee to go?"

"Certainly, sir," the young woman said. "Getting ready to fly out?"

"Yes, got the last seat on the noon to Minneapolis."

"That was lucky."

"You're telling me. I thought I was here all week and then this morning I got called back. No offense, but I don't know how you people stand it here."

"I'll just go get your coffee," the woman said, ignoring the jab.

"That's him," Shay said in an amused voice. "The guy Scott sent home so he could have his room. His job was probably wiping Scott's ass or something, and now Scott is going to have to do it himself."

Shay had told her the whole story as they got ready. Colleen had been both impressed and vaguely sickened. She'd been certain she couldn't have pulled off what Shay had—and then she realized that if it meant getting information out of him that could help her find Paul, she probably would have done whatever he asked. The difference was that she wouldn't have been sharp enough to get the upper hand at the end the way Shay had.

"Thank you," she said stiffly. "For coming to get me, for getting us the room."

Shay didn't say anything for a moment. She set down her fork and stared out the window, across the parking lot to the airport. Banks of plowed snow glittered in the blinding morning sun, and a small plane like the one Colleen had arrived on waited outside the terminal.

"That room you said Andy got?" Shay finally said.

"Yes."

"You owe me now. That room's half mine. As long as we're here, as long as it takes." Her face had darkened slightly.

"Of course."

"And it's not charity. This isn't you doing me a favor. We need to get that straight."

"I never said—"

"Let me finish. I just want it understood between us, I did my part last night. You probably think it's easy for me, with him, letting him put his hands on me, just because you look at me and think I give it away every chance I get."

Colleen wanted to object, but she kept her mouth shut, her hands clenching in her lap.

"Look. Okay, I see people, *men*, it's all casual. I'm not all hung up, like, what society thinks if there are two of us having a good time, responsible adults, whatever. But last night? I don't *do* that. Not with a guy like that. Thinking he was going to have me in that bed when he could barely remember my name? His hands on my ass while I could hear his phone buzzing because his wife was calling for the third time?

"He made me *sick*," she said, her voice a little shaky. "So no, that wasn't easy. I did it for the same reason you asked that girl to come meet you, because we've got to do *everything* we can."

A moment passed. "That's it," Shay said, her voice nearly back to normal. "I guess that's all I have to say."

"I understand." Colleen pushed her plate to the edge of the table, no longer hungry. "I don't . . . take it for granted. I don't take you for granted."

The bill came, and while Shay signed it to their room, Colleen remembered something else she had thought of, a way to do her part.

"Listen, I think we need to get some better media coverage. Not just the papers, but TV."

Shay snorted. "Right. Didn't you hear what Chief Weyant said? They have guys walking off the sites all the time. How are we going to convince them this is any different?"

"You aren't going to like this, Shay, but hear me out. This is different because it's two white boys with money. Back in Boston, who do you think gets covered? In Chicago? In any big city? How about Sacramento, out by you? Kids from rich families."

"But Taylor doesn't—"

Colleen stopped her with a shake of the head. "They're together," she said firmly. "That's the story. Look, I'm sick of trying to explain myself all the time, but there's some things in this world you can buy. Let's go out to the affiliate and see if we can talk to someone. I'll get Andy to call the bigger outlets."

Shay nodded slowly. "Okay. You know where it is?"

"Yes, I looked it up while you were in the shower." She allowed herself a small smile. "On my *phone*. See, there may be hope for me yet."

THEY TOOK A poster off a drugstore window on the way. The affiliate was located a few miles out of town on a flat, snow-thatched field, the transmission tower spearing the chalky sky. There were only a few cars in the lot, and inside, there was a lone woman sitting at a desk, cleaning her glasses on a cloth and staring at her screen.

"Help you?" she said.

Colleen had reapplied her lipstick in the car and arranged her scarf carefully around the neckline of her coat, while planning exactly what she wanted to say. Now she raised her chin and took a breath.

"My name is Colleen Mitchell, and this is Shay Capparelli. We are the mothers of the boys who went missing from the Hunter-Cole job site that has been plagued with shocking safety violations. The local police have been unwilling to help, and there are rumors that someone in the department is being paid to stonewall the investigation. We're ready to speak out on camera to get the message out that we need to get Paul and Taylor home."

She was shaking when she finished speaking. The women lowered her glasses to the desk and frowned. "Seriously? You think the cops are covering it up?"

"We don't—there's no proof, but we were hoping that KUXC might be willing to do an investigation," Colleen said, some of her certainty slipping. "We're also working with several media outlets in Boston and Sacramento, where the boys are from, as well as Bismarck." With any luck, that would soon be true.

"Wow, I wish you luck. I can try to get someone to call you this afternoon," the woman said, reaching for a pen.

"Isn't there anyone we could talk to now?"

The woman waved at the closed door to her right. "Honey, there're only three people here besides me. Lester at noon and Anna on weather, and one engineer."

"You can put on the news with so few people?" Shay asked. "What about all the reporters? And the, you know, sound and camera people?"

"It's all automated now." The woman shrugged. "Ten years ago there would have been more than a dozen people running the show. Now we got cameras that think for themselves. Hey, do you want me to go ask if you can come in and watch?"

"Thanks, but we don't have time," Colleen said, deflated. "It would be great if you had someone call. And here's a poster with the boys' pictures."

She wrote down their names and cell numbers. The woman wished them luck again on their way out.

BACK IN THE car, Shay didn't turn the key right away. She looked out on the desolate horizon, a few snowflakes drifting aimlessly in the steely cold winds. "You did good," she said quietly. "You knew how to talk to her."

"I don't think it's going to do any good, though. I've got to figure out how to get to the programming director, or whatever they call it." Colleen had her phone out and was tapping away.

"Who are you texting?"

"I'm not. I found an app for taking notes this morning. I'm writing down the anchors' names." She glanced up. "Don't look at me like that, Shay. You're the one who inspired me to figure it out."

When Colleen had come out of the shower this morning with the thick white towel wrapped around her head, smelling of the fancy soap the hotel provided, she'd looked not so much relaxed as relieved. As if she was finally back in her own skin. She'd called someone to come up to their room to get their laundry, something Shay hadn't even known you could do, and showed him the rip in her pants and told him she was happy to pay a surcharge for them to be repaired right away, and then she'd given him a ten-dollar bill.

Shay, who had been sitting at the desk writing Mack an email, pretended not to pay attention to the conversation. But she added her own laundry to the pile and wondered what it would be like to live that way. She could see that it would be a comfort, but the risk was that you would be helpless if it was taken away from you.

She was finally understanding how much farther Colleen had had to fall.

And not just because she'd had to sleep on a table for two nights or wear dirty underwear. Somehow, seeing her in her own environment— the Hyatt that was probably the closest thing in Lawton to what felt like home to Colleen—Shay got a glimpse into what it must have been like at home, for her and her husband, and also for Paul. When Taylor came home, as often as not trailing a couple of guys from the team, or his study group from Spanish, Shay didn't make them take their shoes off at the door or call her "Mrs. Capparelli." They helped themselves to whatever was in the fridge and didn't seem to care that the dinette chairs didn't match, and when the pizza came they all threw in a few bucks unless Shay had just gotten paid, in which case she'd send one of them to the Freshway down the block with money for sodas and a salad from the deli, and give the pizza guy a big tip.

She guessed that in the Mitchell home, you paid for the thick carpet and the gourmet groceries and the maid by never causing a fuss. Never leaving crumbs on the coffee table or the toilet seat up or yelling during a football game on TV.

Taking Colleen out of her environment had shaken her badly. But for Paul, maybe it had been his first taste of real freedom. Taylor had told her how happy Paul was in the camp. He sang dirty songs in the shower, changing the lyrics and getting people to sing along. He loved when they all gathered around the big-screen TV to watch games, half of them on the floor because there weren't enough chairs, almost getting into fistfights when Alabama played LSU. He even loved when the girls at the desk got mad when they tracked mud in and made them all go back outside and put the little booties on.

"Look, there's something you need to know," Shay said, when Colleen finally put her phone back in her purse.

"Please don't tell me anything technical, because I swear to you I

can't learn one more new thing right now." Colleen gave Shay the little self-deprecating half smile that Shay had finally figured out indicated her most confident moments.

She took in Colleen's carefully drawn-on eyebrows, her hair
sprayed in place. She knew that Colleen felt like she finally looked
decent again, but to Shay she looked like the moms who'd never talk
to her in the pickup lines at the school, the ones who stared at her
when she took Leila to the park, not because Shay was too old to
have a two-year-old but because Leila was biracial.

She missed the woman who'd first stumbled into the motor
home, with her mascara smudged from crying and her hair standing
up. But that wasn't the version of Colleen who was sitting with her in
the car, and she had no choice but to make things right with this one.

"What I said about Paul. What Taylor told me. It was true.
When he first got there, he did have trouble fitting in. But not the
way I made it sound."

She peeked at Colleen. Her face was a mask; she'd gone rigid.
Keep breathing, Shay wanted to say. *Honey, just stay with me here.*

"They just didn't know what to make of him, is all, and he was
shy, and every time he'd do something that they made fun of, he'd
get all embarrassed and go back to his room. Like even if it was a
little thing, like I guess he had this belt with anchors all the way
around it, nobody had ever seen anything like that. And you know
how guys are."

Colleen's lips trembled and Shay knew she was going to cry if
she didn't get this out right.

"Okay, look, the one who gave him that nickname? Who got everyone calling him Whale? It was *Taylor*. But he wasn't making fun of
him, he was trying to give him something to hang on to. And all of
this was just the first week. Taylor said the minute Paul figured out

that everyone didn't hate him, he was like a different guy. He went to Walmart and got all new clothes and wore them with the wrinkles from the package still in them, he started joking around with the desk girls, he played poker . . . Taylor said he always won at poker. What I'm saying is, everybody *liked* him."

Colleen was crying now, silently shaking while tears tracked down her cheeks. She took a tissue from her purse and dabbed at her eyes. "You can't know," she whispered. "You just can't know."

"It's okay," Shay said, and then she really needed Colleen to stop because there was still that other part, that thin, dark shadow behind the friendship between their sons.

The boy with his skull caved in. The boy in the locker room. And because of that boy, the gift she had just given Colleen was tainted, it was spoiled at the core.

But let Colleen hold on to that solace for now. Because if she found out that Paul had gone crazy again, there would be ample time for her to pay. And pay and pay for the rest of her life.

"Okay," Shay said. "We'd better get back to town."

"No, wait. Before we do . . . there's something I haven't told you, either. Kristine . . . she's pregnant. With Paul's baby."

"*What?* How do you know?"

"I didn't tell you because . . . I guess because I was embarrassed. The girl at the truck stop, the one who gave me her number, she told me. And when Kristine came and I asked her about it, she didn't deny it. Oh, Shay, listen, if Paul knew his girlfriend was having a baby, there's no way he'd do anything to jeopardize his job."

Maybe, Shay thought darkly. She herself had had to tell a man that she was carrying his unplanned child. His response gave her little confidence in men's ability to absorb that kind of news. "How do you feel about it?" she asked carefully.

"I don't know—so many things. I mean, shock, I guess, mostly. And worry. And—oh, I don't know, we just have to get through this and then I'll think about what comes next. I mean, it's new, she can't be very far along, they just met at the end of October."

"Then she could be almost three months."

"Well . . ." Colleen frowned, her forehead wrinkled. "I mean, if it happened . . . I don't know when it happened."

Shay didn't say anything, letting Colleen reach the same conclusion, if she hadn't already. If the baby was only a few months along, it could still be made to go away.

"Maybe that's what she wants to talk about." She told Shay about the text, about Kristine's insistence she come right at twelve twenty. "We still have plenty of time to get there."

"Is it okay if I come along?"

"Of course. We . . . I could stand to have another set of ears. You know, to talk to her."

"There's one more thing. Even though I feel like this is nothing, I'm guessing it wouldn't hurt to let someone know where we're going."

"You mean like Andy?"

"Sure, that works. I just figure whenever we go somewhere, we should text someone, either Andy or Brittany or her husband, Robert, so there's a record. Not to be all paranoid, but we're stirring up some big shit now. Like at the rig, what if that guy had run you down?"

"Well, I guess you would have had to run faster." Colleen's attempt at humor was forced.

"Yeah. Anyway, at least we'll be building a record you can give your detective or, like if they ever get *real* cops in on this. Or OSHA, or the Feds. You give your husband the names and numbers of everyone we've talked to, tell him not to use them unless . . . you know. Unless something happens."

Colleen was silent for a moment. "This is crazy," she said. "I came here to look for my son. All I wanted was to find him, not to get involved in some huge cover-up. And now I'm trying to leave a trail in case something happens to us too."

"We didn't ask for any of this, Col," Shay said. "But this is what we got."

twenty-five

COLLEEN CALLED ANDY on the way back to town. "I'll explain more tonight," she said. "For now I just need you to write a few things down."

"What the hell's going on there, Colleen? I got a call today from Hunter-Cole corporate. The *head* of Hunter-Cole. He says there was an incident yesterday where Shay assaulted an employee on one of their sites."

"*What?*" Colleen hadn't told him the whole story in the message she'd left the night before, only that they'd gotten a chilly reception.

"He says they've turned up the heat on their own investigation, but they can't move forward until they have a guarantee that you'll stay off their property. Colleen, that woman is a menace. Have you given any more thought to me coming out there?"

"It's . . . complicated, Andy. But listen, I was there, Shay didn't do anything. I mean, not until after the guy hit *her*, anyway."

"Look, Colleen." She could hear the frustration in Andy's voice. "I understand you have feelings of loyalty to her, that you've been through something very emotional together. But I'm coming out there Thursday. Vicki's working on my flights. She's helping me sort through the calls we've been getting. And I talked to Steve—he'll fly out this weekend and use the other room you booked. Hunter-Cole has offered to work with Steve, to share their findings as the case progresses. And they're in full cooperation with the Lawton PD."

He waited. Colleen knew he expected her to respond, but she was still stuck on something he'd said: *Vicki's working on my flights.* Not so much the words, but the *way* he said it. There was that . . . faint sense of intimacy, of arrogant familiarity. To Andy's credit, he lapsed into that tone only with his assistant . . . and with Colleen.

With the women he bedded.

Colleen sucked in her breath. Had she really just thought that? About her husband, about her best friend? She couldn't even prove the thing with the assistant, and she wasn't at the firm anymore—the girl had gone back to grad school—but *still*.

"Listen, Col, I think you're too close to it," Andy pressed. "You've been under a lot of stress, but I think you need to step back a little. Come on. Be reasonable."

Colleen had said nothing when she found the texts from the assistant on Andy's phone a few years back. And since Vicki seemed to be spending most of her time trying to help find Paul, Colleen supposed she didn't care all that much if she screwed her husband on her breaks. And she had to admit that Andy would probably make more headway with the authorities than she ever could.

But this was the last time he would ever tell her to be reasonable.

"Are you ready to write these names down?" she asked coldly. "Otherwise, you can hang up and I'll just text them to you."

"Colleen, come on, I—"

"I really don't have time for this."

"*Fine.*"

Once she'd hung up, Shay glanced over. They were almost back to town, taking it slow on the icy roads. "You okay?"

"Yes." Colleen didn't bother keeping the irritation out of her voice. "I didn't even get a chance to tell him about Kristine and the baby, because he lit into me about yesterday the minute he picked up. Get this—he says that guy who hit you is thinking of filing assault charges."

"Of course he is," Shay said, rolling her eyes.

"And then I feel like he didn't even listen to my side. You ever feel like everyone in your life thinks you're incompetent?"

"Only most every day of my life," Shay said. "Fuck 'em. You really need to get past that, Col. Tell you what. You can do the talking in there. Just keep repeating it to yourself—*fuck 'em.*"

"Hey, better slow down," Colleen said. "Look at all that."

At the intersection ahead, police and fire vehicles were taking the right turn, lights and sirens going.

"They're headed toward the Hunter-Cole rig," Shay said.

"Not necessarily, they could be headed anywhere."

"Seriously, what else is even out there? We didn't see a single damn house on the way to the rig."

"We can't do anything about that now," Colleen said. "We have to get to Kristine."

"Kristine will be there later today. What if this is important? If we get there now—if there's been another accident, there's going to be chaos, no one will pay any attention to us. Maybe we can find something out."

"No," Colleen snapped. Panic clutched at her throat. She couldn't miss Kristine, couldn't miss the chance to find out the truth. "We can go as soon as I get done talking to Kristine, I *promise.* If it's any kind of big accident, the rig will be shut down for hours."

Shay hesitated only a moment longer, then she peeled forward, her jaw tight. "I'll drop you off. Then I'm coming back here."

"Fine."

They got to the apartment complex, a seventies-looking three-story brick building, in less than five minutes.

"Just let me out here," Colleen said impatiently, already opening the door as Shay pulled in front of the building. The dash clock said twelve twenty-one. "Come get me when you're done."

"Good luck," Shay called. As soon as Colleen shut the door, she made a U-turn and headed back the way she'd come.

Standing in front of the homely building, Colleen adjusted her scarf and ran a hand through her hair, thinking that she should have freshened her makeup in the car.

Apartment 102 was dead center, its view obscured by the stairs outside to the building. Sheer curtains hung in the windows. Before Colleen could knock, the door opened, and Kristine was standing there in a black skirt and emerald green blouse. She was wearing black tights and, incongruously, fuzzy blue slippers. Her hair had been pulled back into a tight bun, and her eyes were accented by carefully drawn eyeliner and a thick coat of mascara. She smelled like shampoo and toast.

"Come on in, Mrs. Mitchell." She seemed nervous, stepping out of the way for Colleen to enter, and then shutting the door quickly behind her.

The apartment was a tight little box with a pass-through to a tiny kitchen. To the right was a narrow hall. Through the partially open bedroom door, Colleen saw a neatly made bed topped with a pile of pillows in various pastel shades; one was embroidered with the words LIVE LOVE LAUGH. The furniture was neat and scrubbed, but it looked hand-me-down, with sagging cushions and worn trim. An old TV sat on a large doily on a pressboard stand.

"I have tea," Kristine said. "Or soda?"

Before Colleen could answer, a girl came out of the bedroom. She looked about sixteen and was startlingly pretty, with wide blue eyes and thick pale hair that cascaded around her shoulders. "Hi," she said shyly, not quite meeting Colleen's eyes.

"Okay." Kristine clasped her hands together and took a breath. "Mrs. Mitchell. This is my cousin. Elizabeth. She's on her lunch break from school."

"Hello," Colleen said, confused.

The girl burst into tears. "Oh, my *God*. I'm so sorry. I'm sorry, I'm such an idiot. Maybe I should just go."

"You're not going anywhere," Kristine said sharply. "Sit down."

The girl sat on the edge of the love seat, twisting her hands in her lap. Colleen grabbed a box of tissues from the coffee table and handed it to her. Elizabeth accepted one gratefully, dabbing at her eyes.

Kristine took a seat at the far end of the sofa, leaving Colleen the other side, between the two girls.

"I need to apologize to you," Kristine said. "Mrs. Mitchell—"

"Please, just call me Colleen."

"I wouldn't blame you for being furious. You have so much to deal with. The thing is, I'm not really Paul's girlfriend. I was covering for Elizabeth."

Colleen looked from one girl to the other. Elizabeth looked miserable; she'd taken the decorative pillow from the love seat and was clutching it to her stomach.

"Covering . . . how? You mean *you* were dating Paul? But you're . . ."

"I'm almost eighteen," Elizabeth said quickly.

"Not until June," Kristine said. "Elizabeth came to the Halloween party where I told you I met Paul. She told Paul she was nineteen. She made up this whole story about how she waitressed with the rest of us. None of us knew about it until they'd been dating like a whole month."

"I told him right away." Elizabeth's voice had gotten very small. "The second time I saw him, I felt so bad about lying. I just . . . I wanted so bad to talk to him. At the party. And I knew he'd never talk to me if he knew I was still in high school."

"Wait a minute," Colleen said, putting her hands out on either side of herself on the couch. "Wait just a minute. You're telling me you're his girlfriend? Even after he knew how old you were? Are you . . . are you *pregnant*?"

"Oh, Mrs. Mitchell, I wish I didn't have to meet you this way," Elizabeth said, tears dampening her cheeks. "I've been thinking about it so much, the way I wanted it to be, Paul and I wanted to come tell you ourselves, we were going to come see you on my spring break. And now . . . now . . ."

She couldn't speak, she was sobbing so hard. Colleen patted her knee awkwardly while Kristine watched in stony silence, her arms folded across her chest.

"Why—why did you lie?"

Both girls started talking at once, but then Kristine pressed her lips together and rolled her eyes. Elizabeth blew her nose.

"My dad would kill me if he knew. He's super protective. He and my mom are very strict, they're really religious. The only other boy I ever went out with, my dad hated him. So now I'm not supposed to date at all. When Paul and I got serious, I told Kristine. She's all I have. She's like a big sister to me. She said Paul and me could meet here after school while she was at work. So whenever Paul had night shift, we met here before he had to go to work. And if he had to work days, I'd just say I was going to study over here after dinner and meet him."

"Mrs. Mitchell, do you remember I told you I stayed with relatives when I came back from college?" Kristine said. "I stayed with the Weyants. My aunt and uncle and cousins. Elizabeth and I shared a room."

"She always made me feel better, whenever my parents—"

"Wait," Colleen broke in. "*Chief* Weyant? Your dad's the police chief?"

Elizabeth nodded. "He'd go crazy if he knew I was pregnant . . ."

"You don't have to be," Kristine said tersely. "Mrs. Mitchell, I'm sorry, it's not my place, but I've been trying to tell Elizabeth that she has options. I can't keep covering up for her. I can't keep lying."

"It was only supposed to be until I graduated," Elizabeth said earnestly. "I'll be eighteen. I'll be an adult. Paul and I were going to get a place. We were going to get married. He proposed."

"Oh, God." Colleen put her hands to her face, unable to process everything she was hearing. Her son had not only found a girlfriend, his first; he'd gotten her pregnant and fast-forwarded to marriage. "You're underage. If anyone had found out—"

"Once I'm eighteen they can't prosecute," Elizabeth said hurriedly. "I went online. I mean they could but they won't, not if we get married. Oh, Mrs. Mitchell, I miss him so much, I can't even believe how much."

"Do you—do you have any idea where he and Taylor are? What happened to them?"

For a moment Elizabeth said nothing, her hand twisting the tiny cross she wore on a gold chain. Then she shook her head, not meeting Colleen's eyes.

"This baby is everything to me," she said, pressing her hands to her flat stomach. "Mrs. Mitchell, I miss Paul so much. I can't breathe sometimes, thinking about him, and then I think he's with me all the time, in this tiny baby we made, and . . . and that way I can keep going through each day, even though it feels like I'm in a daze."

"*Elizabeth*," Kristine said impatiently. "That's not what she asked you. Is there anything you've thought of? That would help Mrs. Mitchell and Taylor's mom? Anything you remembered from the last time you saw him? This is serious. Come *on*."

Elizabeth turned to her cousin. "I've gone over and over it, every minute we were together after he got back from Christmas. He came to see me the first night he got back. I told my parents I was at a movie with friends and since it was a Friday they were okay with that. I told him I was pregnant before he left, and he . . . the night he came back he asked me to marry him." She blushed and tugged at one of the thin chains around her neck.

Something glinted at the end of the chain. When Colleen realized what it was, she gasped. "Oh, my God. That's . . . that's my mother's ring."

Elizabeth undid the clasp and let the ring fall into her palm. The diamond glittered between the two tiny sapphires in the antique platinum setting. She held it out to Colleen.

"I don't feel right keeping it now, Mrs. Mitchell. I couldn't let my parents see it, and I didn't know where to keep it safe, but Paul said he wanted me to have it. He said as soon as I turned eighteen I'd put it on and we'd drive to see you and . . . and . . . I've been keeping it in a little box in my dresser but I'm worried sick my mom will find it. If you would keep it safe for me . . . if Paul . . ."

Trembling, she put the ring in Colleen's hand.

Colleen folded her fingers over the ring, the metal warm from Elizabeth's skin. Her mind raced, thinking back to Paul's last visit home. He'd said he needed his passport to take back with him, for employment verification. Colleen had thought it was strange that he was being asked for it now, after being on the job for several months, but he said it was because they'd been so backed up. He offered to pick up dinner, since her favorite Thai restaurant was next to the bank, and she'd been so glad to see this change in her son: taking responsibility, getting things done, offering to help.

And of course she hadn't been back to the safety-deposit box . . . and even if she had, would she have looked in the velvet box to make sure her mother's ring was still there?

"I was so afraid of what my dad would do if he found out."

"Elizabeth," Kristine said, "your dad loves you. Both your parents do."

"You don't *know*." Elizabeth's voice was agonized. "You have no idea what they get like."

"I lived with you guys for most of a year," Kristine said, exasperated. "They're strict, but they're not mean."

Elizabeth was shaking her head. "They have *everyone* fooled. Oh, my God, Daddy practically killed me when he found out I started dating."

"That is *not* true."

"He hardly ever lets me out of his sight. That's why we're so careful. Paul parks a block away and goes through the parking lot out back and I let him in through the slider door."

There was a knock at the door. Kristine jumped up and went to answer it.

"You must be Kristine," Colleen heard Shay say. "I'm so sorry to barge in like this, but is Colleen still here? Oh, you are, thank God."

She pushed past Kristine into the room. "Hi. I'm sorry, I don't mean to interrupt. I just . . . Colleen, it was a fatality. One of the workers fell off the rig. He's dead."

twenty-six

"IT *COULD* HAVE been an accident," Colleen said.

"Don't you think that's a hell of a coincidence?"

"I don't know. I just don't know. Right now everything feels like it's all twisted up. Like I don't know what caused what. Where it started and where it ends. *God.*"

They were back in their warm hotel room, drinking room service tea, the sky outside going steely as thick, low clouds moved in and obliterated the sun.

"Okay, look." Shay was sprawled on the love seat, tapping on her iPad. "We know a lot that we didn't know a few days ago. And we're starting to get pulled in different directions. We need to separate what we know from what we're just guessing at. Maybe then we'll be able to figure out what we're not seeing here."

Colleen went to the desk and came back with the notepad and pens with the hotel's logo. "I have to do this on paper," she said. "I can't think about it unless I can see it all laid out." She pulled a chair close to the coffee table and tore a piece of paper off the pad.

"Okay. What we know. There were safety violations that the boys knew about." She wrote *Hunter-Cole safety* on the paper.

Shay set her iPad down and sat up facing Colleen. "Is it okay if I write on these too?"

"Yes, that's the point." Colleen handed her a pen.

Shay tore off two more sheets. She labeled one of them *fact* and marked the other with a question mark and set them at opposite ends of the coffee table. She pushed the *Hunter-Cole safety* paper to the fact side. "We know that a worker is dead after an accident today. And that there have been a lot of other accidents on Hunter-Cole rigs. We also know that the foreman, or whatever he was, was willing to assault me to keep us off the rig." She wrote *fatal accident* and *cover-up* and set it by the question mark.

They were quiet for a moment. "So now . . ." Shay said slowly, "let's say Weyant found out about Paul. If what Elizabeth says is true, that he's crazy, what if he . . . did something to Paul?"

"You can say it," Colleen said hoarsely. "If we're going to do this, we have to look at all the possibilities. If he hurt him, if he went after Paul . . ."

"And somehow Taylor got in the way, or something. And he goes nuts and kills them. So then he's responsible for both of them."

"Just to keep Paul away from his daughter? It just seems . . ."

"We're brainstorming, Col. Come on. So he . . . got rid of the boys. Now we're here stirring things up. Of course he's not going to do anything to help us."

Shay grabbed another piece of paper and wrote *Elizabeth/ pregnant* and added it to the question-mark pile.

"That should go in facts," Colleen said.

"No. We don't have any proof. Yesterday you thought it was the other girl. Maybe both of them are lying."

"Why would they do that?"

"I don't know. But it's not a fact. Not until I see her pee on the stick, anyway. And really . . ." She wrote *Paul's girlfriend* on the paper too.

Colleen slowly nodded. She took the paper back and wrote

abusive/protective father underneath. "So really, we don't know any-thing about her."

"Except the ring."

Colleen wrote *Mom's ring* on a fresh sheet and slapped it down on the fact pile.

"Now, the Indian angle." On another piece of paper she wrote *Reservation, mineral rights/lease.*

"This is really just part of this one," Colleen said, tapping the paper marked *Hunter-Cole.* "Hunter-Cole is only at risk of losing their rights if their safety record is exposed. We haven't come up with any proof that the boys had anything to do with the reservation."

"Okay, one more," Shay said. "If we're thinking outside the box. Kristine wanted you to come exactly at twelve twenty—"

"Because of Elizabeth's schedule—that way she'd be sure Eliza-beth could come without anyone missing her at school."

"What if we're thinking about the wrong girl?"

"What do you mean?"

"What if this all started with *Taylor?* Remember I told you that when he was home over Christmas, he was talking about a girl. That she was special—he hadn't ever known anyone like her. Told me she looked like Dakota Fanning."

"Kristine? Is that what you're thinking?"

"No, her roommate. Chastity. That's how they all met. I thought her name sounded familiar. She and Taylor party, they all get to know each other. Chastity introduces Taylor and Paul to Kristine. She and Elizabeth are close, right? Close enough to cover for each other. Kris-tine was willing to pretend she was dating Paul, for Elizabeth's sake. But then today, you said that she was impatient with her. When she was telling the story, right? What if she was upset because Elizabeth was screwing it up?"

"I don't get it."

"Elizabeth screwed up by actually falling for Paul. That wasn't supposed to happen. She was supposed to be easy to manipulate because she was young and—sorry—Paul was gullible. No wonder Kristine put the two of them together."

"I'm way lost, Shay."

Shay grabbed a clean piece of paper off the pad. "Okay, let's look at this another way. Think about Nora. She has coffee with one guy from the rig, tells him which guys are complaining to Roland in the break room, and he gives her an envelope full of cash. What do you think they would pay to find out about something potentially way more serious? Guys with the brains and the determination to make *real* trouble for them?"

"So you're saying . . . Kristine was doing the same thing? Selling information she got from men she dated?"

"Worse than that. What if she's not the only one? What if she and Chastity specifically targeted guys they thought they could get information from?"

Colleen was silent for a moment. "You're saying these girls have a whole scam going where they spy on workers and sell information for money." She thought about it for a moment, the pieces falling into place. "Hunter-Cole has a problem—they've got safety issues that are getting out of hand, and these leases are coming under challenge. They stand to lose their whole stake on the reservation. The next council meeting is coming up. They know they've got potential troublemakers on the inside, guys making noise about reporting them, and they're trying to control it the old-fashioned way. Like with Roland. He makes a complaint, next thing he knows, he's demoted. But they know it's a ticking bomb. The way they handled it was the stupidest thing they could have done, because they've taught the workers not to come to management with their complaints. Which means they'll collect data and take it not to their supervisors, where it can be contained—"

"But to people that Hunter-Cole *can't* control. Just like Scott said. Their biggest fear is that someone gets the media involved, calls in CNN or even the Bismarck news stations, they wouldn't be able to resist a story like that."

"But they know it's only a matter of time before someone comes along whose conscience is bigger than his fear of losing his job. Or even just someone who doesn't need the money that bad."

The women stared at each other.

"Taylor didn't blow off his friend to go fishing that day because he didn't want to get in trouble," Shay said slowly. "He did it because he didn't want to get his *friend* in trouble. So he took Paul. Because he knew Paul would land on his feet if he lost his job."

Colleen pressed her hand to her chest, feeling her heart pound under her palm. "And meanwhile, Elizabeth is no good to Kristine anymore because she's fallen for Paul . . . but at least Elizabeth tells her everything. Because she's young, and dumb, and in love. So she accidentally gives Kristine the information she needs. She knows what the boys were going to do, and when."

"And when she let Hunter-Cole know they were about to blow the whistle, someone made sure that they never got there."

"Oh, God," Colleen said. She felt like she'd been punched in the gut. "How are we going to get her to admit all of this?"

"Not her. Think. We need the weakest link. We need Elizabeth."

"She'll never talk to us. She'd never turn against Kristine . . . that's her cousin. Her *family.*"

"But so are you. Colleen, think about it, she can't depend on her parents. She's afraid of them. She was in love with Paul. And

now you're the only person who can protect her and this baby. She
needs you."

IT WAS AS easy as Shay had predicted it would be. When Colleen
called Elizabeth after school, Elizabeth burst into tears. Colleen
asked questions until it was clear that she was overwhelming the girl:
no, she didn't know she was supposed to take prenatal vitamins; no,
there wasn't a doctor anywhere in the county she could trust; no,
she had no idea how she would support herself when she started to
show, because she was positive her parents wouldn't let her stay in
the house around her younger sisters.

When Colleen suggested they talk about finding somewhere safe
for her to go to wait out the pregnancy, she hadn't meant to bring up
Boston. She didn't want to scare the girl off. But when she blurted
out that she and Andy would take care of her, Elizabeth seized on the
thin hope she offered. "I'm just so scared, Mrs. Mitchell," Elizabeth
whispered into the phone. "I don't know how much longer I can keep
all these secrets from everyone."

"I'm not going to let you down," Colleen said. She explained that
her husband would be arriving in three days, that they would all figure it out together. "Can we meet tonight? Just to talk?"

"There's no way. Mom's already upset because I got a tardy in
fourth period because I was late to class after lunch, and the office
called her. I told her I was at Taco Bell with friends but she didn't believe me."

Colleen tried to hide her dismay. She had to cement this bond,
make sure Elizabeth trusted her enough to confide in her, before
Kristine had a chance to intimidate her into silence. "Is there any
other way for us to get together?"

"I could see you tomorrow at lunch," Elizabeth said. "We just have to be really careful that I get back in time."

It wasn't ideal; Colleen didn't like the idea of being constrained by the short lunch period. She was sure Elizabeth had no idea of the danger Kristine was putting workers in by reporting them to Hunter-Cole, but it was delicate; if the girl sensed that Shay and Colleen were threatening Kristine, she might not be willing to speak to them at all.

"I don't like that she's by herself tonight," Shay said. "Now that we've made Kristine nervous, she's going to try to keep tabs on Elizabeth. She could easily decide to go to see her, make up some excuse about studying or visiting or . . . or anything. When Elizabeth talked to you, all she was thinking about was Paul. But what if Kristine manages to get her thinking that her loyalty is to *her*?"

"But if Elizabeth thinks that Paul is really gone—"

"Kristine won't let her think that. The only thing keeping Elizabeth from telling someone about Kristine's little scam now is that she doesn't know who to tell, because her dad's the chief of police. So Kristine is probably doing everything she can to reassure her that Paul's okay, that he got nervous and left on his own. And that's another way she might talk Elizabeth out of telling us any more—by convincing her it would be endangering Paul."

"Well, we're not doing anything else tonight," Colleen said. "I guess we could go over to the apartment building and keep an eye on Kristine."

"No. Better if we watch the Weyants' house instead. That way, anyone comes to see Elizabeth *or* the chief—someone from Hunter-Cole, Kristine, whoever—we know about it. If we feel like there's any threat, we're right there."

"You're suggesting we do . . . a *stakeout*? On a *cop*? Have you forgotten that we're a couple of middle-aged women with absolutely no experience?"

"That's exactly why this has to work. They'll never guess we'd do anything so stupid."

twenty-seven

RIG TRAFFIC NEVER changed: weekday, weekend, holiday, it was always the same. Hitches ended and new guys came on, and the trucks rolled back and forth all day, every day.

There wasn't a lot of reservation traffic in the store because the Lucky Six, on Central Street half a block from the old folks' home, sold everything Myron stocked, cheaper in most cases. And most people planned ahead, bought their handles of rum and vodka and their cases of beer and soda at the Costco in Minot. Right now, as another moonless, cold night settled in, they were putting together dinner and turning on their TVs and preparing to get their numb on.

T.L. tried to get through his physics homework between customers, but after a while he gave up and settled for flipping through the newest ink and gaming magazines that Myron stocked. Around seven thirty a couple guys came in, headed back home after their twelve-hour shift, coveralls streaked with drilling mud. One of the men bore the imprint of his hard hat on his wiry hair. The other was much younger, with a long, bushy brown beard like some of them grew. The older one interrupted their conversation to slap down a bill on the glass counter and say, "Pack of Newports. You got any Tylenol? Just the single serve, not the bottle?"

"The one's from Massachusetts, is what I heard," the other one said as T.L. got the items from the racks. "I ain't ever met anyone from out east up here." "I met the other one," the wiry-haired man said. He was old enough to be his friend's father. "When I was on the Hunter-Cole job. California boy. Nice kid."

"Can't figure where the fuck they went. I mean . . . sure, you think about it. Ditching. Like, if he didn't have anyone?"

T.L.'s fingers tightened on the pack of Newports, denting the cardboard. He forced himself to relax his grip and smoothed out the dent while his heart thudded in his chest.

"Everybody's got someone somewhere," the older man said. "Eventually, people notice when you don't come home."

"What do you think happened?"

There was a tremor in his voice, and—beard or no—he suddenly seemed even younger, too young to be so far from home, wherever home was. T.L. pushed the cigarettes across the counter and rang up the purchase. He fished two quarters and two pennies from the cash register, not looking at their faces.

The older man shrugged. "Pissed off the wrong guys on the job," he said, ticking off the options on his fingers. "Took off for Mexico for an early spring break. Or maybe they run into a couple of radishes up here and got scalped."

T.L. froze, hand extended across the counter with the man's change. As slurs went, *radish*—red on the outside, white on the inside—was hardly the worst. The man looked past him in the direction of the road, then back. "Hey," he said. "Hey."

T.L. dropped the coins into the man's hand, laid two dollar bills on top.

"I didn't mean nothin'." The young kid was snickering, headed for the doors. But his friend stood his ground, clearing his throat and looking at his change like he was going to give it back.

T.L. shrugged. He could feel the heat on his face and didn't trust himself to speak. A memory came to him, one that had escaped him before: the taller one—he'd had something around his neck that glinted in the sun.

"Look, I'm sorry," the man insisted. "That was . . . I had no call."

"It's okay," T.L. managed.

"I mean, I got no issues with you people. Guy on my rig . . . maybe you know him. David Youngbird. He's from here, right? Good guy."

"Yeah, okay. Thanks." T.L. just needed the guy to go. He'd get Myron's folding chair, the one he kept around for when his back was acting up, and he'd sit down until the next customer came in. Maybe watch the little TV Myron kept under the counter. Pretend to watch it, anyway.

The man turned and followed his friend out. He had a slight limp, favoring one leg and coming down heavy on the other one. A moment later the lights from their truck cut across the doors as they made the tight turn.

Silver chain. Dog tags, like a soldier would wear.

T.L. felt like he was losing his mind. At least Myron knew now. Not being alone with it anymore—that was a comfort.

But there was at least one other person who knew. Which was why he had been trying so hard to get Kristine to talk to him. Because the only way to get to Elizabeth was through her. After Chief Weyant found out that T.L. was dating his daughter, he took away her phone and forbade her to go out. For a while they'd been able to communicate through a Hotmail account she set up and used at school, so that they'd arranged to see each other at football games and outings with her friends. And there were those four times she'd pretended to be at sleepovers, and instead they'd gone for drives in his truck.

Around Halloween, Elizabeth seemed distracted, too busy to see him. She stopped answering his emails. Then right before winter break, he got the news about the scholarship. A full ride to UCLA—a way for them to be together, far from North Dakota, far from her family, her parents' crazy rules. It was what she wanted most in the world—to be somewhere else. To put North Dakota in her rearview mirror and light out for the coast, any coast. And California! When she found out he was applying, she'd been so excited that he felt bad about telling her the odds, telling her that UCLA was nothing but a dream.

A dream that had somehow come true, and she was the first person he texted. That night she snuck out and met him with news of her own: she was pregnant—that was why she'd been so scarce. She'd waited until she was sure, she said, evading his eyes.

They'd cried together; this wasn't what they had planned. It would be all right, Elizabeth promised through her tears. They'd get a tiny apartment near campus, and she'd find a job. They'd take turns watching the baby, and he would study and she would work, and they'd go to the beach on weekends. After all, the beach was free— and it was worlds away from the rolling hills, the endless frigid nothing she'd grown up in.

T.L. was dismayed. They couldn't raise a baby that way. A baby needed family, stability, tradition—everything his mother had denied him and that Myron had provided. There was no way he was starting a family far away from home. He'd never wanted to go to California anyway—he had only been trying to please Myron, but he always intended to come back once he got his degree. T.L. wanted to draw and paint, to work hard and create the family he always wished he had, and he didn't want to do it far from the wide-open sky he'd grown up under.

It was an uneasy parting. Elizabeth had made him promise he'd think about it. That he'd consider L.A. She said she could never be happy living in Fort Mercer, especially since it would be the last nail in the coffin of her relationship with her parents. She'd hinted before that her father was racist, but now she was adamant: *He'll never accept you. He won't let us go anywhere near the reservation.*

T.L. had marshaled his arguments. He'd planned exactly how he would convince her. But he never got the chance, because the next email she sent was to break up with him.

He wrote increasingly frantic emails back. She couldn't do this to him. There was no way he would turn his back on a child he had fathered. He couldn't make Elizabeth love him, but he could make her share custody. He researched it online, sent her the links. The Department of Children and Family Services had a whole program that would help establish paternity—he could force her to take a test, if it came to that. Just hear me out, he begged. He even offered to reconsider the scholarship in California. But he got no response.

Until the week he told her that he had no other choice but to come and talk to her father. That he would get a lawyer if he had to. He had been bluffing, but she didn't know that—it was what finally got her to call him on a borrowed phone. He asked her to meet him. Told her his schedule: a couple of shifts at the store, fishing on Saturday, studying for a math test on Sunday. She said she would find a time and let him know.

Now, in the empty store, his only company the game turned down low on Myron's little television, T.L. thought about what an idiot he was. He'd walked right into the trap, and he was no closer to understanding what had happened than he had been a week and a half ago. He couldn't reach Elizabeth, Kristine wouldn't help him, and Myron had counseled him not to say a word.

twenty-eight

SHAY TOSSED COLLEEN the keys as they walked across the parking lot in the dark. "You drive this time," she said. "This snow's going to kill me."

Colleen drove slowly through town, joining the parade of trucks returning from the rigs and heading back out into the night. The Weyants lived in a sprawling trilevel house in the nicest part of town, a gently sloping subdivision near a nine-hole golf course. She parked in the street that ran parallel above the Weyants' street, where they had an unobstructed view of the driveway, which was helpfully illuminated with a powerful spotlight.

Through the house's back window, they could see the family sitting down to eat. "One, two, three, four, five," Shay counted. "Mom, dad, and all three kids."

"Cozy."

Dinner took less than half an hour. The kids carried plates to the sink; a light went on in the family room, followed by the blue glow of the television. Someone did dishes at the sink.

At seven o'clock the garage door went up. Colleen almost missed it. They'd been turning the car on for a few minutes to warm up whenever it got too cold, running the windshield wipers to clear the snow from the glass, and the blades obscured her view.

Then headlights came on and a little Toyota RAV4 pulled slowly out of the garage.

"Can you see who it is?" Shay demanded.

"I think the driver has long hair. So, Elizabeth or her mom."

"Could be her mom running to the grocery. Or to see friends."

"Let's find out."

Colleen's heart pounded as she started up the truck and drove slowly down the hill, hanging back as far as she dared. The SUV turned right out of the subdivision.

Away from town.

It kept up a steady fifty miles per hour, below the speed limit, which seemed prudent given the weather.

"Where the fuck is she going?" Shay muttered as the miles went by. After they'd been in the car for nearly fifteen minutes, the RAV signaled a right turn onto one of the rural routes that crisscrossed Ramsey County. Colleen took the turn and dropped back even farther, until a set of headlights approached close behind.

"I can't believe there's other traffic on this road," she said, speeding up.

Shay turned her head to look. "They're carrying a load," she said. "They're probably on the clock."

After that Colleen didn't bother to maintain as much distance. If there was traffic at this time of day, even in weather like this, whoever was in the SUV wouldn't give much thought to a vehicle behind them.

It was another several miles before the SUV turned down an unmarked road so narrow that Colleen wouldn't have known it was there except for the fresh tire marks.

"She's meeting someone," Shay guessed.

"Out here? Where are we?"

Off in the distance to the left, they could make out the orange glow of a rig. To the right, a couple more glowing dots studded the distant hills. The SUV drove steadily ahead, headlights bouncing along the road.

Colleen pulled off the road and idled. "What the hell do I do now?"

"Try cutting the lights. The moon's probably enough."

The SUV was far ahead now, disappearing over a gentle rise. With the headlights off, the road in front of the truck was illuminated eerily by the moon, its silvery light shining on the tire tracks. Cautiously, Colleen started forward.

Neither of them spoke. Colleen stayed as close as she could to the other set of tire tracks. The road was marked by bright yellow poles on either side, and she tried to keep between them so they didn't end up in the ditch.

She thought she'd lost the SUV several times, but each time it popped up again on the gently rolling road ahead. As they started down a long incline, Colleen realized that the placid field stretching far to the right at the bottom of the hill wasn't a field at all, but a lake.

The SUV was slowing in front of a tiny boxy shed.

"Hunting blind," Shay said. "Or fishing shack, one or the other. I'd bet money."

The SUV made a lazy turn and pulled up with its lights shining on the shack. A figure in a bulky parka stood in front of the little structure. Behind the shack, Colleen could see another truck.

"There he is, whoever she's meeting," Shay mumbled. "What on earth . . ."

Colleen slowed, the truck crawling along the road, wondering if they'd already been spotted. They descended a swell and were momentarily cut off from the view of the shack. When they came up the other side, Colleen decided there was no way they could assume they were still hidden. She had to hope the driver didn't turn around and look up the hill.

A gasp from Shay made Colleen twist around to see what was wrong. Shay's mouth hung open, her face contorted in an expression of shock. "Oh, God," she said, and then her hand was on the door handle and she was opening the door. "That's Taylor's truck. Oh, my God, I can't believe it, that's Taylor's truck!"

She was in the snow, trying to run, her legs sinking almost to the knees. Colleen jumped out and raced after her. When they got to the tire tracks, it was easier going. Colleen strained to see the figure that had turned now and was looking up the hill. A man. There was something wrong; he seemed to be stumbling, losing his balance. His face was lit white and featureless by the headlights as he lifted a hand to shield his eyes.

He stepped out of the bright glare of the spotlights and for a moment he hesitated, staring at the two women running toward him in the snow.

Then he lurched forward. "Mom!" he yelled. He took three steps, the word still on his lips as he fell to the snowy ground.

twenty-nine

ELIZABETH RAN, HER feet plunging through the crusted snow, desperation the only thing keeping her from falling.

She had been moving toward Paul when he fell. The sound of the car doors behind her were like bullets in her back. It never occurred to her that someone would follow her out here, once she slipped the knot of her family, once she got behind the wheel of her mother's car. Everything in her life was moving forward, toward Paul, toward her future. Paul was still trapped in the net of the past, but Elizabeth would be strong enough for both of them, strong enough for them and for the baby too. Everything had gone wrong and she was to blame, and she was sure she would pay for that later, if there was justice in the world. But for now she could not look back, because it wasn't just her anymore: she had a baby—a family—to take care of.

So she ran. But Shay was faster, wild like a dog racing with its head down and its ears flying, every cell in its body focused on being where it wasn't. Elizabeth witnessed the exact moment when Shay realized that the man on the ground was not her son. Too short, too wide, the wrong clothes—if it weren't for the desperation of her love she would have seen it sooner.

She staggered and Colleen ran into her, she was so close behind. Colleen pushed Shay out of the way as if she was nothing, a rack of clothes, a shopping cart, and Shay's hands went to her mouth and Colleen reached her son and threw herself to the ground.

By then Elizabeth was there too. She knelt on his other side: the two women, like when Jesus died and it was his mother and Mary Magdalene who grieved together, keening over the body and tearing their hair. Except Paul wasn't dead, he couldn't be. Elizabeth found the tab to his coat zipper and pulled it quickly down. Then, more carefully, she unbuttoned the soft cotton shirt with the stiff brown stain she knew she would find there.

The headlights from the car illuminated them in harsh white light, leaching the finer features from Paul's face and the color from his skin. Elizabeth worked carefully, terrified of hurting him further.

"Is he dead?" Colleen screamed. "Oh, my God, please don't let him be dead!"

"He's hurt, Mrs. Mitchell. Can you call nine-one-one?"

Colleen dug frantically in her coat pockets, coming up empty. "My phone—it's in my purse. Oh, God. Oh, *God*."

Elizabeth was going to tell her to run to the car and make the call, when she changed her mind. Paul's skin was hot, much too hot. The heat radiated from his skin, shimmering in the freezing air. *Fever.* He was burning up with it. There was a faint crust of white on his dry, cracked lips. A smell came from him, sweetish and terrible.

He was so much worse than he'd let on. But she would fix this.

"Mrs. Mitchell, stay here with him, please. He's hurt, here, on his stomach. I think it's infected. I'm going to get help."

She didn't wait for a response. She ran toward the car, picking out Shay's footsteps in the snow so she could be faster. Shay had gotten to her feet and was staggering toward the shack. She was looking for her son. She wouldn't find him. Elizabeth felt a crush of emotion—guilt, shame, fear—and then she resolutely pushed the feelings back.

The door of their car was open, and she slid into the driver's seat. Two purses sat on the floor of the passenger side. Elizabeth grabbed the black leather one and pawed through it, found the cell phone in a pink case with a scrolled floral design. No passcode—thank God. Only one bar. She tried the call: nothing.

She felt for the keys, and yes, they were still in the ignition. She slammed the door shut, the car dinging its seat belt warning, but she ignored it. A seat belt was nothing to her. She floored the gas, turning the car in a wide turn, remembering too late that she could easily end up stuck in a drift. Her wheels spun, then—miraculously—bit down into the snow. She let up on the gas and ground her teeth together and willed the tires to find purchase in the tracks they'd made driving down. Slowly she inched up the hill, then picked up speed at the top before slamming on the brakes. She stabbed at the phone, trying again.

When the dispatcher answered, she gripped the phone tighter.

"What is the address of your emergency?"

"A man's hurt. He's, I don't think he's conscious. He got stabbed. We're on the southwest side of Lake Kimimina. There's a fishing shack? It's the only one on this side of the lake."

"I need to know the address."

"It's not marked, it's a farm road. A mile . . . maybe a mile and a quarter past Abernathy Road." She could hear keys tapping, fast.

"You said the victim was stabbed?"

"With a knife. A fishing knife." She thought fast. "I don't think it hit anything important, though."

"Who stabbed him?"

"No—no. He's not here. It didn't happen today. It was days ago. Eleven days. It got infected, it's bad—"

"You're sure the suspect isn't there?" the dispatcher cut in.

"Yes. I'm positive."

"They're on their way as fast as they can. I'm going to give you some medical instructions now, okay?"

"No, no—I can't," Elizabeth said, already hanging up. She couldn't stay in range and also be with Paul, and nothing the dispatcher told her was going to help him now.

She had to get her wits about her. She had to do this exactly right, for Paul. She had to start thinking, fast.

Weeks ago, when she found out about the baby, she had panicked. All her life, Elizabeth had wanted only one thing: to get away. But now it was for real. Now she had to get the baby out too. There was no way on this earth she would let her baby grow up the way she had: trapped, scared, desperate to leave this bleak and empty place.

She grabbed at the first chance that came along. Stupid, *stupid*! Even after Paul had told her he loved her, after they had fallen in love with *each other*. God had listened to Elizabeth's prayers and given her the gift of Paul, and instead of keeping faith the one time it mattered most, she'd turned away, she'd brought disaster down on them all. And let there be no mistake: she knew she was guilty and she knew she deserved to suffer.

But Paul didn't. Not Paul, her Paul. Her love.

With the engine idling she dialed one more number. It took two rings for her father to answer.

"Dad."

"Elizabeth? Where are you?"

He sounded more confused than angry. Elizabeth took a deep breath. "I'm at the fishing shack down that farm road on Lake Kimimina, on the southwest side. You know the one I mean?"

"You're—what the hell is going on?"

"You know where I mean?" she pressed.

"Yes, but—"

"I called an ambulance. Paul Mitchell is here. The boy that disappeared. His mother is here and the other mother too. Paul's hurt bad."

"Wait, wait, slow down. You're with Paul Mitchell? Are you safe?"

"Yes, I'm safe, Dad. Everyone is. But Paul's hurt bad and—and things are going to get . . . They're going to get . . . Dad, I have things to tell you. Everything's gone wrong."

There was a silence—just a short one, but Elizabeth could picture her father's face, the way it looked when he was paged. She'd seen it a hundred times, how he could shut everything else out, narrow down to the phone in his hand and the job in front of him.

"Don't talk to anyone," he said in a clipped voice that sounded nothing like she expected. "I'll be there as soon as I can."

"But, Dad—"

"I mean it, Elizabeth. *Do. Not. Talk.* No matter who gets there, not if you know them or if you don't."

"*Dad,*" she pleaded in a small voice, surprised when a tear dripped off her cheek and onto her lap. "There's something else. You have to make sure Paul is okay. Not just at the hospital. But later when you talk to him, you have to protect him. Don't let them—don't let anything bad happen to him. Promise me."

"What are you talking about? Elizabeth, you're not making any sense, you're—"

"I'm having a *baby*, Dad. I'm pregnant. It's Paul's."

She could hear his sharp intake of breath and then a muttered curse. "Don't talk," he repeated, and hung up.

Elizabeth allowed herself to sit for only a few seconds before she put the phone back into the black purse. Her heart was racing, but she had done it. She had finally told. Now she had to make sure Paul was all right. She turned the truck and headed back down the hill.

The tracks were deep now; she could see the dark undergrowth poking through the snow in places. A thin, wispy cloud slid past the moon, making flickering shadows on the field of snow. As she descended, she looked down on the scene below. Colleen was bent over Paul; her hands flitted over his torso, adjusting, touching, talking, whispering. Shay staggered toward her, coming in the direction of the white truck. The one that had belonged to Taylor. Even with the windows rolled up, even across the distance, she could hear Shay screaming.

Elizabeth felt the terrible thing she had done seep into every corner of her body. She had already accepted that she would pay in ways that she didn't even understand yet. If hell waited, she'd go willingly—after she raised this child and spent her life with Paul. She'd pay when payment was due and not a moment earlier.

But watching Shay lurch across the snow, her hands opening and closing around nothing, Elizabeth understood for the first time that she had ended a mother's life too. She pressed a hand to her flat belly, imagined the tiny embryo inside her, growing, waving its hands languidly in the warm liquid world of her womb, blind and not even aware that there were colors and sounds in the world, two parents to love it. Elizabeth made a wordless promise to her baby and gained speed down the hill.

For the first time she understood that she was just like them now. Mothers: they were all the same, even if only Elizabeth's child was still protected and unharmed. But someday her baby would go out into the world as well, and things would happen, joyful things and terrible things and things he or she would never recover from and others that would feel like revelation.

She parked where the car had been before and turned the ignition off. She left the keys where they were and got out, closing the door gently. She walked through the snow, unblinking, watching one mother's joy and another's agony. She was numb with the new understanding that it wasn't her love for Paul that had transformed her, after all. She loved him and she would love him more tomorrow and even more the day after that, but it was motherhood that had made her something new.

"They're coming," she called. "Help is on its way."

Colleen only nodded, unable to tear her gaze away from Paul. His lips were parted and he was breathing fast and shallow, his eyes rolling up in his head.

Elizabeth needed to go to him, but there was one last thing she had to do first. She went to Shay, who was shivering in the wind, arms locked across her chest. Elizabeth stood directly in front of her, but even then she wasn't sure the woman saw her. Her pale hair whipped around her shoulders, knotted and snarled. Her eyes were wide with shock. Her eyelids were purple and finely veined, bare of makeup.

"Mrs. Capparelli," she said. When the woman turned her unfocused gaze Elizabeth's way, she put her hand on her arm. "Mrs. Capparelli."

"Where is he?" Shay rasped, her voice like dried leaves stirred on pavement.

Elizabeth swallowed and forced herself to look into Shay's eyes. "I'm so sorry."

"Tell me he's alive. Just tell me he's alive."

But Elizabeth could only keep repeating "I'm sorry. I'm sorry."

thirty

THE PARAMEDICS SWARMED around Paul and told Colleen to step aside, but it felt like only part of her backed away. Like that TV show from long ago, when an angel came to escort the dead to heaven, and a ghostly shadow of the person clambered out of the motionless body in the hospital bed or at an accident scene.

With Colleen it was the opposite. Her soul, the essence of her—certainly everything that was good and worthy about her—stayed behind with Paul, praying and promising to always love him best, while her poor, tired body carried on. She would not allow Death here. She looked around, past the strobing lights and all the police and paramedics trampling the snow, as if Death might appear in a guise she hadn't thought of, creeping and finagling its way toward Paul with its greedy snatching fingers. She had to be on guard for what others couldn't see, the terrible things that came when you were least expecting them, when you thought it was an ordinary day and yours was an ordinary family.

No day was safe, and no sacrifice was enough. If life had taught Colleen nothing else, it had taught her that. She thought she had been vigilant before, but she hadn't been able to protect her son from the threats that waited, always, just out of reach. Still, she had nothing to give besides her total dedication, her disregard for her own self.

But maybe her selflessness was a more potent weapon than she had realized. It had gotten her here, hadn't it? And it made it possible for her to endure Shay's screaming, over there, kneeling in the snow. One of the paramedics had been trying to help her, talking to her, trying to help her stand, but then he got called over to help with Paul. He left Shay there, on her knees, so Colleen watched over Shay as she picked up handfuls of snow in her bare, red hands and smashed them down, like a child too young to make a proper sand castle. Her hair had escaped its barrette and strands of it stuck to her face. Smudged makeup ringed her eyes, and a narrow strip of her back was exposed where her jacket rode up above her jeans. She had been screaming so long that her voice was going hoarse.

Someone should go to her. Someone should comfort her.

Colleen looked back at the paramedics and police. She counted six, seven, eight of them, two ambulances and two police cars and an unmarked car. Elizabeth was standing between the two cruisers, talking to a man in a parka and a knit hat. Everyone else clustered around Paul. They were getting ready to put him on the board, adjusting things around his face, doing things with the straps.

When Colleen had touched Paul's face, he was burning hot, raging hot. It had been eleven days since he was wounded, but she still didn't know what had happened. Who had done that to him? Where had they gone? Who had cared for him after? Had he been afraid?

And what had happened to Taylor? Had Paul . . . ?

No no no.

Colleen bit her lip hard enough to taste blood. She followed the paramedics' progress toward the ambulance, watched them lift Paul through the open doors. The man standing with Elizabeth broke away from her to talk to the paramedics.

Colleen hurried over to take his place. "Elizabeth."

The girl turned her face toward Colleen and it was obvious she had been crying. She dabbed at her eyes with a crumpled tissue. "Oh . . . Mrs. Mitchell."

"Did he do it?"

The question hung in the air between them, and Colleen knew she couldn't turn back from the answer. If Paul had done something, if he had . . . if he had lost control of a situation, if the anger had taken hold of him the way it used to, then what? It had been such a long time since Paul had slipped, and Colleen had believed he had outgrown it because she wanted to, because she had to. A devil had been purged, a problem had been handled.

She remembered Paul on his knees in the kitchen the day before he left for North Dakota, cleaning up the shards of glass and crockery, his eyes swollen from crying. She had convinced herself it ended there. He'd had a bad moment, but all it had cost was a few plates before he got himself under control. And he'd been so remorseful, anyone could have seen that.

If it had come back and taken hold of Paul, this consuming evil, then Colleen would not fail him. She would take this poor battered echo of herself and find the strength to face his future, and gird herself with whatever it took to save him.

But in this trembling second, between speaking the damning question and finding out the answer, she was as vulnerable as anything on this earth.

Please God.

In front of her, Elizabeth shivered and blinked, hugging herself in her too-thin coat. "Did he do what, Mrs. Mitchell? Do you mean Paul?"

"*Did. He.*" Colleen squeezed her eyes shut and clenched her fists and ground her teeth together, trying to make the words.

"Oh, my God, no!" Elizabeth's eyes widened with shock, and she reached for Colleen's hands, squeezing them through her pink mittens. "It was an accident. I swear to you, Mrs. Mitchell, Paul didn't do anything on purpose, this was all my fault. I asked him to . . . Paul was trying to help me. *Us*. He did this for us, the baby. Taylor was . . . he just fell in. It was no one's fault, he just didn't know. Paul tried to save him. He lay on the ice and he . . . it was cracking underneath him but he stayed until, until he was all the way gone, until there was no hope. Mrs. Mitchell, I swear to you, Paul was a . . ."

She blinked. Colleen thought she was going to say *hero*. Instead, Elizabeth shook her head.

"He fell in?" Colleen felt the edges of something sharp crowding her heart. Like joy, but more painful. "Taylor fell in the water? He drowned?"

"Yes, in the lake. The ice broke."

"Were they fighting?"

"Taylor and *Paul*? No, no. They were best friends, Mrs. Mitchell. It was T.L."

"But that's . . ." There was more to the story, so much she didn't understand, but Taylor's death had not been Paul's fault. Colleen started backing away, desperate to see her son again, knowing what she knew now.

"It was my fault," Elizabeth whispered, as Colleen turned and left her there.

thirty-one

T.L. HAD BEEN sitting in the interview room for an hour and ten minutes, checking his phone and tugging at his collar whenever the heat cycled on, when Weyant finally came.

The chief of police paused in the doorway, holding on to both sides of the frame as though he was trying to remain standing. He looked terrible, his hair pushed forward, his shirt wrinkled and not all the way tucked in on one side. Stubble made the skin of his face appear pale and waxy, as if a thumb pressed into it would leave a dent. His eyes were red and unfocused like a drunk's, but T.L. knew that Weyant didn't drink.

"My daughter's knocked up," he said, his voice shredded and hoarse. "I just came from the hospital. They confirmed it. She says you're not the father. Is that true?"

T.L. went still, his fingers curled against his legs. He was wearing the jeans he'd had on yesterday, the ones he'd dropped on the floor when he'd gone to bed, exhausted, after closing up the store. They were softened from wear, the seams frayed. He tugged at loose threads while he tried to look Weyant in the eye.

"That's what she told me." *Sir*, he added automatically in his mind, but he wouldn't give the man the satisfaction. Not now. Too much had happened, he'd been accused once too often. All he'd done was what seemed right, every step of the way.

At first, Elizabeth said the baby was his. It was only later, when he refused to consider moving to L.A. with her and the baby, that she changed her tune. He should have believed her then. He should have backed off then. But T.L. had known only one direction since he went to live with Myron: ahead. Keep moving ahead, because behind you was a place you never wanted to return to.

"What do *you* say?" Weyant leaned in, as though some barrier prevented him from coming into the room. He brought with him a faint smell of cooked onions, not unpleasant. Whatever Elizabeth's mom had made for dinner hours ago.

T.L. felt the fight drain out of him, like air from an inner tube that had run over a nail. He'd thought he would stand up to Weyant, take full advantage of his youth and anything else he could think of to blunt the man's attack. Now he just felt exhausted.

"You can't keep me in here," he said. "I didn't do anything."

"So get up and fucking walk out."

The word, coming from the chief, was shocking. He was strait-laced to the core, the sort of man who parted his hair and shined his own shoes. They regarded each other for a moment, and then the chief seemed to change his mind. "Your uncle's sitting out there in my waiting room."

"Yeah, I know. He followed the car over here when they brought me in. Nobody said he couldn't."

"It's a free country." The chief rubbed the bridge of his nose with one of his meaty hands. "You know he broke my nose once. He ever tell you that?"

"What?"

Weyant regarded him carefully. "You know we knew each other. Back in the nineties."

"You wrestled," T.L. said uncertainly, something Myron had told him when he started seeing Elizabeth. *Be careful of him*, Myron had cautioned. *He doesn't fight fair.* "You went into the army when he was still in high school."

"Yeah. But I'm asking you, did you know me and your uncle have a history?"

T.L. shook his head, bewildered.

Weyant waited him out, drumming his fingers on the table. "All right. Never mind that. I want a statement from you. What happened that day, to that boy. Taylor Capparelli."

"Could I . . ." T.L.'s voice was dangerously close to cracking. He cleared his throat, sat up a little straighter in the chair. "I want Myron here. I'll tell you everything right now, you let him come in here."

"Your uncle's got the res lawyer out of bed. He's heading over now. Might as well wait for him." He ran a hand through his hair, messing up the part. "Might as well make it a fucking party. Christ."

THE LAWYER, JACK Cook, had taught T.L. to tie flies. There had been five or six eight-year-old Cub Scouts around a banquet table in the rec hall where the troop held their meetings. Mr. Cook and Mr. Whitecalf wore their tan scout leader shirts over their work clothes, their polyester button-downs and stained ties. Mr. Whitecalf sold insurance, and the two men were the only dads T.L. knew who wore ties to work.

Mr. Cook's son had already been in high school then, living with his mother downstate. As far as T.L. knew, they'd never reconciled and Mr. Cook never remarried. He had a stroke a few years ago; he was hard to understand now and didn't use his left hand. He still drove and fished, but the limp appendage added to his general air of disheveled shabbiness, and for a fleeting second T.L. wished there was someone else who could come in here and make Weyant feel small.

The recorder was on and they had moved into a bigger room to accommodate all four of them. It smelled of burnt popcorn and air freshener. There was a fake Christmas tree wrapped in a garbage bag in the corner, its stiff branches poking through the plastic.

Mr. Cook had accepted a cup of coffee, which seemed like poor strategy. Also, he had an actual yellow pad. T.L. suspected that a better attorney would have a laptop. Myron sat with his arms folded across his chest, staring at Weyant as though this was a livestock auction and the chief was leading one underfed calf after another up across the block. It was nearly four in the morning.

"I'd caught a walleye but it was less than a foot long and I threw it back," T.L. began, choosing a scratch on the table to focus his attention on. "I'd had good luck at that spot before, but it was early in the afternoon and I wasn't catching much."

He'd gone farther out that day than he should have, but he had his ice picks at hand, laced through his sleeves so that he'd be able to pull himself out in seconds if worst came to worst. He'd learned about the ice in Boy Scouts too. It had been his friend Alan's dad who demonstrated how to distribute your body weight if the ice started to give out under you, facedown in his Carhartt jacket on a sloping field of switchgrass since the lake had only begun to freeze for the season. How they threw themselves into it, a bunch of ten-year-old kids in dirty Wranglers and stiff shirts that their mothers sewed their badges on, all but T.L., whose badges were glued in place by Myron, so that the shirt could never be washed. They pressed themselves into the scratchy ground and giggled as Alan's paunchy, bald father yelled, "This is *serious*, boys, this is life and death—"

T.L. had no death wish, but he was in a gloomy mood. On that frigid day, the postholiday pall lay heavy on the town. Plastic garland hung twisted and limp from street posts, and the Walmart parking lot was full of people returning the gifts they'd received. He'd texted Elizabeth twice the day before, and again she'd ignored him.

He was on the ice by one, having spent the morning helping Myron retag the remainder of the holiday merchandise, the crap that didn't sell at half off. Now it was 80 percent off and the reservation kids would come and buy it. T.L. had stopped for a Subway sandwich on his way to the lake and he ate it after he got his line in the water, tossing the crusts into the water and watching the fathead minnows come to the surface to nibble at them, tiny mouths jerking, bodies twisting and bumping against one another.

It was almost two o'clock when the white truck came down the road to the public beach and parked a hundred feet back from his own truck. Two figures got out; from this distance it wasn't possible to make out much about them other than one was tall and one was average. The truck was new, shiny and big. T.L. figured it was bought with oil money.

Both men dug knit caps from their pockets and pulled them over their heads. They were the type of cap with holes for eyes, the cheap orange ones you could get for six bucks at Walmart. They walked down to the lake, struggling through patches of jutting weeds and scabs of dirty snow, and started out on the ice toward him.

The shorter one had a baseball bat.

That was when T.L. got scared. He would have run, but he couldn't safely go any farther out on the lake. Behind the ice was honeycombed and uneven. Two hundred yards away he could see water shimmering in the sun.

That left only one escape route. If he didn't go toward the men, he could go to the right, but the shore dipped at that point and he would have an extra fifty yards of ice to cross. A man on land could easily outrun him. Two men could trap him and take away his options.

T.L. stood his ground, hand on his belt where he kept his bait knife in a leather sheath that had belonged to his grandfather. He eyed the auger lying on the ice, wondered if he should make a grab for it.

His considered the possibilities. Most likely, these were nothing but hopheads—there were plenty of them these days, guys who couldn't get through a shift without a hit of meth or Adderall. They went on benders between hitches, coming back on the job more strung out than when they'd left. In town, the pharmacy had been broken into twice, looted of prescription uppers; men coming out of bars and nightclubs were held up for their cash and phones.

Maybe these two would take his truck. It wasn't worth more than three thousand, thirty-four hundred tops, and there they were with a new Silverado. Still, desperation made people do crazy shit. In his wallet was thirty bucks and Elizabeth's senior portrait, which he had promised himself he would get rid of.

"T.L. Collier," the short one said, passing the bat from one hand to the other and ending that line of thought. They knew him, but T.L. didn't recognize the voice.

"Yeah?" He stood with his hands hanging at his sides, his legs slightly apart. He'd played football in the fall, putting in a dismal season but welcoming the distraction from the breakup, and he was feeling strong. He'd take either of these guys in a fair fight. Together—and with the bat—he didn't stand a chance. "Tell me what you want and you can be on your way. I'm going to reach for my keys, now. Keys to my truck? Okay? You want them?"

His hand hovered outside his pocket, considering going for the knife. But one swing of the bat, even a clumsy one, would knock it from his hand.

"I know what you did to Elizabeth," the short one said. "I *saw.*"

T.L. blinked. Everything shifted. Elizabeth flashed in his mind— the last time he'd seen her, before her dress rehearsal for her fall choir concert. It had a Halloween theme, and she'd been wearing a glittering mask that she pushed up on her forehead. It held her hair back, and as she turned away it gave the illusion of a jeweled crown, and she'd looked like a movie star from the old days, like Grace Kelly. That was when she'd told him she couldn't see him anymore.

"I haven't seen her in months," he said. Then he told a lie. "She doesn't mean anything to me."

"That why you *beat* her, man? That why she's black-and-blue under her clothes? You're a fucking coward, hurting her where no one can see it!"

The taller one said something that T.L. couldn't hear, his voice low and steady.

"You're going to stay away from her, man." The tall one stepped forward, close enough that T.L. could see the fringe of light brown hair coming out of the bottom of the cap. His eyes were narrowed and intense through the holes. "You hear? Don't talk to her, don't call her, don't text her, don't even say her name."

"Yeah, sure, whatever," T.L. said. He had no idea what they thought he'd done. *Beat* her? The last time he'd touched Elizabeth, he'd wound that silky hair of hers around his hand, pulled her gently closer, inhaled her perfume, and she had whimpered—but not from pain. Her body, pale and almost shimmering in the faint light of the setting sun, stretched across the truck's bench seat in the middle of an alfalfa field early in October, had been perfect. Flawless.

Had someone else done something to her? But who? He'd never seen these guys in his life, and besides, how would Elizabeth meet a rig man? As he cast about for an explanation, out of the corner of his eyes he saw the shorter one get a two-hand grip on the bat and get ready to charge him.

T.L. tried to sidestep, but he was too slow and the bat caught him across the hip. He heard wood on bone before he felt it. The blow was hard enough to knock him to the ice, pain shooting through his body. The guy raised the bat and T.L. was sure he was going to bring it down on his head. His friend tried to stop him, grabbing for the bat, blocking the hit, and it crashed down on T.L.'s groin, glancing off his thigh in an agony of pain that made him gasp. He rolled onto his side in time to throw up on the ice.

"Stop! Paul, Jesus!" The tall one wrestled for the bat. T.L. forced himself to roll to his knees. He'd absorbed most of the hit in his gut. He didn't think his hip bone was broken. Maybe a rib or two. He tried to crawl, got a few feet away and felt rather than heard a cracking deep in the ice.

The others must have sensed it too because they paused, long enough for T.L. to grab his knife. He nearly dropped it before getting a good grip on the handle.

The tall one had wrested the bat free. He flung it toward shore, and the sound of it skittering across the ice reminded T.L. of pickup hockey games, a handful of boys and a single chipped puck, half of them with branches for sticks. "Paul!" the guy yelled again, holding onto his friend's sleeve. "Enough!"

"It's not enough until I know he's going to stay away from her," he said, kicking T.L. as he tried to crawl sideways out of the way. He reached for the guy's foot as he landed another kick, and held on. He slid and fell, his friend losing his grip on him, and landed on T.L., causing waves of agony through his battered hip. As he writhed in pain, the guy went for his throat, clutching and shoving. T.L. tried to push him off, but he had leverage, his knee on his gut.

It happened without thought—T.L. arced his wrist out and then slammed it into the other man's side, into the puffy orange down coat. It was only when it lodged fast that he realized what he'd done. He let go immediately, the handle protruding from the jacket only for a second as the guy lurched clumsily off of him, before falling to the ice. A blooming spot of red appeared on the torn fabric of the coat.

T.L. had no idea how badly he had wounded the man, but he was coming toward him again, ignoring the injury, so that had to be good, right? T.L. scrambled on his hands and knees like a crab, trying to ignore the pain, and it wasn't until the lake sighed and splintered again that he realized he had been heading backward. The wrong way.

"Watch out!" he yelled, because if they didn't get off the cracking ice, they were all dead. The injured man went still, cocking his head, and T.L. knew he heard it too. The cracking was splintering and racing toward them along invisible fissures and fault lines below the opaque white surface. Underneath, the black water was hungry for them.

He went flat on his stomach, arms and legs spread like a child making snow angels, and T.L. knew he'd learned the same thing, wherever he came from. How not to die when the ice reaches for you.

The other one hadn't.

He was looking at his feet, dumbfounded, as the first large crack split the ice and the water rushed over his boots. At first that was all it was, an inch or two, flooding the listing plane of ice. T.L. was already scrambling backward, body pressed flat and legs and arms extended, his weight distributed as widely as possible. The injured man was flat on his stomach too, but he wasn't moving. He was screaming and reaching for his friend.

"Get down get down get down—"

But he didn't. And then the ice took him.

"HE ALMOST DIDN'T make it," T.L. said. Someone had put a plastic cup of water in front of him. He was thirsty, his throat raw and his lips dry and cracking. But he didn't reach for the water.

"Who? Paul?" Weyant had barely reacted to the story, fixing him with that unblinking gaze. Jack Cook seemed to be trying to stay awake, his eyelids drooping more than usual. Only Myron looked upset, putting his hand flat against his sternum and swallowing hard.

"Paul. Yes. When Taylor went in, Paul was back two, three feet from where the ice broke. He went forward a few inches and I turned back around. I thought—I don't know, I guess I thought maybe I could grab his boots and pull him, keep him from going in. But, you know . . ."

"He'd been *beating* you." Finally unable to restrain himself, Myron burst out. "He was irrational. You would have been crazy to help, he could have got you both killed."

T.L. didn't meet his uncle's gaze. He pressed his teeth together, welcomed the ache in his skull. "He tried to reach out for Taylor, but Taylor was fighting the water. You know. Doing everything wrong."

No one said anything, but everyone in the room could visualize what had happened. It took only ninety seconds in the water before you had no chance of saving yourself.

"What did you do after, Theodore?"

The chief's voice had a hard edge. The name was jarring in a small way; no one had called T.L. by his given name since he was a child. Even his driver's license said T.L. Weyant knew that; when Elizabeth had brought him to dinner, he'd shook his hand and stared him down and said "T.L." as though it was a curse.

"I . . . went to my truck."

"When you left, you believed that Taylor was dead and Paul was injured."

"Hey," Myron said, placing his hand flat on the table. A warning. "Those boys tried to *kill* him."

"We don't know that." Some dull animosity lingered between the two men. "I understand Theodore feared for his life, but Paul and Taylor may have been just trying to send a message. A warning."

"He said that kid had the bat raised up in two hands, coming down on his skull. You want to tell me that ain't attempted murder?"

"It's okay," T.L. cut in. "Myron, it's all right." He shifted his gaze back to the chief. "I got off the ice, first thing. That's what I learned to do. Once it starts to go, you don't know where it reaches to. I stayed down until I was close to the shore. Then I got up and I ran to my truck."

He crawled and slithered and felt the ice's angry drumline pounding its finale through his body. Ice got in his mouth and scraped his face and caked every crevice of his clothes, and Paul was yelling something that T.L. couldn't make out. Panic, that was for sure, terror and grief.

T.L. had never watched a man die on the ice, but there was that winter when the deer broke through and three of them watched from the shore, him and Mark and Keith. They'd been getting high around a driftwood fire, the joint burning down to nothing as they watched, transfixed by the sheer desperation in the deer's thrashing, the stillness when it finally gave up and sank, something he would never forget.

When he finally stood up and ran for the truck, he didn't turn around. He slipped and fell on the slope up from the shore. When he tried to get his keys out of his pocket, his hand was numb and clumsy. He didn't look back when he drove away: after revving the engine twice, he turned the heat to full blast, letting the harsh sound block out everything else except the snowy road ahead.

"So that's it. He told you everything."

"You didn't tell anyone what happened." Weyant ignored Myron, watching T.L.

T.L. shook his head. "No one."

"Even though a boy was *dead*."

"Sir." T.L. held his gaze. "I know how you feel about me. You've hated me ever since I first went out with your daughter. If I came in here and told you I got into a fight, and one of the other guys is dead, you think I'm going to expect you'll believe my side?"

He was breathing hard. The recording device made a *whir-click*, but otherwise the room was silent.

Weyant reached across the table and shut off the recorder. He pushed back his chair.

"You're wrong," he said tonelessly. "I haven't hated you since you took my daughter out. I've hated you since the day you were born."

thirty-two

COLLEEN WOKE AGAIN and there was light seeping through the windows. Morning, then, finally. She'd been lying on a vinyl couch in the hospital waiting room. Earlier, when she was tossing and turning, there were other people here. An old woman with a scarf wrapped round and round her neck, who sat with knitting on her lap, unmoving. Later, a big man with a T-shirt that didn't cover his belly came and sat next to her, faint music coming from his earbuds. Angry, cacophonous music, turned up so loud Colleen could hear it across the room.

They were both gone now. She sat up, feeling the ache in her hips, the cottony bad taste of sleep in her mouth. Her phone was on the end table, where she'd left it so she wouldn't miss a call. But there was only a text from Andy: Got on 2:00 arr. Lawton 4:58. Got car. Call when you get this.

She dialed, glancing around the waiting room. The nurse at the desk was turned away from her, talking softly on the phone. It was a different one from earlier.

"Andy," she said, the minute he picked up.

"How are you?"

"I'm—I'm fine, I guess. A little achy from sleeping on the couch."

"They didn't give you a cot? Or one of those bed chairs?"

"They didn't let me stay in the room. They've got—there's a police officer there. Sitting outside." With the straight-backed chair, the paunch, the radio—just what you'd expect.

"Aw, hell. Did you ever get to talk to him at all?"

"For a few minutes." She blinked at the memory. "He was pretty out of it. He just said . . ."

He had an IV taped to his arm, a bag slowly dripping. Equipment glowing in the dim room. His eyes were swollen and heavy. When he looked at her, it took a moment for him to focus. The first thing he said: "I'm going to marry her. When I get out."

"He thinks he's going to jail," she said quietly.

She had tried to call Andy in the middle of the chaos at the fishing shack, after they loaded Paul into the ambulance, but she didn't have cell reception. The police let her drive Shay's car out, after she agreed that she wouldn't try to keep pace with the ambulance. She kept her eyes on the road and the speedometer, and as she drove she murmured a prayer, over and over: *Thank you, God. Oh, thank you, God.* It wasn't until she was in the hospital parking lot that she tried Andy again. He'd answered right away—he was already up and getting ready to go to the office—and she'd said, "He's all right, Paul is alive," and then both of them were talking and crying at once.

It had been a moment of such pure joy, a moment that was lost to memory now, with reality shadowed over with doubt and dread. How quickly she had gone from gratitude that her son was alive to worry about what came next.

"Colleen, I'm not going in today. I'll leave for the airport around noon and I'll come straight to the hotel when I land. Remember, it's the Homewood Suites, right? Will you be able to get over there and get checked in?"

It took her a moment to catch up, and then she remembered.

The room Vicki had found, just a few days ago when everything had been different.

Her things were still in the other room, the one Shay had gotten for them. Shay: there, alone. At least, Colleen assumed she was still there; it was where the cops took her last night. Had they stayed to make sure she was all right?

What did it say about Colleen that she had not bothered to wonder, all the long night on the waiting room couch, how Shay was doing, in her first hours as the mother of a dead child?

"Andy, I need you to do something. Before you get on the plane."

"What?"

"Get Shay's daughter on a flight. And her son-in-law if he can come, and their daughter. Can you do that?"

There was a pause. "Colleen . . . last night you said . . . with everything that happened, and the police being involved—"

"Taylor is *dead.*" She was impatient now, even though she knew she had no right to be. "I know. But it wasn't Paul's fault. It *wasn't.*"

"Colleen . . ."

Colleen gripped the phone harder and hunched over. The nurse was talking to someone else now, paying her no attention. She could smell coffee coming from somewhere down the hall.

Last night it had all tumbled out, Andy trying to get her to slow down, to sort out the facts. The *facts.* What had it mattered then? Their son was *alive.* Taylor was dead, and that was all she knew.

In the few short moments that she had spent in Paul's hospital room, she hadn't learned much. She touched his face, kissed his forehead, smoothed his hair back. He asked for water and she held the bent straw to his lips. He didn't seem especially glad she was there. She thought he might have gone back to sleep, but then his eyes fluttered open and he looked at her and said, "It's all my fault."

But that couldn't be. Elizabeth said it was all *her* fault. *He did this for us, the baby.*

Taylor had drowned, and there had been another boy there. Why hadn't she asked Elizabeth the rest? What could have possibly happened that night? And worst of all, why did Paul think he was responsible?

The other boy. The one who ran away. He was complicit. Paul had been there when the tragedy happened, and he felt guilty about it and ashamed. He thought he was letting his parents down again, letting himself down. And he was sensitive. No one ever understood that Paul felt everything more deeply than most people. So even if it wasn't his fault that Taylor had died, he would blame himself. It would all get sorted out, and maybe they had all played some part, maybe they all bore some responsibility, but eventually Paul would come to understand that he alone hadn't made it happen.

Darren Terry's face came into her mind, the face she never allowed herself to think about. His yearbook picture, taken before it happened. Everyone acted like *that* was black and white, but it wasn't. It was shades of gray. Darren, and he wasn't the only one, had tormented Paul, pushed and pushed until something had to give.

This was different. Paul had friends now. He had a *best* friend. Whatever had led them out onto the ice, whatever was at the heart of the conflict, it wasn't just Paul, it was all of them. And Taylor was dead and that was unbelievably tragic, her heart was breaking over it, but he had been there too, he had been a part of it.

"Just get them out here, okay, Andy?"

So he recited the names back, Brittany and Robert and Leila Litton from Fairhaven, California. He said he would text their flight information when he had it. "You'll need to call Shay and let her know."

Colleen was silent, biting her lip. She had to go to the hotel room anyway. Her things were there. Shay was there. Alone.

"All right," she said softly, and hung up without saying good-bye.

I'm going to marry her. The first thing Paul had said last night, but she hadn't told Andy. She wanted to go back into that hospital room, to hold her son, to see him for herself, but something about the way he had looked at her last night made her hesitate.

The other thing he'd said: *It's all my fault.*

And finally, when she started to protest, to beg him not to think about that now—*Don't talk, just do what the doctors tell you. Daddy will be here soon*—the confusion had drained out of his eyes and he had pushed her hands away. "Leave me alone," he'd said. "I don't want you here."

IT WOULDN'T HAVE mattered. The door to Paul's room was closed. The police officer was pushing his chair down the hall. "The chief is in with him now," he said over his shoulder. "I'm sure you can see him after. Chief's lifted guard detail. I'm going home."

Colleen was suddenly exhausted. She needed to see Shay and then she needed sleep. Tonight, when Andy got here, they would come back to the hospital. They'd visit with Paul together. She wouldn't tell Andy that Paul had said he didn't want her there; by to-night everything would look different, to all of them. Paul would feel better. He would be sorry for the way he'd spoken to her—he always was. She wouldn't mention it and they would just start again.

But there was one more thing, first.

Elizabeth had been here, in the hospital. Colleen had seen her last night, during one of the many long, anxious fits between her rest-less dozing. She had been walking down the hall with a thin, blond woman who had to be her mother. Only now did it occur to Colleen that the girl had experienced a shock too. What if it had been too much for her? What if the baby—?

"Are you sure she wasn't admitted?" she demanded, and the nurse glared at her. She didn't understand, how could she? *She's carrying my grandchild*, Colleen wanted to explain. Didn't that mean something? Didn't that give her rights?

thirty-three

COLLEEN THOUGHT ABOUT Elizabeth as she drove through the pale, wintry morning to the Hyatt. The girl, standing in the dark last night, hugging herself, watching Shay fall to her knees, screaming. What had she been feeling? What did she know?

The hotel lobby was empty, classical music playing softly. There was the muffled sound of a vacuum cleaner down the hall. A gas fire burned behind glass in the faux fireplace. The silk flower arrangement, the sofas, the patterned rug—all of these were exactly as they had been when Shay brought her here two nights ago. Only two nights since she and Shay slept in the same bed, bound by their desperation and their hope.

"May I help you?"

Colleen put a hand on the sofa to steady herself. She was suddenly feeling shaky. Food . . . when was the last time she had eaten anything? Her face felt droopy and waxy. She could smell her own odor mixed with the faint scent of her hair spray.

"Oh," she said, trying to force a smile. "If you'll just give me a second."

The wave of dizziness passed. Colleen clutched the collar of her coat tightly despite the hot air blasting from the heating system.

Shay hadn't answered her phone or Colleen's texts. Colleen approached the desk, thinking fast.

"I've . . . lost my key," she said, reaching in her purse for her wallet. She opened it and showed the clerk her driver's license. "I think my friend put my name on the reservation . . . Shay Capparelli."

The young woman typed at her keyboard, the pleasant smile never leaving her face. Every girl in Lawton seemed to have the same friendly demeanor, the same sweet and compliant nature.

"Here you go," she said, taking a card from under the counter and sliding it into a paper sleeve.

"Thank you." Colleen realized she had no idea what the room number was. "Um . . . that was . . . three fifteen?" she said, guessing wildly. "I'm sorry, it's just—"

The young woman looked at her curiously, and Colleen blushed. What must she think? That Colleen was returning from a hookup?

"There was an accident," she said, attempting a weary smile. The lies came so much more smoothly now. "I was a witness. I had to go to the police station to give a statement, and now I'm exhausted."

"Oh *no*," the girl said. "Is everyone all right? Oh, I'm sorry, what a stupid question, if they were, you wouldn't have had to go to the station."

"No, no, everyone's fine, just a few scratches. It was just the cars that were damaged. Totaled, both of them."

"Oh, thank the Lord," the girl said. Her relief seemed genuine. What was it with these people, here in the overlooked center of the country, that they were willing to pray for strangers, to take on others' pain? "Anyway, it's room three thirteen. Is there anything else I can do for you, Mrs. Mitchell? I can schedule housekeeping for later this afternoon so you can get some rest . . ."

Colleen thanked her and headed toward the elevators. She found the room and paused in front of the door. It was painted a rich orange shade, a detail she hadn't noticed the other night. All she had to do was knock. It was time, it was the next step.

But she was so afraid. That Shay would slam the door in her face—that would be the least of it. Maybe she would try to hurt Colleen, kill her even, an eye for an eye.

Kneeling in the snow, Shay had never stopped screaming. She lashed out at everyone who came near her, as if she was trying to pull them down onto the ground with her. Colleen had been focused on Paul; she turned her back on Shay and tried to block the screaming from her ears. After they loaded Paul into the ambulance, she looked for Shay and saw her leaning on one of the police officers, all the fight gone out of her as he walked her to a cruiser.

That had been around three in the morning. Six hours had passed since then. What had Shay been doing? Had the police officer walked her up to the room, at least? Had she slept? Had she woken up and remembered and started screaming again?

All was quiet now. Colleen knocked. She waited a long time, but there was nothing, no sound from within the room. She tried again, and still nothing.

She let herself in with the key.

The room was dark, the drapes closed except for a gap of an inch or two. It took a moment for Colleen to spot Shay. She was lying on the floor next to the window, curled into a ball, still wearing her coat. The hood served as a sort of pillow. She was turned away from Colleen, staring through that small gap. Or maybe she was asleep.

Or—

"Shay!" Colleen raced across the room and knelt next to her, grabbing her arm and turning her over. What if she'd come back here and decided she had nothing left? Colleen's sleeping pills were still in her toiletry case, hers and Andy's—enough, maybe, if Shay took them all—

Shay's eyes fluttered open and she looked up at Colleen. She was so light, like a child, her limbs thin and flopping.

"Are you all right?" Colleen demanded. "You didn't do anything, did you?"

Shay made a sound that was almost a laugh, an expulsion of breath. She leaned up on her elbows and sighed. "You want to know if I tried to kill myself?"

Already Colleen saw that it was ludicrous. Shay was so much stronger than that. She would never choose the easy escape—that was for women like Colleen. Her face burned with shame.

"I don't know," Shay said, sitting up the rest of the way and leaning against the sliding door. Her voice was raspy. Her hair was knotted and tangled; combing it out was going to be a big job. Mascara was smudged under her eyes. "Maybe I should. I hadn't thought that far ahead. Can you get me my purse?"

Colleen found it near the door, where Shay must have dropped it. Shay got out her cigarettes and lighter, her hands shaking. "Can you open that?" she asked, inclining her head toward the sliding door. "Wouldn't want good old Scott Cohen to get stuck with the bill if they figure out I was smoking in here."

Colleen slid the door open a few inches. The balcony held a plastic table and chairs that were crusted with ice. Cold air rushed into the room. Shay lit up and took a deep inhale, closing her eyes and holding the smoke in for what seemed like forever. Then she leaned over and exhaled toward the gap in the sliding door.

Colleen sat down cross-legged next to Shay and watched her smoke. She did it so prettily. Her thin wrists and fingers curled languidly as she held the cigarette so lightly between her fingertips. Shay made smoking look like the most natural thing in the world, like the French girls Colleen had envied when she spent her junior year abroad. She had never even tried to imitate them, knowing it was beyond her.

When the cigarette was spent, Shay stuck her hand through the door and ground out the butt on the balcony floor. Then she closed the door and leaned back against it.

"Shay," Colleen said hesitantly. What could she say? What the hell could she say?

Shay looked at her. She scratched at her chin. "How's Paul?" she asked tonelessly, as if she was asking about a bus schedule. "He have to stay in the hospital?"

"He's . . ." *Going to live. Going to see his twenty-first birthday. Going to have the chance to get married, get a job, grow old.* "Shay, Andy is working on flights for Brittany and Robert, to get them out here as soon as possible. Tonight if he can. Leila too."

"I know. Brittany called." Shay lit another cigarette. "I had to tell her, you know. I had to be the one to tell her that her brother is dead."

Colleen moaned quietly. She didn't mean to, but the sound leaked from her, the frayed grip she had on her composure starting to sever. "Shay. Shay."

Another woman would know what to do. Another woman would reach for Shay and hug her, let her cry on her sweater. Colleen didn't care about her sweater, her coat, anything. She would give anything at all to help Shay. Everything. But what did she have?

When the thing had happened with Darren Terry, the word had spread quickly through the school. A few days later, after Paul had been suspended for two weeks, Colleen went to the school to pick up his homework. She had waited until half an hour after school let out, hoping not to see anyone. She'd walked, head down, taking the back stairs, and still she had run into a knot of mothers. Who knew what they had been doing—an academic booster meeting, teacher appreciation planning, sister school fund-raiser, it could have been a thousand different things, meetings and activities that Colleen herself had once been a part of.

The knot of women split apart for her to pass through. She knew nearly every one of those mothers. One or two murmured greetings, the rest looked at the floor, the walls, pretended to check their phones. Anything but look at her.

And then Sandy Prescott had stepped in front of her. Colleen had never liked Sandy. No one did. She didn't fit in and, worse, she didn't seem to know it. She had the faint traces of a New Jersey accent and she chewed gum with her mouth open and people tended to roll their eyes when she spoke up in meetings.

"Colleen," she said, reaching for one of her hands. "I've been thinking about you ever since I heard. I'm just so very sorry your family is going through this hard time, I can't even imagine." And then she'd hugged her, hard, patting her back and giving her a peck on the cheek before she let go. "If you need anything, to talk, or, I don't know, just to get away from everything for an hour—oh, I don't even know what would help. For something like this. But if you think of it, let me know, okay?"

The mob had moved on, and Colleen had stood in the hall, feeling the ghost impression of Sandy's arms around her.

She reached a hand, tentatively, to touch Shay's leg. Shay had taken her boots off and was wearing gray leggings and pink socks with yellow stars. They knew each other's wardrobes, after spending the last few days together. Colleen settled her hand on Shay's thin calf. Shay didn't move, and after a moment Colleen lifted her hand.

"Thanks," Shay said, in that same dead voice. "I should thank you and Andy. For buying the plane tickets. You know I can't pay you back."

"That's—of course." Colleen recoiled, stung. "It's, it's what we want to do. The least we can do."

Shay narrowed her eyes and her lips thinned. So she wasn't going to give Colleen any help. Maybe she even wanted to hurt her a little. Or a lot.

Colleen would endure it. She had no choice. She took a breath. "And Andy's assistant is trying to get another hotel room, for Robert and Brittany, and he had this one billed to us. As long as you want it. We have that room Andy reserved at the Homewood Suites. So, uh, that worked out. And then—"

"Since you have that room," Shay interrupted, taking another cigarette from the pack, "could you just go? Just take your stuff and go?"

As Colleen gathered her toiletries and stuffed them into her suitcase along with the laundered and folded clothes, Shay stayed on the floor, smoking steadily. Colleen could feel her watching as she moved around the room. When everything was packed, she stood in the middle of the room with her coat over her arm, her hand on the handle of the rolling suitcase, and tried one last time.

"If you want me to come back—I'm just down the street. I can get back here in no time. I'm going to try to get a little sleep before Andy gets here but I'll keep the phone by my bed."

Shay raised one eyebrow. "Right," she said through a cloud of smoke. "Thanks."

It felt like a curse.

COLLEEN HAD LEFT Shay's car keys on the nightstand. She decided to walk to the Homewood Suites, but it was farther than she remembered. The sidewalk petered out into a gravel shoulder. She trudged by the Dollar Store, a gas station, an Arby's. Passing cars sprayed dirty slush on her pants and coat.

By the time she arrived at the hotel, she was past the pretense of dignity. "I think I have a room reserved," she said meekly. "Under Mitchell?"

The tapping, the fresh-faced girl, the sweet smile—all of it all over again. "Oh, I'm so sorry, Mrs. Mitchell, but that room won't be ready until three." She looked genuinely regretful. "That's when check-in is."

"Oh." Colleen's mouth collapsed on itself. She looked at her watch: barely noon. "I just . . . can I just wait here, in the lobby? I don't have anywhere else to go."

"Of course, Mrs. Mitchell. Or if you want to go somewhere, I can call you when the room is ready. You never know . . . maybe they'll get to it a bit early." She didn't sound very hopeful. "Maybe you want to get some lunch?"

Lunch. Yes. She should eat. "Where?" she said, and then she was swaying again. She gripped the edge of the counter and tried very hard to hold on, but her very best effort wasn't enough. She let go and went down.

thirty-four

AFTER COLLEEN LEFT, Shay set her phone alarm for four o'clock and crawled into the bed, but she was awake again long before then, her mind going a thousand directions at once. She pulled the covers off the bed and sat on the floor wrapped up in them, staring out the window. The view wasn't much, just the parking lot and the dumpy strip mall next door, and a few houses and then the open fields started, the rolling hills all the way out to the horizon. She didn't see a lake, but somewhere the lake was out there too, and Taylor was there, trapped in the black water below the ice.

That was all she knew right now. She should have asked Paul more. He was lying on the ground and Colleen was talking to the girl, almost shaking her, asking her what her precious little darling had done, ready to clean up the latest mess he'd made.

"How?" she'd finally asked him, after the first wave had knocked her senseless, after the snow had soaked through the knees of her pants, and her throat was raw from screaming. She'd crawled over to him and demanded to know, just as the ambulances were cresting the hill, their lights strobing across the snowy lake.

He'd used the last of his strength to tell her, quickly, before his mother came back. He wanted to tell her. He wanted her to know. You could see in his eyes he was sorry, Shay would give him that. So he wasn't a monster. But he was still alive, and Taylor wasn't, and there was no balance in that.

"He drowned," he had said. "It was an accident."

Then the paramedics were running toward them and Colleen was shouting something and his eyes rolled up and there was nothing else to learn at that moment.

But now, Paul was lying in a bed at the hospital and Britt and Robert wouldn't be here until later, and Colleen was safely out of the way and this was her chance.

She pulled off all her clothes, leaving them puddled on the floor. She turned on the shower and twisted her hair into a knot while she waited for it to get hot.

She let the water splash on her upturned face. It was hot enough to hurt, running into her eyes and pooling in her mouth, coursing down her body, across her belly and down her shoulder blades and the backs of her legs. Taylor. *Taylor.*

She might have stood there forever, waiting for the heat to reach into her bones, to burn away the thought of him frozen in that terrible brackish lake. Long ago, Taylor had swum in Lake Tahoe's crystal blue depths. She had stayed on the beach with her friend Marian drinking G&Ts from a thermos while the boys, eight or nine at the time, swam like seals until their lips were blue, and then lay on the beach shivering in the sun. Taylor had the makings of an athlete even then, with his long sun-browned legs and arms. "He's going to take over the world, that one," Marian had said, while her youngest buried her feet in the sand.

Shay still saw Marian sometimes, though she was on her third husband, and the little one had grown up reckless and got into a motorcycle accident and was in a wheelchair now.

What would it have been like, if it had been Marian here this last week instead of Colleen? For a moment Shay hesitated, holding the damp towel she'd dried herself with. Marian made a sound like a donkey when she laughed. She poured a whole bottle of Red Bull on her living room carpet and told the insurance adjuster her nephew did it, as a way to get new carpet. She met her third husband at a debt-counseling seminar. It was safe to say that Marian would have been a disaster to lean on when the chips were down.

On the other hand, Colleen had come back. She had tried hard to talk to her today. Shay hadn't let her. She'd looked down at Colleen's hand on her leg, and she'd seen only the diamond as big as a walnut, the remains of a French manicure still clinging to the nails, and she'd wished that it had been not just Paul who had died instead of Taylor, but Colleen too, and Andy and all their rich, boring friends back in Boston. All of them.

She wished they'd never been born, that they were obliterated from history. Anything to reverse the course of fate. But she had been here once before.

When Frank had died, she knew the minute the cop came up her walk. She'd only been surprised it hadn't happened sooner, when he enlisted and went off to Iraq. Frank was reckless, fearless to a fault. At some level she'd been preparing their kids to lose their dad long before he left them for real, and still it hit her like a wrecking ball. As they lowered his casket into the ground, Brittany in her little pink dress tossing rose petals on top, Shay had wished that she'd never met Frank, just so she'd never had to lose him. That the driver of the car who hit him had a heart attack that morning instead, that she had collapsed in her Shredded Wheat.

But Shay had known deep in her heart that life doesn't work that way. You don't get to choose from a menu of tragedies and losses, don't get to consider which you can survive and which will crush you. God simply serves them up and there you are; you either play the hand He deals, or you give up.

Shay hung the towel carefully over the shower curtain rod. Someone was going to have to clean this bathroom and she might as well not make the job any harder. She dressed in clean clothes and combed her hair, yanking hard and taking a handful of hair out with the knots.

When Brittany and Robert got here, she would be ready. She would hold her daughter and let her cry her heart out and she would tell her it would be all right. She would survive this.

But there was something she needed to do first.

IT WAS DARK by the time she left. The Explorer complained and sputtered before it started. "Come on," Shay encouraged as she fed it gas, "come on, you motherfucker, come on."

Finally it coughed to life. Shay idled for a few minutes, letting the engine warm up. She'd timed her departure to the shift change— it was a quarter to six, and the boys with the farthest to drive were getting in their trucks, ready to head out for the night shift. They carried lunch pails and coolers, and half of them were bareheaded. Some of them didn't even bother zipping up their coats.

It was the sort of bravado she could identify with. These men risked their lives on the rigs, all so casually. Shay had a lifetime's experience with men and their dumbass risk taking. The way they'd take a turn too tight with you on the back of their motorcycle, just to show off; or toss another man a wrench that could take his eye out; or stand on top of a roof beating their chests, pretending to be Tarzan to get a laugh from a three-year-old. They gambled their lives as though they were worth no more than a quarter flipped for luck.

She drove to the hospital, asked for Paul at the desk, and went up to his room. So easy. Too easy. Didn't they understand?

They'd decided he was innocent. There would be no arrest made, no charges brought. Shay wasn't really surprised. He was a golden boy. Soon his father would arrive with their lawyers, and he and Colleen would form a wall around Paul just like they always had before. By this time tomorrow, the story—whatever it was—would have been molded and smoothed, the parts they couldn't explain away would be recast, and history would be altered. There would be no justice. And Shay could learn to live with all of that. After all, nothing was going to bring Taylor back.

But now, in this narrow period of time before the wagons were circled, she was here and Paul was alone and unprotected.

Shay slipped into his room.

The lights were low. Paul lay sleeping, propped up on two pillows, a blue blanket pulled up to his chin. His lips were slightly parted but there was no sign that he was breathing. She could see faint blue veins tracing his eyelids, charcoal-colored smudges underneath. But his eyelashes were still pretty, as black as coal.

She knocked against a chair and he jerked, then woke in twitching stages. "No, I can't," he said, or something like it, as his eyes fluttered open. His fist clenched the thin blanket and then relaxed. He looked around the room and licked his lips. His head came up off the pillow and then he lay back down, seemingly exhausted by the effort.

He noticed her standing there, but it took a moment for recognition to dawn in his eyes. Last night her face had been streaked with makeup and constricted with grief. Now she was calm. She was surprised that he recognized her at all.

"Mrs. Capparelli," he said. "You came to see me?"

What had she been expecting? That he'd cower, or cry, or start making excuses? He had a young man's voice, not quite a man's, liable to crack at any moment. Taylor had been that way too. He used to come into the kitchen and pick her up and she was helpless to do anything but laugh and slap at his arms as he spun her, singing along with the radio in a big loud baritone.

"I want to know everything," she said. "You owe me that."

He nodded. "I can't believe he's gone," he said. "Every morning I wake up and for a minute or two, I don't remember. Those are the best minutes of the day. They're the only time I feel—the rest of the day I . . ."

He couldn't seem to find the words. Shay stiffened her resolve and crossed her arms across her chest. "If he had never met you, he would be alive, wouldn't he? Whatever happened, you dragged him into it."

Paul swallowed. He looked like it hurt. "After it happened, I thought about killing myself. I think about it every day, every single day."

"Then *why don't you*?" The words shot out of her. Shay clapped her hand over her mouth, horrified. How could she really have just said that?

She backed away from the bed, tripping against the same chair, nearly falling. She stumbled out of the room, gasping for breath. There was no one in the hallway and she bent at the waist, leaning against the wall, feeling like she might throw up. *God*. Was that what she really wanted? For Paul to be dead? If they both died, would it somehow make it even?

She wanted so much to hate him. She *did* hate him. He had stolen the most precious thing in the world from her and she could kill him with her own hands, she could take a dull knife and stab it into him, over and over, until he was dead . . .

Except that this wasn't him, this wasn't Paul. Not the Paul she expected him to be. The boy in the hospital bed looked like the pictures Colleen had showed her, with those long eyelashes and that tentative mouth and that thick dark hair. But he wasn't ruthless and he wasn't crazy. His eyes weren't empty. There was no guile there, only desperate sadness.

"Mrs. Capparelli . . ." There was a clattering in the room. Shay went in without thinking. Paul had managed to sit up and was trying to get out of the bed. He'd lowered the side bar and pushed off the covers, and she could see a spreading rusty stain on the bandage around his waist.

"What are you *doing*?" she demanded, putting her hands on his shoulders and pushing him back against the bed. "I'm calling a nurse."

"No—wait. *Please.*"

She froze, standing over him the way she had stood over both her children on days when they stayed home sick from school, when they had fevers and the flu and chicken pox, wanting to tuck the covers back around him.

"If you want me to kill myself, I will," he said quickly. "I just need . . . I would just ask that you not take it out on my parents. Please. They . . . I've already hurt them too bad."

"Oh," she said. A wave of exhaustion as palpable as a seizure passed through her. She sat down on the edge of the bed.

"I loved Taylor," he went on. "I never told him that. He was my best friend. I was scared—because, you know, I've had friends before, where they didn't end up being what I thought, where they weren't really there for me when things got bad. But Taylor, he was the best. Everybody loved him, Mrs. Capparelli." He swallowed again, as if he couldn't get his throat to work right. "Everybody wanted to be like him. He was funny. He made everyone laugh. And it was like it always got fun when he was there. We could all be sit-

ting around doing nothing, and Taylor would come in and then everyone was laughing and . . ."

He wiped at his eyes with his hands. "And I couldn't believe he
wanted to be friends with me," he said, his voice cracking. "And
Elizabeth—when I found out she was only seventeen, and I didn't
know what to do, and Taylor said, *Do you love her?* He kept telling
me if I loved her, then everything would be all right, that love was the
only thing that mattered. And that was before I even knew she was
pregnant. And then . . . I was so worried about what my parents
would say, and what we'd do, how we would make things work, with
a baby, and he told me about you."

"*Me?*" Shay said. "What do you mean?"

"He told me you got pregnant with his sister by accident and did
your best anyway, and found someone to love and it wasn't perfect
but it was a good family, and even though he lost his dad and you
didn't have much money, he never felt like he was missing out on
anything. He made me feel like it would be okay."

Shay's eyes welled with tears. She grabbed the box of tissues from
the bedside table. "He was special," she said, dabbing at her eyes. "He
was such an old soul. I can't believe it. I thought . . . I thought he'd
come back to California once he got tired of working up here, that
he'd save some money for a fresh start near me and his sister."

The plan she had come here with, to make Paul tell her everything and then, somehow, to figure out how to hurt him and his family the worst way possible, had splintered into shards.

"I'm getting the nurse, you should be looked at," she said. "I just
need to know what happened. Why you went there that day and
what you were fighting about."

Paul blinked. "It wasn't her fault," he said. "She was scared."

"Whose fault? Elizabeth's?"

"Yes. She got beat up bad, she showed me pictures. She was worried about the baby. She told me T.L. did it. He thought . . . he thought the baby was his. But it wasn't. Elizabeth didn't know what to do, she said I should talk some sense into him, scare him enough to make him leave her alone.

"That's all I wanted to do," he said, his eyes pleading. "Just to make him understand, once and for all. That she was with *me* now. That we were having the baby and he had to leave us alone."

"Wait wait wait," Shay said. "*Who* beat her?"

"T.L. did." Paul's breathing had steadied again, but that spreading stain, that couldn't be good. "They used to go out. He was in love with her but she didn't love him anymore. She was with *me*. But the timing . . ." His face flushed, in embarrassment or anger, she couldn't tell. "He thought the baby was his. But it isn't. When Elizabeth tried to tell him she was with me, he wouldn't leave her alone. He kept bothering her, telling her that he wanted her back. One day he came when she was walking home from school, and she went with him, just to talk. And things . . . they got out of control and he hurt her. He left bruises, up here and here." He touched his upper arm, the top of his rib cage.

"He was careful, it was places no one would see. But she texted me the pictures. He could have hurt the baby. I had to do something."

Shay's mind raced, trying to factor all of this into the story. It had gotten away from her, shifting and changing, taking what she knew and making it into something different. She didn't know how she was supposed to feel now. "Do you still have those pictures?"

"No. I got rid of the phone. I smashed it and got one of those prepaid ones. I wasn't thinking real well, after . . . you know, when I left."

"But Elizabeth might have them."

"Why?" He fixed her with his pretty olive-colored eyes. "I figure he's paid enough. He hasn't bothered her again, not once since then. That's all we wanted. Just for him to leave her alone. And now it's just me that has to make up for all the rest. For Taylor."

Shay gripped the side of the chair. The metal was cold and sharp. These chairs were shit—you'd think they could put something a little better in a hospital room, where people watched their loved ones suffer. Where they prayed and castigated themselves and wished for do-overs, for another chance.

"Court might not see it that way," she whispered, the words a struggle to get out. "If he hurt her . . . that's something they'd think about."

She wasn't actually sure. It was getting too complicated. It wasn't black and white anymore. The blame had been what she held on to, a hard, furious kernel that was as real as her own flesh. But now it had splintered like the view in a kaleidoscope, all the pieces winking and mirroring one another, mocking her.

"If she was afraid for her life, or the baby's life. And you were . . . trying to protect her." The words were like chalk in her mouth. "And Taylor was just there to help you."

"I wanted to take a gun," Paul said. "Taylor had one. His dad's."

"Oh, Jesus," Shay said. How could he have been so stupid? That thing had been locked up in the case Frank had made for it, a plywood box bolted to the garage wall. She hadn't looked at it for years. Knew where the keys were, of course, because you don't fuck around with that sort of thing with kids in the house.

Evidently Taylor had known where the keys were too.

"It was just for hunting," Paul said hastily. "Our friend Luther— he was going to hunt duck, he invited us to come along. I . . . couldn't, I mean, I've never shot anything."

"Taylor didn't tell me," Shay said, shaking her head. "I should have gotten rid of that thing years ago. There just, there wasn't that much that belonged to his father, and I don't know, I thought someday he or Brittany might want it. Fuck."

"He always had his dad's army tags on," Paul said, fingering an imaginary chain around his neck. "Anyway, I asked him to bring the gun and he said no way. If it wasn't for that, I would have had it and I could have shot him. Only . . ."

His voice grew thick and hoarse. "Taylor's dead so maybe it would have been better. I would have killed T.L. and gone to jail for murder, but Taylor would still be here. I mean, how do you even figure that out?"

Shay sighed, trying to do the mental calculus. One boy or another. One life or another. It was too much to think about, too big. She laid a hand on the mattress, the sheets thin and cool under her touch. After a moment she moved her hand to his arm. Paul's skin was hot, hotter than she thought it should be. She had to get that nurse.

"You can't," she said softly. "That sort of thing, only God can sort it out. But losing you too, that doesn't add up, it doesn't help. Leave it now, let's figure out how to move on."

"But I'll never be able to make it up," Paul said. "I'll never be able to do enough."

"You don't know that," Shay said. "You got a whole life ahead of you still. See what you can do with it."

SHAY WAS DIGGING in her purse for her keys when the elevator doors opened and Colleen was standing there. Their eyes met, and for a moment Shay forgot everything. Colleen looked terrible, her eyes sunken and her hair greasy and lank. Behind her was a tall man with short gray hair and round glasses. Andy—exactly what she would have expected.

"What are you doing here?" Colleen demanded.

Then everything fell back into place, the terrible truth. The things that couldn't be undone.

Colleen moved toward her, stumbling, zombielike. She grabbed for Shay and Shay jerked her arm away.

"Were you in there? With Paul?" Her voice rose into a shriek. Spittle collected in the corners of her colorless lips. Andy tried to pull her away, but she shook off his hand. "Who let you in there?"

"You don't control him," Shay shot back. "Or me. You don't control *anything*."

She shoved past Colleen and Andy as the elevator doors started to close. She stabbed the buttons and watched Colleen stumble down the hall, her purse dangling from her thin arm. Her Walmart boots had already torn and a piece of the faux fur was flapping loose. One pant leg had come free and sagged along the floor, soiled and ragged.

There was little evidence of the woman who'd arrived in Lawton just a few days ago. All the polish, all the refinement had been stripped away.

And what about me? Shay thought, as the elevator descended. *Who am I now?*

thirty-five

"I'M GOING WHETHER you come or not," T.L. finally said, the only way he knew to end the argument.

Myron was convinced the meeting would lead to nothing but trouble. For a while he insisted he wasn't coming unless Jack Cook came too. But when T.L. was getting ready for school that morning, filling his commuter mug from the old coffeemaker, Myron came into the kitchen dressed in his good sweater and khaki pants.

"I'll meet you over at the place," he said. He wouldn't say *Ricky's*. He thought the restaurant was a ridiculous place to meet, with its banks of big-screen TVs and baskets of sticky hot wings and beers as big as a carton of orange juice.

But T.L. had chosen it for a reason. When he pulled into the parking lot at three forty-five, fifteen minutes before Andy Mitchell had asked to meet, most of the parking spots were empty. At seven forty-five that evening, the lot would be packed and overflow would be taking up half the church parking lot next door. But for now, most of Ricky's customers were either working or sleeping.

When T.L. was a kid, the restaurant had been a Chuck E. Cheese's. He hadn't been invited to many birthday parties that didn't take place in someone's living room on the reservation. But a kid from a soccer camp had invited him, the mom standing at the door of the place greeting the parents and kids as they arrived. Myron had carefully wiped his boots on the mat at the door, handing over the clumsily wrapped gift, a plastic dart set he bought at the drugstore, and then stood there looking like he didn't know what happened next. The mom had given Myron a thin smile and told him that he was welcome to stay, there was plenty of punch and cake. T.L. had wanted nothing more than for Myron to leave.

Now he stood inside the restaurant and waited for his eyes to adjust from the brilliant sun. There, in a corner booth, was Myron, his hands resting on top of a folded newspaper. His reading glasses were pushed up on his forehead. If T.L. had to guess, Myron had been here for half an hour already, sweating in his acrylic sweater.

He looked terrified.

T.L. slid into the booth. "Myron . . . look. Nothing bad is going to happen."

"Yeah?" Myron's face was deeply lined. He had aged in the last six weeks. "Andy Mitchell had three lawyers out here before that kid of his was even out of the hospital. He threatened the police department with a *lawsuit*. And you want to tell me you're some kind of bulletproof?"

Fear was the only thing that could make Myron angry, a fact that T.L. didn't fully understand until he was in high school. He did his best to ignore it. "Thought you'd be happy to see someone get the upper hand on Chief Weyant."

Myron looked up sharply. There was something on his face, some troubled depth that T.L. hadn't seen before. "Why would you say that?"

"What aren't you telling me?" T.L. demanded. After he'd been questioned and released back in January, he'd asked Myron why Weyant hated him. All Myron would say was that he and Weyant got into it after T.L.'s mother died.

Myron sighed. "Okay, look, your mom and Weyant used to have a thing."

"I figured it had to be something like that. Did she break up with him?"

"You . . . look, you can't understand what it was like back then. Nowadays a kid like you and some girl from Lawton High go out, it's no big deal. Back then it meant something. When Weyant started coming around, people talked. Your grandpa was sure your mom was going to end up hurt. He told her this was Weyant's big walk on the wild side, seeing a Fort Mercer girl."

"How . . . serious did it get?" T.L. asked carefully.

"Well, more than any of us expected. Weyant didn't just take her to the prom and cop a feel and drink some Boone's Farm and put it all behind him when he went off to Bismarck. He and your mom . . ." He wiped a hand over his forehead. He was perspiring in the afternoon sun streaming through the windows. "They saw each other whenever they could. She was a year behind him. Her whole senior year, every time he was home from college, he came around. Even after he was engaged to some girl he met at school. Nobody could stop your mom. Your grandpa used to yell . . ."

Myron never spoke about his parents, dead before T.L. was born. He never talked about the past at all, about T.L.'s mother's hard times, her descent down the meth pipe, her collision with a truck carrying gravel on an afternoon when she'd left him with a neighbor and gone to meet a girlfriend for happy hour in town. T.L.'s only memories of his mother were perfume and cigarette smoke and a brand of wafer cookies she had liked.

"When your mom got pregnant by some guy she'd gone out with a few times, Weyant went nuts. I was working at the plant and going to community college. Your mom was living at home again, between jobs, and Weyant was a rookie in town. He came over when your grandfather was at work, and she went out on the porch to talk to him and you could hear him yelling up and down the block. I got your grandfather's gun and I went out there and told him I wasn't afraid to use it, he couldn't arrest me if he was dead, and he turned around and got in his car and left."

"That was it?" T.L. said. He wasn't sure what to do with this glimpse of the past. "That's what you've been afraid to tell me all these years?"

"No, son," Myron said, curling his fingers around the paper, wrinkling it. "That was nothing. Your mom had you a few months later, and within a month after *that*, Weyant had found a girl, different girl from the one he'd been engaged to, knocked her up, and that was Elizabeth. They had a shotgun wedding. I figured that would be the end of it, but then he kept coming around and your mom still kept sneaking out to meet him. Those two—it was like you couldn't keep them apart."

"Wait." A rushing in his ears, a pain in his heart. For some reason, the mother T.L. had imagined for himself had never been capable of anything like a grand passion. *Love.* She'd been a junkie on the pipe and he figured Myron was the best thing to ever happen to him and nobody ever told him different. "She was in *love* with him?"

"Or *something*," Myron said darkly, his eyebrows lowered. "The rest you know. She had the accident. You came here. But on the day of her funeral, I came back here after the wake at the church, had you in a little red snowsuit, I remember that. There's Weyant in his car, his personal car, parked in my driveway. Right out there,"

Myron gestured, as though he had forgotten they were sitting in Ricky's. "Drunk as a skunk. He gets out of the car when he sees me, and I think, You bastard, you couldn't even come to the church. He's got a bottle in a bag and I can smell him a few feet away. He opens his mouth and I figure I don't want to know what he's going to say. *Shut your fucking mouth,* I tell him, *you got nothing to say to me.*"

Myron was shaking, he was so angry, his skin a mottled red, the paper shredded between his fingers.

"I went inside and turned on the TV and I didn't even wait to see what was on, left you sitting on the couch in your snowsuit and mittens. I went back outside and I hit Weyant so hard he fell down. When he was lying on the ground, I saw he'd pissed himself. He kept saying he loved her. Over and over. And that just made me angrier. See, in my mind, if he had been braver, if he'd stood by her, married her the way it was supposed to be, she never would have become a junkie and she never would have died. He was lying on the ground and I kicked him, once in the ribs, and I was getting ready to kick him in the head, I think I would have killed him. But then I thought about you, sitting on my couch. And I picked him up and kind of dragged him to his car. He wasn't fighting me by then. He got in and I closed the door on him. Went inside and turned the TV up loud and sat with you, and when I had waited long enough I went back to see and he was gone. Car was gone. I didn't care if he died in a wreck on the way home, I guess that might have been some kind of justice. Anyway, so now you know."

T.L. tried to absorb what Myron had told him. He'd always known Weyant hated him, but he and Elizabeth had never questioned why. They just figured that the fact that he was her first boyfriend had been enough.

"Why didn't you tell me? When she and I started going out?"

Myron laughed, bitterly. "You got to be kidding. I won't deny it was kind of satisfying, knowing he couldn't do a damn thing about it. But mostly I figured you were entitled to your own life, without all that crap from the past hanging over you."

T.L. wondered what he would have done if he'd known. Probably wouldn't have made a difference. It still would have ended anyway; she still would have gotten bored with him and taken up with Paul. Got pregnant.

She'd be almost five months along now, if what he'd heard was true. He'd pieced together the story from the scraps that ended up in the paper. There hadn't been a court case. No one had been arrested. T.L. had been asked to come in a second time, and they made it sound like his decision even though he knew it wasn't, and he brought Jack Cook, who sat at the other end of the table from the Weyants' attorneys. All the lawyers took notes and everyone was polite to him. Weyant was nowhere in sight. When he was finished, the police officer shook his hand and told him they'd be in touch if they had any further questions.

And that was the last time anyone contacted him, until Andy Mitchell emailed, asking to meet with him. "Off the record," he'd assured T.L. "Bring anyone you want."

In the weeks since everything quieted down, T.L. had kept his head down, tried to ignore the news, and recommitted himself to school. He quit baseball and started painting again. Myron asked him to reconsider UCLA, and after thinking about it for a few days, T.L. had made a call and explained what had happened, leaving out some of the details. The scholarship was still his. He had until the end of the month to decide if he wanted it. He was leaning toward yes.

The door jingled. They both looked up. Andy Mitchell was

dressed casually, but even so he looked nothing like Myron. He was wearing a wool coat with a leather collar. His belt buckle gleamed. He had his hand out before he ever got to the table. Myron, seated against the wall, couldn't stand all the way up, so he had to lean across the table to shake hands.

The waitress arrived as they were stumbling through the pleasantries. T.L. ordered a root beer. Andy glanced at Myron's glass of iced tea and ordered the same.

"I want to start by saying how grateful I am that you agreed to talk to me," Andy said.

"One thing," Myron said. "T.L. can't talk about that day anymore. It's too much. It's just too much to ask from him."

"Of course, of course." Andy nodded.

T.L. was surprised—that was a conversation he had never had with Myron.

Andy pulled out a folder full of papers from his leather portfolio. He laid the papers on the table, squaring up the edges. Then he started talking—about Hunter-Cole Energy.

"The safety lapses that have been going on, the handling of accidents, have gone beyond unconscionable to outright illegal," he began. He had reports and graphs and incident reports. He had figures and statistics. He told them that he was speaking confidentially and that he couldn't reveal his sources—but then he listed several names from the tribal business council.

"Why are you telling us this?" Myron asked. "What do you want from us?"

"It's . . ." Andy looked like he was choosing his words carefully. "I guess it's a courtesy. I wanted you to know before it gets into the news. I mean, it could be a very good thing for Fort Mercer. The reservation can only benefit from the exposure. Lease renegotiation could happen as early as this summer, and any pressure we can put on Hunter-Cole . . . Well, you get the picture."

"So you're going after Hunter-Cole," Myron said. "You're not the first."

"No," Andy said calmly. "But I do bring a lot of experience—and a lot of resources—to the table."

Myron nodded. "Okay. Say you shut down their operations in Lawton, get the leases to revert. That's good for us, you're right. But how does it help you? How does it help your boy?"

T.L. had been wondering the same thing. When Andy had asked to meet, T.L. guessed it had something to do with the lawsuit. That maybe he wanted ammunition to use against Weyant. Or possibly to defend against a civil suit.

Myron had asked the question he'd been thinking: what about Paul? T.L. had never seen him again after that day on the ice. Paul had disappeared once he was released from the hospital, somehow eluding the news media. The way T.L. figured it, his parents could have driven him to Bismarck and paid cash for a flight on one of the big carriers. Anyway, it didn't matter now.

Andy looked pained. "It doesn't help Paul, not directly," he admitted. "But I just . . . I took a leave from my firm, to sort through this mess. When it was over, when we got Paul home, I wasn't ready to go back yet. I wanted . . . I guess the word that comes to mind, and I hate to use it, is *closure*. I wanted something good to come out of this, if at all possible. Regardless of what happened, there were significant failures of the system on the rigs. Men were hurt. People need to be held accountable."

It wasn't a very convincing explanation, and neither Myron nor

T.L. made much of an effort to pretend otherwise. Andy gathered his papers and pushed his untouched iced tea away. "There's one more thing I wanted to tell you in person."

Here it is, T.L. thought. This is where he tells him that Paul is sorry, that he'd do anything to go back to that day and do it differently. That he knows now that T.L. was innocent all along and he blames himself. And so on.

Andy took a deep breath and looked into his eyes. T.L. felt his body tense. He could get through this. He'd prepared for just this moment. He wouldn't know if it was true until he spoke the words, but he planned to say that all was forgiven.

Andy cleared his throat. "Elizabeth has come to live with us. She and Paul are getting married this fall."

T.L. THOUGHT ABOUT that moment often in the weeks that followed. He put in extra shifts at the store when the day worker broke his collarbone falling off a ladder. He called the admissions department at UCLA and accepted. On Facebook, he friended the boy he'd be rooming with. Myron gave him the watch his father had owned as a graduation gift—he'd taken it all the way to Minot to be replated.

It wasn't that hard to put it all together. The bruises on Elizabeth's body, the ones that had provoked Paul to come after T.L.—it was pretty obvious now that she had made them herself. Maybe T.L. was even partly responsible. If he hadn't pushed Elizabeth so hard about the baby, if he had believed her the first time she said it wasn't his, if he hadn't been in such a rush for a family, a life whose outlines he'd imagined since he was a kid—if he had just let her go when she asked, none of this would have happened.

Already it was hard to remember why he'd fought so hard, but the road that brought him to that place was a long one. T.L.'s earliest memories were colored by his mother's inexhaustible longing for a different life, a life that didn't include him. He'd wanted a mother, a father, a brother, a dog—instead he'd gotten Myron. Things, needless to say, looked different now. How long would T.L. have lasted with a baby, a girl he barely knew, a couple of shitty jobs cobbled together to make the rent, while they pretended to be a family? How long before he became as taciturn, as resigned as Myron?

The chief must have drawn his own conclusions, coming close to the mark on his own. Elizabeth must have backed off her story. Maybe she'd even confessed to making the bruises herself. That would explain why T.L. was never accused or held, why Weyant hadn't barred him from walking out of the police station. Why the Mitchells' lawyers kept their distance.

T.L. couldn't help wondering what version of the truth Elizabeth had saved for Paul. It would have been a convincing one, artfully delivered. She would have given it everything she had—the story she spun, the promises she made—since her entire future depended on whether he believed her. As long as he had known her, the thing she'd wanted more than anything in the world was to escape Lawton, and now, with some sort of sleight-of-hand, she had made it happen.

T.L. was left with an emptiness where the entire last year should have been, lodged in his memories, the stories he would someday tell his children and his wife. T.L. had won a scholarship and dated a pretty girl and helped take the baseball team to the state finals, and seen his uncle look old for the first time. For another boy, in another place, these events would have slowly taken on the patina of nostalgia: the girl would grow prettier, the game-winning triple would be epic, the friends he went on the class trip to Bismarck with would be legend. But for T.L. it was like all of those things had happened to someone else.

He remembered a night with Elizabeth, the second time they'd had sex. T.L. had peeled the condom off as discreetly as possible, shoving it into the Walmart bag he kept in the truck for trash. He'd shifted his body so Elizabeth wouldn't be pressed uncomfortably up against the door handle. Outside, the stars over the rolling hills were sharp as needles, the moon full and heavy on the horizon, and T.L. had cradled Elizabeth in his arms as they stared out at the sky together.

"A night like this, you could think this was the most beautiful place on earth," he'd said.

"This?" Elizabeth had said sleepily. "But there's nothing here. Just miles and miles of nothing."

Now he realized that she was already way beyond him, that these stars would never be enough for her, that she had always been dreaming of leaving.

thirty-six

THE TEXT ARRIVED at six forty-two on an early June evening when Colleen was at a BodyPump class. She didn't see it until nearly eight, when she'd finished the class and stayed behind to talk with one of the other women, and then swung by Safeway for three bottles of the pinot noir she had been drinking lately and the steel-cut oatmeal Andy ate every morning for breakfast. She had arrived home and put the groceries away and looked in on Andy, who was working in his office, and then stood at the foot of the stairs with her hand on the newel post listening, as she so often did in the evenings, to the sound of the television upstairs.

The upper floor of the house had become Paul and Elizabeth's quarters. It hadn't taken very long at all for the dynamic of the house to shift, for it to no longer be all right for Colleen to go upstairs with a load of laundry or a package of toilet paper for the linen closet. Elizabeth had moved in nearly two months ago, and now, at twenty-eight weeks, she finally looked like a woman expecting a baby, her stomach tight as a melon, jutting in front of her thin frame. Colleen had taken Elizabeth to her hairdresser, where they'd used a vegetable-based rinse to cover up the bad bleach job, and given her a few layers around her face. She no longer looked like a Midwestern mall rat but like a girl who might be headed back to Penn in the fall, a girl who wore corduroy jeans and angora sweaters. Unless you looked at her stomach.

Elizabeth and Paul were unfailingly polite to Colleen and Andy, and that was a relief, wasn't it? Only they didn't go out, didn't call Paul's old friends, hadn't taken Colleen's suggestion to check out the events page at Sudbury Community College where Paul would be going in the fall. They studied together—Paul had two math classes he was trying to get out of the way over the summer, and Elizabeth was getting ready to take the GED, since she'd stopped going to school after everything that happened.

Colleen had been prepared to go easy on Elizabeth, since the rift with her parents was still so fresh. She didn't know the details and hadn't asked, and Elizabeth was starting to talk to her father on the phone again, which was encouraging, even if her mother was apparently still barely speaking to her. Colleen had thought that wedding planning might be a good distraction for Elizabeth, though the wedding wasn't going to happen until Thanksgiving, when many of Colleen and Andy's relatives would be in town. The girl dutifully paged through the bride magazines that Colleen brought her and went to lunch with her at various restaurants that they were considering for the reception. Of course it wouldn't be anything elaborate: the small chapel in the church, a luncheon for fifteen or twenty guests, a few days on the cape with Colleen and Andy watching the baby.

When she wasn't studying, Elizabeth fussed around their rooms and talked to her friends and sisters on the phone and texted and seemed to eat nothing but sliced apples and cheese sandwiches. She and Paul took long walks together, and sometimes Colleen wished she could follow them and find out what they talked about. In the evenings, they watched television together, Paul with a textbook on his lap and Elizabeth with the Sudoku book Colleen gave her. Their conversations were quiet.

Elizabeth would have made a perfect daughter-in-law if the kids were, say, twenty-six. Or even twenty-three. And maybe if she had been to college, but there would be time for that, later, when the baby was old enough for preschool. Colleen reminded herself every day how much there was to be grateful for, and was she certainly ready to pitch in, but she wasn't up for full-time caregiving. She just didn't think she had it in her, especially once the baby's arrival changed the balance among all of them, and Elizabeth would have opinions and maybe even rules about the baby's care.

Besides, all of that was just a way of avoiding what was really on her mind, of pretending to have the same set of challenges and joys as any other grandmother-to-be, a fantasy she had test-driven at the church women's club golf outing. Some of the women knew what had happened, which meant that by the end of nine holes and cocktail hour, *everyone* knew. The ladies at her table had been unfailingly polite—overly effusive, perhaps, although that may have been the wine—but she still knew they knew.

She'd had decades of experience, after all. She was *that mom*: "You know, the one with that kid . . . ?" Colleen had forged her game face since kindergarten, bearing the weight of it for both her and Andy, and if they ever handed out awards for nodding and smiling like you didn't know what people were saying about your family, she'd take top honors.

Would it ever, ever be her turn? To simply *be*, to shop for a bridal registry with a future daughter-in-law, to sit in a park watching a toddler in a sandbox, without wondering who was watching and talking about her?

But even that wasn't the worst thing that lodged itself like a bitter seed, deep inside her. Colleen had two concerns about Elizabeth that could keep her up for hours at night. The first, of course, was what she had done to herself . . . the bruises, the pictures she had texted. Colleen had Steve, the detective, to thank for that particular nugget, though it couldn't be proved and had come at the cost of a fair amount of up-front cash for which Steve could not provide a receipt. Someone in the police department had come through, Steve told Andy, someone close to the chief who was nonetheless willing to spill a few details of a case that was dead anyway.

Elizabeth was young, and immature, and maybe not the brightest top in the box, and she must have seen the glow of a better future in Paul's guileless eyes. Only T.L., the clinging boyfriend, stood in the way, and Elizabeth had needed a way around him, and perhaps she'd thought she'd found a solution where no one got hurt besides herself. But to pretend to have been beaten? It was the stuff of tabloids, of soccer sideline gossip, the sort of thing that might happen in Revere or Swampscott but never, ever Sudbury. It hadn't leaked yet, and maybe it never would, but Colleen wouldn't forget. For Paul's sake, she would forgive, but she wouldn't forget.

The second thing was the reserve with which Elizabeth held herself back from Colleen. And now she'd got Paul doing it too. Always polite—never-endingly, eternally polite, so that sometimes Colleen had a rogue impulse to slap the girl across that pretty face, just to get a reaction out of her—but never intimate, the way Colleen always thought she would be with a daughter-in-law. They didn't laugh together, didn't share knowing glances over Paul's little quirks and habits. Instead, Elizabeth and Paul sat together at the dinner table, did all their errands together, pitched in around the house together. Made their decisions together, decisions that excluded Colleen.

Like: They had refused to tell Colleen and Andy if the baby was a boy or a girl after the last ultrasound.

That was the oft-returned-to hurt that Colleen was dwelling on as she stood at the foot of the stairs, listening. The television, their soft voices. Finally Colleen dug in her pocket for her phone, mostly out of boredom. And saw the text:

They found him

BRITTANY HAD PICKED up right away but was interrupted before Shay could tell her the news. "I'll call you right back, Mom, I just need two minutes to find this invoice before Nan leaves for the day."

So Shay was left with this heavy, strangling knowledge, barely able to breathe. She had been gluing pale pink crystals in a swirl pattern on a box decorated with tiny decoupaged images of ballet slippers, and her fingertips were crusted with dried glue. She ought to clean them. She had bottles of solvent and lotion on her workbench. At the very least she should put the cap on the glue. It dried so fast.

She sat motionless, the phone dangling from her hand. Through the window she could hear the Cho boys kicking a soccer ball against the side of their garage next door, a sure sign their mom had left them home alone.

Shay had known this day was coming, known that as the lake warmed and the ice thinned, things buried for the winter would break free and come to the surface. She'd set the weather app on her phone for Lawton, and every day—every balmy, sunny central California morning—she stared at the forecast and thought about Taylor, finding his way home.

But now it was real and she was here and he was there and everything that had to happen next felt like a slab of marble pressing her down. She didn't feel the relief she'd expected. She felt dead. She felt like a better alternative would have been for her to wade into the lake herself and join Taylor in the mud-bottom tomb.

Just yesterday Paul had sent her a prayer he had found somewhere on the Internet. One line of the three verses had stayed with her, echoing in her mind as she dried the dishes last night: *Make my eyes ever behold the red and purple sunset.*

Paul had taken to signing his emails *love*. As in, "Love, Paul and Elizabeth." She had stared at the word for a long time, wondering if she had a right to it. Or if she even wanted it. Besides the prayers and inspirational quotes he sent, he always said the same thing. He prayed for Taylor and for her every day. He was studying hard—Shay knew that was a reference to his promise to make his life mean something. In the last email he had reported that the baby was a boy, adding that neither he nor Elizabeth cared as long as he was healthy.

Paul was Colleen's son, not hers. Shay hadn't lured him away, not on purpose. She never took his side, never discussed his parents, never did anything but remind him that he was strong enough to get through each day. Shay couldn't help it if Colleen had learned nothing from everything that had happened. Her job was not to teach. Her job had only been to raise her son to be a man, a good man, and she had done that, and she had earned her peace. And if some days peace came in the form of Paul's brief emails, then she would be a fool to question the gift.

She had stood at the sink last night, the evening breeze carrying the scent of star jasmine, and dried the plate that Leila had made for her at day care. Leila's tiny handprint was surrounded by colorful scribbles; one of the staff had lettered her name and "I Love Grandma" around the rim.

This, Shay had thought, setting the plate down carefully on the counter, *this* is precious. This is what I have.

Now she waited for her daughter to call back so she could tell her about Taylor's body. Another difficult task, and Shay would get through it, but she would not feel sorry. Not about Paul, not about Colleen. Let Colleen sit in that echoing mansion, with no one for company but her husk of a husband and a son who had finally found a way to leave her.

COLLEEN WAS ALREADY looking up flights before it occurred to her to tell Andy. His response: "Have you told Paul yet?"

He said he'd finish with the airlines and line up a car for her. A hotel would have been a challenge, but in the last months, more housing had been completed and more man camps erected—and besides, over his last few visits to investigate Hunter-Cole, Andy had forged a relationship with the manager of the Hyatt with generous amounts of cash.

Colleen went up the stairs slowly, her hand on the polished railing. The television was off. Music was playing. She cleared her throat, self-conscious. The "media room" was an oversize landing at the top of the stairs, big enough for a sectional sofa, a few tables, an entertainment wall with a television in the middle of it. When they bought the house, Colleen envisioned Paul and his friends as teenagers, drinking sodas and joking around, playing foosball and video games. Needless to say, that had never happened.

Paul was hunched over his laptop. Elizabeth was stretched out on the chaise, one hand resting on her stomach, her feet in the fuzzy slipper socks that Colleen had given her. Seeing that she was wearing the socks buoyed Colleen a little, despite everything.

"Paul."

They both startled, Paul twisting around and Elizabeth scrambling to sit up, as though they'd been caught doing something wrong. Paul's expression quickly turned to annoyance, which he did his best to cover up. "Sorry. Didn't hear you."

"Listen, honey." She took a breath. "They've found Taylor's body. Shay will be able to take him home now."

For a second, his face was completely bereft of expression. He blinked, then put his hand on the edge of the coffee table, as if for support. "When? How?"

"I don't know any details. I'm assuming it's the thaw, like they predicted . . . he probably just washed up somewhere."

"You haven't talked to her?" His voice sharper now.

"No, honey, I . . . she just texted me. Dad's trying to get me a flight now."

"I'm going." He went back to his laptop and began typing furiously.

"Paul, that's not a good idea." The tightening of the chest, the girding for an argument. When he'd been younger, she had learned to physically steel herself—for the tantrum of a five-year-old, the stomping of a nine-year-old, the slamming doors of a thirteen-year-old. Now he just typed faster.

"You've been doing so well," Colleen tried. "You've got As in your classes. There's a test Friday, right? You can't risk jeopardizing those grades, or you might not get your core classes in the fall."

"I'm fine," he said tightly. "It's under control."

It was true that Paul seemed to have gotten through the worst of it. His torso had healed, a shiny knotted scar the only evidence of the infection that kept him in the hospital for three days, and he'd been to the half dozen therapy sessions Andy and Colleen had asked him to attend. Their own counselor had suggested they take his lead and not bring up anything from the past unless he initiated the conversation. Give him time to process and heal, while dealing with the new realities of his life, was the idea.

Who knew what this could bring up for him, how far back it would set him?

Colleen was trying to find another objection, when she glanced at Elizabeth. The girl's expression stopped her. She was staring at Paul with her eyes narrowed and a calculating frown on her face. "Honey," she said softly, putting her hand on his arm. "Please. Don't go. I need you here."

His fingers went still on the keys. He took a breath and let it out slowly. Then he stopped typing and took Elizabeth's hand between his.

He wouldn't be going. That much was clear.

But Colleen had lost anyway. Paul no longer belonged to her.

IT WAS FOUR o'clock in the morning when they pulled out of the driveway, Andy at the wheel. Neither of them spoke on the way to the airport.

Colleen had seen Vicki exactly once since returning home, in the cleaning products aisle at Target, and Vicki had turned on her heel and walked away, pretending not to see her. Colleen wasn't sure if she and Andy were still doing whatever they had been doing. She wasn't sure what they had been doing, for that matter. Her name no longer came up in conversation, and Andy had been waging his war on Hunter-Cole alone.

When he leaned across the seat in the departure lane at the airport, his kiss barely brushed her cheek. "Text when you land," he said. She got out of the car without answering.

The plane touched down in Lawton at one thirty in the afternoon. Unlike last time, Colleen had fallen asleep and had missed the descent with its bird's-eye view of the rolling hills, the rigs.

Andy had navigated the terse conversations with Lisa Weyant, and Colleen was grateful for that. She'd rather spend the night on the bench in the gas station parking lot than in their guest room, but Andy said all the right things. *It was so good of the Weyants to offer, but perhaps it would be best if Colleen were to stay at the hotel where she could be near Shay.* There were no more objections after that, no exhortations to come for a home-cooked meal.

They were a long way from a cozy relationship with their future daughter-in-law's family, but now wasn't the time to work on that. Especially given the nature of the trip. In the calculus of blame, it was their daughter who had knocked over the first domino.

Colleen had no idea if Shay blamed the Weyants. Shay had ignored her calls and letters. Not that there had been many. For every time Colleen actually wrote an email, put pen to paper, dialed Shay's number, there were a dozen times that she couldn't face the challenge, that she didn't feel strong enough.

She filed off the plane along with the men in their work boots and faded T-shirts. Waited in line for her suitcase. Walked to the rental car counter with only her dread for company.

thirty-seven

THE CONNECTING FLIGHT was delayed, and Shay spent the time in the air trying to distract herself. Robert and Brittany, at a joyless dinner to celebrate her birthday three weeks earlier, had given her the newest iPad, smaller and lighter and faster than the one they'd given her two years ago. Robert downloaded a few games and showed her how to play them, and Shay popped bubbles on a spinning disk by tapping with her finger and wordlessly willed the women sitting on either side of her to keep their eyes on their *Redbook*s and leave her alone.

When they landed, she had half a dozen texts. One was from Brittany: I love you mom call me when you get there

The rest were from Colleen:

1:52 I arrived. Will check in and meet yr flight

3:11 Saw yr flight delayed will check on app

4:44 Coroners office says they will stay open late for you

5:01 Says you're on the ground I am here. Have car

Shay shoved the phone back into her handbag, harder than necessary. She had told Andy everything she knew, that Chief Weyant would have someone meet her at the morgue, that there were papers she would need to sign before Taylor could be released. That since Taylor's death had been ruled an accident, and the coroner had stated the cause of death was drowning, she was free to take him home for burial.

She hadn't been prepared when Andy told her that Colleen was planning to come out. Andy's voice on the phone was reassuring, smooth, probably good for the lawyer business. When he explained that he had already contacted a mortuary firm and arranged transport to one in California, she knew that he meant that all the expenses had been covered, and she couldn't find the words to tell him not to let Colleen come.

While she was talking to Andy, she felt that there was a certain dignity to the proceedings. But the minute Colleen got involved, it stirred up the bitter resentment she'd been nursing since that night at the hospital. Shay knew it was irrational. Or maybe *displaced* was the right word. But still, why did Colleen have to barge into everything like she was in charge? Even if she was trying to be helpful, even if she and Andy were the ones paying for it—that wasn't *her* child lying on some cold steel table.

Shay spotted her suitcase on the luggage truck. She pushed her way through the crowd of passengers and yanked it off herself. No one stopped her. She had to watch herself, had to keep her temper under control. She knew the source of her simmering rage, but knowing didn't make it go away.

She stared at the cinder-block airport terminal. Inside that building was Colleen. Shay wasn't ready. She stood, hidden in the shadow of the plane, and called Brittany, but she didn't pick up.

Slowly, Shay put the phone away and walked toward the terminal, dragging the old suitcase behind her. The terminal was busy; another flight would soon be leaving, and the men were lined up, impatient to get home. They carried paper cups and duffel bags and stared at their phones and iPads. They paid her no attention as she walked past.

It took a moment for Shay to recognize Colleen. The last time she'd seen her, in the halls of the police station, she'd had her hair pulled back in an indifferent half ponytail. Her clothes had been slept in. Her lips were colorless and chapped, her eyes sunken, her jowls trembling.

The intervening months had brought Colleen back to life. Her hair was colored a rich chestnut with lighter highlights and cut shorter. She had on makeup: eyeliner and lipstick and foundation that evened out her skin tone. She was wearing a coral pink short-sleeved sweater with a scooped neckline that showed off her long, elegant neck, ivory capri pants, and the same unlaced canvas sneakers that Brittany wore, the ones with the little rectangular patch that Shay had teased her daughter about: *fifty dollars for a label?* Her bag looked a lot like the one she'd lugged around during the week they'd spent together, except a lighter shade of brown. She looked, Shay thought unkindly, like a magazine ad for a feminine product: competent, happy, even a trifle smug.

Well, to be fair, Colleen didn't look all that happy right now. Her brow was creased, and she searched the arriving passengers anxiously, twisting her hands on her purse strap. When Colleen saw her, a wealth of emotions passed over her expression before she smoothed it into a bland greeting: dread, guilt . . . and longing.

She rushed toward Shay with her arms outstretched. Shay wasn't sure if Colleen was going to grab her hand or hug her or what. In all of that terrible week that they had spent together, they had never hugged. They had touched only when it was made necessary by their close proximity. Even the terrible night, when Shay was being led to the police car, Colleen had stood apart, consumed by her relief at having Paul, and maybe that was forgivable, but Shay had ridden in that car alone. Shay had been alone when the policeman asked her if she was having thoughts of *hurting herself or others.*

Colleen settled for an in-between gesture: she reached for both of Shay's hands, then stood there clutching them. Her hands were cold. "Shay, I don't even know how to begin to tell you . . ." she said, and then stopped. Shyly, almost, she stepped forward, closing the distance between them, but at the last minute Shay pulled her hands away and twisted out of Colleen's grip. She seized the handle of her suitcase and dragged it between them. A barrier—an emergency one.

"You didn't have to come," she mumbled. She knew how she sounded and she knew she couldn't stop. Not yet. "Tell Andy thanks for the flights, the hotel—everything. We'd better go, right?"

She made a show of looking at her wrist, though she hadn't worn a watch in years.

"Yes," Colleen said softly. "Of course. We don't want to keep them waiting."

After that Colleen didn't try so hard. She led Shay out to the parking lot to a dirty white car. It had a crack in the windshield and smelled of cigarettes. Grime was crusted in the console. "This is a rental?" Shay said, not bothering to hide her disgust. "Hope you didn't pay much for it."

She stole glances at Colleen as they drove toward downtown. Her face was pinched and tense. Good—that felt like a small victory. If Colleen was a smoker, she'd be wanting one now. As for herself, Shay had stayed off them completely since going back to California. She thought it would be hard to quit, but it wasn't. The idea of smoking held no more appeal than eating cardboard. She wasn't drinking much, either, and Brittany had to remind her to eat when she stopped by. Shay's only coping indulgence was Mack: seeing him whenever he could get away, taking him to bed without preamble, fucking him as hard as she could and crying after, his sweet bewildered face hovering over her in concern. But even that had died down. She hadn't bothered to let Mack know about Taylor.

"*Here?*" Shay snorted. They were back at the police station. Behind the brick-and-glass box was a building Shay had taken for the utility plant: pale cinder block with a ramp leading up to the entrance.

Colleen parked and waited for Shay to get out of the car before she did. They walked together toward the entrance, Shay keeping some distance between them. A dozen yards from the ramp, she stopped.

"I don't think I want you there," she said, but then it hit her, and she suddenly had trouble breathing. Inside this building were the poor tattered remains that were all that was left of her beloved, her best loved. She would gather him in her arms if she could, she wouldn't mind the condition of the body, she had already endured the worst. Except, what then?

Tomorrow she would fly home, and in the plane would be a sealed casket packed in a plain brown box provided by the airline. It had been explained to her by the man from the mortuary Andy had made arrangements with. He had been patient, repeating himself several times until Robert gently took the phone from Shay and wrote everything down neatly on a sheet torn from the grocery list pad on the fridge. So yes. She knew the logistics.

But that wasn't what made the terrible hole inside her. What, then? After he was transferred to the casket Brittany and Robert were picking out today, after the service, after he was lowered into the plot next to her mother—it had been purchased long ago by her father, but he ended up being buried with his second wife—after the stone was laid and the flowers placed there and everyone had gone home and Shay finally took off the black dress and Brittany and Robert took Leila home—what *then*?

"Oh, God," she said, stumbling against Colleen. And Colleen caught her.

INSIDE WAS AN officer Shay vaguely recognized. "I made sure they waited," he said. "I talked to your son-in-law. The papers are all ready. You only have to go as far as this front office. Tomorrow everything's going to be taken care of for you, you can get back on the plane and then on the other end the other company is going to handle it from there."

It took only about ten minutes. The staff, one woman and one man, didn't meet her eyes as they guided her through where to sign. The officer stood beside her. Colleen stood against the wall, clutching her purse like her life depended on it, a strange little grimace on her face. When Shay pushed back her chair, finished at last, she realized that Colleen was trying not to cry.

"Thank you," she said stiffly on the way back to the car. She let Colleen open the passenger door for her.

"You must be tired," Colleen said falteringly. "Coming all that way."

Shay shrugged.

"I was thinking . . . would you like to have dinner? We could go somewhere quiet, where we could talk."

"Like Swann's?" Shay barked out a harsh laugh. "That would be great. We'll invite Kristine to sit down with us after her shift."

"No, no, that isn't—" Shay could see how uncomfortable she was making Colleen, but it was too hard to care. "I just thought, somewhere that we could take our time. I mean it wouldn't even have to be, we could stay in the room, get room service."

"Which room, mine or yours? Since you guys got two. What did that cost, anyway? What's my tab up to?" She had heard that the cost of transporting a body could run as high as five thousand dollars, a figure that made her mouth go dry. Robert was trying to deal with the insurance company, to see what might be covered, and Shay had backed completely away from the details.

Maybe that was what was making her feel guilty: between Andy and Robert, the two of them were handling everything. Shay was used to taking care of herself. She'd been on her own since she was eighteen. Sometimes she screwed up, but she was usually as proud of surviving the mistakes as she was of her successes.

She turned away from Colleen, suddenly stiff. She had pushed too far. She was—at least the fragile part of her that still experienced normal feelings, that still participated in the world around her even while the rest of her drowned in grief—sorry for what she was doing.

And grateful. Yes. She could still do gratitude, though it was a rusty tool, degraded from lack of use.

She watched the town go by outside her window. There . . . the gas station where she'd left Colleen on the curb. In the concrete planters were marigolds and petunias. An old man in a greasy white apron tied over his jeans stood outside, washing the windows with Windex and crumpled newspaper. Shay knew that trick—best way to clean glass with no smears. There, on the left, was the lumberyard. The shack in the middle had been demolished, and in its place was a sign announcing COMING SOON LUXURY 1- AND 2-BEDROOM APART-MENTS ALL THE AMENITIES LEASING THIS FALL. It was hard to believe that an apartment complex would go up in the next six months— around Fairhaven, there were half-finished projects that had been abandoned after the housing crash, weeds growing up between the lots.

Soon Colleen pulled up at the Hyatt.

"For old times' sake?" Shay said. Making the joke was an effort. An olive branch.

Colleen glanced at her, eyes wounded, looking for the barb. Ready for the blade. "Andy just wanted you to have somewhere comfortable," she mumbled. "Listen, whatever you need, I'm here. If all you want is"—her voice hitched, and she coughed in an effort to cover it—"is to be left alone, I understand. Maybe in the morning, you might . . . I mean, if you want to talk, you have my cell number and I'll just be in my room. And of course I'll take you to the airport. I've got all your flight details and—"

"Colleen." Shay cut her off, then didn't know what else to say. "It's okay," she finally managed. "Give me fifteen minutes to splash some water on my face, maybe we can find a place in this town where no one knows us."

That was supposed to be a joke too, but it was clear Colleen didn't get it. She nodded and ducked her chin. When she got out of the car she held onto the doorframe for support, like an old woman.

thirty-eight

COLLEEN WAITED FOR Shay's text, eyeing the minifridge. Inside, she already knew, was a split of Sutter Home chardonnay and another of Riesling. Neither was her first choice. Either would do.

Last week, she'd white-knuckled her way through three consecutive nights with no wine. She'd scared herself Sunday night, when she'd waited until Andy was in bed and there were no sounds from upstairs, and then drunk what was left of one bottle and another full one of her pinot noir. At twelve fifty-four, when she was finally stumbling to bed, she'd had the foresight to take one of the bottles to the garage and shove it underneath a pile of mail and newspapers in the recycling bin. That way there was only one empty in the kitchen bin.

Not that any of them had noticed. She did her drinking quietly. A glass with dinner, or not; she didn't need it then. It was bedtime that drove her need, the prospect of a long night with nothing but nightmares for company. At first, she'd convinced herself it was better than relying on the Ambien, and that the two, sometimes three brimming glasses of the ruby-colored wine were a reasonable substitute.

But Monday morning she was hungover. She woke with her face on a drool-damp patch of pillow, Andy in the shower and her head thick and aching. It wasn't even six, but she knew she'd never get back to sleep, so she got up and brushed her teeth twice, combed her hair and washed her face, and promised herself she was done. It was a long and difficult day, her fatigue made worse by the tremors and dizziness, not to mention the headache.

That night she'd gone to bed at ten with a stack of magazines. Andy was reading, his glasses sliding down his nose, the cover of his hardback crackling every time he turned the page. Colleen stared at images of kitchens and living rooms, beautifully decorated, and tried not to think about the wine sitting downstairs in its familiar bottle. The peeling of the copper-colored foil, the swirl up the sides of her bell-shaped glass. The taste on her tongue, smooth and rich, a promise. The first lovely tendrils of numb.

She didn't need it. She wasn't an alcoholic. But when she turned out the light and lay, open-eyed, in the darkness, her heart raced with something like fear.

Tuesday and Wednesday, she convinced herself she didn't miss it. It had just been an ill-advised self-soothing spree, a temporary bump in a single-glass-most-nights habit.

But Thursday, the half glass she allowed herself turned back into several, and now here she was again.

A text buzzed. Ready to go, meet u in lobby

She shot her reflection in the mirror a quick, determined smile and ran her fingers through her hair. *I'm here for* her, she reminded herself. *I can do this for her.*

"HOW'D YOU FIND this place?" Shay said, setting her laminated menu on the scarred pine table and looking around the room. The restaurant was small and dim, its walls covered with fake paneling and beer advertising signs. It was called the Honey Do, and they'd spotted the blinking neon chicken from the road, fifteen miles from

Lawton and past the turnoff for Turnerville, just as the Yelp review had promised. They'd gotten the last empty table.

Colleen felt her cheeks flush. "I did a little research," she said, not adding that in her purse was a neatly folded piece of paper with a list of half a dozen restaurants.

There was just this to get through. Being there for Shay. It was going to be uncomfortable. Downright painful, even, but Colleen was ready to do the right thing. It wasn't just that she was the one whose child had survived. She wanted to think that even if their roles were reversed (no, she couldn't allow her mind to go there, couldn't imagine Paul being the one under the ice all of those months, Paul thrashing in terror as the darkness closed over his head and the ice water filled his lungs), she would still have felt some sort of . . .

What was it, exactly? *Kinship* was the word that came to mind, but she and Shay were no closer to being kin now than when they first met. They were different in so many ways, and enduring misery together hadn't changed that. Colleen ducked her head, pretending to read the menu, to hide the twitch in her eyelid. *Friendship.* That was the word she had been thinking. She wanted to believe Shay was her friend. Even more, she wanted—desperately—for Shay to consider *her* a friend.

"We could split the chicken and catfish platter," she said brightly. "It comes with hush puppies and onion rings."

"Jesus, we could just roll our arteries in cornmeal and pan-fry them," Shay said, but she didn't object. When the waitress came over to their table, Shay ordered a carafe of house white wine without consulting with Colleen. "I need a drink," she explained, handing her menu over.

Colleen abstained until the food came, but when she looked at the sheen of grease clinging to it, she reasoned a glass of the house

Chablis didn't stand a chance against all those calories. She took a sip from the glass Shay had poured. It was terrible, as she expected.

Conversation had been stilted. Colleen had asked whether Shay had started taking custom orders again (she had), how Robert and Brittany were doing (their house was on the market and they had put a bid on a model in a new development that was ten minutes closer to Shay's house), what Leila was doing for the summer (camps, mostly, and two afternoons a week with Shay). She'd gotten her old job back and even managed to arrange her schedule around Leila's afternoons by working four ten-hour shifts.

Shay answered every question in a monotone. She cut her chicken into tiny pieces with her knife and fork.

Colleen drank more of the terrible wine. Let the slightly sour, cold liquid sluice down her throat. After a while she felt better. Stronger. Enough to ask the question she had been rehearsing.

"I just wondered if you would like to talk about it. About knowing, finally . . . and getting him home."

Shay looked at her through narrowed eyes. "You want to know if I feel closure or something like that?"

"Well, or . . ." Shay wasn't going to make it any easier for her, which Colleen supposed was fair. "I can't know what it's like. Obviously. But I feel like . . ." She had been going to say that she felt like she *knew* Taylor a little, from the time she and Shay had spent together and from the things Paul had told her. Not that there were many; he parsed them out only occasionally, in context of other things. Like, "I first heard that band one time when Taylor and I drove to Minot." Or, on July Fourth, "A year ago Taylor and I were setting off fireworks, you could see them so much more clearly away from city lights."

And now she felt cautious, unsure how Shay would respond. "I only thought that you might want to talk about it." She swallowed. "I wish I could make today even a little less awful for you."

"Yeah. Thanks. I don't really think I can talk about it right now." Shay picked up a french fry and chewed, never taking her eyes off Colleen, looking not so much devastated as calculating.

"So, you and Andy must be excited," she said, after she had taken a delicate sip of her wine. There was a shift in her tone, and her eyes gleamed in a way that put Colleen on alert.

"About . . ."

"The baby. That he's going to be a boy."

Colleen froze, her greasy fingers in her lap, a rime of salt on her lips. "We don't—they actually haven't told us yet. They're keeping it secret."

"Oh," Shay said, and was Colleen imagining it, or was there some faint note of triumph in her voice? "Never mind, I guess I was just—you know how some people have a sense for these things? I'm usually right, but I've been wrong too. A girl would be sweet, especially if she got Elizabeth's coloring."

"Wait," Colleen said. She felt like she was wading out into the undertow. There was a pounding in her ears, the conversations around them blending into a dull buzz. "Wait. Tell me why you said that. About him being a boy."

Shay pursed her lips and stared over Colleen's shoulder at the wall behind her. "Look, I'm sorry I said anything, and I don't want to—I mean, there's so much going on, people are kind of stretched to the limit. I don't want to make a big deal out of something that really isn't."

"Shay." Colleen leaned across the table and covered Shay's hand with her own. She squeezed her wrist, as Shay stared at her hand there. "Please. Don't do this. I need to know. How do you know?"

"You'll take it the wrong way," she finally said, staring directly into Colleen's eyes. "You'll read things into it."

"Into what?"

Shay sighed, drummed her fingers on the table. "Okay, look. I thought you knew. Paul wrote me a few times. Just emails, short ones."

"When?" Colleen was stunned. Paul never mentioned Shay, or Lawton, and barely spoke about his in-laws-to-be; she and Andy had assumed those subjects were painful for him, and avoided them. "When did he write you?"

"It was only a few times, like I said. Not like every day or anything."

Colleen's head was filled with a painful rushing, but the only thing she thought to say was, "Do you write him back?"

"Not much," Shay said, after a pause. She went on, quickly, "Now look, I know you're probably mad at me that I didn't answer *your* emails or calls. And I'm sorry. But I was counting on you to understand. I just couldn't. Seriously, it would have taken me right back—and I was trying to move ahead, trying to get my job back, and take care of Leila and I didn't have . . ." She waved her hand, not specifying what she didn't have enough of. Strength? Time? Motivation?

"But Paul—"

"He was Taylor's *friend*, Colleen," Shay chided. "Taylor wouldn't have wanted me to ignore Paul now."

Colleen pushed her plate away; suddenly the grease-sodden pieces of chicken, the crumbling hush puppies, nauseated her. "All of a sudden he's Taylor's friend."

"What's that supposed to mean?"

"The whole time we were trying to find them, you were convinced he was—was some sort of monster. You blamed him. You were ready to cut him loose, him and me both."

"That was different," Shay snapped. "That's not fair."

"Not fair?" Colleen felt the anger inside, which she kept so carefully coiled, the twisted strands of rage she had hoarded with such care, all these years. Her biggest secret, the only one she'd successfully kept. "Not *fair*? How was any of this fair—for any of us? Did any of us ask for our boys to come here? Did you ask for Taylor to lose his dad? Did I ask for Paul's brain to work differently from other kids'? Did either of us ask for the ice to give out that day?"

"Don't put me on the same level as you," Shay hissed. "I didn't have any problem with Taylor coming here to work. He was old enough to take a man's job and that's what he did. Paul too. You never seemed to get that he was just trying to go out there and do something of his own. Maybe if Paul thought you and Andy supported any decision he ever made, he'd tell you things more often."

The knotted fury twisted painfully, making Colleen gasp. "You can't—"

"I can't what? Challenge you, Miss Perfect? You and Dr. Spock? I guess you did every damn thing by the book. Probably nursed him until he was three and made homemade baby food and washed his diapers with organic detergent. But you never let him grow up. If you'd let him off his leash with the other kids, instead of putting the poor kid through hell with all your tutoring and assessing and psychologizing, he would have figured out how to deal with his frustration the way normal kids do."

"Stop," Colleen said, almost begging.

"I *won't* stop. I'll tell you what, you were right: I did misjudge him. For that I'm sorry. I read about what he did to that kid and I jumped to conclusions. But you know what I think now? I think that was *your* fault as much as his."

"*My* fault?" Colleen was shocked, not bothering to keep her voice down.

"Yeah. Look what happened when he came out here. Sure, he had a few tough days, a lot of them do. And then he got his balance and he did fine—because there wasn't anyone here to prop him up. Maybe a few guys gave him a hard time, but for the first time in his life he didn't have Mommy to come and make them stop. And he figured it out. That's what you can't forgive him for, Colleen, he was able to do just fine without you. And you can't *stand* that."

"You have *no* idea," Colleen said, her voice trembling. Around them, a few of the other diners had noticed the argument and were casting them glances. "His mind doesn't work the way other people's do, you're oversimplifying—"

"Oh, you are so full of *shit*, Colleen!" Shay smacked her hand on the table, making their silverware jump. "He *is* like the others. Or wants to be, if you'd stop smothering him. Oh, maybe he's got ADHD or anger issues or whatever the fuck you want to call it, but so do half the kids these days. Haven't you noticed that? Taylor went to a speech therapist in preschool, he had a thing where he didn't say the end of his words. I thought it would clear itself up, and they were trying to convince me that since I didn't go to a specialist right away, he was going to end up with a permanent defect or some bullshit. And you know what, by the next year you'd never know he ever had a problem."

"Don't you *dare* compare a mild speech impediment to what Paul had to deal with!"

"Oh, for Christ's sake, Colleen, I'm not. I'm just saying that if you had just backed the hell off, he might have learned to deal with some things on his own. And it wouldn't even matter—and I should know that better than anyone, because no matter what happens my son will still be dead—but you're still doing it."

She was digging in her shoulder bag for her wallet. Colleen pushed back her own chair and picked up her purse. "You don't say something like that to me and then just leave," she said. She was so angry that she thought she might pick something up and throw it. She could imagine it—she longed to pick up a glass and hurl it, to grab the stainless coffeepot off the serving cart and throw it against the wall, to knock over the chairs.

"Say what? That you're still treating your son like a child? Even though he's got a baby on the way and a family he needs to provide for?" Shay pulled out two twenties and threw them on the table. "He might have grown from everything that happened. God knows he's trying to. You know what he told me in the hospital?"

Colleen had been reaching for her own wallet, to throw more money down. To make sure there was enough for the bill and then some; she couldn't afford to give up even this thin advantage, of always paying. But Shay's words stopped her. She had never asked Paul about Shay's visit. Like so many things, she'd been waiting for it to fade from her memory.

Shay leaned across the table. "He asked me if I thought it would make things even for him to kill himself."

Colleen staggered, her heart lurching. She grabbed the back of the chair to support herself. "Stop it," she whispered.

"He was ready to do it. Your son—your *son*—would have done anything to make it right. He worked that out on his own, without any of your help. Paul knows right and wrong. I bet he has for a long time. But every time he tries to work it out for himself, there you are, with your Mommy-knows-best shit. Your *lawyers*." She practically spit the word. "Your money and your influence. You just made it all disappear. And now he and Elizabeth are stuck in your house, hating every minute, trying to figure out how to get out. He told me, Colleen. He emailed me when he told you they wanted to move to an apartment, that he asked you for a loan just until he could find a job. That you turned him down."

"That wasn't his idea," Colleen said. "That was *her*. Elizabeth."

Shay was already shaking her head. "Oh, no, it wasn't. And I *know* he didn't ever blame her. You came up with that on your own."

"She hates it there, she doesn't even try to hide it!"

"And Paul is the one who wants to give her a chance to have her baby in her own home! They don't hate *you*, all they want is their own life."

"They have the entire upstairs," Colleen said. "Over a thousand square feet."

"Where she feels like she's in jail. Only she's too polite to ever tell you, especially after everything you've done for her. She knows not everyone would take her in after what she did. So you get credit for that, Col. But I promise you, if you keep playing that card much longer, you're going to be the mother-in-law from hell. You think I like everything Robert does? You think I was thrilled to have a twenty-seven-year-old man knock up my nineteen-year-old daughter? Hell no. But I found something to like about him because I knew that if I didn't, I'd never get to see their baby."

Shay started toward the exit. Colleen had to race to catch up, after finally getting more money out and adding it to the bills on the table. Shay kept talking as though she didn't care if Colleen heard her or not.

"I'd lay odds they'll be out of your house in a year one way or another. Meanwhile, you want to know the baby's name?"

She glanced back at Colleen, then pushed through the heavy wooden door.

Colleen followed. The warm evening had cooled down, and Shay's words were lost to the roar of traffic passing on the road. She kept walking, and for a moment Colleen thought she meant to walk directly into traffic, but then she stopped and put her thumb out. Immediately a passing truck put on the brakes and started coasting over.

"What?" Colleen yelled. "What did you say?"

Shay turned. Her face was lit in the reddish glow from the brake lights. Her hair was wild around her face.

"Taylor!" she yelled. "They're naming him after *my* son."

COLLEEN HAD BOOKED them both on the same afternoon flight to Minneapolis, where they would part, she had imagined, with tearful hugs. That, or she would change her own flights and go with Shay back to California, where she thought she might be able to assist in planning the memorial. She could take a week off—the school volunteer job was over for the summer, and everything else—BodyPump, the cooking class her neighbor had signed them both up for, even Elizabeth's Lamaze classes—would go on without her. She'd gently steer Shay toward the right choices, discreetly paying for whatever was needed. It was to have been her final gift to Shay, because she suspected that once Taylor was buried, they would slowly lose touch.

By six o'clock in the morning, when she had been awake for a restless hour and a half, she knew that wasn't going to happen. She'd drunk both splits of wine, telling herself that Shay could change her mind and call at any moment.

(There had been an ill-advised call to Paul at around eleven, midnight back in Massachusetts. Colleen remembered asking Paul when he was planning to tell her about the baby's name. Paul had hung up on her, eventually, but she couldn't remember everything that she had said first.)

She showered and dried her hair before texting Shay. When she didn't get an answer, she tried calling Shay's room. Finally, she went down and knocked on the door.

But she already knew. And when Shay texted her, at one thirty, to say Took earlier flight, she didn't really expect an apology or an explanation.

All she wondered was how Shay had paid for the ticket.

thirty-nine

ANDY PICKED HER up at the airport. Colleen had been hoping maybe Paul would have come instead. They needed to talk. But it was probably for the better; she had been slightly hungover most of the day, and the six-hour trip hadn't improved her mood any.

"How did it go?" Andy asked, taking Colleen's roll-aboard from her and stowing it in the trunk. He leaned in for a kiss, and Colleen turned away, afraid he would notice the faint trace of her hangover on her breath, despite the fact that she had popped a piece of gum as soon as they landed.

In the car, putting her seat belt on, she gave him the answer she had prepared.

"She wasn't ready to talk yet. I understand that. But at least we were able to go out to dinner and spend some time together. Robert and Brittany are working through the rest of the details on their end, so the memorial should be able to happen by the weekend." All of which was true, and all of which she had pieced together before the disastrous dinner.

"Ah, that's tough. So we'll need to head out there this weekend, then. Do you think we should let Paul come?"

If you had just backed the hell off, he might have learned to deal with some things on his own. Colleen winced as Shay's words echoed in her mind. It had been painful to hear, but now as she listened to Andy, she couldn't help questioning. Should they *let* him . . . as if he wasn't old enough to make even that decision on his own.

"I don't know," she hedged. "Honestly, I was thinking . . . maybe we should all stay home."

"And miss Taylor's memorial?" Andy said, glancing at her. "You can't be serious. Or did something happen with you and Shay?"

"What do you mean?" Despite herself, the question irked Colleen—why would Andy immediately think she'd picked a fight?

"Just, you have had a volatile relationship from the beginning. And it was . . . hard, those last few days."

Colleen hated it when he was careful with her. It was a signal that he thought whatever she was saying or doing indicated fragility in addition to being mistaken.

"Yes, it was hard," she said, her voice tight. "Because *she* had just lost her son and *we* were trying to deal with our own son in the hospital, plus the inquiry and the media. And Elizabeth's pregnancy. Shay and I barely even saw each other."

"That was my point," Andy said tiredly. "You don't have to bite my head off, Col. I just meant that you had a pretty intense week together there and then it suddenly ended, before you had a chance to really resolve anything between you."

"There isn't anything *between* us, there's just each of us trying to put together the pieces of our lives and move on." Why was she lying to him? At first it was just to avoid having to go through the painful retelling now, when she was so exhausted. But the lie had been dug in, and now she was committed to it. "Look, she's got her family, and her own friends out there, and that's who she wants to do this with. I'm not going to question that. Maybe later in the summer, before Paul starts the fall semester, I can go out and visit for a few days."

Andy said nothing for a few moments, his jaw clenched. He drove slowly through the parking pay lane and merged onto the highway. It would be an easy half-hour drive home at this time of the night.

"Even if we don't go, we should still let Paul go," Andy finally said.

"What? A minute ago you were saying—"

"I know what I said. But I thought about it. Taylor was his friend. Of any of us, he has the most reason to be there for a memorial for him."

Colleen actually agreed, but how was that going to happen now? She wasn't about to confess to Andy or Paul the way things ended with Shay. So she would have to tell Paul that Shay had requested it be family only.

But what if they were still emailing?

"It's really great that you have opinions all of a sudden about what's good for Paul," she said sarcastically, playing for time. "Since you've been holed up in your office all summer, harassing Hunter-Cole."

This time he looked at her incredulously for several seconds. "I've been talking about taking a sabbatical for years. I thought we agreed that this was the time, with Paul and Elizabeth getting settled in. And yes, I've found . . . comfort, and meaning, in what I have been doing."

The other partners at Andy's firm, with a spirit of generosity that Colleen had to believe was firmly rooted in the fervent hope that Andy wasn't losing his shit altogether, had encouraged him to take the time to "tie up loose ends." From what Colleen could see, Andy had been keeping his usual hours at the firm, and he often worked into the evenings. At least, that's what he said he was doing when he didn't come home until late.

"I don't understand you," Colleen said, though actually, she did. If she'd had a way to distract herself from the things that had happened, she would have taken it. That's what those stupid BodyPump classes were supposed to be—otherwise, no one could have gotten Colleen in that ridiculous studio with all the other sweating, yoga-pants-wearing women. "Taylor's death had nothing to do with the safety violations. So how does running Hunter-Cole into the ground help you process what happened?"

Andy didn't answer, his mouth going tight, his hands gripping the wheel. He'd been featured on the news both locally and in Lawton; the Bismarck and Minneapolis affiliates had sent reporters to interview him. He had flown out to council meetings twice last month. Already it looked as though the Fort Mercer leases would all be renegotiated, but there was no sign that Andy intended to let up until he'd gotten all the eastern North Dakota Hunter-Cole rigs shut down.

"Are you still having an affair with Vicki?" Colleen asked, almost lazily.

"For God's sake, Col," Andy muttered.

It wasn't much of a denial. By the time they pulled into the house, she was still trying to decide if she cared.

PAUL AND ELIZABETH had gone to bed already when they got home, but when Paul came downstairs in the morning, showered and dressed, at eight thirty, Colleen was ready for him. She'd made a fresh pot of coffee and run out to the Bruegger's to get him a couple of everything bagels, and a whole wheat raisin one for Elizabeth.

But when he came into the kitchen, he wasn't wearing his usual perfunctory, faintly sullen expression and he didn't mumble his usual truncated greeting. Instead, his face was blank and pale.

"I'm going to the memorial, Mom. Elizabeth's staying here, her doctor doesn't want her flying this close to her due date if she doesn't have to. I'm leaving first thing tomorrow morning."

"But we haven't even—"

He held up his hand to stop her. "Don't. Just . . . don't. I've still got money from my last paycheck, since you won't let me pay for anything. I already booked it. If you won't drive me to the airport, I'll take the shuttle."

Colleen leaned back against the kitchen island, dropping the dish towel she had been holding. "Shay talked you into it?"

His eyes sparked dangerously, while he kept the rest of his expression impassive. "She just told me when it was and said she understood if you didn't come. What the hell, Mom? Seriously, you're going to blow it off?"

Colleen shook her head. "You don't understand."

"No, that's an understatement. All summer long you've been telling me that you and Dad don't blame me for what happened. Even when I'm trying to take the blame, you won't let me. And now you won't even go out there, and what am I supposed to think? If you're too ashamed to even—to even honor Taylor's life—"

Paul lost his battle for composure, and his face crumpled the way it had when he was little, his lower lip trembling and his freckles standing out.

"He was my *friend*," he said. "You can't even understand that."

"Oh, honey, I—"

"*No.*" Paul shrank from her touch. "I'm so sick of you trying to make everything go away. Just once I wish you and Dad would—would . . . oh, forget it." He glanced around the kitchen, didn't seem to see what he was looking for, and stomped out of the house.

For a long time after he left, Colleen stood in the middle of her kitchen, doing nothing. Then she slowly, carefully, turned the top of the paper Bruegger's bag down in several neat folds so that the bagels wouldn't get stale.

She was taking the bedroom drapes down that afternoon, sliding the hooks from the rings one by one while standing on the step stool, when the phone rang. She was down to the last two hooks, and she was afraid the weight of the drapes would put too much pressure on the last rings, so she worked quickly, getting them freed just as the phone rang for the fourth time and went to voice mail.

She stepped off the stool and dug out her phone: Shay.

She sat down on the bed, next to the drapes, and stared at the phone until it buzzed to indicate a voice mail had been left. Then she stared at it awhile longer, wondering if she should listen to the message now or let it wait. But if she did that, the day would become all the more difficult, the burden of the empty house unbearable.

Making a snap decision, she tapped Call Back.

Shay answered in two rings. "You get my message?"

"I didn't listen to it. I mean, I was taking the drapes down when you called and I couldn't get to it in time and I figured I'd call back right away instead." Maybe this hadn't been such a good idea. Her pulse was pounding, her hands sweaty and metallic smelling from the drapery hardware.

There was a long pause, and then finally Shay said, "Why the fuck are you taking the drapes down? Is this some East Coast thing you people do in the summer?"

"I . . . they get dusty," Colleen stammered. "If you put them in the dryer on the fluff cycle with a damp towel, it gets rid of the dust. And you can go a lot longer between taking them to the cleaners."

Shay laughed. It startled Colleen, but the laugh went on for several seconds, a deep and throaty belly laugh. "Oh, God, Col, I swear, only you. I don't think I've ever washed curtains in my life. I didn't know you could. I just wait until they're disgusting and buy new ones at Penney's."

"Oh. Well . . ." Colleen wasn't sure what to say next. She supposed Shay knew all about Paul's flights and arrival time. "Is . . . is he staying with you?" she finally asked, plaintively.

"Look, Colleen." Suddenly Shay was all business. "This is stupid. We said some things the other night—you were right, that was a hell of a day, I had a lot of emotions going on. When I got home, I slept for fourteen hours. Anyway. I appreciate you coming out to help in Lawton. And now you need to come out for the memorial. Andy too, if he wants. But you need to be here. Okay?"

Colleen tried to answer, but she couldn't talk around the lump in her throat. "I don't want us to set each other off again," she said. "I mean . . . I take responsibility. It was my fault. I just don't think that it's a good idea. You don't want—you don't want anything to add to the, ah, the difficulty of the day."

"That's fucking ridiculous," Shay said. "That's a cop-out. I'm asking you for something that you know you can't say no to. The memorial's Saturday at eleven. We're just doing a barbecue after, at Frank's parents' ranch. It's casual, so don't dress up too much. Definitely no heels, because the barbecue's outside. It's supposed to be nice, probably up in the eighties."

"All right. I'll come," Colleen finally said. She pressed a hand to her forehead. She was suddenly very tired. When she hung up, maybe she'd lie down and pull the drapes over her like a blanket and take a midday nap. "All right."

"I'll send someone out to pick you up, text me the flights. I need to go, Colleen. Just promise me you'll be there. Okay?"

"Okay," Colleen whispered. She set the phone on the bedside table and slowly sank onto the bed. The sun slanted through the bare windows, warming her body. A breeze came through the screens. June was nice. A good season for cleaning, for clearing out the dust.

She closed her eyes.

forty

THEY DIDN'T OFTEN all have dinner together. Andy usually stayed late at work and picked something up downtown. Paul had a late class three days a week. And Elizabeth, until recently, had said the sight and smell of food at that time of day made her ill.

But tonight was the last night before Paul left for the memorial. Colleen texted Andy and asked him to be sure to come home. She stopped by Stazzo's and picked up mushroom béchamel lasagna, which both Paul and Andy loved and might be bland enough for Elizabeth too. She made a special trip to the bread stall for a loaf of their olive multigrain, and chose a half dozen fancy cupcakes from the bakery, with elaborate poufs of frosting with glazed fruit embedded like jewels. The salad she made herself, from a recipe that her mother-in-law had given her years before she died.

She took her time setting the table. She had opened the china cabinet, thinking she might use the Lenox that came out only at holidays and Paul's and Andy's birthday dinners, when she had an idea. She picked up one of the dinner plates and went upstairs.

"Elizabeth," she called from halfway up the stairs. "Okay if I come up for a minute?" She could hear the television on quietly, the sound of studio laughter. It was silenced abruptly.

Elizabeth was sitting on the couch, knitting. She hastily set the yarn and needles down and pushed a couch cushion on top of it. She was struggling to get up, but her bulk—her stomach was perfectly

round, the rest of her thin frame barely puffy—made the task difficult.

"Don't get up," Colleen said, surprised by the knitting. What had
she imagined the girl was doing up here, between her twice-daily
walks and endless texting?

She sat down gingerly on the sofa. Between them the knitting
peeked out from under the couch cushion: a beautiful shade of peri-
winkle blue. Because it's a boy, Colleen thought automatically, but
then pushed away her resentment with a heroic effort. "I didn't know
you knew how to knit."

"Oh. I . . . my mom taught me and my sisters. I mean, I'm not
very good."

"Will you let me see?"

"It's just . . ." Elizabeth reached out to touch the edge, a two-by-
two ribbing. Maybe the band at the bottom of a baby cardigan. "It
was supposed to be a surprise."

To Colleen's mortification, she sniffled in a way that didn't dis-
guise the fact that she was about to cry. Colleen jumped off the sofa
and got the tissue box from the table and set it in front of Elizabeth.

"About that," she said. "I'll admit I was kind of, um, taken aback
that Shay knew that the baby is a boy before I did. But really, it's up
to you kids to share that when you want to and with whomever you
want to." Had the girl told her mother? Did everyone know but her?

"No, that's not what I meant. But just so you know, I didn't want
Paul to tell her, I was kind of mad at him for that. I thought . . . we
were going to have a dinner. Paul and me. It was my idea. I wanted to
cook for you. Like a thank-you? For letting us stay here and everything? And we were going to tell you then. And I was going to . . ."
She reached out and shoved the knitting all the way under the cushion. "I was making this for you, for a present."

It took Colleen a second to understand. The knitting. It wasn't for a baby. And that beautiful blue, the color of a scarf Elizabeth had once complimented her on . . . hadn't she told the girl it was her favorite color?

"Oh," she breathed. "Honey."

"It's just when Shay texted Paul, you know, after they found him, Taylor—well, I think he wanted to give her something to hold on to. I mean we'd already talked about naming the baby after him. But that—once Shay told him, it was like, yes, that's what we're going to do. Both of us, we thought it was right. And so he told her."

They'll be out of your house in a year one way or another, Shay had said, trying to hurt her, and succeeding more than she could know.

She had tried so hard to keep them close. But what she had lost. Oh, what she had lost.

Colleen felt a tiny loosening inside, a relaxing of a pain she had been holding on to so hard it was practically pulling her apart from within.

"Paul," she started, and then had to stop and collect herself. Elizabeth was dabbing at her eyes with a tissue, and she reached for one herself and cleared her throat. "Paul is *good*. On the inside. He always has been. He's made mistakes . . ."

Darren Terry, in the locker room. So many ruined playdates, the incidents at school. The middle school suspension, the screaming matches between Paul and Andy after every semester's report card. The hurled words and curses.

The broken dishes on the floor. Paul on his knees, looking up at her like it would never, ever be all right again between them, and then returning to the task, his fingers cut and bleeding as he swept up the shards.

"We all make mistakes," Elizabeth said. "I did something so

bad . . ." She squeezed her eyes together as if trying to shut out the thought itself.

Tentatively, Colleen reached for her hand. It was small and cool, the fingernails cut short and bare. She folded it in both of hers. "I know this is hard to believe now," she said, "but after a while, that's not going to hurt quite so bad. You'll get more experience and you'll learn that everyone does stupid things when they've run out of ideas. You'll start to forgive yourself. I promise."

Was it a lie? Colleen wasn't sure she would ever be able to for-give herself for all her wrong turns with Paul, for every time she looked at her little boy and found him wanting, every day that she spent trying to bend and shape him into something he wasn't.

But this wasn't about her right now. Couldn't be.

She squeezed Elizabeth's hand a little harder. "You love my son. Don't you?"

Elizabeth blinked, her watery blue eyes finding Colleen's, her lips parted in surprise. "Of *course* I do, Mrs. Mitchell."

"Well, then." How could she make Elizabeth see that that was enough, that for that gift Colleen would never, ever betray her? So far, she hadn't found the right way to show the girl. Hadn't even begun to understand her, much less befriend her. All those hours, up here, she must have been so lonely.

An idea came to her.

"Honey, would you like to invite your mom out for a visit? Or a few of your friends? Get some time with them before the baby comes?"

"Oh, I . . . I'm not even sure my mom would come."

"Whyever not?"

"She's not exactly . . . she's kind of mad at me." Elizabeth's voice had gotten very small. "I made her one of . . . the thing I'm making you. Hers is pink. I had Paul mail it last week but I haven't heard anything."

"But you've been talking to her, haven't you? On the phone?"

"No, not really. She'll get on the phone for a few minutes after I talk to Daddy, sometimes. And sometimes I'm pretty sure she's there but she makes Daddy tell me she isn't. She's—I don't know. Because I did the same thing she did, you know, getting pregnant by accident, when I was too young. And she feels like Grace and Brookie will see me and, I don't know, like somehow that will corrupt them or something. It's . . ."

She couldn't seem to find the word she wanted. "Well." Colleen sighed. "That will change too, I'm pretty sure. Once she sees her grandson."

Elizabeth hung her head. "I hope so."

Colleen picked up the plate. She had chosen the pattern with her own mother, ivory bone china with a delicate tracing of white and gold around the edge. *Timeless*, her mother had said. *You'll never get tired of it.*

It was so funny, the things women pretend are important, generation after generation, standing among the glittering displays of tableware, outside jewelry stores looking at the diamond rings, stroking the lace of a dress suspended from a silk hanger. If Colleen had had a daughter, would she have done the same? Probably. She would have stood by, feverishly spinning a web of sterling iced tea spoons and eternity bands and satin pumps and organza veils, praying it would be enough. And having so little to offer when it wasn't.

"This is my wedding china," she said, showing the plate to Elizabeth. "It's yours, if you and Paul want it. But more important, I was wondering if you might be willing to come downstairs and keep me company while I set the table? I'm frankly bored out of my mind down there. And I'm sick of all this sad stuff. Let's just pretend for one afternoon that none of it happened, okay? I'll fix you a virgin daiquiri." She smiled. "With an umbrella. I think I still have a few of those left over from last summer. How does that sound?"

The girl gave her a tentative smile, wiping her eyes. "I'd love to."

forty-one

THIS WEEK WAS for the poor kids, the ones recruited to boost the university's diversity statistics. They didn't call them "poor" or "disadvantaged"—in fact they didn't call them anything at all, something T.L. had noticed during orientation. Everything was left vague. Even the program's name didn't really mean anything—Special Transitional Enrichment Track, so when a term was needed they were just the "STET kids."

The faculty in charge of the program kept emphasizing that the friendships T.L. and the others made this week, before returning to their shitty lives for the rest of the summer until they came back for real in August, would last them throughout their years at college, and beyond. *Beyond*, into the futures the adults kept describing as limitless, spectacular, larger than not only the lives they'd led so far but also larger than their own imaginations.

But look at them, T.L. thought, from his seat at the back of the classroom. Balding and paunchy men, women with loose flesh in their upper arms and ugly shoes. Had this been their dream, to usher the underperforming and unremarkable into the hallowed halls of UCLA? Was this the limitless future they'd imagined for themselves, a degree from a respectable school and a cinder-block office with a mini-fridge and a view of the quad? Half the STET kids wouldn't graduate, and the university didn't care, as long as they stuck around long enough to make their numbers.

T.L. had arrived at LAX on his first plane trip and a wave of uncertainty, unsure how deep his debt to Myron went. He supposed he owed his uncle the whole four years, the degree, a job with a 401k. In the suitcase borrowed from Wally Stommar, he'd packed one pair of shorts from Abercrombie & Fitch, bought in Minot last week, and a half dozen T-shirts culled with care from the stack in his dresser. Boxer shorts from the Gap and a new bottle of Axe. New flip-flops, the very same ones he'd seen the kids in Lawton wear, that summer he'd spent with Elizabeth.

Elizabeth. Andy Mitchell had promised that if T.L. ever needed anything, all he had to do was ask. But what T.L. needed from the Mitchells was only for them to keep her, to enfold her into their remote and unknowable world, with his failed first love sloughing from her like a snakeskin. The baby would take her the rest of the way, and then finally his home would be *his* again, all of western North Dakota and its brilliant stars and rustling grasses and birds and sky and mice and foxes. The reservation and the lake, the highways and summer storms and snowdrifts, the mud in his boot soles and the grit in his eyes on windy days.

In L.A. everything was shining and temperate. There was no humidity, no mosquitos. T.L. was offered weed, a place to stay if he was ever in East St. Louis, a harmonica, dried mangoes, a hand-knotted bracelet made of colorful threads, a blow job, an invitation to prayer. He went to one study skills refresher class and skipped the rest. He went to a subtitled Turkish film and, before he could figure out the plot, a girl from the Sierra foothills—T.L. had not known California had inland mountains—put her hand in his pocket.

The night before he was to fly home, he and that same girl went up on the roof of the dorm. She brought a huge plastic tumbler of homemade sangria. Bits of orange rind floated among the ice cubes.

The girl's lips were spicy and cold, but they quickly warmed. She had a tiny silver stud in her cheek, and T.L.'s fingertips brushed against it as they kissed.

The sky in L.A. was chalky and diluted at night. But not far away, past the buildings and the hills and the highway, was the ocean, which T.L. had seen for the first time three days ago. He licked the salt from his fingers and watched the Ferris wheel spin above the Santa Monica pier. The sand under his feet didn't belong to anyone. The kelp and broken shells, the shrieking of children and the smell of fried food, these were all his if he wanted them. He could stay here. He could stay.

forty-two

SHAY WAS ALONE in the bride's room of the church.

A thousand years ago, she had waited in here with her mother and three of her friends all fussing over her dress. It had had puff sleeves you could hide a loaf of bread in and sequins embroidered over every inch of the bodice. Her aunt was outside in the church trying to console Brittany, who was supposed to be a flower girl but had thrown such a huge fit over the basket of petals that they decided to skip her part.

Shay had married Frank. She had found a father for her daughter and then she'd had a son. She'd tried hard to hang on to her marriage, and when they split, she worked to keep it friendly. When he died she tried to be both mom and dad to her kids.

All her damn life, she had just tried so hard. She'd shown up at school for mothers' teas and choir concerts and See's Candies fundraiser meetings. She'd worked extra shifts to pay for softball team fees and prom dresses and orthodontia. She made sure her children knew how to clean a bathroom and write a thank-you note and pay for what they broke or, in one memorable case, shoplifted. She'd confined her rogue needs to late at night or weekends stolen for trips to Reno, dates at the Red Lobster in the next town, hurried couplings in backseats and cheap motel rooms and guest rooms in the middle of the day. She'd never brought a man home and she'd convinced herself she was only borrowing them for a while, the ones whose wives wouldn't really miss them.

She looked at herself in the full-length mirror, the one for brides to do a final primping before they headed down the aisle. She was wearing a simple black scoop-neck top with butterfly sleeves and her favorite jeans and black sandals with leather flowers stitched to them. No one knew, not even Brittany, that she had cut the small "26" from the sleeve of Taylor's game-day jersey and had been carrying it in her pocket for weeks. She touched it now, the soft cotton fabric a comfort.

Father Greg had retired, but he came back for this. He'd done Frank's service too. The church had been full when she took refuge here fifteen minutes ago. Brittany had come with her, and she'd only stepped out now to confer with Father Greg about where they would stand to receive the overflow crowd afterward.

Shay had asked Father Greg to keep it short. She didn't want to spend this day falling apart. She figured she could keep her shit together for fifteen minutes. There weren't going to be any eulogies, hell no. Later, maybe, at the barbecue, after everyone had eaten and had a few drinks, people could get up and say whatever they wanted. By then Shay would be all right with it. And she could take Leila down to see the goats if she needed a break.

But here . . . she'd always had a special reverence for churches, even though she hadn't been a believer since she was in grade school. She liked their cool, chemical floor polish smell. She liked the leatherette covers of the hymnals. She couldn't have chosen a better place for all of the flowers than the marble altar. But Taylor was up there, in the shiny dark casket that Brittany and Robert had chosen. And Shay just didn't know how she was going to survive having to look at it, even if it was just for a few moments.

There was a sound at the door. "Britt?" Shay said, turning from the mirror.

The door and a woman slipped through, closing it behind her.

"The flight was late," she said quickly, breathlessly. "I got here as fast as I could."

Only then did Shay see that it was Colleen, transformed again. This time she was wearing one of the shirts some of Taylor's old friends had printed up—his beautiful grin, in his football team photo, posed on one knee. Shay knew that on the back the shirt read TAYLOR C. ALWAYS AND EVER IN OUR HEARTS, because the boys had one made for her. The shirt was much too large for Colleen, and she'd knotted it at the waistband of her black slacks. The rest—the low patent pumps, the pearl earrings, the shiny stiff hair—was all Colleen. But the expression on her face was new.

She stood there looking completely peaceful, like she was ready for whatever Shay might dish out. Her brown eyes were solemn, but the deep hollows under her eyes were gone, and the creases in her forehead seemed to have smoothed out.

"You don't have to go," Shay said. "I'm just . . . all those people."

"I know," Colleen said. She didn't say she was sorry and ask was there anything she could do. Which was good, because Shay didn't want to hear that one more fucking time. They were all sorry, and no one could do a damn thing.

"You saw Paul?" she asked.

"Yes . . . he introduced me to Brittany and Robert. And Leila. She's beautiful."

Shay didn't miss the pain that passed over Colleen's face. Well, she wouldn't have been able to miss Brittany's condition, not in that black jumper.

"So I guess we're both going to be grandmothers the same month," Shay said. "Paul says Elizabeth's due the fifth. Brittany's not due until the eighteenth, but Leila was almost two weeks early, so . . ."

"You're so lucky," Colleen said softly, almost wistfully. Then she looked stricken and slapped her hand over her mouth. "Oh, my God," she said. "I'm so sorry. I didn't mean—"

"It's okay," Shay said. "Come on. Today, let's just cut all the shit. Me and you—we earned that, right?"

After a moment Colleen nodded. "All I meant was . . . Brittany and Robert, it's just so clear how much they love you. They told me you're going to cut back to half time so you can watch the new baby. I . . . I would give anything for Paul and Elizabeth to . . . well, to want to be with us, like that."

Shay bit her lip, wondering when Colleen was going to figure it out. "There's no magic," she said. "We don't get along any better than anyone else. Robert came home drunk Tuesday from poker and Brittany came over and stayed with me. Then they patched that up and suddenly Britt's mad at me for letting Leila watch *Real Housewives* and neither of them are speaking to me." She smiled at the memory. Brittany had hung up on her last Thursday morning, but then that night she'd brought Leila over, since Robert had the evening shift, and they'd all done their nails after dinner. Shay had done Leila's, holding those tiny hands and dabbing at the little perfect fingernails and then doing the wave-your-hands dance with her until they were dry.

"We never fight," Colleen said miserably. Then she took a breath. "I've decided something. When we get home I'm going to kick them out. I mean, as soon as they can find an apartment. And if Paul wants to take a break from school . . . well, I'm not going to stop him."

"Damn, girl," Shay said, holding up her hand. "You rich people are so fucked-up." Colleen gave her a high five. And then Shay gave Colleen a quick, hard hug, pulling away before Colleen could hug her back.

Colleen stood there with her mouth open for a moment, then smiled. It wasn't much of a smile, but it was a start.

"We should probably go," Shay said, checking her hair one last time in the mirror. She'd managed not to mess up her eye makeup yet, and she had a pocket mirror and a tube of concealer in her purse just in case. "Is Andy saving you a seat?"

"I, uh . . . well, I told him not to come, actually," Colleen said. "He stayed in Boston with Elizabeth."

Shay raised her eyebrows. There was a story there for sure, one they could get to later, when the day wound down and everyone went home. They'd take a bottle and a couple of glasses and sit out on the back porch, where Frank's dad had rigged a swing so you could watch the sunset.

"Well, all right, then," she said, putting her hand on the door. "Turns out I don't have a date for this thing. Want to walk me to my seat?"

"It would be an honor," Colleen said, and the two of them went out into the waiting crowd together.